Trashed

Stolen Hope, Innocence Lost - The Chase is on

P G Robertson

Contents

This book is dedicated to my father, a supremely capable and kind man with an intense love of fishing that defies all sense. Born on the land and never far away, the stories of Ange's family property are heavily informed by my father and grandfather, both hoarders of some magnitude.

In a separate dedication, I spare a thought for our dear friend Will, a beguiling and intriguing young man taken far too soon.

Brilliance sits on the edge of darkness.

In memory of WRA

Prologue

The woman painstakingly moved aside the cardboard boxes, straining to make as little sound as possible. She knew them to be pizza boxes, yet she had never eaten pizza until a few nights ago. In her opinion, pizza was overrated and not the delicacy suggested by the countless bootlegged movies she had watched back home.

Once clear of those smelly boxes, she carefully pushed open the lid of the large plastic bin and took in a deep breath, savouring the fresh air, a stark contrast to the putrid odours that she had endured for the past few hours. She had experienced worse back home. Ironically, she had been running for her life then as well. It had taken weeks to rid herself of the smell of those pigs.

Despite it being the dead of night, the surrounding countryside was awash with the sounds of unfamiliar birds and animals, going about their nocturnal business. She heard the bleating cry of a calf somewhere off in the distance, no doubt urging its mother to provide food or comfort, perhaps both. The woman slowly raised herself up and carefully folded over the lid of the bin, taking a moment to stretch muscles that had started cramping. The next move was tricky, and she could not risk a sudden muscle spasm.

A mere slip of a girl, with shoulders that barely broached the rim of her smelly hiding place, she stood silently and surveyed her surroundings for a moment. She slowed her breathing as best as she could, forcing herself to remain calm. A rushed or panicked move at this point could spoil everything. She looked skyward and saw a heavy cloud moving across. Timing would be crucial.

Satisfied that nobody was watching, she then carefully pulled herself up and straddled the two sides of the bin. Luckily, the woman was still young and flexible, able to balance herself precariously and avert tipping the bin over, a disaster that would destroy the solitude that was both an ally and an enemy of her escape.

A crow cawed, fracturing the dead of night, as if warning that death and evil were afoot. Fear and superstition overcame the woman, causing her to slip ever so slightly. She steadied herself and waited for a handful of seconds until she was certain that only the crow was watching. Those ominous birds missed nothing, especially when food was involved.

As soon as her extraction was complete, she stood perfectly still, waiting for the cloud cover to extinguish the slivered moonlight. Once under cover of darkness, the woman moved away from the buildings as quickly as she dared, suppressing any temptation to run and potentially trip over. The night was now as black as that crow, yet she knew that there was a road straight ahead somewhere, having heard cars rumble past during the day. The young woman eventually came up against a barbed wire fence, and she stopped for a moment to look back, straining to see the outline of the farmhouse where those men were staying.

She turned to her right and followed the fence line until she came to an opening. She was pleased to have taken things slowly; otherwise, she might have broken her leg on the strange contraption that lay on the ground. Made from a series of metal bars, spaced perfectly to catch the unwary, it was an obvious trap of some sort. She had seen nothing like it. Whether it kept things in or out, she couldn't be sure.

Having painstakingly negotiated that torture device, she walked onto the road that would be the conduit for her escape. The woman looked left and then right, weighing up her only two options. In the distance, to her right, she could see the faint glow of a yellow light, so she started walking in that direction. She already knew that cars were not a concern at this time of night, so she stuck to the middle of the road and moved as quickly as she could. Without shoes, the gravel and sharp stones cut at her feet, and she knew she would struggle to go much further than that yellow beacon.

After what seemed an eternity of pain, the woman stopped and surveyed the situation. Fear gnawed at the pit of her stomach as she decided whether to seek refuge or keep walking. No torture device guarded this entrance, confirming her suspicions about the place she had just escaped from. Hopefully she could find safety here.

The tiny woman climbed over the gate and silently made her way toward the house. She waited for a dog to bark. She had heard them off in the distance before. Surely it would smell the remnants of her past few hours. Thankfully, she remained undetected.

She spied a pickup truck in the shadowing light cast by the lone light bulb and decided in an instant that this would be her best option. She climbed into the bed of the vehicle and slid under its canvas tonneau cover. The overwhelming smell of cattle and stock feed was strangely comforting, and except for a spare tyre that she bumped into, her new hiding place was empty. The woman pushed herself into a corner, where she curled up as tight as a ball and promptly fell asleep.

Woken after what seemed only seconds, although it was probably hours, she listened as a door over at the house opened and then closed. She held her breath as thumping footsteps came her way, assuming the worst. A man muttered to himself and secured the corner of the canvas cover that she had used to enter her hiding place. Phew.

She breathed another enormous sigh of relief when the truck barked into action and drove toward the road. The driver left the vehicle running while he got out to open the gate. She heard him mutter a curse to himself. Although she didn't speak his language, she knew from all her movie-watching that it was a curse, repeated as he completed this little dance for a second time to close the gate.

Finally, they were off, heading away from that dreadful place. So far, so good.

Chapter 1

A Testy Start

Detective Ange Watson was barely weaned off painkillers and lay sprawled on a large and luxurious three-seater couch, her plaster-encased leg perched elevated on the armrest. She was reading an early Don Winslow novel, something light and easy to follow as she slipped in and out of repeated catnaps. Her body was struggling to deal with the effects of a long and complicated surgery and the naps delivered a welcome respite.

The comfortable couch on which she was sprawled belonged to the delectable Gus Bell, CEO of Bell Surfboards and makers of the coolest boards in the world—at least in Ange's eyes. It had been her best friend Kerrie, a hugely successful lifestyle influencer of some renown, who had been responsible for her comfortable accommodation. While she was in hospital, Kerrie had been busy in the background facilitating Ange's move to recuperate at Gus's place.

It was quite a commitment by Gus to look after an invalid. Ange would have surely pushed back had she not been so beaten up. Gus lived in a magnificent estate, perched in the hinterland above Byron Bay, and had kindly let Ange use his guest house, a decidedly five-star set-up that was way beyond her pay grade. The view from her couch stretched all the way to the ocean.

She looked up from her novel and gazed longingly across at the sparkling ocean. In a moment of self-doubt, Ange wondered if she would ever surf again. Her surgeon had insisted that a full recovery was almost certain, but she could not imagine ever being strong and fit again. Learning to surf was the greatest thing that had ever happened to her. Paddling out into the ocean and communing with nature was her salvation from dealing with the rigours of her taxing job. Surfing was a physically and mentally demanding sport and, as things stood, she was nowhere near as confident as her surgeon.

If surfing was the high point, getting shot ranked as the low point, certainly never part of life's plan. Sure, that was something that any police officer needed to face up to, especially during those early days when she'd pounded the streets as a junior constable in Western Sydney. However, being shot on the job was something relatively rare in Australia and quite unlike the crime shows of the USA, where guns were more freely available. Once she'd joined Major Crimes, being shot had seemed the remotest of possibilities.

Every night since the shooting, Ange would jump awake in a cold sweat as memories of that fateful day haunted her dreams. Who would have guessed that those Ndrangheta mafia hitmen would have snapped like that and opened fire? Lomax and Smith didn't sound like surnames of the Calabrian Mafia, but their fully fledged membership of the Ndrangheta was handed down from their mothers. Once the red sniper's dot appeared on their chests, they commented they were dead anyway, almost as a casual observation, before trying to take Ange with them. The federal snipers, deployed in the scrub for cover, had no option but to take the two thugs out. Ange and her team had seriously underestimated the clinical ruthlessness of the Ndrangheta.

Ironically, once her leg was safe within its plaster-of-Paris cocoon, it was her cracked rib that proved the most painful, an injury where involuntary laughter at the hands of her friends became a bittersweet experience. Thank goodness for that high-tech vest that her federal colleagues had provided. Some marvel of science called nanotubes had done the trick and saved her life. That and good fortune, when the other bullet had missed her femoral artery by a whisker.

Knowing that Ethan Tedesco, the crypto-tsar and the architect behind this trauma, was probably living the high life overseas still infuriated her. Tedesco had cleverly faked his death in a fiery car accident, carefully staged to allow sufficient time to slip away on his corporate jet. Pursuit of Tedesco and the theft of around seven hundred million dollars in crypto assets had passed into the hands of Interpol. According to Ange's boss, the unflappable Senior Detective Sally Anders, Interpol seemed disinterested. One couldn't blame them. As it stood, a clever lawyer would easily obfuscate any case against Tedesco, particularly when cryptocurrency and NFTs were involved. Few people understood that stuff, least of all the courts.

The situation concerning Chief Superintendent Bold, Sally Anders' former boss, was even worse. It was Sally's belief that Tedesco had helped Bold fake his death while ocean swimming. Most likely, the pair had escaped together on Tedesco's jet and Bold was also living it up in Europe somewhere. Unfortunately, this was just a working hypothesis. Without a shred of evidence to go on, Bold was being pursued by nobody; such was the brilliance of his deception. That a Ndrangheta mole could show such discipline and bide their time to rise to the upper echelons of the police service was both breathtaking and chilling. It would not surprise Ange to learn that Bold's supposed ocean swimming hobby had all been part of his escape plan from the very beginning.

Her phone buzzed with an unrecognised number, interrupting her wandering thoughts of the past few weeks. She put down her book and realised that she hadn't read a word for ages. Letting her phone ring four or five times, she accepted the call, her finger poised ready to drop the robocaller in an instant. 'Hello,' she answered tentatively, having learnt never to say your name to an unknown caller lest it form part of a campaign to steal your identity. She soon regretted answering that call.

'Detective Watson?' questioned the caller.

'Yes. Who may I ask is calling?'

'It's Special Investigator Ben Carruthers from Internal Affairs. We're in town today and would like to pay you a visit.'

'It's not convenient. I'm still in a lot of pain,' explained Ange, genuinely not in the mood to be interrogated—especially not by Internal Affairs.

'It's not a request, Detective. Text me your address and we'll come straight around,' said the officious Carruthers.

Ange felt instantly on edge, somehow guilty of something or another. She agreed and texted the address of Gus's house to Carruthers' number. 'That was stupid,' she thought to herself. 'I'm here on my own and I don't know if Carruthers is who he says he is.' She quickly rang her boss, Senior Sally Anders.

'Hi, Ange. How's the recuperation going? By the way, you're not supposed to be ringing me. Remember, we agreed that you have three months' leave ahead of you. Stop thinking about work for a moment and get better,' said Anders.

'Well, I was doing a passable job of that until I just received a call from a certain Ben Carruthers, purporting to be from Internal Affairs. He's on his way here right now. Is he who he says he is?'

'I'll ring you straight back,' instructed Anders, her conversational tone quickly displaced by one that was all business.

Ange sat twiddling her thumbs for two or three minutes until Sally Anders rang her back. 'Yes, he is from Internal Affairs. I'm so angry with them for this. They were supposed to wait until you had your psych assessment.'

'What! I need to see a shrink as well?' explained Ange.

'Absolutely. You've been through a traumatic experience. We need to ensure that you're OK. Mentally as well as physically. Anyhow, you and I have already workshopped this situation with Internal Affairs. Don't let them badger you or box you into a corner. Ring me back when you're done,' said Anders.

Ange heard a car scrunch down the gravel driveway. 'They're here now. I'll let you know how it goes. Speak later, boss.'

Ange then texted Carruthers, trying the pleasant version of herself for a starter.

> *I'm at the guest house on your left. Forgive me for not coming out, but I'm not mobile at present.*

Ange heard the crunch crunch crunch of two people walking her way—then a knock at the door.

'Come in. It's open,' politely offered Ange.

'Hello, Detective. I'm Special Investigator Carruthers and this is my assistant, Sheena Wadley. Nice place you have here. Looks somewhat above your pay grade, Detective?'

A more obsequious individual Ange had not yet met, and she was instantly on high alert. 'It's a friend's house who offered to help after my surgery. Do you have a problem with that?'

'Not on the face of it,' replied Carruthers, his voice trailing off as if he had more to say on the topic. Ange's blood approached its boiling point. She took a deep breath to calm down.

'So, how can I help you?' asked Ange sweetly. As things stood, helping them out the door with a sound whack of her crutches was her preferred approach.

'We have some questions about the botched incident that you were recently involved in,' replied the self-righteous Carruthers. Wadley just stood sporting a smug smile, as if catching invalided detectives unawares was a fun game to play.

'How to win friends and influence people,' thought Ange. Her competitive and obstinate streak swiftly replaced any remnants of professional courtesy towards her colleagues of sorts.

'Are you OK if we record this interview?' asked Sheena Wadley, the first time that she had uttered a word since the pair had arrived.

'That will be fine,' said Ange. Before Wadley turned on the little recording device, Ange pulled her up. 'That's on the proviso that you agree to send me a copy of the recording and any transcript that you prepare.'

'Sorry, that's not how we work,' sharply shot back Carruthers.

'OK. Well then, I'm sorry that you came all the way out here. My boss, Senior Detective Sally Anders, will help facilitate an alternative time when either she or a lawyer can be present.' Ange looked them both in the eyes, then beckoned at the door. 'You can let yourselves out.'

'You cannot refuse to be interviewed, Detective. You should know that,' said mister self-righteous.

Ange had had enough of his attitude. 'And you should know that I can also demand that someone else be present. Plus, I understand you were told not to interview me until I've completed a psych assessment.' Ange paused for effect. 'So, what's it going to be?'

The two investigators looked at each other before Carruthers nodded. 'OK, we'll agree. We've got nothing to hide. Getting back to it, we have some genuine concerns about the botched operation.'

'Not so fast,' interrupted Ange. She reached for her trusty notebook to find a fresh page and hastily scribbled up an agreement of sorts, straining to recall her best bush-lawyer skills.

I, Detective Angela Watson, agree to be interviewed by Investigators Ben Carruthers and Sheena Wadley from Internal Affairs on the proviso that I am provided with a copy of any recording or transcript made from said interview.

Signed:
Dated:

I, Senior Detective Ben Carruthers, agree to provide Detective Watson with the above-mentioned and unaltered recording and tran-

script within 24 hours of the date below.

Signed:
Dated:

She handed over the notebook and pen to Carruthers and pointed to the second signature block. 'Sign here, please.'

'Don't you trust us, Detective?'

'Of course not. You try to hijack me in direct contravention of protocol and against medical advice. Tell me why I should trust you?'

Carruthers refrained from answering Ange's pointed question, but signed and dated the page. He handed the notebook back to Ange, who did the same. She took out her phone and took a picture, which she immediately forwarded to Sally Anders. She handed the notebook back to Carruthers. 'Here, you can do the same with your phone and then we can get started.'

'Sergeant Darren Billings didn't raise such a fuss. In fact, he was far more agreeable to being interviewed,' muttered Wadley.

'Of course he didn't. He's lucky not to be in jail already. When did you see him?' asked Ange.

'This morning. He's in worse shape than you, Detective. He gave us an interesting account of the events.'

'Taking seriously any account by Darren Billings is certainly a brave approach. Anyhow, happy to answer your questions, Investigators,' said Ange in a steely tone. Evidently, being shot had not invoked contrition in the corrupt sergeant, and he likely remained as slimy as ever.

Once that little tête-à-tête was over, Carruthers wrested back control of the interview and got down to business. 'We have some concerns about how you came to be engaged in the gun battle at Namba Heads in the first place, Detective. We'd like to understand how officers from Major Crimes, the sergeant of the Byron Bay station, the sergeant of the Namba Heads station, and the Australian Federal Police all became involved. It seems like a lot of firepower to confront two individuals.'

'Not if those two individuals are Ndrangheta assassins, it isn't. I presume you've seen the video footage of how things went down. The entire operation went perfectly until those thugs snapped and opened fire. Our guys had to take them out. If we made one mistake, we needed four federal officers hidden in the scrub instead of just three.'

'That's what we're confused about. Why were federal officers involved at all?'

'Well, there are two reasons for that. First, we had a Ndrangheta informant in our ranks, a high-ranking mole, as you're no doubt aware.'

'Let me stop you there, Detective. What mole are you speaking about?'

'Chief Superintendent Gary Bold. Where have you guys been?' responded Ange in exasperation.

'But the chief superintendent went missing while ocean swimming, Detective. Surely you've been following the news. He was an accomplished swimmer, by all accounts. A real tragedy.'

'I see,' was all Ange trusted herself to say. That Bold's supposed swimming tragedy had been so readily accepted as the explanation for his demise was disquieting. Internal Affairs was supposed to play the role of a relentless sniffer dog stalking the stench of corruption, not a puppy that eagerly lapped up popular headlines. The timing of said *tragedy* alone, coinciding so nicely with Tedesco's escape, should have been enough to wrinkle noses. All that Ange could sniff was someone's arse being comprehensively covered up.

'Moving on, you were saying, Detective.'

'We needed the support of the federal police as we were being pressured from above to abandon our investigation and we lacked resources. I believe Internal Affairs also tried to bully my boss into dropping the case.'

Wadley visibly bristled at the accusation that her department was guilty of the B-word. 'There was no such pressure from Internal Affairs, Detective. So why the federal agents?'

'Because the feds are running a task force dedicated to reining in the Ndrangheta mafia. They alerted us that Lomax and Smith, the two thugs killed by the federal marksmen, were Ndrangheta hitmen. The feds also identified the link to Bold, just before his death.'

'Putting aside your delusions about the former chief superintendent, it sounds as if Major Crimes might have been guilty of bullying tactics. At any rate, the federal police officers who I've spoken with haven't mentioned these supposed links between the Ndrangheta and Chief Superintendent Bold. Prominent people have a habit of dying during your investigations, Detective. Some might even call it a personal vendetta,' accused Carruthers. An arrogant smirk crept across his face.

Ange was positively fuming by this stage. 'So, you're telling me categorically that Internal Affairs never pressured my boss, Senior Detective Sally Anders, to drop our investigation?'

'Correct,' said Carruthers.

'And the federal police deny contacting my boss to confirm a link to the Ndrangheta?'

'Correct again, Detective. You're getting the hang of this,' replied Carruthers, his smug smile growing even more resplendent.

'Well, you clearly know more than I do. I guess Peter Fredericks is also in the clear?' said Ange, crossing her arms indignantly. She was referring to her former colleague, the snitch who had been feeding information to Bold, which was then passed through to the Ndrangheta. Fredericks had been turning a blind eye to the realities of his duplicity, ambition for Sally Anders' job his justification for being a snake in the grass.

'Detective Fredericks did nothing wrong. He was doing his job perfectly and keeping the chief superintendent abreast of your unauthorised activities. I understand that he's being favourably looked upon for a position in Internal Affairs,' returned Carruthers smartly.

Ange could not help but sneer. 'I think Fredericks will fit in just perfectly.'

'Which brings us to Sergeant Billings. Why on earth was he involved?' asked Wadley in an accusatory tone. There was no attempt at any good-cop, bad-cop approach by this duo.

'Because Billings was a snitch for Lomax and Smith and the conduit that we used to lure them into the open. He was on the take in return for paying off his gambling debts. We convinced Billings that it would be in his best interests to contact Lomax and Smith and help us apprehend them.'

'It didn't quite end that way—did it, Detective? From what you just described, you basically admit to bullying Billings to get involved in your botched operation, with him ending up being shot?'

'Did Billings tell you that?' asked Ange, now convinced that she was being set up. She knew that Billings couldn't lie straight in bed, and she shivered at the stories he might have dreamed up for the benefit of his own salvation.

'Not in so many words. It looks to me as if he really was an unfortunate casualty of this mess,' replied Wadley, her tone suggesting that she might harbour some sympathy for the loathsome Darren Billings. A cringeworthy memory flashed by of the first time that Ange had met Billings, when he had looked her up and down as if appraising a racehorse. In a moment of vindictiveness, Ange wondered if Wadley might enjoy a man like Billings paying her such attention. She pulled herself back to the present battle.

'Did you interview Sergeant Jim Grady?' she asked, forming air-quotes over the word *interview*.

'No, Sergeant Grady refused to be interviewed without legal counsel. We're arranging that,' said Wadley.

'Well, at least you've proven that Sergeant Grady is much smarter than I am,' observed Ange.

'And then, let's not forget the suicide of Mr Eddie Falconi on the Gold Coast. I understand that was also you who pushed him over the edge,' pressed Carruthers, leaning forward in his chair as if he had just parried the killer thrust.

Ange had not met a sleazier individual than Falconi. After Ange had upended his cosy drug importation and money-laundering operation on the Gold Coast, Lomax and Smith had killed Falconi in a faked suicide. He was a big wheel around town, and it seemed as if some powerful friends were protecting Falconi's reputation in order to safeguard their own. She had had enough. 'I see where you're trying to take this. I think it's best we stop this conversation right now. If you need to interview me again, please go through the correct channels so that I can arrange legal representation.'

Carruthers and Wadley looked as if they had scored the winning goal. 'I think we've gotten what we came for,' said Carruthers as he rose to leave. His face could not have been any smugger. Conceited and arrogant were two other adjectives that sprang to Ange's mind. Ironically, they had gotten no worthwhile information from her, yet seemed quite pleased with themselves. If anything, it was Ange who had benefited most from their visit.

'This has been fun,' said Ange sarcastically. 'Please close the door on your way out. Oh, by the way. I will expect the recording and transcript by this time tomorrow.'

'You'll be hearing from us,' was all that Carruthers said as he shut the door behind him.

As soon as Ange heard the investigators' vehicle drive away, she rang Sally Anders and gave her a full account of the interview.

'That was good work, Ange, getting them to agree to a recording and to supply a copy of any transcript. This is a set-up and a massive cover-up designed to protect some delicate reputations. Can you forward me the recording and transcript as soon as you receive it?' said Sally Anders, her tone decidedly upbeat, seemingly happy with Ange's discomforting interview.

'I gather they plan to keep running with this, boss,' concluded Ange.

'Don't worry, Ange. I've got your back. By the way, I've chased up getting your psych assessment out of the way. I've organised for a Dr Kirby Hall from the Gold Coast to pay you a visit. She's offered to come and see you tomorrow. Will that be OK for you?'

'Sure. I'm not going anywhere. Keep working on watching my back. I've only just dealt with the target that Lomax and Smith had put there. I don't need a fresh one,' replied Ange, laughing ruefully at her present predicaments.

Ange had absolutely no idea how Sally Anders was going to cover her own back, let alone Ange's.

That evening, after work, Gus Bell popped over to the guest house bearing gifts of takeaway curry and a bottle of wine. They had fallen into this habit each night, having dinner on the terrace overlooking the coast when the weather permitted. Ange had insisted on contributing to their meals, something that Gus had initially resisted. He only conceded that point after Ange argued she was no freeloader and would not feel comfortable about the situation unless she could contribute.

It was nice to have that time together, where their conversation would wander over the past and present. That was another subject that she had tackled him about. Gus ran a substantial company with national, even global, connections. She was suspicious that he should have been regularly travelling with the demands of his work. As it was, the pair had shared dinner every night since her arrival. When Ange had expressed concern that she didn't need to be babysat, he casually brushed aside these worries, blaming the difficulties of travel and the convenience of Zoom calls for his attentiveness.

As Gus had walked through the door, his arms laden with bags, a look of concern had come over his face. 'What's up? Are you OK?'

'I'm OK, Gus. Thanks for asking. I had an unfortunate visit from Internal Affairs today. They showed up at short notice. I feel as if I'm being set up.'

'I was thinking of your injuries, but clearly this is worrying you. Do you want to talk about it?'

'Not really, Gus. I'd need to speak in riddles. My boss, Sally Anders, assures me she has my back, but I can't fathom how she's planning that feat. You haven't met her. She's very impressive. Anyhow, I'll get to talk about it enough tomorrow. Sally has organised a shrink to come visit.' She saw Gus's concern over that last revelation. 'Don't worry. Apparently, it's a routine procedure in my situation. To be honest, I'm not really looking forward to having my brain probed, especially after the way Internal Affairs held my reputation for ransom today.'

'OK. Let me know if I can help. By the way, I bumped into Kerrie today. She and Mike are coming around for a BBQ lunch on Sunday.'

'That sounds fun. I hope my ribs can cope with the laughter that Kerrie normally brings to the table. Would there be room for another?' asked Ange.

'Yes, sure. Who?'

'It would be nice to include Bree if she's not playing hockey. She might be at a loose end now that Billy has gone back to Sydney. You briefly met them both at the hospital one day. I get the sense that their relationship has gone way beyond being purely professional. I'll text her.'

By the time they went their separate ways to bed, Ange had relegated the trials of her day to the background, only to have them rudely return that night. Her nightmares were now a melee of whizzing bullets and heavy-handed accusations. In one dream, she was back at school, hauled in front of the headteacher and accused of sneaking her boyfriend into the boarding house. Ange had spent countless hours plotting how she might achieve that feat back in the day, however the boarding mistress at her school had been a formidable opponent, one who Ange had never bested. As she struggled and strained to fall back asleep, she knew this dream had its genesis in her rapidly developing fantasies about Gus. It was only after fully exploring those prospects that she could board the sleep train again.

Chapter 2

Let's Chat

A nge received a call from her new psychiatrist first thing the next morning. She would arrive mid-afternoon after completing some patient visits in Lismore. Having her own psychiatrist was another experience that Ange had never contemplated during her many dreams and aspirations for her career. If someone had mentioned this possibility at the police academy, she would have recoiled at the thought, thinking that she was made of tougher stuff.

It was just after 3 p.m. when Ange heard the scrunch of a car in the driveway, followed soon after by a knock on her door. She still had a nasty taste in her mouth after the odious visit of Internal Affairs of the previous day, so she was not looking forward to being probed and prodded by a shrink. 'Come in, the door is open,' she shouted from the comfort of her couch.

Dr Kirby Hall came over to introduce herself. Ange noticed her psychiatrist looked fit and moved with the confidence and grace of someone who didn't spend all her time behind a desk. Younger than Ange had expected, Hall couldn't have been much older than herself, she guessed. Ange admonished herself for being surprised by this. She needed to face facts—she was no longer the twenty-some-thing woman of her imagination.

'Hello, Detective Watson. Nice place you have here. That's quite a view,' observed Dr Hall as she took in the spectacular aspect of the hilltop estate. She pointed towards a rocky island a few kilometres off the Byron Bay coastline. 'Is that Julien Rocks out there?'

In an instant, Ange felt her resistance towards her psychiatrist wither and fade. It was impressive how easily Hall had dismantled Ange's defences. It was hard to pin down how she had done that. Ange wished that she could bottle that skill for herself, something that would make her job so much easier.

'Call me Ange, please. Yes, that is the infamous Julien Rocks. No doubt you've read about the all-too-frequent shark attacks around those rocks.'

'Call me Kirby, by the way.'

'Cool name,' said Ange.

'It can be a stretch for most people. I get Toby, Kerrie, Cody, you name it. Hardly anyone hears Kirby when I introduce myself.' Hall looked down at Ange's cast. 'How is the recovery going?'

'Slowly. I'm hoping that I don't go mad. Lucky I have this view. It's a friend's house. No stairs,' replied Ange by way of explanation. She didn't want to suffer a repeat of the not-so-subtle accusation that the view was beyond her means.

'I hear you,' said Kirby Hall, pointing to a large scar on her right ankle. 'Reconstruction after a wind-surfing accident. I've spent way too much time on crutches. You can't even carry a cup of tea with those darn things.'

With that connection made, the conversation meandered through Ange's life as Hall deftly explored the inner workings of her patient's mind. Ange felt increasingly comfortable and revealed far more than she had planned. 'This is a much more agreeable conversation than I had expected, certainly a lot more pleasant than I suffered yesterday. Internal Affairs paid me a visit.'

'Oh yes. Your boss said that you might mention that. She told me to reassure you she has that under control,' said Hall, glancing up from her notepad to fix Ange with a penetrating look. 'Sally never strikes me as someone to be trifled with.'

Never a truer word had been spoken. 'That would be a massive understatement. I'm intrigued about how she's going to remove this latest target from my back. I could almost feel the cross hairs being drawn yesterday. It made for an uncomfortable night's sleep,' Ange admitted.

'Tell me about that' asked Hall, effortlessly manoeuvring the conversation to take advantage of Ange's insight.

Ange explained her latest nightmare in some detail. 'I reckon Miss Anderson, my boarding house mistress, should have been a spy. Heck, she was good. I never once got the better of that woman.'

Hall laughed at that. 'I still have those headteacher dreams myself sometimes. I was a bit of a rebel at school. All that you describe is completely normal, Ange. It's just your brain processing the trauma that you've experienced. Based on our discussion today, I'd expect nicer thoughts will soon replace these disturbing ones as life marches on. I'm going to text you an invitation to a mindfulness app that can help.'

Hall must have noticed how Ange screwed up her face at the concept. 'It's very good. I use it myself. There are several modules covering things like meditation and yoga, even Pilates classes.' She gestured at Ange's crutches. 'Those classes can be for the future. What I want you to do is to keep a set of earbuds and your phone by your bed. When you wake up in the middle of the night and are having trouble falling back to sleep, play one of the sleep-casts. They cover things like a thunderstorm, a train journey, a boat trip, the ocean, the night-time sounds of the bush. They really work. You should also give the guided meditation classes a go while you're incapacitated.'

'OK. You've convinced me. I promise to give them both a go. I have real trouble getting back to sleep after some of my more sinister nightmares.'

'You will have times when unsettling images spring into your head and anything can trigger them. That's also quite normal and they will gradually become less frequent. The human mind is amazing at sorting this stuff out. Do you have a good support network?'

'I enjoy working with my boss and one of my work colleagues in Sydney, but I'd only just moved there. I do have some close friends here in Byron Bay,' commented Ange.

'Your boss told me you have three months' leave ahead. It sounds like you should stay here, where your friends are. Do you have a partner?' probed Hall.

'Well, that's not one of my strong suits. I call them *male fails*. My girlfriends and I joke about the fact that I can solve a murder, but not my relationships. There was a guy in my life until recently, but he's moved back in with his ex-wife to be with his children. I'm not bitter about that. I'd probably make the same choice in his shoes. It was probably going to end in tears anyway, as he was also a colleague of sorts.'

Almost as if on cue, another car scrunched its way along the driveway. It was Gus Bell.

'That can be fraught, but I've seen it work,' commented Hall, glancing over towards their visitor.

'I didn't realise he was a colleague at first. We met through surfing. Anyhow I've moved on from that relationship,' commented Ange, shutting down any further avenues for discussion as Gus Bell popped his head through the door.

'Gus, I'd like to introduce Dr Kirby Hall, my psychiatrist. I never thought I would say that. Kirby, meet Gus Bell, the maker of the world's coolest surfboards and owner of this estate. Should I call you my landlord, Gus?'

Hall laughed easily. 'Well, by the look of this view, you certainly aren't Ange's slumlord.'

In a moment of disquiet, Ange felt an unexpected pang of jealousy, worried for the briefest of moments that Gus might find the impressive Dr Hall more appealing than her. Kirby was also a markedly cooler name than plain old Ange. In reflex, Ange smoothed her hair, suddenly insufferable in its unshowered greasy state.

She was still supposedly an edgy brunette sporting a short bob, having taken on the persona of a savvy online NFT trader for the takedown of Lomax and Smith. It had been fun for a short time—until she got herself shot, that was. Ange instantly felt like a dishevelled grub, in total contrast to the stylish and accomplished Dr Kirby Hall. The full-length cast protecting her damaged leg didn't help matters.

'How are things going? Will Ange be OK?' asked Gus, a look of genuine concern written across his handsome face, helping calm Ange's misgivings of moments before.

Hall seemed to perceive what lay behind this subtle exchange and stole a glance at Ange before answering. 'Refreshingly normal, would be my professional opinion. Believe me, I don't say that about all my patients. You will be fine, Ange, but you need to take care and let your body and mind heal. You've been through trauma that few people will ever experience. Don't underestimate its effects.'

Hall stood up and handed Ange her card. 'Ring me anytime. It's all part of the service that your department offers. Please don't hesitate. The sooner that you can talk through any issues you're having, the better. Whatever you do, don't let things fester unchecked.' She looked towards Gus. 'Friends play a crucial role, and sometimes you will recognise an issue before Ange does herself. You can also ring me if you feel Ange's recovery is going off the rails.'

With that, Dr Kirby Hall took her leave. As she walked toward the door, Ange realised that Kirby Hall, the person, probably suffered nightmares of her own, as Dr Hall, the psychiatrist, sought to lessen the nightmares of others. Ange waited until Hall had closed the door. 'Well, Gus, are you relieved to know that you don't have a crazy woman living in your guest house?'

Gus smiled broadly in his typically laconic way. 'I think that anyone who would get themselves shot in a gun battle with Mafia hitmen probably begs that question. By the way, I'm cooking whiting with Greek rice and a salad tonight. Do you think we could get you up to the main house for dinner?'

'I think I'm up for that challenge. It's nice to know my sanity is beyond reproach—despite your own uneducated point of view.'

'Great. I'll come over at 6:30 and give you a hand.'

As Gus walked back to the house, Ange checked her emails. She saw that Ben Carruthers from Internal Affairs had at least been true to his word and attached the transcript of their interview. The email also included the hyperlink to a file share service containing the recording. Ange had no desire to relive that affair, potentially ruining both her evening and her night's sleep. She simply forwarded Carruthers' email to Sally Anders.

Sally instantly replied.

> *Great. I'll come back to you. Take it easy. Don't give that interview another thought.*

That was something easier said than done, all things considered.

Senior Detective Sally Anders downloaded the audio file Ange had forwarded onto her phone. She figured that it was something to relieve the boredom of her stop-start drive home. As was her habit, she waited until the commuter crowd thinned before leaving the office. She lived on the northern side of the harbour and chose the Sydney Harbour Bridge over the tunnel as her means to traverse this impressive body of water. The harbour sparkled under a waterfall of light, spilling from the countless apartments and high-end houses that clung to the harbourside cliffs. The normally somewhat bland skyscrapers were pillars of brilliance, still crammed with workers chained to their desks, perhaps striving to afford the mortgage on their own private view of the harbour. Many would be too tired to enjoy their expensive vistas once they finally made it home.

Sally Anders hardly noticed the impressive spectacle. She was intent on following the accusations of Carruthers and Wadley as they interviewed her star detective. Had any of the swarming commuters glanced her way during the innumerable stand-still moments, they would have assumed that Anders was listening to a favourite song to ease the tension of the tedious Sydney traffic. Her increasingly satisfied grin suggested that she was enjoying herself immensely.

Sally took her exit off the Cahill Expressway and wound her way east into Northbridge, the accurate, if not simplistic name for a suburb immediately north of the harbour bridge. She rolled through the leafy streets, lined with an eclectic collection of expensive homes. Most ignored the southern hemisphere convention to face north, such was the magnetism of a slivered view of the harbour. Sally's house sat on a T-junction at the bottom of a long street, almost in a gully and certainly not any abode that enjoyed water views. It was all that they could afford back then, and there was no chance to upgrade given the stratospheric North Shore prices. Even if they had won the lottery, she and Max were too busy with their careers to invest the time and energy needed to move again. It was a lovely home, not the worst home in the best street by any means, but modest compared to their neighbours.

Perhaps having a family might have changed their perspective, but the couple had been putting that prospect off each year, as each successive career milestone or opportunity had come along. Then, suddenly, Max was gone, his insidious disease stealing away any option to have a family together. Sally sometimes blamed herself for that tragedy. Perhaps she should have been more vigilant and seen how the deadly condition had snuck up in the night to take away her husband. They had both been too damned busy to worry about trivialities such as health and well-being. Her therapist had helped rationalise those destructive thoughts.

She drove straight across the intersection and up the narrow driveway into her garage, then walked down to the mailbox to empty the pile of junk mail that had arrived during the day. The distributors of this forest carnage, paid piecemeal for each delivery, had long ago ceased to take any interest in her stickered warning that they were unwelcome. As if to serve as a constant reminder of her loss, she found some mail addressed to Max. Despite her best attempts, companies, even government agencies, were happy to waste their money trying to contact him. Maybe employing a psychic would prove a better investment. Sally still tried to speak with Max, yearning for his counsel to discuss a problem, or uncover his smile to laugh about something funny that had happened in her day. Many in her situation would have sold the house, but it somehow provided her with comfort.

The place held far too many fond memories of her beloved husband impregnated within its walls. She was not yet ready to move on.

God, she missed those endless debates, where Max's insightful interrogation would cut her many theories and propositions to shreds. She had learned to make sure she had explored every avenue and resolved all inconsistency in her thoughts before standing toe to toe with her husband. Max had undoubtedly honed her skills as a detective, and he remained the secret behind her success. Even after half a decade, she still mentally prepared for their spirited debates on the drive home. Sometimes, she walked around the house alone, speaking out loud as she argued with herself, channelling the memory of her husband to expose her stupidity.

As she sat and waited for her meal, Sally sipped her wine amongst the artwork which she and Max had collected, a shared passion that seemed much more fun than investing in the stock market. She became lost in the distant hills of a mesmerising landscape by Garry Shead until a ping from the microwave jumped her back to reality. By the time her wineglass was empty, she had settled on her plan to deal with Internal Affairs.

Over a rare second glass of wine, she reflected on the persistent nightmares of her damaged detective and pondered the impact of the past few weeks. As things stood, Detective Ange Watson was better off staying in Byron Bay to recover from her gunshot wounds, perhaps even for good. Sally was loath to lose such talent from her ranks. She rarely saw an investigator with such intuition and tenacity to see things through. The memories of Sydney would incite temptation, and Sally was sure Ange would not resist a renewed pursuit of the Ndrangheta. Some water needed to flow under the bridge before that could happen.

As Sally finished her wine, she recalled an email she received a few days ago. A plan for how to deal with Ange came in a flash of inspiration, the perfect solution for the right moment.

Chapter 3

Revelations

After two long days, Ange finally heard back from Sally Anders. It was just in time, as Ange was doing a poor job of avoiding being pulled into a black hole of despair.

'Hi, boss. I guess you're pleased to know that I'm not crazy—not yet, anyway. That could all change after another four weeks of this.'

'Yes, Kirby rang me. Isn't she great? She was such a help to me when Max passed a few years back.'

This uncharacteristic admission, a telling insight into the building blocks that made up the real Sally Anders, startled Ange. This was quite a revelation of what lay behind the titanium exterior that Ange saw day-to-day. It was one moment when time expanded, allowing Ange to consider that her boss was human after all. This immediately placed Ange's own plight into perspective, a mere fraction of the trauma that would be associated with losing one's partner, particularly when you had plans for a long life together. Sally Anders was not all that much older than her, and Ange could not imagine the pain of that experience.

In comparison, Ange had nothing to worry about, although that didn't stop her from trying. She often thought about that moment when the flat line of time made a sudden detour. It was as if a year's worth of memories had been crammed into the flicker of an eye. That split second, between the thump of Lomax's bullet and losing consciousness, was being replayed over and over in the middle of her nights with disturbingly crystal-clear fidelity.

Whether because of adrenaline or shock, Ange's own insignificance had been illuminated, exposed under the glaring light of a fragile mortality. She had sought to rationalise these thoughts of irrelevance during the many reruns of that fateful moment, but it didn't matter. The conclusions were always the same. She was nothing more than a pinprick within a pinprick that formed one of the infinitesimal and minuscule dots on the human continuum. Those moments, or perhaps the moments since, had blessed her with an insight—focus on what was genuinely important in her life and ignore what was mere froth and bother. Ange knew things had to change.

Sally Anders snapped Ange from this reverie, recognising her own rare slip-up and needing to move on. 'Upstairs finally gave me approval to secure some much needed additional resources. With you being on medical leave and the extermination of our resident carpet snake, we're already two down. I'm planning to secure four more investigators when the final funding approval comes through. My strategy is to beef up our digital capability. This last investigation has highlighted how woefully under-gunned we've been in this area.'

'Wow, boss! That's quite a change of fortune. I thought it more likely that upstairs would disband us. In my case, after that hatchet job by Internal Affairs, I imagined being posted as a traffic cop out the back of Whoop Whoop. Maybe Broken Hill—if I was lucky,' commented Ange, admitting to some doubts which had been circling in the days since that infuriating interview.

'You don't need to worry about Internal Affairs. I've well and truly clipped their wings. Well, for the time being, at least. In fact, that recording of your interview did the trick.'

'Well. Out with it. Fill me in on how you achieved all of that since we last spoke,' said Ange, pleased to see some light at the end of her dark tunnel of uncertainty.

'Let me start at the beginning,' said Anders, taking a breath, as if gathering her thoughts into order. 'I was becoming suspicious when the pressure started piling on during our investigation of Falconi, but I had assumed that was simply a case of Falconi having connections in high places. I didn't start joining the dots until Internal Affairs joined in the party. We seemed to be perpetually one step behind and I sensed that something stank to high heaven, although I didn't realise where the smell was coming from. I started recording any conversations which I felt were inappropriate. I'm pleased that I did.'

'How do you manage that? Record those conversations, I mean,' asked Ange, always on the lookout for something that might make her own job easier.

'It's quite easy. I purchased this phone app that sits in the background and can be activated mid-call. The recordings are timestamped and sit in the cloud somewhere. It's quite seamless. I'm not sure that it would pass as evidence in court, but it's perfect for covering one's own backside and keeping the record straight. I'll text you the name of the app sometime.'

'That's the way now, isn't it?' Ange observed. 'There's an app for anything you think might be useful, as well as plenty of things that aren't. I'll add your recording app to the basket of handy helpers that I'm collecting. Apparently, I need one to sleep, meditate, and even exercise. I sometimes reckon that even my job might be replaced by a clever AI app, something with an inane name like *CrimeSolverAI*.'

Sally Anders was well used to Ange's thought bubbles and chose not to go down any AI rabbit hole. 'Anyhow, our former chief superintendent, Gary Bold, was clearly worried that we were getting close and must have set about maligning us within the hierarchy. Even the police commissioner herself rang to accuse me of overreach, throwing in Eddie Falconi and the Gold Coast disaster for good measure. Then Internal Affairs piled on. That recording of your own interview with IA brought it all together nicely.'

'Well, I'm pleased that interview was of use to someone other than the people trying to bury me under a pile of you-know-what,' laughed Ange.

'It's still hard to determine who was acting alongside Bold and the Ndrangheta, and who was simply duped by Bold. Either way, I accept it looks bad for everyone involved and I needed to work out where everyone stood. Once I had been through the recordings, I set about organising an urgent meeting with the commissioner and the commander of Internal Affairs. They both tried to fob me off—however, I can be rather forceful when I put my mind to it.'

'Based on your tone of voice, I presume that your meeting went well,' observed Ange.

'I suspect they wanted to see if I would toe the line to support their fake news about Bold. This would allow them to sweep the whole affair neatly under the rug, with you as the sacrificial lamb. While I don't agree with her methods, the commissioner's desire to bury this mess is predictable. She's closer to a politician than a police officer. Imagine the furore if word got out that organised crime had infiltrated the uppermost echelons of the police service. For heaven's sake, the public already doesn't trust us.'

'It is concerning that the people we work for would scuttle us so readily. I'll never look at the commissioner quite the same again,' observed Ange.

'It's the way the world works when politics and position are involved. It was the jelly-spined commander from Internal Affairs who really riled me, and I let him have both barrels. Even though Bold was effectively his boss, he must have known what he was doing was downright dodgy, yet he was totally happy to go along with the charade. That they were gunning for you so flagrantly made me furious. Internal Affairs can do what they want with me, but I see red when they try to throw my team under the bus.'

'I found IA's interrogation quite intimidating. It made me doubt myself.'

'That was exactly what they wanted. However, when they realised I had them on record and in complete contradiction to your interview, that slimy commander tried to threaten me with the law and that I had made my recording illegally. For goodness' sake!' remonstrated Anders.

'How did you deal with that?'

'I mentioned that my lawyer, amongst others, has a comprehensive account of this affair, including the recordings. He has strict instructions about what to do should anything happen to me or any of my staff—including anyone being posted to Whoop Whoop. We can't be certain we've eliminated all the Ndrangheta moles. The fact that the feds went AWOL soon after they alerted me to the plausibility of Bold being Ndrangheta is also disturbing. Anyhow, the commissioner came round when I mentioned that Sue Elkington from *The Times* will also receive a full transcript in the event of my demise—professional or otherwise.'

'Knowing you, I guess you asked for a pound of flesh?' asked Ange.

'Of course. Clearly, the commissioner was always ready to pay me off with a deal to avoid embarrassing the service. I offered her a quick and easy resolution. Once she was on board, IA had nowhere to go,' said Anders, pausing briefly as if signalling an end to her story. 'So, there we have it. You're in the clear and I got my hands on some badly needed additional resources. You'll notice some new faces around the office.'

'Any word of Tedesco or Bold?'

'Nothing. It still irks me that Bold has so successfully staged his death and is being portrayed as a wonderful servant of the people. However, he's effectively out of the picture and can't return to Australia. Allowing the public to believe that lie is a small price to pay. In that respect, I guess I'm no better than the commissioner,' observed Anders in a rare moment of self-admonishment.

Ange had not yet finished, wanting to put to bed some of her own concerns.

'Do you think Internal Affairs will come back for a second bite?'

'I doubt it, not for the time being, at least. However, I don't trust them as far as I could kick them, so we should stay alert to their nonsense. Anyway, all's well that ends well is how I see it. Well, except for the part about you being shot, of course.'

Ange laughed at her boss's black humour. 'What about the feds? I don't want the guys who helped me to cop any heat over this.'

'Whether the feds are worried about a mole in their own ranks, or whether they would simply prefer to distance themselves for political reasons, I'm not sure. The hierarchy can wait, but I'll reach out and give your mates a heads-up. They can get me involved if they feel anything untoward is going on. Who knows, we may need their support again someday.'

'Boss, those guys are good. I would be happy to have them on my team any day. Hopefully, we don't need their type of firepower too often,' observed Ange.

'Oh, I forgot to mention. Those resources that I mentioned, the ones I extracted from the commissioner, they included Ted Kramer's crypto assets. It came with the proviso that they only get used for investigative purposes, which doesn't include more surfboards for my new lead investigator. Billy reckons his stash is worth close to a million dollars, even after this last market correction.'

Ange laughed while she figured who she might work under in the future. 'Wow. That was brilliant, boss. The way this stuff works, you need to be properly in the game. I'm sure we can do something with a million-dollar stake. I imagine it would have taken a month of Sundays to convince the bean-counters to exchange hard cash for crypto when we needed some. Who's your new lead investigator?'

'You, you idiot. Who else in my team would be at risk of buying a new surfboard with Kramer's cryptocurrency? Did that concussion mess with your powers of logic, Detective?'

'Wow,' replied Ange, the third time in this conversation that she had used that expletive, otherwise lost for alternate words. Anders' reveals usually took on the form of Russian nesting dolls, the ones made up of layers upon layers. 'That gives me a lot to think about, boss. Thanks for the support and your faith in me. And your name is again?'

Sally Anders laughed out loud at Ange's joke. 'You're welcome. Sleep easy, Detective. Oh, and happy birthday for the weekend.'

'Thanks, boss. How did you know that?'

'I've been poring over your service record way too much lately. Have fun. No dancing on tables.'

'I'll do my best, boss. To have fun, that is.'

Once Ange had finished the call, she reflected that her boss would make a fearsome politician herself, perhaps the perfect party whip. She was one formidable woman, a word that she increasingly associated with Sally Anders. Having the foresight to secure Ted Kramer's crypto nest egg was impressive. Hopefully, the sorry mess that had started way back in Namba Heads would amount to something. After all, Kramer's fortune was no use to him after the Ndrangheta had despatched him to the afterlife.

Ange's conversation with her boss represented a substantial change in fortune. Only yesterday, she was fretting over how she might deal with being relegated to serving as a traffic cop, posted far out west and away from her precious surf, potentially needing to put her precious surfboards into foster homes. Now, she had just gained a promotion of sorts.

It was yet another lesson on managing one's worries and fears. Worry could be a useful thing, forcing one to contemplate the options. However, the trick was to not let this worry take control and send your brain into fibrillation. Regrettably, that was something easier said than done.

The next day, she got a somewhat unexpected call from Special Investigator Ben Carruthers. He made the mistake of starting the call with a superior tone. 'Hello, Detective Watson. I'm just ringing to say that we don't see any avenue to take your case any further. This will be the last you'll hear from me on the matter.'

Ange knew it was the wrong thing to do, but her blood boiled uncontrollably. Fear and a misguided sense of superiority were currencies that the likes of Carruthers deployed to break spirits.

'You've been told to ring, haven't you, Special Investigator?' Ange raged at the fellow officer on the other end of the call. 'I get that you have a boss, but you guys are supposed to protect us and weed out this type of behaviour. It's part of your job description. Yet, you were quite prepared to protect your own backsides and stitch me with that pile of shit.' Ange knew from her time growing up on the farm in Tamworth, dealing with shearers and farmhands, that resorting to gutter language could be of strategic advantage in certain situations. This was one of those situations.

'It wasn't like that, Detective,' pleaded Carruthers. 'We can only go on what we're given in our brief.'

Rather than his excuses placating Ange, Carruthers failed to realise that he was only making things worse. 'That's complete bullshit and you know it. Your job is to look behind the smokescreen and check every nook and cranny. I know what you did, and if you try to pull a stunt like that on me or any of my colleagues ever again, I swear I will file a humongous harassment claim, one that you will never weasel your way out of. Believe me, you won't know what hit you.'

Stony silence met this last tirade, as the last crumbs of Carruthers' superior attitude were well and truly swept into the dustpan. She quit while she judged she was ahead, lest she spoil the lovely mood she had created. 'I never want to see or hear from you again. Goodbye.'

It took Ange some time to calm down. She craved a glass of wine, even though it was still not yet midday. Anyway, trying to navigate a glass of wine from the fridge to her couch would be another exercise in frustration.

She felt good, as things stood, despite her unrestrained rant.

Chapter 4

Birthday Wishes

J im Grady was one of the many well-wishers who rang the next Monday, the day of Ange's birthday. 'I hope you like your new surfboard.'

'It's beautiful, boss—I mean, Jim. Thanks for chipping in.'

The pair were referring to her birthday present, a beautiful powder-blue longboard that her friends had given her during a long and relaxing Sunday afternoon BBQ at Gus's estate. Kerrie had put the hat around and everyone had chipped in, although Ange knew that the major donor and source of inspiration had been Gus. On the bottom, in the style of Andy Warhol, was a custom mural showing an Ange-like figure, fashioned as a superhero. She could not wait to get that baby into the water.

'There was no way to resist your friend Kerrie, even if I'd wanted to. Her and Barb hit it off.'

'Kerrie has a way of doing that,' laughed Ange. 'Watch out. Barb will soon kit herself out with a new wardrobe, courtesy of Kerrie's lifestyle blog.'

The pair laughed again before Ange's fears and insecurities came knocking at the door. 'Boss?' she asked, failing again to break old habits. 'I had a grilling from Internal Affairs last week. It's been really messing with me. Did I make any stupid or naïve errors when we confronted Lomax and Smith in the bush? Be brutally honest with me, please.'

'Ange, the only error you made was having Billings by your side. That sleazebag of a sergeant would have jumped ship at the first opportunity. It was lucky for all of us that his Ndrangheta colleagues shot him before I did. Stop overthinking this. You did everything perfectly, except for getting yourself shot, of course. I won't hear another word about this, Detective,' replied Jim Grady emphatically.

'OK, boss. Thanks for having my back—again! By the way, could you keep a special eye on Bree while I'm out of action?'

'Sure. That is my job, you know,' replied Grady in a matter-of-fact tone of voice.

'Yes, I know, but I think Bree's got some special sauce. Just look over her shoulder like you looked over mine. That should do it.'

At Gus's invitation, Constable Breana White had come along to Ange's birthday BBQ following a hockey game on the Gold Coast. Bree, as she was commonly known, was a member of the national hockey team and hoped to become an Olympian. Ange was also mentoring Bree in how to become a detective, one that didn't get herself shot. Bree had easily held everyone's attention, exuding a vitality that was intoxicating. It was hard not to be impressed as she talked about her goals and aspirations.

The fact that Bree made money out of trading her NFT collection was something that always intrigued Ange's friends. Understanding how this curious technology made sense took some serious imagination. Ange was not surprised when Kerrie's partner, Mike, popped the question on everybody's mind. He was an early-stage venture capitalist, but what that entailed was forever opaque to Ange. Kerrie and Mike were a curious couple. Kerrie's social media persona was on permanent display, yet Mike played the part of an international man of mystery. 'So, Bree. How's your NFT trading been going?' he asked pointedly.

'That is a rollercoaster like you cannot imagine. My CoolCat NFT shot up to over two hundred thousand dollars but has since dropped back to forty-four thousand. This all happened in a matter of days and when I wasn't watching the market. Of course, I'm kicking myself. I could have put a deposit on an apartment with that sort of cash,' Bree explained.

'I suspect I know what might have distracted you, Bree,' wryly observed Ange. 'How does that even happen? The NFT rollercoaster, that is.'

Bree laughed at Ange's not-so-subtle reference to her week's holiday with Billy. The pair had taken some time off together after the gun battle incident, and Ange had quickly deduced what they'd been up to during their sojourn. Billy and Ange's own relationship went back to when the pair were stationed in Byron Bay. She relied on Billy as her personal tech maestro and had leaned on Sally Anders to enlist him into Major Crimes. Considering Ange's own patchy past performances, she was keen to see how Bree and Billy might manage a relationship at a distance, but that was a conversation for another day.

'Well,' said Bree, focussing back on the question that Mike had asked, 'there was a rumour that Nike or Adidas, I can't remember which, had plans to acquire the company that minted the NFTs. The market immediately spiked on that rumour, but crashed soon after it was exposed as a pump-and-dump scam.'

'What's a pump-and-dump scam look like, Bree?' asked Gus.

'Exactly like what happened to me. It's basically someone who gets in early and then uses social media to pump up the price before they cash out. The idea is nothing new and has been going on in the stock market forever. It's why I don't trust the stock market myself. Too many advisors and spruikers who need to make their money off me. Kerrie, with her incredible online following, could easily do this. I wouldn't recommend it though, as the marketplace will call you out and you may have to emigrate. Since NFTs are global, even emigrating wouldn't help you from being shamed and trolled. The CoolCat bubble that I missed was a brilliant pump-and-dump, where the anonymous rumour had its roots in some real live examples.'

Ange was struck by Bree's point of view and her generation's abject lack of faith and trust in age-old structures like the bourse. Yet, she was quite comfortable swimming with sharks in the crypto and NFT markets. Bree's generation took a similar approach to the media. Ange had once asked Billy about something she had read in the news, to which he'd confessed that he didn't read the news, instead relying on the social media news created and edited by his peers. A monumental shift was underway in how society communicated.

Ange spent the next four weeks in deep study. If only she would have applied herself even half as diligently at university, she would surely have secured a University Medal. As it was, her mildly above-average results had confined her degree deep into the bell curve of mediocrity. Naturally, she had totally aced any of her courses that involved the criminal mind.

She was like a sponge for any insights into the vulnerabilities of cryptocurrency and blockchain derivatives. As best as she could determine, the technology itself was bulletproof. It was always human behaviour which delivered any weak points to be exploited by the morally bankrupt.

One thing Ange realised was that many of the perpetrators did not consider themselves criminals. To them, this was a giant game, not unlike the video games that they played, a trait for which there was a high correlation. Of course, there were organised criminal gangs who went about fleecing punters from their crypto assets, gangs like the Ndrangheta, but these were in the minority. In fact, Ange had formed a view that the Ndrangheta had exploited Ethan Tedesco to learn their way around blockchain and how they might further exploit human frailties.

In that respect, narcotics and crypto seemed a perfect match. However, this alliance seemed to be largely that of small-time dealers and users finding a new way to transact—now that actual cash was becoming a novelty item. Even her friend Lisa only took dribbling amounts of cash at her market-day cake stall, with contactless pay now the norm. Covid had accelerated this trend, and crypto-entrepreneurs were intent on gaining market share. Even crypto-lenders had popped up, although Ange was having great difficulty with the mental gymnastics necessary to understand that business model. She had read with interest how one of the high-profile crypto-based lending platforms had recently collapsed—and in spectacular fashion.

In between these dark thoughts, Ange imagined what she would do with her liberty. Of course, there was her new powder-blue superhero longboard, a vessel that would undoubtedly ferry her to new pleasures and countless hours of fun. She was itching to wax up that baby and paddle out into a sun-infused turquoise sea, sparkling under a deep blue Byron Bay sky. Ange often stared longingly towards the sea during her recuperation. Her temporary hilltop lookout surveyed the entire coast around Byron Bay, which sat tantalisingly off in the distance. Getting back into the water was a future challenge to be navigated—a challenge to be relished.

Then, there were the nagging thoughts about what might happen once normal life resumed. She was scheduled to move back to Sydney in just over two months' time. Ange loved her job and the mental stimulation it provided. Sure, there was a lot of disturbing stuff that came her way, like getting shot, for instance.

However, working in a supportive team and trying to make the world a better place was an intoxicating experience. Despite her delusions that the ageing process did not apply, she was no longer in her mid-twenties with endless relationship opportunities in front of her—like Bree, for instance. She wasn't sure that she could manage a long-distance relationship with Gus if things panned out in line with her early-morning musings. The thought of slowly drifting away, using one's career as the excuse, was a reality that Ange could ill afford at her stage of life.

One Sunday, Gus had misinterpreted her distance-gazing, and they had taken a drive down to the ocean's shore. It had proved a catastrophe of sorts, creating an uncomfortable and embarrassing moment when she had fallen in a tangle of crutches and legs getting out of the car, badly grazing her elbow. Gus had felt terrible, but it was none of his doing. The falling part was all Ange, trying to stamp her independence and failing badly. There was no actual harm done, and her wounded elbow quickly healed. However, her wounded ego remained tender, so Ange vowed to stay put in her crow's nest until she could walk unaided.

Chapter 5

Cast Off

The day had promised to be a big one. A ginormous day, in fact. Ange had an appointment with her orthopaedic surgeon to remove the incredibly annoying full-length cast from her left leg. For the past six weeks, even the smallest of tasks had been a source of frustration. Forbidden from imparting any weight on the damn leg, she had been like a child again, unable to do anything for herself. Even going to the toilet had been an exercise in exasperation, although that was one task which she still preferred tackling alone. Crutches prevented simple pleasures like a good-old cup of tea in front of the TV, and she had needed to develop workarounds for almost everything. Ange had developed a newfound respect for anyone who suffered a permanent disability.

The first thing that she had planned was to take a long shower and wash her hair. Forced into wholly unsatisfying one-legged baths—plaster-of-Paris being allergic to water as it is—she thought she might even try to return her hair to something resembling her natural auburn hue; well, at least the natural hue provided by a bottle. She checked with Kerrie and learned that a solid bleaching was required to erase the edgy brunette she had assumed for her last case. The lengths that women went to. It all sounded like hard work.

Gus had kindly offered to drive her to the Lismore Base Hospital to visit her surgeon. Every cloud has a silver lining and Gus Bell was hers. Their relationship—friendship; courtship; whatever one called it—had developed slowly and naturally. Ange sometimes worried that she was victim to a variant of the Stockholm Syndrome, but their comfortable daytime banter and easy laughter erased those midnight misgivings. Gus seemed to sense that Ange needed some space in which to heal, and she had been playing it cool.

'God, he is handsome,' she thought, catching his glance in the mirror. Her straightened leg required Ange to fully recline the car seat, so the mirror was their only way of making eyes at each other. There was definite tension in the air.

Save for her humongous and unbecoming plaster cast, they would surely have already consummated their relationship. Ange knew this step was hers to take and she would need to weigh up the pros and cons after she appraised the state of her leg. While the pros were currently winning hands down, she didn't want to risk that crucial first time. Having him recoil from her hideous form was not a preferred outcome.

First impressions mattered, at least according to Kerrie. A consummate stylist, she had generously organised a new wardrobe to keep Gus's eye off Ange's mummified leg, and her ministrations seemed to have worked. Ange had wanted to pay for her 'war wardrobe', as they called it, but Kerrie insisted the clothes were gifts from well-wishers. Her bedside social media post, entitled *My Hero—Detective Ange Watson*, had apparently secured a bunch of new followers and grateful sponsors. Ange did not believe any of that story for an instant.

Despite her lustful urges, there was something that she needed to resolve before she shared a bed with Gus. Every other night, she would jump awake in a cold sweat as memories of that fateful day haunted her dreams. She needed to consider whether frantically sitting up in bed amidst cries of fear would turn Gus off. Perhaps he might feel that he was sleeping with a madwoman and not the hoped-for woman of his own dreams.

When all else failed, it was thoughts of surfing that calmed her down and drowned her nightmares. She would imagine carving down an expansive unbroken wave face, deep blue and feathered by a light offshore breeze. The epitome of style, Ange would then make a slow and elegant bottom turn before ducking under the crashing lip and into an epic tube ride. With her right hand trailing against the wave, leaving her mark on this unblemished canvas as she calmly raced toward the sunlit opening, her relaxed smile suggested that this was an everyday occurrence. Surfing had also brought Gus into her life, who was the other source of escape from her midnight panic attacks.

Ange prayed he would not devolve into one of her patented 'male fails'—of which there had been many. 'This time things will be different,' Ange promised herself. It had certainly started out that way, her invalid status keeping them out of the bedroom, instead focussing their attentions on becoming friends. Their night-time conversations habitually ranged over wide and open ground. Gus had been refreshingly open about his own chequered history regarding relationships. The only son of a surfing legend, he was facing the prospect of becoming a somewhat farcical middle-aged playboy before 'growing up', in his words. When he'd taken charge of the business side of his father's iconic surfboard manufacturing company, this exalted position had delivered a plethora of beautiful Byron Bay girls to keep him company. As bad as he may have been with relationships, not so with his business sense. Bell Surfboards went from strength to strength and somehow Gus had grown the business while still preserving the mystique of their iconic brand.

'Are you OK, Ange? Where have you been on the drive over? You seem distracted,' asked Gus as he painstakingly unpacked her from his car.

'I'm great, Gus. Just thinking about getting my leg and my liberty back,' she lied. 'It's been a long six weeks.'

The sign said 'Waiting Room', which it was, but other descriptors may have been equally appropriate. Worry; Vanity; Self-Doubt; Insecurity—these alternate adjectives made equal sense. As excited as Ange was with the prospect of being relieved of her cumbersome cast, she was also anxious about what it might uncover. Would she bear hideous scars, her leg reduced to a permanently disfigured mess? Ange had always considered that her legs were her best feature—well, had been her best feature before a bullet ruined the picture. Would she now feel self-conscious when her legs were on display at the beach? Worse still, in coital intimacy? These were not the concerns of a battle-scarred and gritty detective—more those of a woman unsure, shallow and insecure about her looks. It was all most disconcerting.

When her turn came, she was grateful that Gus offered to wait outside. She needed to deal with this test on her own, although she appreciated his helping hand to retrieve her crutches when they slid off the metal arms of the waiting room chair and clattered loudly on the vinyl floor. She could not wait to hand those suckers back. Her orthopaedic surgeon was a burly man, not the type that Ange would have normally associated with surgical precision, although she noticed that his touch was light as he helped her onto his examining table/bed, already prepped and ready for her breakout. She hoped this would be nothing like when her post-surgical drip had been extracted. That had felt as if her thigh was being turned inside out. She shivered at that memory.

The reciprocating saw whined into action, starting on her lower leg, and cutting through the hardened cast with ease. Now discoloured and grubby from the past six weeks, her cast had taken on an increasingly buttery hue with each spill or mishap. When she was at boarding school, it had been a ritual to scrawl messages over the casts endured by schoolmates. These were visible symbols of affection and well wishes, not the puerile scrawls of immature teenagers that rolled her teachers' eyes. Why, as an adult, did this seem inappropriate somehow? At what age did we lose the ability to express our feelings so readily and demonstrably? Ange had probed these memories a few days prior, considering how she might express her own feelings in the coming days or weeks.

Although it was an otherwise painless experience, once her cumbersome plaster cocoon was peeled back, Ange realised she had good reason to be worried. Her leg was a mottled and disconcerting appendage she failed to recognise. The scar from the gunshot wound shone purple, a raised welt that screamed loudly. Surely this withered and pathetic object belonged to someone else? Her hands instinctively slid along her left thigh, passing over the wound itself, as if tentatively checking it was hers. The surgeon asked her to roll over slightly whilst he examined his handiwork. He seemed pleased, muttering 'that's good', perhaps a rote observation to ease his patients' angst.

'OK. Let's get you up,' he said matter-of-fact-like, as if this move was a mere trifle.

'What do you mean? Now? Without crutches?'

'Yes. Your fracture is completely healed. That point will be stronger than the rest of your femur. There's some scar tissue that we still need to deal with, but you're good to go in terms of weight bearing. We may need to consider removing your screws at some point, but that's a decision for another day. I understand that you have your first physio appointment straight after mine.'

'Do you deal with gunshot wounds like mine very often?' asked Ange as she gingerly swung her legs off the table and bent her left knee for the first time in ages.

'You'd be surprised. Farmers mostly. Either distracted or sloppy. Nearly always involving feet and lower legs. OK. Up you get,' replied her surgeon decisively. Evidently, this was often a time-wasting point of contention amongst his patients.

Simple things are rarely that when properly examined. Walking, something that Ange had always taken for granted, was one such simplicity. She could not recall learning to walk as a toddler, although she had observed the many falls and tears of her friends' children. The toddler would invariably take each stumble in its stride, the embodiment of flexibility and malleability, immediately making a fresh attempt at this wondrous defiance of gravity. Her friends would always complain about the challenges of restraining their liberated children once they had achieved two-legged mobility, a state that quickly escalated into a wobbling run as they yearned to escape custody.

Most everything exists as the pinnacle of the evolutionary process. Take surfing, one of life's *simple pleasures*. The surfboard was an incredibly sophisticated blend of chemistry, fluid dynamics, design, and style. Then there was the wetsuit that kept one warm on winter days. And let's not forget the transport that delivered you to your surf spot. When one looked under the hood, surfing was no *simple pleasure* at all.

Engaging unused and stiff muscles, each needing to fire off in a finely tuned sequence, was not the perfunctory act that Ange remembered. When she finally stumbled back out to reception, she felt like a toddler herself. There was quite a deal of pain as each step stretched muscles and tore apart scar tissue, but at least she brandished those bloody crutches in one hand, a victory wave of sorts. She shot off a determined smile towards Gus before lurching straight over to the dispensary. The woman working behind the counter commented that retrieving hire crutches was a highlight of her job.

As she staggered back towards Gus, he met her halfway and simply enveloped her with his arms, their first ever fully fledged and unrestrained full-body hug. It was lovely. She didn't want this to end, but the physio beckoned.

'I have a physio appointment now, Gus. Are you sure that you're OK to wait? I can catch a taxi back to your place.'

'All good. Take your time. I have my laptop with me, so I'll find a quiet corner and get some work done. Text me when you're done. I'll also make some dinner reservations for tonight so we can celebrate. Kerrie has already rung me to ask how you are. She's been driving me crazy checking up on you,' Gus laughed as he picked up the laptop satchel that had been resting against the waiting room wall.

This feeling of being loved, on top of the morning's emotional roller coaster she was riding, suddenly made Ange teary. 'What the heck?' she thought. This was not the person she wanted Gus to see. She glanced away sheepishly, embarrassed by her own emotional fragility. Gus just put down his satchel and gave her an even bigger hug. Her tears fell unchecked, making a conspicuously damp patch on his polo shirt. Once she had finally stopped crying, she reluctantly pulled herself from that embrace and wiped her watery eyes.

Ange turned to make her way to her physiotherapy appointment, probably to encounter more tears. No more was said. Nothing needed to be said.

Chapter 6

Liberty

Her first physiotherapy appointment was painful. Apparently, Sally Anders had insisted that the physio practice schedule daily sessions until she was sufficiently mobile. By the time she had finished for the day, damaged muscles massaged and stretched beyond their comfort zone, she felt worse than when she'd started. The therapist lent her a walking stick and showed her how to use it properly, on the opposite side to her injury ironically. Tough love seemed the order of a physio's day.

Gus drove her back to his house. He went to help her from the car, but Ange resisted his offer. She needed to regain a normal existence. First thing, however, was an excessively long shower, something she had missed terribly. A hot shower was surely one of humanity's greatest inventions—if one ignored the amount of water that was used. She had read somewhere that, in a similarly arid South American country, residents were being directed to pee in the shower to save water. In her rush to get into the shower, she had forgotten that basic need and was thankful knowing that it wasn't poor form at all, especially for the environment. Despite Australia being one of the driest continents on the planet, Ange doubted that any similar directive would take off here.

Hair shampooed, then again, then conditioned, glistening with body lotion, Ange spent an hour or two doing all the little personal grooming chores that had been neglected on account of her ungainly cast. Her body and soul rejoiced at this attention, and she felt human again, although the deep blue scar on her leg still looked unearthly. The surgeon had made a neat anterior incision to repair her bone; it was in a place that Ange could not properly see without the help of a mirror, although she knew it would be obvious to others. Unlike the 'I'll show you mine if you show me yours' scenes popular in the movies, Ange was not yet proud of her wounds.

After giving her some space, Gus came over to confirm that they had a booking for dinner at her favourite Japanese restaurant. Japanese food was a delicacy that she had missed desperately during the past month and a half. Ange needed to tackle the elephant in the room, at least the elephant that she was sitting on. 'Gus, you've been so generous. Don't feel obligated to keep looking after me. I don't wish to outstay my welcome, let alone start driving your cars. You can move me on, you know.'

Gus looked positively hurt. 'Do you want to leave? I understand if you do, certainly now that you're regaining some independence.'

'As if I would want to leave this view,' replied Ange, gesturing towards the ocean in front. 'The company's not too bad either. I'd love to stay—if you'll have me. But on the proviso that you tell me when I've outstayed my welcome.'

'I'm pleased. It's cool having my very own detective staying in-house. If anything, I reckon you'll get itchy feet before I get sick of you. Now, the dinner reservation is for 7 p.m. I'll come over and collect you around 6:15. You can drive there, and I'll drive home. That will give me an opportunity to show you the ins and outs of the Subaru.'

Ange wondered what would become of their friendship. She didn't quite know what to think. Despite her late-night fantasies, she had set aside the question of how to progress their relationship. This had been something to tackle once she was back on her feet, so to speak. She wondered what Gus might be thinking. Was his generosity borne of charity or compassion for the victim? Was she guilty of evoking the hurt puppy dog feelings in him?

She pulled herself from these answerless questions to try on some of the new clothes that Kerrie had progressively dropped over on her many visits. Ange's new Byron Bay recovery wardrobe was now considerably more impressive than her old one. She tried on every piece before settling for a slinky singlet top over a long, flowing peasant-style skirt. Not trusting herself with any sort of heel, she chose some ballet flats.

Kerrie rang in the middle of Ange's private fashion show. 'What are you wearing, Ange?'

Ange gave a description of her preferred outfit. 'Perfect,' replied Kerrie. 'I love that skirt. I'll introduce you to the designer one day. She owes me big-time. I got her stuff into some upmarket stores in Brisbane. See you at 7 p.m.'

Ange was sitting on the balcony, her legs crossed for the first time in ages and admiring the first tinges of the incoming sunset, when she saw Gus walking her way. She stood up and retrieved her walking stick.

'You look amazing, Ange. That skirt really suits you.'

'That's all Kerrie,' she replied somewhat sheepishly, before finding her smile and good humour. 'I think the walking stick sets off the ensemble nicely, don't you think? Although I'm doubtful that this is the look the designer was going for. Who knows, gunshot chic could be a whole new genre once Kerrie and her camera get cracking.'

Gus somehow struck the perfect balance between style, comfort and cool, in keeping with his image as a major surfing identity. Ange thought he looked perfect.

Gus jangled the keys to his second car, a Subaru wagon. 'Ange, how about you drive down and I'll drive home? You can keep using the Subaru as long as you need. It's an automatic, which should make it easier for you. I'll drive the old Volvo for a bit. The clutch on that thing is a beast. When you're ready, the Subaru should be ideal for your surfing, although it is not as cool a ride as the Volvo,' he said with a broad smile, referring to his uber-cool and fully restored 1974 Volvo 240 station wagon.

Getting back in the driver's seat for the first time in ages was confronting for an instant, before familiarity born of countless cars and countless hours behind the wheel took over. Gus showed her all the important switches and off they went, winding their way down from the hinterland into the township. Ange even pulled off a perfect reverse park, which was lucky, as she feared that putting a dent in Gus's car might have put a dent in their relationship. Her performance left him suitably impressed.

Kerrie and Mike spied her the moment she hobbled into the restaurant, and they both came over to give her a big hug. Kerrie stood back and surveyed her outfit. 'Hopefully you can lose the walking stick soon,' she commented offhandedly, confining the whole gunshot chic movement straight to the dustbin.

'Come on, show us your scar,' she asked, as subtle as a sledgehammer and showing no restraint, despite the look of discomfort in Ange's eyes. 'What, you haven't shown anyone yet? You should be proud of it, Ange.'

Proud was not the word that Ange had in mind, but she knew from long experience that Kerrie would not be dissuaded. She sat down, and as demurely as was possible, pulled up her skirt to display her wounded thigh.

'Wow, my first gunshot wound. It's looks just like in the movies. You know that I'm trying to convince Mike to fund a miniseries about you.'

'That would be a total snoozefest, and you know it, Kerrie,' said Ange as she unfurled her skirt and let it drape over her wounded leg. She noticed that Gus had stood back during her showing, looking decidedly uneasy. Was his discomfort borne out of care for her privacy, or was he confronted by her damaged leg? Kerrie gave no time for these doubts to spoil the evening as she handed her a present.

'What's this, Kerrie? You need to stop this. You've already given me too much stuff.'

'It's just a little something to go with your outfit. I've been looking for the right person to give it to.'

Ange opened the box to reveal a multicoloured necklace, the perfect match for her skirt. She leaned across and gave Kerrie a hug of thanks.

The formalities concluded, the two couples fell into a series of spirited conversations that ranged over wide and open country, some of it familiar and some of it new. It was 11 p.m. before they knew it. After goodbyes, Gus drove the Subaru back to his home. Their self-conscious peck on the cheek was almost awkward, leaving Ange with a nagging concern that she had somehow put Gus off. That was not what she had wanted.

Chapter 7

First Day

After two long weeks of physio, each visit as painful as the last, Ange was ready to take her beautiful new baby for an outing. She had been desperate to let her glorious birthday present loose in the water and had remained diligent with her exercises during her recuperation. As her strength built, she focussed on jump-ups, a strenuous exercise to imitate the move that a surfer makes on take-off. This was by far the most fragile moment of any ride, where strength, timing, experience, and guts all came into play. The more confident and precise the jump-up, the better the outcome—well, mostly. There was always lots to go wrong in those first few milliseconds. Her physio had insisted she could do no actual damage by getting back in the water, provided she did nothing stupid—something easier said than done in the heat of the moment.

A couple of nights back, she had finally fallen head over heels in love. It had come as a shock, borne of a dream where she was travelling with Gus on a yacht, off on some surfing adventure. The confluence of these desires was obvious in hindsight. Ange had spent months suppressing the horror of what had happened in the scrub that fateful day and had used thoughts of Gus and surfing to ease her terror.

However, there is no more apprehensive feeling or greater fear than when you have fallen in love with someone—especially when they don't know it yet. Ange struggled to recall the last time that she had felt this way. That honour most likely went to Scott Partridge. She had almost forgotten about Scott until her mother had reminded her a few Christmases ago, showing Ange where she had scratched the words 'I love Scott Partridge' under the kitchen table. Goodness knew what her mother was doing under the table. One might wonder what Ange had been doing, scratching the name of her infatuation in this way—although she had only been seven years old at the time.

She had since proven to be a gross disappointment to her mother, failing to add to the growing herd of grandchildren. Her brothers had delivered some relief from this pressure, but she knew that her mother yearned for Ange to experience that joy. It was a topic her mother broached indelicately each year, an unsatisfying discussion that usually accompanied the Christmas plum pudding. Which was where Scott Partridge had come into the conversation, a fresh twist in the festivities. For goodness' sake, Ange almost felt as if her mother expected Ange to look him up and rekindle their friendship of three decades past.

It had been almost three months since she had packed for a proper surf excursion. Once she had folded down the rear seats of Gus's Subaru, she was pleased to find that her new longboard slid in nicely. It was her preferred way to carry her boards, tucked safely in the cabin. She recalled a time when she had seen a surfboard fly off the roof of a car she was following. Fortunately, the board had spun and spiralled up and away like a gigantic gum leaf, before disappearing into the roadside bushes. As a police officer, she had felt obliged to stop. The board's owner was almost in tears as they walked back down the highway, searching amongst the vegetation. It was a brand-spanking-new surfboard, and in his haste to get to the beach, he had made a poor job of securing it to the roof. Fortunately, the accident hurt no one, and the board had remained remarkably intact. It had suffered little more than a couple of depressions on the deck, the least important part of any surfboard. Ange had let him go with no fine or serious reprimand. He was unlikely to make that mistake again.

Out of rhythm with this ritual, she triple-checked everything before driving down towards Byron Bay. Ange had judiciously planned the right day for her surfing comeback and had chosen a truly magnificent morning, the best that Byron Bay could offer. The light south-westerly wind was predicted to swing slowly around toward the east and the conditions would be perfect until lunchtime, more than enough time for Ange to test herself. She had made a half-hearted invitation for Gus to join her, but he seemed to sense that she needed to do this on her own. She marvelled at his self-confessed transformation from being a selfish playboy to someone so caring.

Ange chose The Pass for her comeback, a surf spot which had options and offered waves of varying degrees of intensity. Hopefully, she could range across the various sections until she found a break that suited her confidence level. Before any of that could occur, she needed to wax her new board for the very first time. This seemingly routine act was an almost intimate experience, where a covenant is made between surfer and board. After that first time, applying wax becomes a rushed and urgent affair, a chore which steals away surfing time. She had a new leg rope, a lifesaving device that she attached to the special plug fibreglassed into the deck. Her new leash was bright red, in stark contrast to the soft powder blue of her beauty, perhaps a warning that her special pet must not stray too far. Ange was yet to name her new love, which was unusual for her. All her other boards had personalities and names to match. Hopefully, today would deliver clarity on that point—amongst others.

The weather was warm, but Ange knew that the water would still be cool, so she pulled on a new spring suit that she had purchased online. Pleasingly, the fitting guide had been accurate, and it sat snug against her body. Despite her stretching and physiotherapy, the heat of battle would undoubtedly expose her lack of flexibility. The spring suit would hopefully keep her muscles warm and flexible for those moments. Importantly, her new spring suit covered up the deep-violet scars on her thigh, something she remained self-conscious about.

So, there she was, standing on the foreshore, checking out the waves. She glanced up regularly from her stretching exercises to determine the most appropriate section for her tentative state of mind. The surf report had been spot-on and waves were shoulder high and perfect for her plans. Her new board was a handful to carry, wider and longer than any she had owned previously. She needed two hands to carry it down to the water's edge, taking care not to trip on her bright red leg rope, an easy trap for the unwary. The sea before her shimmered turquoise, rippled in places by the light breeze that moved across its surface. The breaking waves flashed mother-of-pearl, in stark contrast to this blue-green hue, a confluence of colour that had surely offered inspiration to countless artists and fashion designers for centuries—such was this brilliance.

After wading in a few metres, she laid the board on top of the ocean and used its buoyancy to help her balance. The cold seeped into her spring suit and somehow focussed on her wounded thigh, a stabbing sensation that intensified her feelings of self-doubt. She pushed off the sand, leapt atop her baby and paddled enthusiastically outward. The first thing she noticed about her new longboard was how much easier it was to paddle, buoyed by its extra volume and lighter modern construction. Her old longboard had been an ancient clunker that weighed an absolute ton. Ange had sold that monster for a mere one hundred dollars before she moved back to Sydney and had all but forgotten about the difficulties presented by whitewater, longboards being virtually impossible to duck-dive under a wave of any size and power. After a few botched attempts, she remembered how to execute this tricky manoeuvre and eventually reached the unbroken water beyond the waves. The session was not exactly going to the plan that she had fashioned when lying in bed that morning.

Once she was safely out the back, she sat on her board and looked around. A flock of coastal birds was feasting out wide, picking up the scraps left by some feeding fish, most likely early-season spotty mackerel or late-season long-tail tuna—they were too far away to be sure. That was a good thing, as even more aggressive feeders followed these schools of pelagic fish. Larger mutton birds were making kamikaze raids, dive-bombing the ocean to secure larger fish that swam deeper. A lone albatross swooped along distant swell lines, perhaps heading south for summer, using the updraft to its advantage, the epitome of grace in flight. She looked back towards the shoreline, which was still deeply scoured after an episode of headland bypassing, a natural phenomenon which had stolen millions of tonnes of sand from the beach. The sand was slowly coming back, but the scars remained, an obvious allegory for Ange's own state. The entire scene was deeply cathartic—a cleansing of the spirit.

A nicely formed shoulder-height wave finally came her way. The time had come. Ange clumsily manoeuvred her board around to face the shore, finding this to be a more laborious exercise than expected. There would be no late take-offs that day—she needed time to prepare for that moment of truth. With the wave now in her sights, Ange paddled her board up to intercept speed. A key benefit of a longboard is that it allows the rider to pick up waves earlier and further out than those riding shortboards. It surprised Ange how quickly the swell collected her, still some way off breaking. Thankful for the extra stability offered by the long and wide board, Ange popped onto her feet, adrenaline overcoming apprehension to make a successful take-off. She quickly turned to glide across the unbroken face.

Her new board was fast, particularly seeing as the swell was of modest size. She swept along the wave face, making a series of slow, graceful turns, tentatively testing how her new baby performed. A section formed ahead, threatening to break and spoil her fun. Ange turned to the very top of the wave and then down again, garnering as much speed as possible and making a long skating turn around the white-water spoil, easing back into the clean wave face and off again. She was determined to make this wave last as long as possible and sought to eke out every pinch of pleasure. In the last few metres, as the wave was petering out, she looked up to see the magnificent albatross coming towards her, swooning on the next swell across. Ange held out her arms and mimicked the giant bird as its wings tilted this way and that. It was a breathtaking moment.

She wasn't entirely sure how long her ride had lasted. The usual measures seemed inadequate for such events, where each microsecond was jam-packed with sensory encounters, experiences to be replayed and savoured frame-by-frame and in all their splendour. All sports people know about those precious moments, in-the-zone, when time stretches and perfection is attained.

At the end of her time-bending ride, Ange collapsed back onto her board, sobbing with joy, relief, perhaps shock at what she might have missed had the bullet struck mere centimetres to her right. She paddled out on autopilot, flushed with emotion and grateful for her existence. A fellow surfer saw her face as she paddled past. 'Are you OK?' he asked, perhaps wondering what could be so wrong on such a day.

'I'm incredible. Thanks for asking. My first ride on this new board,' said Ange, as if this might deliver some explanation for the volcano of emotional outpouring that was behind her tears. 'What a day.'

She must have surfed for over two hours that morning, forced to leave the water due to cramping calves and a left thigh that finally refused to cooperate on take-off. After the second embarrassing fail, face-planting down the wave and being rolled over and over, she decided it was time to call the session. Her morning surf had been an all-round success and there seemed no point in pushing her luck. As she was walking off the beach, she recalled her many moments of joy that morning. It was no normal surf, as there was a sense of relief and thanks embedded, where she had faced the alternate reality that had passed so close by.

The name for her new surfboard came in a flash. It could only be called Bluey, named in honour of Ted Kramer's super-smart blue cattle dog that she had met some months back. 'It' became a 'he' at that moment. Bluey, the barking 'he', was not only skilled at sniffing out bad eggs but had helped bring Ange's pursuit of the syndicate to its violent conclusion. Of course, it turned out to be a su-per-syndicate, one that was hundreds of years old in the form of the Ndrangheta

Mafia. None of the part involving Ange getting shot was the fault of Bluey the dog, but without him, she would never have met her beautiful powder-blue Bluey Longboard—he wouldn't hurt a fly.

It felt good to have this settled. Her surfboards were not mere inanimate objects, and they did not deserve to remain nameless—important friends and companions as they were. She would only be half the person she was without them. Gus had chosen Bluey Longboard well, knowing that her recovery from injury would make a shortboard hard work. As it was, even with the help of Bluey Longboard, there was still some way to go. Certainly, her session today was not one of a superhero, despite the mural beneath.

Once rinsed and changed, her new pet safely tucked away, she drove into town. After finding a strategically located carpark, she enjoyed an early sushi lunch, before walking to her physio appointment. After some punishing pokes and stretches at the hands of her physiotherapist, Ange took immense delight in handing back the borrowed walking stick.

She had promised a special meal to celebrate her return to the water and had settled on making a Sicilian fish dish, the recipe for which she had found online. She chose flathead as the fish, one of her favourites. The moment called for something with bubbles, so she also picked up a bottle of sparkling Tasmanian Riesling to accompany the meal. It was nice to be busy again. Idleness was a profoundly overrated state.

Ange drove back to Gus's estate to prepare dinner. Gus was still not home, so she let herself into the main house and started preparations. The sauce was a salsa of olives, garlic, tomato, carrots, and zucchini, with capers and anchovies serving as the two special ingredients. Once the salsa was complete, she laid her flathead fillets onto an oiled cast-iron casserole dish she found in one of the kitchen drawers, poured over the salsa and put it into the fridge. Although none was required, Ange still whipped up a simple salad of lettuce, shaved parmesan, and some avocado. Ange had been keeping a close eye on her carbohydrate intake, but nibbles were essential. She whipped up some guacamole, extra spicy, accompanied by thin crispbread, something she felt sure would go well with the sparkling wine she had chosen.

Once dinner was ready and with the time approaching 5 p.m., Ange walked across to the guest house to prepare herself. She took her time showering and washing her hair, a feature that had grown only halfway to nowhere, still far from appealing in her eyes. Doing the best she could with what she had, she still felt like one of her childhood rag dolls—decidedly uninspiring for what she had in mind.

She tried on several outfits from her stylish *war wardrobe*, before settling with a simple linen dress in the palest of blue, perfect after the day she had just enjoyed. She was still not comfortable wearing shoes with any heel, but the dress looked great with ballet flats and the necklace that Kerrie and Mike had given her some weeks back. Despite her rag top, she felt pleased with the overall result. She heard Gus's Volvo drive up to the gravel courtyard and into his garage. She met him outside and he looked dusty and worn out, certainly not the look of a successful CEO.

'Hi, Gus. Dinner is ready and in the fridge. When do you want to eat?'

'Wow. You look amazing. I guess I'd best get myself cleaned up. We had a tough run in the factory today. Two staff off with Covid and a backlog of orders we can't jump over. I spent the day in production, helping whatever staff remained. I haven't been on the factory floor for years and I'd forgotten how tiring it could be. It was good, though, as I picked up quite a few ideas on how we can improve things. I probably should make a habit of that—Covid or no Covid.'

'Perhaps we should start dinner early, seeing as you're so tired. Is thirty minutes enough time for you to get all handsomed up?'

'I'd need a year and Kerrie's help for that. See you in twenty minutes. I can't wait to hear about your day.' Gus smiled before he shot off to the house for a much-needed shower.

Ange was laying out her guacamole dip and drinks on the balcony when Gus walked out. 'I love that shirt,' she commented, appreciating his bright floral shirt over bone jean-style pants and soft brown moccasins. His longish hair was still wet, and he'd done nothing more than smooth it back through his fingers—a complete contrast to the blowing and brushing ordeal that Ange had endured. She considered Gus had made a fine effort in getting himself handsomed.

As they settled into their nibbles and a flute of sparkling wine, the first question on Gus's mind was about her surf.

'It was amazing to be back in the water. Bluey Longboard was perfect for me. We're going to be firm friends,' answered Ange. Seeing the quizzical look on Gus's face, she explained. 'Bluey Longboard is the name I christened my birthday present. All my boards have names. There's JayTee, who you already know, since you sold him to me; then there's Franky, my Sydney public transport bruiser; then

Maverick, my pintail thruster for when the waves are fast and steep; and finally there's Malcolm in the middle, my midsize for when nothing else is quite right.'

'They're all men's names,' observed Gus.

'Of course! I'm not inclined to get so intimate with another woman. But that's just my inclination, in case you might be wondering,' she explained with a mischievous smile. 'Let me put dinner in the oven. Back in a minute.'

Dinner underway and drinks in hand, Ange gave Gus a full description of her day, including her moment of communing with the majestic albatross. Gus's day had been nowhere nearly as exhilarating, but he seemed satisfied. He expressed a desire for them to have a surf together soon. Now that Ange had conquered her first day back in the water, she was just as eager to share her passion with him.

With the meal served and more wine poured, dinner fell into an easy rhythm. Although Ange had fashioned her plan the previous evening as she tried to fall asleep, she was unsure how to execute. She instinctively knew that any move was hers to make. Gus had been so compassionate and understanding of her situation over the past two months, it was unreasonable to expect that he would take the next fateful step.

The moment, when it came, flowed naturally as they were cleaning up after their meal. They brushed past each other in the narrow galley kitchen, and a spark ignited. Without thinking, Ange turned and kissed Gus, a tender kiss that quickly raced out of control.

The pair stumbled and fumbled their way into Gus's bedroom, scattering discarded clothes along the way. There was no time for foreplay, such was the sense of urgency. The act of joining, when the universe collapsed in an intoxicating implosion, one of indeterminate duration, was everything that Ange had hoped for—her second such experience in one day.

Chapter 8

Almost Bliss

The next two weeks were magnificent, the happiest that Ange could ever recall. It was a sensation that was perhaps only challenged by that first day of summer holidays, being released from boarding school and back on the farm in Tamworth with Buddy, her much loved red cattle dog.

Her fortnight of bliss had fallen into a routine. Surf by day, come rain, hail, or shine; a shared dinner, either with friends or just with each other; with the day bookended by lovemaking. Ange had fully moved into the main house and had remained a permanent fixture in Gus's bedroom. After that first night, she had quietly tried to get up and leave Gus to return to the guest house.

'Where do you think you're going?' he asked, grabbing her arm and pulling her gently back into his bed. After a few days trudging back and forth, retrieving clothes and other of life's paraphernalia, Gus had put his foot down. 'This is ridiculous. Go over and bring all your stuff back here. Anyway, I need my guest house back.'

Even amongst such contentment, her nightmares persisted, but Gus helped soothe the demons that were chasing, when her cries in the night would wake them both. Ange leaned on Dr Kirby Hall several times, chats which had helped far more than she could ever have imagined. Mostly, these chats came because of those incessant nightmares, poorly named given that not all of them came in the dark of night.

One day, as she was walking through town, a hotted-up car had backfired loudly as it cruised down the main street. Ange had impulsively leaped sideways and cowered into a shopfront, almost knocking over a young girl on the sidewalk. She pulled herself together when she realised that the loud bang was not that of a gunman. She had apologised and made her peace with the young girl, but the incident left her shaking, her own peace not regained for the rest of that day.

This inability to let go of her trauma worried Ange. Did this mean that she wasn't up to being a detective again, like one of those police dogs that never recovered from being shot? Ange preferred to work through her problems on her own, but these fearful moments were debilitating. The car incident tipped her over the edge, and, with some sense of failure, she rang Dr Kirby Hall again.

'I'm still having nightmares all the time. Is this normal or will I go crazy? Will I ever be able to do my job again or will I constantly be jumping at shadows?' Ange blurted out, not knowing the best way to approach one's psychiatrist with such problems.

'Tell me about it,' asked Hall easily, as if she was asking about a fabulous restaurant that Ange was raving about.

Ange was hesitant at first before blurting out a complete account of the incident.

'I'm not concerned about the backfiring car. That could happen to anyone, even someone who hadn't been shot. Is there a theme to the nightmares?' probed Hall.

'Yes, probably. It always involves someone, probably Lomax and Smith, although I can't see their faces. They jump out of everyday places and start shooting. I always freeze and can't seem to move or do anything to protect myself.'

'What happens when you wake up?'

'If I yell out, I always wake up Gus. He's been good about it and helps calm me down,' replied Ange before realising that the last time she had seen Dr Kirby Hall was before her relationship with Gus had progressed to another level. 'Oh, I forgot to mention that I've started a relationship with Gus Bell. You met him briefly when you came to visit me.'

'I'm pleased for you. I could sense something smouldering in the background when I visited. Do you talk about your nightmares with him?'

'No, not really. He seems to drift back to sleep, and I usually lie there for ages.'

'Well, I could give you a prescription for something that will help with that, but sleeping tablets can become addictive, so let's leave that as a last resort. Can I suggest you try talking over these nightmares with your partner? Even though they seem real, they're in your imagination. Talking these episodes through with him might help put them into perspective. If you don't wake him, then talk about your nightmare the next morning. If you can't get back to sleep, document the episode in a notebook, a type of sleep journal.'

'That will help—writing them down?' asked Ange, thinking that this was a slightly macabre use of her trusty notebook, although it had probably seen worse.

'The absolute worst thing you can do is bottle them up, so don't do that—whatever you do. There's also an app that can help deal with PTSD, which is what you're experiencing. The app senses when you're entering this phase during the night and will wake you up before the nightmares set in. Do you have a smartwatch?'

'I didn't wish to burden Gus with my crazy dreams. And, no, I don't have a smartwatch,' replied Ange.

'They're your fears, not his. Talking about them won't bother him as much as it will help you. Can you ask him to call me, and I'll give him some strategies to work through? I'm also going to send you some recommendations for a smartwatch and a link to the sleep app. You can claim it back from the department. I'll let your boss know. Don't mess around with this. Go out and get the watch straight away and I'll ring you in a week to check how you're doing. Remember to get your partner to ring me. Today would be good,' pressed Hall.

Her recuperation had been a torrid period in her life. She would never have survived without the support of Gus, Kerrie, and her other friends. Kerrie, of course, took total credit for easing Gus into Ange's life. She would be forever grateful to Kerrie for that. Yet, the level of concern shown by her psychiatrist had worried Ange. She had purchased her smartwatch and Gus had a long conversation with Dr Hall, which had made Ange annoyingly jealous, childishly so.

The decision about what to do with her career had been stalking her for days. With her extended leave rapidly evaporating, Ange finally made her decision and rang Sally Anders.

'Hi, boss. I'm sorry to do this to you, but I can't come back to Sydney. I don't know exactly what I'll do yet, but that's my decision,' Ange blurted out before her boss even had time to answer. Tension and discomfort about this news had forced her straight to the crunch.

'I thought this might happen. I presume this is about Gus Bell?' asked Anders. Ange's silence was an adequate answer. 'Your old boss gave me the heads-up. Apparently, Barb had torn strips off him when he mentioned that he was worried you might throw your career away—his words, not mine. Kirby Hall rang me as well. She was very supportive of your relationship with Gus. I'm pleased that he's not a colleague this time around,' said Anders, referring to Ange's former relationship with Brett Tompkins.

It shouldn't have been a surprise to discover that her old boss, Sergeant Jim Grady, had spoken with her current boss. Gus had accompanied Ange to dinner at the Gradys' a fortnight earlier. Barbara Grady had seemed most impressed with Gus Bell. Apparently, Jim Grady and Sally Anders had been friends for ages, although Ange had never fully established the source of their connection. To be fair, when Ange had fallen into that relationship with Brett, she hadn't realised that he was working undercover for Major Crimes. If anyone was at fault, it was Brett, but Sally Anders knew all of that. Nonetheless, Ange did need to concede that the second round of that affair, relationship, infatuation, or whatever they had been doing, had been mostly her fault.

'So, I gather that the cat's well and truly out of the bag about Gus,' observed Ange, allowing Anders to have her fun by letting the friendly ribbing about Brett Tompkins go through to the keeper.

'You should know that I have my sources. Moving on, I see I approved an expense claim for a smartwatch. That's a first,' commented Anders in a questioning tone of voice.

'Kirby told me to get one. Don't worry, I was looking after your finances and went for a budget model. Apparently, you can even take calls on the high-end models while you're surfing. You can ring me when I'm asleep, boss, but not when I'm out surfing,' joked Ange.

'Your expense claim didn't exactly scream *budget model,* but how is this smartwatch working out for you?'

'It's working well. I'm not sure how it does it, but the app somehow anticipates where my dreams are heading. This week, I had my first night without a nightmare for a long time. My leg is healing well—the daily surfing and walking are doing the trick. It's my mind that isn't cooperating. I didn't think it would be like this.'

Sally Anders' voice softened from that of a boss worried about expenses, to one worried about the wellbeing of her staff. 'It sounds to me as if you're making excellent progress on several fronts. Anyhow, that all works out rather well.'

This was not the response Ange had been expecting. 'What do you mean by that? Did you already decide to pension me off?'

'No, you've completely got the wrong idea. I've had a request from the Queensland Police out of Brisbane, asking us to provide an investigator for a task force looking into people trafficking. Their current lead straddles the state border, so you could work out of Byron Bay. I thought that might work well considering your new circumstances,' said Anders, her sardonic sense of humour never far away.

'One can't help good luck,' laughed Ange, suddenly relaxed after her angst of a few moments ago. 'Sounds interesting. So, who would I be working for?'

'Still Major Crimes, but the members of the task force are all Queensland Police. It might be a pleasant change of pace for you. Hopefully, your Queensland colleagues can do some of the heavy lifting. What do you think?'

'After our messy exit from the Gold Coast, are you concerned that our Queensland colleagues might get their noses out of joint again?'

'I'm convinced that shambles was all Bold's doing,' replied Anders. 'However, there's always that possibility. It would be naïve in the extreme to think that the Ndrangheta didn't also have hooks into the Queensland Police, but I would hope we've learnt a lesson or two about whom to trust and when.'

Ange had spent the past few days working out how she would leave work and what she might do with herself, not how she might tackle a fresh case. Working back at the Byron Bay Police Station was one option, but that would go against her philosophy of constantly moving forward in life. Becoming a private detective, in Byron Bay of all places, would likely be a depressing study of infidelity, perhaps even involving some of her old male fails. Taking a generic office job wasn't any sort of option after her current career—she wouldn't last a week. It was easy to say that a career played no part in defining someone, but that was poppycock as far as Ange was concerned. No matter how hard one tried to compartmentalise, the person and the career would almost always fuse to forge identity. The trick was not to let one side take over the other.

Old habits die hard. 'That's interesting. Why aren't the federal police involved? Now that the borders are reopening and immigration is such a hot topic, people trafficking would seem to be right up their alley,' cautiously asked Ange, striving to strike the right balance between interested and reserved.

'My thoughts exactly, and they are conspicuous in their absence. Apparently, the feds were following up some of their own leads, but my contact in Queensland was dubious and all but accused them of looking the other way. I'm sure that we can refocus their attention if push comes to shove. I have a few aces up my sleeve.' Sally Anders paused before cutting straight to the chase. 'So, do I take it from your questions that you might be interested in this arrangement, Ange?'

Ange had done enough rushing headlong into things, so she took a considered approach. She needed to get something straight before she committed. 'Can I think about it for a day or two? I'm not sure that I'm ready to head back into the fray.' This was a stretch of the truth, but she didn't wish to fully expose herself and disclose the genuine source of her reticence.

'Sure. Take your time. You need to get yourself well. Anyway, the task force has been treading water through Covid and our closed international border policy. My contact felt that things seem to be gathering some pace, but it's a slow burn. By the way, Kirby felt you needed to get that brain of yours back into action. Call her to talk it over if you need to,' said Anders casually, seeming to appreciate that it was best not to pressure her wounded charge.

Sally's proposition seemed like the perfect plan. Ange could get her profession-al life back on track while remaining in Byron Bay with Gus. The only problem was that Gus knew nothing about it.

Chapter 9

Shot in the Arm

Ange opted to tackle the problem over Gus with a day-trip surfing at Namba Heads. He had been burning the candle at both ends, staying up late each night to spend time with Ange while also working extra-long hours at his factory. Christmas orders were strong, and it was a case of all hands on deck, at least all those hands not battling Covid.

Ange sometimes felt guilty when Gus came home in the evening, worn out from a hectic day. In contrast, her day had been crammed with surfing, exercise, and frequent lunch dates with her friends. She was feeling like a kept woman, a state that did not sit well with her. Sure, it was fun, but the activity and mental stimulation provided by her job were a big part of her make-up.

Sally Anders' proposition had come like a shot in the arm. Gus noticed this change in her demeanour the moment he walked in the door the night after her discussion with Sally Anders. 'What's gotten into you? You look like someone who's had too much caffeine.'

'Nothing, Gus. I just looked at the weather forecast and figured that you needed a break. How about we head down to Namba Heads for the day? We can catch some waves at Sliders, grab some fish and chips, even take a nap lying on the headland. By the way, I won't take no for an answer, so you might as well agree with my proposal,' she said with a mischievous but determined smile.

'Look what's happened to me. My life has been hijacked by a demanding woman,' replied Gus, feigning a browbeaten demeanour. 'I'll make it work. Sounds like fun.' His face softened and he came and gave Ange a big bear hug, the type of hug which made her feel safe and loved.

Ange had remained on edge during the drive south from Byron Bay to Namba Heads for their Sunday surfing excursion. Gus had become used to Ange disappearing into periods of deep contemplation, and they had made the trip in silence, choosing to listen to music instead of each other. They were driving Gus's vintage yellow Volvo station wagon. People stopped and gawked at the pristine car as it made its way through the small fishing village. Ange wondered if anyone recognised the driver or the occupant, one of whom made the coolest surfboards ever, and the other having instigated a gun battle in the nearby scrub. She slipped lower in the passenger seat as a reflex. The irrational sensation that someone might be watching her remained a stubbornly persistent problem.

The drive over to the Bushies Beach car park, their jumping-off point for the walk across to Sliders—her favourite surf break on the planet—was carved through low coastal scrub and passed right by the place where the shooting had occurred. Ange had not previously disclosed the intimate details of what had transpired that day to Gus, and the walk across to Sliders seemed an appropriate backdrop in which to fill him in.

Gus brought along a longboard as companion to Bluey Longboard, and the two looked quite the couple, wheeling their boards along the beach. Ange had been responsible for Gus stocking those clever surfboard wheels, which had proven a solid seller in his factory outlet in Byron Bay. As they wandered south along Bushies Beach, Ange recounted the events leading up to the shooting, explaining why she had chosen that place for the takedown. Jake Thompson had been a promising young surfer sponsored by Bell Surfboards before his accidental death one night at sea, or so they had concluded. Lomax and Smith, the Ndrangheta hitmen who had shot Ange, had crudely buried Jake in the low coastal scrub nearby, nothing more than a loose end that those mongrels needed to tidy up. Jake was also the source of connection between Ange and Gus. It was indeed an ill wind that blows no good.

Gus had remained silent as she narrated her story, leaving Ange uncertain as to how he felt about sharing his day off with a protagonist in that sorry episode. Though the surf was small, the sun was warm and the water crystal clear, and the pair of surfers kitted up in silence. Once they had paddled out, it was the ocean and the surf that seemed to soothe their minds and break the solitude.

Gus was a far superior surfer to Ange, especially on a longboard. She had expected nothing less of the son of a surfing icon, but the way he moved up and down his longboard was masterful, effortless almost. She was anything but, as every time Ange attempted to shuffle toward the nose of her board, Bluey nosedived and she face-planted, usually in spectacular style. There was a lot to learn about riding Bluey Longboard.

After their surf, they had lain together under a large pandanus palm tree that stretched over the white sandy beach. Once they were out of the cool water, the midday sun was scorching, intimidating even, and the shade from the large sculptural tree was welcome. Ange asked Gus about the large scar on his back as they compared war wounds, a competition of sorts, one that Ange was still winning hands down. Her scar was healing nicely, but it would remain an obvious and permanent reminder of those nearby events.

'It happened in Fiji. It was a day of solid swell, and I couldn't stomach Cloud Break, so we were surfing at Swimming Pools. I probably took the break too easy and went over the falls, board and all, cut by the fin. It put an end to any surfing for the rest of that trip,' answered Gus casually.

'Were you on a surf trip?'

'Not really. I was accompanying my girlfriend. It was a photo shoot, and I didn't realise how good the surf would be. I'd taken the wrong board.'

'What type of photo shoot?'

Gus seemed to realise that he was getting himself in way too deep in this conversation. Ange was a detective after all and would not be easily deterred from her line of questioning. He hesitated before explaining. 'Suzy was a swimsuit model. We were on a boat for a few days, and they wanted some surf in the background,' he replied somewhat sheepishly.

'What became of Suzy?' probed Ange.

'She didn't last long. Beautiful looking, but completely self-centred. I guess that's a moral hazard of always being the centre of attention. She had a fling with the deckhand while I was out surfing,' replied Gus, trying to extract himself from the ditch he had dug.

'So, you got your scar on a photo shoot with a sexy swimsuit model, and I got mine in the scrub at the hands of some mafia thugs. That doesn't seem like much of a comparison, Gus,' stated Ange. Her attempt at humour did a poor job of hiding a lack of self-confidence that wavered in her voice.

Seeming to sense this anxiety, Gus rolled over to stroke the wound on her thigh. 'Like I mentioned, I had a long playboy phase. Even so, Suzy wasn't a high point. She was certainly good to look at,' said Gus somewhat wistfully, slipping back into his ditch with a thud.

'What phase are you in now, Gus?' asked Ange, the smile on her lips a weak attempt at disguising the question mark emblazoned on her forehead.

'I think this will be my gritty and beautiful crime-fighter stage. They're scarce, you know. Particularly ones that can surf,' laughed Gus. The smile that spread from Ange's lips to her entire face relieved any tension, providing some insights to the fact that even superheroes carried doubts and fears hidden in the folds of their crime-fighting capes.

Gus must have known that there was more to this discussion. He cut to the chase. 'So, are you going to tell me what's gotten up your skirt—other than me, of course?'

Ange laughed at his insightful observation, giving her the confidence to pop the question, so to speak. 'Gus, I tried to resign from my job this week. It didn't go quite as planned.'

Gus looked her squarely in the eyes. 'Go on. I get a feeling that there's more to this tale.'

'I don't want to move back to Sydney. Even though we've just begun our relationship, I can't remember being so happy. I don't want distance to ruin it all, so I quit my job so that I could stay somewhere closer.'

'Phew, that's a relief. I'd been cracking my head open, trying to work out how I would spend more time working in Sydney. It was looking almost impossible, given what we're going through at work right now. Does that mean you're thinking of staying here, or are you planning to move to Brisbane or the Gold Coast?'

Before she got into specifics, Ange needed to pop the question that was worrying her. 'Do you want me to stay, Gus?'

He rolled over onto Ange's beach towel and looked her in the eye. 'Of course I do. I feel the same way as you. I've been dreading the prospect of you moving back to Sydney. How did your boss take your resignation, and what will you do with yourself? I just don't see you as part of the Byron lunching set.'

'She didn't take my resignation at all. Instead, she offered me a secondment with a task force. I'd be working with the Queensland Police. I gather the job would be loosely based here, but the details are sketchy. Before I made any commitments, I wanted to speak to you.'

'I'm so relieved, but I'm really pleased for you and your career. You know how attracted I am to sexy detectives.'

With that all settled, Ange felt she was moving forward once more with purpose. Ange's lovemaking with Gus that night was tender and thankful, as if they both sensed that their relationship had moved to a new level. Her sleep that night, when it finally came, was one of peace and contentment, one that no bogeymen disturbed. Dr Kirby Hall had been spot-on, which was not surprising for a trauma psychiatrist.

Chapter 10

Arrangements

E ven though it was Sunday evening, Ange rang Sally Anders to give her the news. With Gus on board and her living arrangements settled, she saw no point in leaving her boss on tenterhooks.

'That was quick,' answered Anders.

'You know me, once I've decided, I'm all in,' replied Ange. 'Anyhow, I need to give one month's notice on my apartment, so I'll need to collect my things before then. I've already informed the letting agent. It came fully furnished and I don't really have much stuff to worry about, other than my surfboards. I think it might be best that I drive down and pick it all up. What I can't fit in the car can go to charity, I suppose. I'll need a car, by the way. I can't keep using Gus's work vehicle. Can you sort that out for me?'

'Hold on, give me a chance to catch up. Let me think about the car, but I'm sure we can sort out something. You will still technically be working for Major Crimes, but your salary gets allocated to the task force and doesn't affect my budget.'

'Excellent,' said Ange. 'That was my next question. I really want to lean on you and Billy. Will that be doable? I don't know who on the task force I can trust. Understandably, I am a touch gun-shy about all of that.'

'That makes sense. I negotiated a thirty percent add-on for admin, so I guess that can work. Well, at least until it doesn't, and I renegotiate. I also told them they cannot use you for anything outside of the people trafficking case. Your work will support our aims as much as theirs. I'm sure that traffickers don't recognise state border lines drawn on maps. In terms of staff, I've been on a recruitment drive, so you'll notice some fresh faces around the office. I'm sure we can let you have Billy when required.'

'Excellent. On that point, do you think I should work out of the Byron station, or work from home?'

'I think work from home if you can, but hot desk at the station from time to time. You've still got a week of leave left if you need it. I'll use that time to get a car sorted and complete the arrangements with the task force. There are lines of reporting and authority that need to be worked out. I don't want our department to get the blame for their screw-ups. I'll take the heat for your screw-ups, but not theirs. When you come to Sydney and pick up your stuff, I suggest we plan to spend a day or two together.'

'You know me boss, I operate best when I'm free range. Anyhow, what screw-ups?' laughed Ange. 'I may as well try to come down to Sydney tomorrow. No point wasting any more time overthinking this. I wouldn't want to suffer a change of heart.'

Ange set off early the next morning. It was a long drive to Sydney, and her aim was to arrive before dark. Summer was in full swing and the coast road was busy with early season holidaymakers. She had loosely asked Gus if he wanted to join her for the drive; she was still driving his Subaru, but he was crazy-busy getting Christmas orders filled. Bell surfboards were as popular as ever and it was a mad panic to a finish line marked by Christmas Eve.

A combination of interesting podcasts and lively music made short work of the long drive, and she soon hit the outskirts of Sydney. Approaching 3 p.m., she avoided the worst of any peak hour traffic and arrived at her Edgecliff address in good time.

It was Ange's first visit back to Sydney since the shooting, and even longer since she had spent a night in her old apartment. With no on-site car parking, she was forced to park around the block in a paid parking station. Her first shock came when she emptied her overstuffed mailbox. The memory of finding that unmarked envelope rushed into her consciousness and sent a shiver up her spine. It had contained nothing more than a photograph of her coming off the beach and hadn't seemed overly concerning. It was only now, understanding how it had started the chain of events that ended in her almost being killed, that the memory made her skin crawl. Today, there was nothing more than junk mail to be binned, but it didn't stop her apprehensively glancing over her shoulder.

Stale air greeted her as she opened the apartment door. She had left in a hurry, expecting to be back soon after her trip to Byron Bay chasing Lomax and Smith. Some interesting smells assailed her as she walked inside, and she quickly opened every window and door. She loved Sydney, but this apartment had never truly been her home. Only living in the apartment for a short time, Ange was pleased to be leaving it now for good. After cleaning out the fridge, she started a pile of things to keep, things to bin, and things to give to charity. The throwing-away pile quickly grew bigger than the keeping pile. Once she was in the swing of things, the job was soon over and she wandered up into Elizabeth Bay to find something to eat.

To say she slept badly that night was a massive understatement. She awoke early to clear skies and crisp air, signalling that a perfect Sydney early-summer day lay ahead. Ange opted to walk the long way to the office and take full advantage of the scenery. Although she had made the trek many times, it was a journey she never tired of. After winding through the inner Eastern Suburbs, she hit the water at Woolloomooloo. The harbourside swimming pool, named in honour of Olympic champion Andrew 'Boy' Charlton, was alive with early-morning swimmers earnestly frothing their way up and down the pool.

As she rounded the point marked by Mrs Macquarie's Chair, Ange was met with Sydney's most iconic sight. The Sydney Harbour Bridge stood high above a glistening Sydney Opera House, a sentinel to the spectacular harbour, deep blue and sparkling in the early-morning sunlight, full of life as commuter ferries filed into Circular Quay. It was hard not to love Sydney, no matter what difficult memories the city held. This walk was one of the many things that she would miss. It was funny how little rituals and engrained habits had taken on a whole new meaning after her near-death experience.

Ange was soon in front of the Major Crimes' office tower. She glanced up at her office floor before wandering into the familiar foyer, smiling as she remembered the very first time that she had visited the office. Ange had had absolutely no idea that Sally Anders was going to offer her a job at Major Crimes, which came as a welcome surprise after being grilled by the state's anti-corruption commission earlier in the day. She remembered having trouble working out the lifts on that occasion, something now familiar.

The lift car spilled her onto her office floor and into the sterile anteroom, serving its role as part reception and part barrier to entry. She waved her pass key over the transponder and was pleased to find that she was granted access to the bowels of Major Crimes. After all, it was well over three months since Ange had last completed this little dance.

Seeing as Ange was still in her exercise gear, she made a beeline for the showers on the opposite side of the lift well. As was common for any normal day in Major Crimes, there were no uniforms in sight, but exercise gear remained a step too far for a first day back. As Ange circled around through the office, she saw that Sally Anders was already at her desk, speaking on her phone as was often the case. She beckoned for Ange to come over and hung up from her call.

'Great to see you, Ange. I'm pleased to see you're walking so well. I didn't notice any limp. Nice exercise gear, by the way.'

'Good to see you also, boss. There were times when I wondered if I would ever be back here. I've been working hard on my exercise regime. My physio was right. One day I suddenly realised that I wasn't thinking about my leg anymore. I guess that was the same day that I stopped limping. The flash exercise gear is courtesy of my friend Kerrie. That girl will see me broke.'

'Maybe I should get your friend Kerrie on board to help style me,' said Anders with a warm smile before beckoning to a yellow manilla folder lying on the corner of her desk. 'In case you're wondering, I don't have any worthwhile information on your new job, other than a pile of background information that your new Queensland colleagues provided.'

Ange sat down in the chair opposite her boss, picked up the file and gave it a cursory flick through. 'I'll look at this later. Unless you have anything pressing for me to do here, I guess I should pack up and head back to Byron and start reading. I'll need a laptop, and that car we discussed.'

'Of course. Our Queensland colleagues have already allocated a car to you, and Billy will set you up with a new laptop. See him before you leave. He's expecting you. Internal Affairs dropped your old laptop and smashed it to smithereens. Idiots. It wouldn't surprise me if Carruthers did it on purpose after I clipped his wings.'

'You know he rang to tell me they'd cleared me? That was evidently after your meeting with his boss and the commissioner,' commented Ange.

'Who rang you?'

'Caruthers. I know I shouldn't have given him a serve, but I couldn't help myself. I told him that if he ever tried another stunt like that, I would bring a case of harassment against him personally.'

'You probably shouldn't have done that. They can be vindictive sons of you-know-whats,' observed Anders. She paused for a moment, as if thinking through the implications of Ange's minor brain snap. 'I guess it makes no difference. Those guys would never admit to themselves of any wrongdoing. By the way, in case you haven't heard, Peter Fredericks is now working for them,' said Anders, her face darkening noticeably. 'I guess that low-down snitch won't be on our side if we cross them again.'

'I gathered that was on the cards. Carruthers had great delight in telling me that Fredericks had applied for a position. I told them he would fit in perfectly.'

The rest of the day was spent meeting unfamiliar faces, all of which were decidedly and disconcertingly younger than Ange. She called by Billy's desk to pick up her new computer, where the pair also arranged to meet for dinner. Billy was Ange's secret weapon in unravelling her cases, and the pair had developed a terrific relationship that was deeper than merely that of two work colleagues.

Over dinner that evening, Ange got a full download of what had been happening while she had been on leave. Ange probed Billy on how his long-distance relationship with Breanna White was going. Bree had been a pivotal character in luring the two Ndrangheta assassins into the scrub at Namba Heads. She was also a member of the national hockey team and a most impressive young woman in Ange's eyes—also Billy's—to risk restating the obvious.

Billy was discreet and a thorough gentleman. He gave away no juicy details, but thoughts of Bree did kick-start Ange's scheming on how she might use some of those crypto assets hoovered up by Sally Anders.

Chapter 11

The Long Drive Home

After many awkward trips up and down the stairs, Gus's Subaru was packed to the hilt and her surfboards tied onto the roof racks. She triple-checked that her babies were safely secured before driving away from her Edgecliff apartment for the very last time. She had downloaded a series of podcasts on human trafficking and soon disappeared into the dark side of humanity. Most Australians confused people smuggling with trafficking, such was the country's fixation on immigration and border control. Being an island stuck at the bottom of the globe did not make life easy for those seeking to enter Australia illegally.

All the podcasts centred on countries with more permeable borders, and she pondered whether the difficulties posed by smuggling people into Australia made it inherently more profitable to criminals. Perhaps the authorities were less vigilant to trafficking because of those difficulties? Maybe they remained focussed on illegal immigrants fleeing their countries and seeking a better life, rather than people who'd been stolen and placed into servitude? Were Australians victims of their own good fortune, thinking that their strong borders were genuinely impenetrable? Whatever the answers to those questions were, Ange knew that wherever there was money to be made, criminals would gather. This axiom formed the basis of her go-to strategy when chasing criminals—*always follow the money*.

She waited until precisely 12:20 p.m. before tackling an idea that had been brewing for weeks. She called up the number for the family property in Tamworth, her first-ever home and one that had endured throughout her many moves. Ange knew not to ring between midday and 12:15 p.m., also not between 7 and 7:30 p.m. These time slots were strictly reserved for ABC news broadcasts, sacrosanct interludes that were not to be interrupted. In summer, her father would have logged six or seven hours of work by midday, having made the most of the cooler mornings. Once news and lunch were complete, he would catch a nap and avoid the blistering heat of the midday sun. Hence why the timing of her call needed careful consideration.

Ange and her parents had a tacit agreement that small talk and inane chatter were to be avoided. Perhaps this trait was a remnant from growing up, when long-distance calls were metered. She could still remember the commotion. Her mother would lean out of the window of their untidy little office and yell at the top of her voice, 'It's a long-distance call. Hurry,' something that was like a starter's gun, prompting her husband to race towards the phone, as if striving to save some money for the caller was of critical importance.

Ange's parents were hardworking countryfolk and more often than not outside whenever the sun was shining. Her father had installed a large clanging bell, linked to the phone and mounted under the eaves of their homestead. After all, it wouldn't do to miss a call from the outside world. The dogs came to recognise this sudden crisis and would bark uncontrollably, such was the chaos unleashed by that bell. As her phone rang, Ange couldn't help but smile at that memory of her youth.

Her mother answered the call. Once Ange had assured her she was OK, her mother promptly passed the call over to Ange's dad. Incoming calls at 12:20 p.m. were always meant for him and nobody else.

'Hello, darling. How's things?'

'Pretty good, Dad. I've moved back to Byron Bay. Same job as I was in, just more fieldwork than office work. Being stuck inside at a desk is not my favourite activity, as I'm sure you can remember from my school report cards.'

'I hear you,' replied her father wearily. 'I've got a pile of bills to pay after lunch.' Ange knew her dad would often make a feeble attempt at completing some office administration after his nap, filling in time until the sun passed its peak and he could venture outside once again. He hated office work with a passion.

'Dad, I'm thinking of getting a dog,' she mentioned casually, as if it were a mere afterthought. This was something that she had been thinking about during those long nights of her recovery, when innocuous night-time sounds took on a sinister tone. Now that she was settled in both her job and her living arrangements, it was time to action those thoughts.

'Don't tell me you're thinking of getting one of the trendy designer dogs bred for apartments?'

Ange knew that to rural folk, a real dog was a valuable farmworker and not something to be cuddled inside. Even cats were workers, hired assassins to rage war against the regular mice plagues that would infest the countryside during a good season. Some bushies owned a small house dog to ease the burden of loneliness, but they were more therapy than any proper dog.

'Actually, Dad, I'm not living in an apartment anymore. I'm thinking about another red dog. Can you put me in touch with any breeders?' Ange knew that her father only purchased his dogs from two breeders, one for cattle and another for sheep. Cattle dogs were more aggressive and trained to nip at the heels of the massive beasts that they manoeuvred this way and that. Sheepdogs, on the other hand, needed a quiet and patient approach to herding flighty sheep, using penetrating eyes rather than teeth to work their magic.

'Well, that's a relief. Tell you what. I've got a terrific dog who suffered some cracked ribs after being kicked by a bull. I don't think he's going to be much use to me anymore. He's just too smart to put himself in that position again. You can check him out when you come down for Christmas.'

'How old is he and what's his name?' asked Ange. The Christmas idea had caught her off guard. She would need to circle back on that.

'He's probably four. His name is Buddy.'

'That's the name of my dog, Dad. How could you?' she teased.

'I can't go around trying to remember names all willy-nilly. My red dogs are either Buddy, Buster or Rusty. You know that. It was Buddy's turn again.'

'OK, Dad. He sounds perfect. I'll get back to you about Christmas.'

Once she had hung up from the call, she knew that this was the first relationship tester for her and Gus to navigate. Custody battles over Christmas Day had torn apart many a happy couple. As things transpired, it was a very wide circle to get back to the Christmas issue.

Memories of her original Buddy kept her occupied for a while. Her youth would have been far less vibrant without her number-one companion. She was just about to get back into her car after a comfort and coffee stop when she received a call from her boss, one that shook away her thoughts of Buddy and plunged her back into the dark world of people trafficking.

'Hi, Ange, when will you be back in Byron?' asked Sally Anders.

Ange knew that her boss was not unlike her parents and rarely exchanged in small talk. 'Later this afternoon. What's up?'

'I need you to get up to Brisbane tomorrow and have a meeting with the Queensland Police. We've finally hashed out the details of how we'll work together. You can pick up your new car while you're there. Jim Grady offered to drive you up. He says that he has some things to do in Brisbane. Assuming you're OK with this, I'll tell him you're fine for tomorrow and get him to collect you around 8 a.m. I'll text you the details of who you'll be meeting and when. Apparently, there has been a recent development. Let me know how it goes.'

'OK. I guess that signals the end of my leave. I'll be there, boss,' quipped Ange, genuinely excited by the prospect and not at all concerned about her truncated leave.

Now that the wheels were in motion, and although she'd been edging towards this moment for some weeks, misgivings and doubts about her readiness now struck home. Would she be like Buddy, who, after being kicked in the ribs, could never fully wade back into the fray? The parallels seemed all too obvious. The sad fact was that Buddy would likely have been put down unless one of the family took pity on him. There was no place on the farm for a real dog that wasn't. Who knew, perhaps the fate of shot detectives might ultimately take the same path?

After she swirled these worries around for a while, her competitive spirit ultimately won out. There was no way that she would let those mongrels in the Ndrangheta ruin a career that she loved, and no way that she was going to be put down by their hand. Thoughts of her last investigation involving the Ndrangheta spun around her mind, the type of wandering reflections that often accompanied a solo road trip. Eventually those thoughts came around to musings about Ted Kramer's crypto assets. She rang her boss back.

'I hope you aren't having second thoughts, Ange?' asked Sally Anders, as if she had been reading Ange's mind over the past few hours.

'Lots of them, actually,' laughed Ange, impressed with her boss's insightfulness. 'Putting those aside, I have an idea to deploy some of Ted Kramer's crypto assets that you so cleverly commandeered.'

'I'm listening,' replied Anders noncommittally.

'Well, we know that crime is rapidly going online, and we can't just sit around and wait for the tsunami. How about we make a set of strategic investments into areas that look suspicious? You know how it works. Once we have a line of sight, we can unleash Billy's amazing software tools to trace what's going on and potentially identify who's involved and if they're up to no good. If our targets turn out to be legit, then we can liquidate our position and move on. If they turn out to be dodgy, then we might help prevent a load of pain for a lot of innocent people. Who knows, we might even turn a profit.'

'I'm sure that there will be a lot of research behind each position, and this sounds like a slow burn strategy running in the background. Billy is way too busy to be chugging away doing grunt work like that. We're still under-gunned in IT. Looking around the office, other than Billy, I don't see anyone with the IT skills to pull off your strategy.'

'I've got an idea about that,' commented Ange.

'I thought you might. Out with it, Detective.'

'What about Breanna White, the constable who helped us flush out Ethan Tedesco? I doubt what I'm proposing would be a full-time thing, so she could continue to work at the Byron Bay station. She is quite ambitious, as she's reached out to me to help with ultimately becoming a detective.'

'Isn't she still young and green for all that?'

'Boss, the more I get into this stuff, the more I realise that we need to recalibrate our expectations. Billy and Bree are the first of a generation of true digital natives. They think differently about how to approach technology and what may be possible. Even I'm a dinosaur with this stuff, and I'm still in my thirties. Theirs is the generation that we need to recruit if we're to have any chance of staying abreast of criminal activity in the digital space. Think about the last case. Without Billy and Bree, the likes of me and you would have gotten nowhere, and Tedesco and his Ndrangheta mates would still be safe and sound in their digital bubble.'

'Point taken. But surely I can recruit for those skills?'

'That's the whole point, boss. The age is part of the skill set, and you'll probably end up in the same place. At least we know Bree and what she's capable of. There's another reason I think she's perfect. She's a savvy trader and will come to the task with that mindset. Did you know about her side hustle trading collectibles from second-hand stores and flea markets? That turned into trading NFTs, where she's made quite a tidy profit along the way. Bree's got initiative and street smarts. With a bit of experience and training, I think she'll be a real asset. Plus, now that I'm staying up here, I can take her under my wing and monitor what she's doing.'

'OK. You've convinced me. Do you want me to speak to Jim Grady or will you do it?' asked Anders.

'I'll do it. It's a slow-burn strategy, as you say, and certainly not on any critical path. I'll check with Jim tomorrow on the drive to Brisbane.'

'It will be your responsibility to monitor Bree, assuming your strategy takes flight. We don't want any more screw-ups.'

'No problems,' replied Ange, involuntarily reaching down to stroke the gunshot wound on her thigh, a residual memory of one such monumental screw-up. In a moment of frustration, Bree and Billy had unleashed a scheme involving rogue NFTs, a crude plan which had backfired badly and precipitated the shoot-out in the scrub.

Ange spent the rest of her drive engrossed in tales of people trafficking and seemed to arrive back at Gus's estate in the Byron Bay hinterland in no time, well before dark. Gus traipsed in just after 8 p.m., totally beaten, and the pair collapsed in front of TV over some packet ravioli and a glass of wine.

She left for another day the subjects of Christmas and their new dog, both touchy topics where timing mattered.

Chapter 12

Brisbane

Jim Grady collected her bang on 8 a.m. ahead of their two-hour drive. It quickly became clear that Grady's offer to ferry Ange to Brisbane was more about a mental health check than any taxi service. Ange pulled him up before they were even halfway to Brisbane. 'Did Sally Anders put you up to this, boss?'

'What do you mean?' asked Grady, staring straight ahead as if the traffic was his sole point of focus.

'I'll be fine. I'm not too proud to admit my own doubts, but you should know that I'm no easy pushover.'

'OK, then,' was all that Grady could reply to that statement of fact. He seemed pleased, and their discussion fell into the relaxed banter that traversed the boundary between friends and work colleagues.

'Boss?' she asked, failing again to break old habits. 'Remember when we were in the cabin at the Namba Heads caravan park, prepping Billings before going into the fray against Lomax and Smith, the two Ndrangheta hitmen?'

'Yeeessss,' said Grady suspiciously, acting as if unsure why she was retracing old ground.

'I've replayed that scene a thousand times in my mind, and I'm certain that I removed the bullets from Billings' service revolver. I can even hear the clink of his bullets as they tumbled into the pocket of those tragic denim overalls I was wearing. How they made their way back into Billings' gun after the shooting has me puzzled. You wouldn't know anything about that, would you, boss?'

'Ange, we've been through this. You must be imagining things. Maybe the shock has scrambled your memory? PTSD, perhaps?'

'Hmmmm. I remember everything else clearly. Why would that scene be scrambled and not others?'

Ange wasn't sure if Grady enjoyed playing poker. If he did, he would be an outstanding player. 'You should get checked out, Ange. Don't you have a psychiatrist now?'

'OK, boss. I get it. Anyhow, I have my suspicions. Thanks for having my back. I know I made the right decision. Billings is a spineless snake and things could easily have turned out differently,' said Ange.

She knew that the pathetic Sergeant Darren Billings would have jumped horses in a heartbeat if he thought the other side had the ascendency. He was surely one of those inveterate lane-changers, the type of driver who pissed off everyone in a traffic jam, convinced of their right to barge back and forth between lanes. Billings would have taken any action necessary to protect his own scaly skin. Letting him loose with a loaded weapon would have been the height of stupidity.

As it stood, Ange had kept him largely in the dark about the level of firepower that hid in the scrub. However, with the benefit of hindsight and Billings' tendency for slipperiness, it might have looked bad, her cajoling Billings into the fray essentially unarmed. Events overtook them, as neither Ange nor Billings had time to reach for their firearms, rendering this point essentially moot. Ange was certain that Jim Grady had reloaded Billings' revolver with those mystery bullets, a move that had conveniently coincided with the video surveillance being switched off. Had he not done so, Ange's interview with Internal Affairs would have been even more challenging.

'I do not know what you're talking about, Detective Watson,' responded Grady, using her official title to signal that there was no point in any further pursuit of this line of questioning.

All things considered, Ange felt comfortable with the line that her old boss was persisting with. 'Sure, boss. Now that I've got you on the ropes, there is one other thing I wanted to discuss.'

'I thought I was supposed to be probing you. Not the other way around. What's on your mind?'

'We would like to second Bree for a few hours each day to do the legwork on a crypto strategy that we've come up with. You know, it wouldn't hurt for you to have some in-house digital expertise, boss. Places like Byron Bay are magnets for people playing games in the digital world. Why wouldn't you live here if you could?' said Ange, all sweet as pie.

'Why Bree? Surely you can use Billy. Isn't he your personal IT guru—the one that you stole from me, if my memory serves me correctly?'

'Billy already has his hands full looking after yours truly. You know that Bree aspires to be a detective down the track, don't you? I can keep my eye on her. She's already asked for me to act as her mentor. I assume that Sally has spoken to you about me hot-desking at the station.'

'I gather that this is your idea that you've talked Sally into going along with,' observed Grady, having previously fallen victim to the same ploy himself.

Ange smiled at her inability to pull the wool over the Grady's eyes. She then gave him a full account of what she had in mind. He listened impassively until she finished. 'OK. Let's get together with Constable White and see how she feels about *your* idea.' He made a point of emphasising the word *your*, but then his tone softened. 'It will be good to have you back at the station, Ange. You can keep Walton and Lynch, your old sparring partners, under control. I assume you heard their story about us having an affair? Morons.'

Ange laughed. 'Yep. And the one where Billy is my toy boy. It'll be fun sparring with those two idiots.'

The pair were soon in the Brisbane CBD and Grady dropped off Ange at the police headquarters, his parting words a simple 'have fun' goodbye. She still had thirty minutes to kill, so she whiled away some time in a nearby coffee shop before alighting to the twelfth floor. Even though she arrived a full ten minutes early, the receptionist whisked Ange straight into a meeting room, where four officers sat around a large table. A man in his fifties stood up to make the introductions.

'I'm Senior Detective David Wallace, and these are Detectives Judy Ly, Henry Chan, and Chris Lambert.'

It's always disquieting to arrive at a meeting already underway, especially when you arrived early for said meeting. Ange's first sense was that she was being set up, so she played off the front foot. 'Ange Watson. I thought I was early. Has the briefing started without me?' She looked around to assess the body language. Wallace maintained a supercilious expression on his face whilst Ly and Lambert cast their eyes downward. Chan looked outright hostile. 'This is going to be interesting,' she thought to herself.

'Not at all. We were just getting ready for you,' replied Wallace. Ange didn't believe him for a second.

She figured that this was probably no outright lie, but his smarmy intonation suggested that they hadn't been discussing the weather. Thinking it was best to stay on the front foot, she pushed on. 'So, what do you have for me, then?' If these Queenslanders thought they would intimidate her, then they were going to be sorely disappointed.

Wallace cleared his throat, clearly not expecting this level of directness from a relatively junior detective. Evidently, he had missed the memo to explain that this junior detective had recently recovered from a violent gun battle. 'We've come across what we believe to be a human trafficking operation.'

Ange made the judgement call that everyone else was fully up to speed on the matter. 'OK. Can you fill me in on the details? How did you *come across* this?'

Detective Ly spoke for the first time. 'Hi, Detective Watson—I'm Judy, by the way. A young Vietnamese woman escaped from what we believe is a trafficking camp. She's Hmong, an indigenous people who live in the mountainous regions along the Vietnam-China border and extending into Laos, Thailand, and Myanmar.'

'How did she escape?' asked Ange. Perhaps they had already planned how to deliver this briefing, but she liked the way Ly was prepared to jump in.

'One of her handlers got sloppy one evening, and she slipped out of the building where she was being held captive. After hiding most of the night covered with garbage, she escaped in the early hours of the morning. She then wandered around in the dark until she came to another house, where she hid under the rear cover of a utility vehicle. Fortunately for her, the driver of that vehicle left at sunrise and drove for an estimated two to three hours before stopping for a break, where the woman slipped from the back and spent the rest of the day in hiding. A cleaner discovered her cowering in a local church the next morning and rang the police. She was so scared and pleased to get away that she has absolutely no idea where she came from. She can't identify the vehicle or give us any worthwhile clues about the place she was being held captive. Given that she was under a tonneau cover, she also doesn't know what direction the car was travelling.'

'Wow, that is quite a lucky escape. Where was she found?'

'Texas. On the Queensland–New South Wales border. You don't need a calculator to work out that two to three hundred kilometres in any direction covers a massive area,' concluded Judy Ly.

Henry Chan, evidently the mathematician of the group, saved Ange any mental gymnastics. 'A circle with a radius of three hundred kilometres is some three hundred thousand square kilometres. The search area won't be as large as that, as that circle crosses the coast, but it will still be somewhere over one hundred thousand square kilometres.'

Ange noted Chan seemed to offer this calculation almost as a challenge. 'So basically, we're looking for a needle in the proverbial. What are your thoughts?'

Chris Lambert spoke for the first time. 'The only thing we've learned is that Border Force is not exactly coming on board with the people trafficking idea. They seem to consider this to be just another vanilla-style illegal immigration or people smuggling situation. The woman doesn't speak any English and the transcripts of her interview with Border Force are all we have to go on, which isn't much. We would have had absolutely no visibility about this if the woman hadn't escaped.'

'What do you mean—transcripts? Haven't you interviewed her in person? How could Border Force assume that this is about illegal immigration?' shot back Ange in a series of rapid-fire questions.

'Once they deemed the woman an illegal immigrant, Border Force had jurisdiction. They sent us a recording of her interview, which was quite detailed. People trafficking has been going on forever, but Covid and all the travel restrictions basically did the job for us and made it too difficult and uneconomic. What happened to hostages before Covid is impossible to know, but it's almost certain that some ended up working as prostitutes. Every victim is still essentially an illegal immigrant and totally unknown to us. It doesn't bear to think what happened to them,' Lambert replied, his trailing tone signalling his conclusion that nothing good had become of those poor unfortunate souls.

'How many other women were being held captive?' asked Ange.

'She said that there were five others, a mix of nationalities, but all from the countries that I mentioned earlier,' explained Ly.

'Isn't that the so-called Golden Triangle? Could this be drug-related?' asked Ange.

The others looked at Ly to provide the answer to this question. 'The Golden Triangle is further south, in the regions where Myanmar, Laos, and Cambodia meet. Vietnam is further east. It could be drug-related, but the woman showed no signs of being used as a drug mule. According to the woman, they lured her from Vietnam, kidnapped her once she arrived in Australia, and then held her captive until she escaped to Texas. I'm inclined to agree with you that this is most likely a prostitution or slave-related case. Border Force believes she's lying to take advantage of our anti-trafficking laws.'

'That's quite a journey. It must be very lucrative to go to all that trouble.'

Lambert replied to Ange's question. 'It is highly lucrative, but it's also likely to be part of a larger suite of services, which would probably include drugs. Before Covid, we know criminal groups were targeting mining and rural areas to provide illegal prostitution services, so this could be the restart of those operations.'

'There is one more thing. Testing of hair follicles taken from the women detected opiates, suggesting that drugs might be involved,' added Judy Ly.

Wallace obviously had better things to do than waste time briefing an obviously junior detective, standing up to signal that the meeting had drawn to a close. 'Well, then, Detective Watson. We'll send you a detailed brief and a transcript of the interview. You can liaise with your three colleagues if you have further questions. Is that all?'

It certainly was not all as far as Ange was concerned and remained seated. 'So why am I here?'

Wallace sighed and sat down. 'You're here because the target area spans the border,' he said wearily, as if that explained everything.

'I'm really looking forward to working with you, Detective Watson. After that amazing undercover work that you did on breaking apart the Ndrangheta cell, I figure you might see this case with fresh eyes. We'd hit a dead end until now,' said Judy Ly, looking around at her colleagues as if to seek affirmation that they agreed with this lack of genuine progress.

The ensuing silence seemed to suggest that nobody else agreed with Ly's assertion, although the looks on the faces of her three colleagues showed that they were unaware of Ange's previous assignments. Judy Ly was obviously the only one to do any homework on their new colleague, although the undercover part was a stretch, something that Ange was going to let ride while it served her needs. 'Thanks, the part where I got myself shot wasn't part of that plan,' she said with a pointed smile. Now that she had their attention, she let this dyslexic group disband. 'OK, then. Do we have a regular project meeting in mind?'

'How about I set up a Teams group and schedule a weekly video call? That way we can keep in contact even when we're on the road,' replied Lambert. 'By the way, we've organised a car for you, a Toyota Prado. It's at the yard over near the Port of Brisbane.'

'I'll give you a lift out and help sort out the paperwork,' Ly quickly suggested.

'Great. Let's go, then,' concluded Ange, finally letting Wallace stand up once again and get on with his other more important tasks.

Chapter 13

Meet Judy

O nce Ange and Judy Ly were safely in the lift, Judy suggested they grab some lunch before they headed out to collect the car. She suggested a gyoza bar on the fringe of the CBD and quite a way from the police headquarters. Over lunch, she explained the dynamic.

'Wallace is OK, but he can be a pompous arse. Jim Lambert is a highly considered man and very capable. You will enjoy working with him.'

'What about Chan? You two seem besties,' said Ange with a wry smile.

Ly smiled back. 'You noticed that, did you? Chan is a piece of work. He genuinely believes that he's superior to everyone else, particularly me. It hurts me to admit it, but he is good at his job. You've probably gathered that I am of Vietnamese heritage? That's probably the only reason that I'm part of the group.'

'I wondered about that. How did you come to be here? Sorry, that sounded all wrong. Let me rephrase that question. How did your family come to be living in Australia? I can tell by your accent that you grew up here.'

'My parents were humanitarian refugees from Saigon during the war. My dad was a motor mechanic and soon found work here. I still have family over in Vietnam, but we've gone our separate ways in the main. I'm fluent in Vietnamese, as my parents still speak the language at home. At university, I studied Chinese, thinking that I may as well follow the money. I never expected to be a detective, but both languages have come in handy and probably given my career a boost along the way. I also speak some Cambodian, so I can usually navigate my way through the language subtleties of the region,' explained Ly.

'I can't imagine being bundled off to another country and having to start from scratch. So, we were speaking about your relationship with Chan?'

'The racial history that sits between us doesn't help. You're probably not aware that China–Vietnam politics have been on a rocky footing for thousands of years. When China came in on the side of North Vietnam in 1975, it split our country and caused a massive loss of life. The Chinese still consider that Vietnam is rightfully theirs, and the Vietnamese people strongly disagree. Tensions have recently been reignited in the South China Sea, but disputes will probably go on for another thousand years.'

Ly didn't need to explain to Ange that Australia had been an active participant in the Vietnam War, a disturbing and fractious period of Australian politics, one that caused a change of government and precipitated a period of considerable political instability. Ange didn't wish to get into this discussion, as it was a topic that still divided. Australia had largely acted as if the war had never happened, including how it had treated its returning veterans. Even though these events had occurred before she was born, Ange knew that Vietnam and its people still bore visible scars from that calamitous period.

'I presume Chan is involved because we feel that there's some Chinese involvement in this case?'

'Correct. He supposedly has some powerful sources and connections with the Chinese underworld. Obviously, I'm involved because of my language skills, but we still have our normal work to do. I feel the task force is more about going through the motions than a desire to solve any case. Other than the young Hmong woman's testimony, there's not much to go on with.'

Ange had a feeling that this was far more complicated and coordinated than Border Force had in mind. The thought that she might get entangled with another equally ruthless organised criminal element was troubling. Ly misinterpreted the look that came over Ange's face. 'Don't worry, he's no snake in the grass. When push comes to shove, I'm confident that Chan will do the right thing,' said Ly, hoping to ease the tension showing in Ange's eyes.

Given her recent experiences with office snakes, Ange mused to herself that time would tell regarding Chan and his loyalties. She changed tack. 'Tell me about the Hmong people and the state of the China–Vietnam border region. Do you know much about this?'

'It's a tragedy on so many fronts,' explained Ly between mouthfuls. 'At the end of the Vietnam War, the country embarked on a baby boom. It wasn't uncommon for families to have nine, ten, or even more children. Vietnam is mostly an agronomic society, and these extra hands helped farm the land. Have you ever been there?'

'No. But it's been on my list for ages. There are a lot of places on my list that I never seem to make time for,' replied Ange, a candid insight into her overblown work ethic.

'You should go, particularly up into the hill tribes out of Hanoi. Take the overnight night train to Sapa. It's really something. When you visit, you will see how young everyone seems, which is the actual source of Vietnam's emerging economic strength. The exact opposite happened on the Chinese side, where the one-child policy stalled reproduction rates. Worse still was the fact that Chinese parents preferred male babies.'

'I've heard about this dreadful situation, men being stronger and more useful for physical labour around the farm and all that. I wouldn't be here if my father had taken that approach,' sombrely observed Ange.

'It's also a cultural issue, one that goes right back to the teachings of Confucius, where males are viewed as superior to females. The prevalence of female infanticide has meant that males are overrepresented in certain areas of China, and this imbalance has resulted in young women and girls being abducted along the border regions. Almost every Hmong family will have a story of a family member who has been abducted in that way.'

'What happens to them?'

'Most end up as child brides and placed in servitude to their husbands. Some are forced into prostitution, usually made into drug addicts to keep them working. Very few escape,' said Ly, leaving that thought to hang naked in the air.

'That's terrible. I never knew,' said Ange, her mind drifting off to imagine the terrible life that those women endured.

'It gets worse,' said Ly, pausing again to eat some more of her lunch, keeping Ange in suspense as to how things could possibly get worse. 'Globalism has struck another blow. Small family farming plots are now unprofitable. Tourism has filled the economic void in many regions, but this has upset the social structure of the towns and villages. Now it's the women who bring in cash to support the family—making artefacts, domestic work, even guiding tourists if they can speak another language. The men, now idle, often take on the domestic duties, including looking after the children. This doesn't exactly fit well with their own sense of worth. Drugs are all too often an escape, with a disastrous effect on both them and the children. The other option for the young people is to abandon the villages and head to the cities to work in the factories. As youthful as Vietnamese cities are, the opposite is now true in many of the small villages. The situation became even more dire when tourism dried up during the pandemic. Many families were left destitute and with no viable means of supporting themselves. Desperate people do desperate things.'

'Where is the young woman now? Will I be able to speak with her?' asked Ange, circling back to the case at hand.

'She's being held in the immigration detention centre near the airport.'

'What? Is she going to be deported?' asked Ange sharply.

'Most likely. She is here illegally. I suppose, looking at this from above, if we spin our wheels long enough, the woman will be back in Vietnam and the case will be closed.'

'That's totally unfair,' said Ange, her blood boiling in an instant. 'Surely we should show some compassion. After all, this is all happening here in Australia, and right under our noses.'

'I had the same feeling as you but was told that Border Force can't make an exception for every sob story that comes across their desk—their words, not mine,' replied Judy Ly with a grim look. 'What's even more disturbing is that the toxicology tests we performed have labelled her as an illegal drug user.'

'I get the picture. Can you explain to me how immigration detention works here? It's not something that I've ever needed to understand before now,' asked Ange.

Judy Ly gathered her thoughts before replying to Ange's request. 'OK. The Australian Border Force handles immigration policy, visas, and the like. The government has outsourced management of the detention centres, and the one in Brisbane is run by a private company called ImDm Corporation. I haven't gotten around to doing much research on the company itself, but I guess they have a website.'

'I'd like to interview her personally. We need to look her in the eye.'

'Not all detainees are eligible for visitors. Border Force makes those determinations. I can ask if you think it's necessary. You should have the file notes from the Border Force interview by the time you get home.'

'Our priorities, and those of Border Force and the managers of the detention centre aren't necessarily in perfect alignment. Can you do your best to set something up? I'm sure we'll learn something. Just getting our own sense of the young woman is reason enough. Now that some time has elapsed, she might remember something new that might help us. As things stand, it doesn't appear as if we have much to go by.'

'OK. Let me work on that,' replied Ly.

It had been a most illuminating lunch, one that forced Ange to reflect on the comfortable bubble that Australia lived within. The island country maintained some of the toughest immigration laws in the world. The onset of Covid had triggered waves of nationalism to sweep around the world, and Australia's border remained one of the tightest.

Ange insisted on paying for lunch. Now that she wasn't even paying rent, she was feeling flush with cash. On the drive over to pick up Ange's new wheels, Ly asked a question that had evidently been playing on her mind. 'What's it like—being shot?'

'To be honest, it all happened so fast that it didn't properly register that I'd been shot. The first bullet hit my chest and was stopped by my vest. I never felt the second one that hit my leg. I was lucky. If the bullet had struck a couple of millimetres to the right, then I probably wouldn't be here. It was our own fault. We should have done more research and realised how the two Ndrangheta hitmen would react once we had them cornered. Hopefully, I won't ever make that mistake again. Anyhow, all's well that ends well, but it's not something that I wish repeated,' said Ange, ending on an upbeat note, neglecting to go into the details of how the altercation had resulted in a barrage of gunfire as the federal marksman took out the two assassins.

'It's so impressive what you did,' commented Judy Ly after hearing all of that.

Ange also neglected to mention the recurrent nightmares that she was still suffering. Notwithstanding Kerrie's viral social media post, Ange considered that her situation was not the cause for any hero worship.

Chapter 14

Team Ange

Ange enjoyed the feel of her new wheels and figured it was the ideal vehicle for her new assignment—also perfect for heading to the farm for Christmas. Once one left the coast and ventured west of the Great Dividing Range, the large mountain range that ran north–south almost the entire length of the country, 4WDs were the preferred choice of vehicle. Affectionately known as 'The Bush', the sparsely populated countryside remained unforgiving, making Australia one of the world's most lucrative markets for 4WDs. By the time she arrived back at her Byron Bay hinterland home, she felt quite at home in her white Toyota LandCruiser Prado.

The drive had given her plenty of time to reflect. Despite the depressing and disturbing nature of what lay behind her assignment, she found herself energised by her day. The case was vague and amorphous, but it felt good to be back on the job and moving forward with purpose, once more doing what she was good at. It was a puzzle of some magnitude, and the sense of injustice that she felt on behalf of the woman and her fellow captives was like a lightning rod. She reasoned that an enterprise such as this, having been operating for an extended period, must surely have the help of the authorities, most likely the very people who should prevent it.

Ange was busy reading up on the Hmong hill tribes when Gus turned up after a busy day. 'Hi, Ange. I know we had plans to go surfing down at Namba Heads tomorrow, but I really cannot get away. I'm sorry. It's crazy at work. With only two weeks until Christmas, I'm going to be flat out for the next seven days to get our orders filled. Is that your new car parked outside?'

'Yes. I think the Prado and I are going to get along just fine. That's OK about the weekend. I have plenty of research to do myself.'

Gus sensed the aura of energy that surrounded her. 'How did your day go? You look different.'

'My day went well. I'll tell you about it when I have a better sense of what the heck is going on. It's still a black box.' Having agreed to Gus's request, she figured it was an opportune time to broach the sensitive topic of Christmas. 'There was one thing I needed to speak with you about.'

'Yeesss?' Gus replied tentatively, as if sensing something touchy might be coming.

'Do you have any plans for Christmas? We're invited down to the farm at Tamworth,' she asked. It wasn't completely a lie, but she should have substituted the word *expected* for the word *invited*. She was also gilding the lily by suggesting that the invitation had included Gus, as her parents really didn't know that she was in a steady, even serious, relationship.

'That sounds like fun. I didn't want to impose, but I was going to be at a loose end. My dad and some of his friends are going to Whistler for a white Christmas. They've missed their last few annual skiing trips because of Covid and plan to make up for lost time. The fact is, that Dad remains at a loss since Mum passed away, so I'm pleased that he has plans to get away and enjoy himself.'

Ange knew that Gus's mother had died some six years ago. 'How did your mum pass? I don't think you've ever told me.'

'Classic Australian way for a child of the beach culture which developed in the sixties and seventies. Melanoma. It was a terrible end, but she was mercifully taken quickly,' replied Gus. 'When my parents were growing up, sunscreen was called tanning lotion—little more than vegetable or coconut oil. I'm pleased to see how diligent you are with applying sunscreen. I only hope that I didn't develop that habit too late in life.'

Ange almost broached the subject of Buddy but left that for their visit to the farm and after everyone had gotten to know each other. After a makeshift fridge meal, the pair collapsed into bed, too tired for sex but comfortable that this was not an issue between them.

Ange texted Bree to check that she was down at the station. Once confirmed, she also texted Jim Grady and gave him the heads-up that she would call by around 9 a.m. to discuss her crypto strategy with them both.

With the rapidly approaching Christmas season, the population of Byron was swelling daily, as early summer holidaymakers flocked into town. The traffic was confronting. She thought briefly about dropping into Bell Surfboards for coffee, but felt trapped in her crawling single-file line of cars inching their way into town. Thankfully, the police station was on her side of town, but she still arrived at the station a full ten minutes late. It would be one of the few places in town where carparks were still available, and she wondered how on earth that massive conga line of vehicles would ever find somewhere to stop.

Bree was working the front counter and her face brightened noticeably as Ange walked in the door.

'Hi, Bree. How's the training going?' asked Ange, referring to the fact that Bree had recently made the national hockey team, endearingly named the Hockeyroos.

'It's brutal right now. Our test series against India starts next week in Sydney. I'm staying with Billy.'

Ange observed how comfortable Bree seemed about her relationship with Billy. 'Don't act as if you're not loving it, Bree. I know how much this means to you. Anyhow, is the boss in?'

'You are absolutely correct, Ange. Yes, he's in, you know your way around,' replied Bree, turning her attention to a sandal-clad, backpack-bearing young woman walking through the front door.

'Could you join me? We have a meeting with the boss at 9 a.m. Tell you what, how about I ask Walton to fill in for you? He'll love that.'

Ange made her way through the station and found Gerry Walton. Walton and his sidekick, Ernie Lynch, delighted in spreading office gossip about Ange, fake news designed to impugn her character. They would be uncomfortable learning that Ange might be hot-desking in their station from time to time, a bolthole from which she would turn some serious heat towards those two imbeciles.

'Hi Gerry,' said Ange, playing out her best good-cop routine. 'Could you take over from Bree and look after the front counter for a moment? We have a meeting with the sarge.'

If looks could kill, Walton would have murdered Ange on the spot. 'I'm not your dogsbody. Do it yourself.'

'As I said, we have a meeting with the boss. I can get him to come out and ask you—if you'd prefer. He probably won't do it as nicely as I am,' said Ange, thoroughly enjoying herself.

Walton stood and grumbled his way to the front counter. Ange knew that his demeanour would brighten when he saw the young woman in reception. She was just his type—female. Bree soon walked through the door, fighting back laughter, and the pair walked over to Jim Grady's office.

Grady saw Ange coming and rose from his desk to greet her. 'Hi, Ange. You really seem to be back to full health. I couldn't see any limp as you walked over. I saw your little game with one of our office clowns. You do realise that your stunt will come back to bite you both?'

'You've gotta give a girl some fun, boss,' said Ange, allowing her expression to blossom into a wide and cheeky smile. 'My legs feels good, all things considered, but I've entered i that danger period of rehab, the point when you forget to do your stretching exercises. Anyhow, I wanted to speak to you both about our idea, the one we spoke of in the car yesterday.'

Ange gave Bree a summary of the project. As expected, she immediately came on board. 'I reckon we need to start on ICOs. Some of them seem as dodgy as all heck,' suggested Bree, her eager eyes brimming with energy.

'What's an ICO?' asked Grady.

'An initial coin offering. It's where someone launches a new digital currency. Some are just out-and-out scams. My favourite is still the Squid Coin that came out of the Netflix series. What a classic opportunistic rug-pull that was,' replied Bree, enthusiasm for her own opportunity bubbling to the surface.

'You realise that you're speaking in riddles, don't you?' said Grady with a bemused look on his face. He was not above realising that his comment was a telling affirmation of Ange's youthful hiring strategy.

'Give me a couple of weeks to get everything sorted. You'll need a new computer set–up, and I presume that the sarge and my boss will need to complete some paperwork. Focus on your test series against India, when you're not at the station, of course,' replied Ange, sensing that she didn't need to push Grady too hard. That Bree had been thinking about where crypto scammers might ply their trade confirmed that she had made a wise recruitment decision.

Ange's team was coming together nicely, and she spent the rest of her day reading the Global Report on Trafficking in Persons report, published by the United Nations Office on Drugs and Crime in 2020. The report was some two hundred pages long and quite an eye-opener.

Gus left for work early on Saturday, whereas Ange had plans for a quick surf followed by some shopping at the markets and a visit to her friend Lisa. The surf breaks were becoming increasingly crowded as Christmas approached. Ange found a small uncrowded beach break at Suffolk Park, but it was more a cleansing paddle than any session worth writing home about.

She called by the Bangalow markets to pick up something for dinner. It proved an ideal place to make a start on the pile of Christmas presents she needed for her family. Once she had made a solid dent in her list, she popped around to say hello to Lisa, the cake maestro. Weekly markets like Bangalow maintained a strict pecking order on who went where, and Lisa had earned herself a prime location. This made sense, as it didn't serve anyone's interests for regular shoppers to be constantly searching for their favourite vendors. The markets were busier than usual, so Lisa was thrilled when Ange offered to take over the stand whilst she took a break.

The bakery and patisserie stand opposite Lisa's was another regular fixture and owned by a young Vietnamese couple. They were exceptional bakers, beneficiaries of a Vietnamese tradition founded when the French had occupied their country. Since her lunch with Judy Ly, she wondered whether the disastrous Vietnam War would have happened if the French had stayed in control. No doubt it had pleased the Vietnamese people to see the end of the French and regain control of their country, only for them to see it fractured under such horrific circumstances. Like most things in the geopolitical space, there were pros and cons—certainly no definitive conclusions.

Until now, Ange had thought of the Vietnamese bakers across the way as nothing more than a part of the multicultural melting pot that formed Australia.

She yearned to pop across and learn their backstory, but they were doing a roaring trade and making the best of the early holiday crowds. Hopefully, their story was better than that of the mystery woman who had shown up in Texas, covered in garbage and scared out of her wits.

In the forty minutes that Ange oversaw Lisa's stall, she observed the mix of people that wandered between the stands, imagining their stories, as was her way. Now, this little game took on an extra dimension as she wondered who may have been a refugee from a war-torn country.

Ange spent a moment admiring the bakers and their hard-working success. She figured that her research could wait for another day.

Chapter 15

Detention

The case notes finally arrived late on Monday morning. Ange had just settled in for an afternoon in front of her laptop when Judy Ly called to say that she had arranged an interview with Cua Kwm, the young Hmong woman, at 2 p.m. on Wednesday at the detention centre in Brisbane. Ange spent the balance of Monday and all of Tuesday bringing herself up to speed with the case.

She left Byron around 10 a.m. on Wednesday, not wishing to chance her arm with the traffic. With only a single highway joining the Gold Coast to Brisbane, accidents could hold up traffic for hours on end. As things turned out, she need not have worried and even had time for a sandwich and flat white at an edgy coffee roastery just off the motorway. Arriving at the main office of the detention centre some fifteen minutes early, Ange was pleased to find Judy Ly waiting for her, giving them time to discuss their impending interview. Ange had been hard at work, and her trusty notebook contained pages of notes and a long list of questions that she hoped to answer.

The office reception screamed *corporate*, with ImDm logos proudly splashed everywhere. Apparently, the company was 'A global leader in the provision of immigration services'. The two police officers settled their interview plan while they waited. As this was primarily for Ange's benefit, she would lead the questions and Judy Ly would translate. A uniformed woman escorted the pair into a bland interview room with four chairs, where they waited until Cua Kwm was brought to them. Ange noticed the security camera and assumed the interview was being recorded. Whether ImDm Corporation or Border Force monitored the video was food for thought. The jurisdictional conundrums of out-sourcing such a sensitive area of government policy would undoubtedly come into play.

Even though Ange had noticed in the case notes that Kwm was only 152 centimetres high, the slight and tiny woman led into the room still came as a surprise. Despite her ordeal, Kwm was extraordinarily pretty, and the combination of her size and beauty gave a juvenile impression. Ange figured Kwm would be of some considerable value as a prostitute, heavily favoured by men of a certain type.

Judy Ly made the introductions, sticking with first names to help ease any tension. Once everyone was settled, Ly activated a small portable recording device and Ange started on her long list of questions, each translated through Ly. The record of that interview follows:

SUBJECT: Transcript of interview with Cua Kwm and Detectives Angela Watson and Judy Ly.

DATE: 14 December 2022

TIME: 2:02PM

PLACE: Brisbane Immigration Detention Centre

[START OF INTERVIEW]

[WATSON] Why did you travel to Australia?

[KWM] My brother arranged for me to come to Australia and take up a well-paid job. I was interested, as it would enable me to send back money and help support my family. My only way to earn money had been selling textiles and locally made trinkets to tourists, but Covid-19 had stopped all of that. We had no money and not enough food to eat some days.

[WATSON] How did your brother find out about the job?

[KWM] He read an advertisement that he found lying around in Sapa. It had a number that he rang and they told him about the job. He convinced me it would be the best thing for the family. They would pay for everything, and I could send some money home to help support the family.

[WATSON] What happened once you agreed to your brother's proposal?

[KWM] I travelled to Hanoi with my brother. Everyone treated me well in Hanoi and I became very excited about moving to Australia to start a well-paid job. They organised my passport and entry visa into Australia. I never had a passport before, but they never let me keep it.

[WATSON] Did you travel to Australia on your own?

[KWM] No. I travelled with a woman called Sue on the plane that we caught in Hanoi. It was my first-ever time on a big airplane. I was told to explain that I was visiting family, and that Sue was my aunty. Sue looked after my passport and spoke English. I was given a suitcase and some new clothes for the trip. It was very exciting.

[WATSON] How did you pass through immigration into Australia?

[KWN] Sue seemed to understand how to deal with airports and border officials. It was easy.

[WATSON] What happened once you passed through borders and immigration in Australia?

[KWM] Sue led me into the back of a van, and some men took me on a long drive.

[WATSON] Can you describe the van?

[KWM] All I remember about the van was that it was white, and it didn't have any windows. There were rows of seats in the back and we waited until another girl joined me before we drove away.

[WATSON] How long did you wait for the other woman?

[KWM] Not long. Maybe ten or fifteen minutes.

[WATSON] OK. Now, how long was the drive from the airport?

[KWN] I am guessing the drive lasted for half a day. We were given water and sandwiches for the trip and we stopped once for a wee on the side of the road. The van was very comfortable, and we watched three movies.

[WATSON] Can you describe any of the people who drove the van?

[KWM] Not really. There were two men. They always wore face masks. They told me it was to protect me from catching Covid-19.

[WATSON] So the men spoke Vietnamese? Is that correct?

[KWM] Yes, but not very well. Just enough for me to understand.

[WATSON] OK. I understand. Can you remember how many nights you were held captive?

[KWM] Six nights, including the night we arrived.

[WATSON] Okay. You are doing well, Cua. Now, I know that you didn't see much, but was there anything special that you remember about the place where they held you captive? Any special noises or smells, for example.

[KWM] I could hear the occasional car during the day, but only a few. I could also hear a rooster in the morning and sometimes a dog barking, but those sounds were weak and seemed a long way away. Oh, there were some loud birds in the morning and sometimes during that day. I didn't recognise most of those bird sounds. One I especially remember sounded like some people laughing out loud.

There were some crows as well. We also have crows in Vietnam. I knew by the smell that we were at a place where farm animals were kept. That smell reminded me of home and made me very sad.

[WATSON] Can you remember which direction those sounds came from, at least in relation to where you were being held?

[KWM] (after pause) Um... The rooster and the dogs were off to one side. The car sounds were off to another. Oh, the bird sounds came from the same direction as the cars.

[WATSON] Tell us about the place where you were being held.

[KWM] I arrived in the night and it was very dark when I escaped, but it looked like there was a large house away from where I was being kept. The men who were holding us captive must have slept in the house. The building where we (the captive women) slept was a long rectangle and had an air conditioner to keep us cool during the day. Except for the bathroom, the windows were all boarded up. Other than a house where I think the men lived, I didn't see any other buildings. The night I escaped was very dark.

[WATSON] So, going back to the sounds you heard, where were they in relation to the rectangle of the shed?

[KWM] (after pause) The dog and rooster came from the short end. The cars and the loud birds came from the long side, the one opposite the door that the men came in and out of. The bathroom window I used for my escape was at the other short end.

[WATSON] Excellent. Well done. Now, moving on, were you well fed?

[KWM] Yes, we were well fed. We had pizza the first night, but dinner was the same every night after that—rice, chicken, and vegetables. They gave us porridge for breakfast, and lunch was mostly bread and leftovers from dinner the previous night.

[WATSON] What were the vegetables like? Did they look like they were fresh, from a can, or frozen?

[KWM] (after pause) They looked the same each time. Not fresh. I think frozen. They definitely weren't from a can.

[WATSON] OK. Now, tell me about the other women. Were they Hmong as well?

[KWM] Some Hmong, but not Vietnamese. We couldn't understand each other, except by using hand signals. We were all terrified.

[WATSON] Were the other women already there when you arrived?

[KWM] No, they arrived all together on the next day.

[WATSON] How many men were guarding you and what did they look like?

[KWM] I'm not sure how many people were guarding us. The same two men who drove the van delivered food and checked on us each day. They always wore face masks and caps. One had dark hair and one was blonde—not natural blonde, Asian blonde from a bottle. They were tall compared to me, but everyone seems tall compared to me, especially here in Australia.

[WATSON] Can you remember what they were wearing?

[KWM] The two men normally wore blue jeans and plain tee shirts. I remember that the man with blonde hair wore a blue Nike cap with the swoosh on the front.

[WATSON] Did you get a sense of what nationality the men were?

[KWM] Asian. Not Vietnamese. They wore masks and caps all the time, so it was hard to be sure.

[WATSON] Anything else about the men that you can remember?

[KWM] The men seemed to spend a lot of time on their phones. This was how I escaped, as one of them was so busy on his phone that he forgot to close the bathroom window.

[WATSON] Did you see what the men were doing on their phones? Were they texting or doing other stuff, like on the internet?

[KWM] One time I could see over one man's shoulder. He wasn't texting. It looked like he was searching through a sort of shopping list or catalogue. I didn't get a very good look, as I wasn't very close to him. It was only for a second.

[WATSON] OK. Thanks. So, how did you escape from the building?

[KWM] Seeing as I am so small, I slid through the bathroom window.

[WATSON] What did you do then?

[KWM] I didn't want to be seen, so I hid in a garbage bin until I was sure that the men would be asleep.

[WATSON] I'm going to show you a picture on my phone now. Did the bin look anything like the one in this picture?

[KWM] Yes, but I think my bin had a red lid. It was hard to say in the dark, but I'm pretty sure it was red and not yellow. The bin was full of lots of things, including some very smelly food scraps. Oh, and some pizza boxes.

[WATSON] That must have been terrible for you, hiding in the trash.

[KWM] It was not as bad as the time I ran from some Chinese men who raided our village looking for brides. I jumped into a smelly pond beside a piggery and they lost interest in me. They took my sister instead.

[WATSON] What happened to your sister?

[KWM] I don't know. We never saw her again.

[WATSON] What happened once you got out of the rubbish bin?

[KWM] Once it was quiet, I crept from the bin and walked away as fast as I could. As I said before, it was a dark night, and I fell over a lot. I found the road and followed it towards a light in the distance. I eventually came to a house where I found a car and hid in the back under the cover.

[WATSON] Can you tell us anything about when you walked to the car? For example, which way did you turn? Was the countryside hilly or flat? How long did you walk for?

[KWM] (after a long pause) I turned to the right. The land was flat, not hilly like home. The road was rocky and very hard to walk on. No shoes. I can't be certain for how long. I was scared and not thinking about the time. (pauses again) I guess around thirty minutes. Oh, before I reached the road, there was a funny thing built into the ground. Sort of like a comb.

[WATSON] Cua, can you look at the picture that I've just drawn in my notebook? Was it like this? It's called a cattle grid.

[KWM] Yes. That was it. Made from metal.

[WATSON] Did the other house have a cattle grid as well, the one with the car you hid in?

[KWM] No. But there was a gate that I needed to climb over. I could tell it was a gate because the car stopped twice and I heard the gate opening and closing. I don't think the man was happy with the gate as he cursed after getting out of the car.

[WATSON] Were there any dogs on either of the two properties?

[KWM] No. That surprised me. I was waiting for a dog to bark and spoil everything.

[WATSON] That was lucky. Approximately what time do you think the car departed?

[KWM] I'm not sure. I'd fallen asleep. I could hear a rooster crowing. Sometime around dawn, I guess.

[WATSON] Tell me about the drive. How was the road? Did you stop anywhere else along the way?

[KWM] The first part was bumpy, then became smoother, and then it became slow and wobbly. (Kwm makes hand gestures to show a winding road). The ride smoothed again and there were more cars on the road. We slowed down and then sped up again many times, but the vehicle only stopped once—when I escaped. I was very thirsty and needed to find some water to drink.

[WATSON] You did very well, and I am impressed. Can you remember anything about the car?

[KWM] I was still terrified and never saw the driver. I remember the car was silver and had a black cover on the back, which I hid under. I was so eager to get away that I didn't notice anything else.

[WATSON] You were in the back of the car for a long time. How did you relieve yourself?

[KWM] I found a plastic bottle in the back that I emptied and used. Not while driving. (smiles)

[WATSON] Can you explain how you slipped from the car? I understand you hid in a church. How come nobody saw you?

[KWM] The church came later. I think the man stopped for fuel and I slipped into the bathroom. When I realised that the place was being locked up for the night, I escaped from the bathroom and found the other place. I didn't realise that was a church.

[WATSON] I thought you went straight to the church. Why didn't you tell this to the police when you were found?

[KWM] I was scared, and they never asked. I think I was just another annoying problem for them. Anyway, police are corrupt in my country. They could have been working with the men who stole me. I don't trust police.

[WATSON] How far away was the church from the fuel stop?

[KWM] Not far, maybe three or four houses away.

[WATSON] OK. Thanks for explaining that. Now, you need to be completely honest with me, Cua. Have you ever taken drugs yourself?

[KWM] No. No. Never. Drugs have ruined our life in the villages where I come from. Two of my brothers are opium addicts and do nothing all day. Their wives work hard on the farms or out selling textiles to tourists, while the children run around with no one to look after them. I hate drugs.

[WATSON] I only have one last question, Cua. Did you know why you were being held captive and what was going to happen to you?

[KWM] I guess I was going to be sold off as a bride. Like what happened to my sister.

[WATSON] Thank you for your cooperation, Cua.

[END OF INTERVIEW: 2:44PM]

Before they left the meeting room, Judy Ly handed over her business card and implored Kwm to make contact should she remember anything else, no matter how insignificant. As they walked back to the entrance to the detention centre, Ange took in the rows upon rows of demountable buildings. Kwm's current detention didn't seem all that much better than the one she had escaped from. It was shocking to be confronted by such a grim reality of life, where Kwm was simply a commodity, ripe for the picking and readily sold, bartered, or discarded.

'That was interesting and worthwhile, Judy. Cua Kwm was very impressive. We gleaned some important new information there,' commented Ange.

'I agree,' replied Ly. 'But why the fascination with the vegetables? That threw me a little.'

'I was raised on a farm near Tamworth. Vegetables are a total pain in the proverbial. Fresh vegetables are either a special treat or grown on the farm, and I don't think I will ever be able to eat canned vegetables again. Frozen veges are the best option, but they can contain listeria and can't be let to thaw out. If they were using frozen vegetables, then they would need to be purchased locally and not transported from Brisbane. It wouldn't do to go to all that trouble, only to poison your hostages with deadly bacteria.'

'OK. Impressive,' replied Ly, with a fresh look of respect in her eyes.

Once the two police officers had parted company and gone their separate ways, Ange stopped at the first roadhouse she came across to sit quietly and summarise her thoughts from the interview.

- *Kwm supplied with forged documents and chaperoned through immigration into Australia by a woman. Shows a highly organised operation.*

- *Why hasn't Border Force been able to cross-reference chaperones with illegal immigrants? Too many people coming through immigration, or just not interested?*

- *Transported from the airport by two men (not Vietnamese) in a large white van with no windows in the cargo area.*

- *Two women. Likely on same flight from Hanoi.*

- *Trip took half a day—meaning a massive search area.*

- *Kwm held captive for six nights.*

- *Four more women joined the next day. Multiple nationalities.*

- *Captive women fed oats, rice, chicken & mixed vegetables (likely frozen). Food may have been purchased from a local supermarket.*

- *Woman may have been housed in a rectangular donga/transportable building with an internal bathroom at one end and an access door off the long side. Likely positioned parallel to road going by car sounds.*

- *Property is on a minor road and well away from other farmhouses. Serviced by council rubbish collections.*

- *Other farmhouses off in the distance and in opposite direction to bathroom. Likely to be a clump of trees between the donga and the road. Access door faces away from trees/road.*

- *Two guards observed but no identification—wore masks and caps. One dark-haired and one blond who wore a Nike cap. Both Asian and heavy mobile data users. Presume more people involved to manage multiple trips from airport.*

- *After escaping, Kwm made her way from property and walked barefooted along a gravel road in pitch-black conditions, for around 30 minutes (uncertain). Need to check how far she could have gone in that time. Assume circa 2 kilometres.*

- *Likely cattle country—cattle grid at the boundary of the property where Kwm was held captive.*

- *Gate, but no cattle grid on the property Kwm escaped to.*

- *Appears that neither property had a dog. Unusual in cattle country.*

- *Car drove along a dirt road that turned into bitumen, then crossed over hills/range before becoming busier.*

- *Assume properties are 2.5 to 4 hours' drive from Texas.*

- *Vehicle probably needed refuelling, or driver needed to go to the bathroom. Perhaps both. Guess three hours for a second wee of the day would be average.*

- *Kwm still traumatised. Might remember more specifics in time.*

- *Expensive operation to run. Must be highly profitable.*

- *Check if her chaperone has left the country—assume fake passport as well.*

All things considered, Ange concluded that Cua Kwm had been both industrious and lucky. She was most impressed with Kwm's steely resolve to risk everything to make her escape, only to be put back in prison again. Yet, despite all of this, she displayed a blunt acceptance of her situation and all that life kept throwing her way.

Kwm left Ange with the powerful impression that she would do well in Australia—assuming that she could stay.

Chapter 16

Last Days

The interview with Cua Kwm had been illuminating. While her testimony was mostly consistent with the briefing notes, Ange and Judy Ly had learned a great deal more about Kwm's story. It seemed as if the initial investigation into her circumstances had been rushed and sloppy.

Why Kwm was being deported was really bothering Ange. She had learned that the two categories of people trafficking and people smuggling were now treated differently, although that had not always been the case. Both were massive problems globally and collectively rated as the second most profitable form of organised crime—narcotics the perennial holder of the number-one spot. Willing participants paid smugglers, and the relationship ended once the participant was in their preferred country. By comparison, trafficking involved deception or force, and Kwm's case was a textbook example.

It was widely known that Australian authorities usually deported illegal immigrants, meaning that victims of trafficking were often unwilling to come forward. For over twenty years, special arrangements had been in place to treat victims of trafficking for prostitution differently than normal illegal immigrants. However, victims often believed that police and officials were corrupt and on the payroll of the traffickers, something that would be entirely plausible for someone from a poverty-stricken country where corruption was often the way things worked. This global environment of mistrust certainly had not helped efforts to stamp out human trafficking.

She contacted Judy Ly to voice her concerns. 'Hi, Judy. I've been mulling over our interview. I cannot fathom why immigration is so quick to deport Kwm. Maybe taking this approach is simply easier than investigating how she got here and who was behind it? A case of see no evil, hear no evil.'

'I agree. It sucks. Unfortunately, she has several problems. First, she doesn't have a passport and the Vietnamese consulate has no record of her ever having a passport. Second, she wasn't the victim of prostitution—not yet, at least. Her medical examination was quite clear on that front.'

Ange interrupted. 'That's totally ridiculous. Are you telling me we need to wait for the crime to happen before we can do anything about it? Surely you know what was going to happen to Kwm in the coming days.'

'Agree again, but Border Force is a bit of a law unto itself, and those are their rules. Her third problem is probably her worst—her positive drug test.'

Ange was so angry that she could barely restrain herself from yelling into the phone at her colleague. It was not her fault, more that of a system where people weren't really individual human beings, viewed as a collective set of scammers vying to get into the *lucky country*. Kwm didn't seem all that lucky from Ange's perspective.

'Can't we lean on immigration to keep her in the country as a key part of an ongoing investigation? Anyway, Kwm did not give me the impression of being a drug addict. I've seen my share, believe me,' raged Ange, referring to her time patrolling the back alleys of Western Sydney.

'We can try, but they haven't exactly been rushing to help. They see their job as one to administer the rules, not deal with the root cause. That's our job—and the federal police's job,' replied Ly.

From her research, Ange knew cases like Kwm were eligible to be considered for a special visa called a Witness Protection (Trafficking) Visa, which would give them thirty days to work out a way forward. Some victims wanted to return home, but that often provided no solution, making their lives worse than before-hand. Others wanted to stay in Australia, but this was a complicated process that took some time to resolve.

As soon as she had hung up from the call, she rang Sally Anders. 'Hi, boss. How is your relationship with the feds coming along? I presume they work closely with Border Force.'

'It's getting there. Why do you ask?'

Ange then gave her a summary of her interview and railed against the prospect of Kwm being deported. Sally Anders waited until Ange finished before offering any promises.

'OK, Ange. I see where you're coming from and I agree with you. Let me see what I can do. It's not an ideal time of the year, being so close to Christmas. On that front, I'm pulling up stumps tomorrow and trying to get a break until the New Year holiday. If we don't speak, have a great Christmas and New Year.'

After returning best wishes to her boss, Ange concluded that at least the Christmas holidays would slow down the process of Kwm being deported. Hopefully, Sally Anders could pull a few strings and get her issued with a stay of execution.

Ange checked on how Bree was going over midweek drinks at the pub, a catch-up that doubled as pre-Christmas drinks.

It seemed as if things had hastened along. Sally Anders had allocated some funding and Bree had consulted with Billy to get set up with a new computer system. Given that some of her work might be sensitive, Jim Grady had installed Bree in a small storage-room-cum-office, positioned at the back corner of the station. Even though it was the worst room in the house, it still bruised certain egos and caused some ructions in station politics.

'Walton has his nose out of joint,' reported Bree. 'I overheard him telling someone that the sarge sure goes for a certain type.'

'How did you react to that? I've gone close to punching that idiot,' replied Ange.

'Oh, I simply laughed in his face. I've seen his type of behaviour plenty of times on the hockey field—players who blame selectors, the state of the pitch, even their teammates. All excuses for why they weren't making the grade.'

Bree then explained how Billy had trained her on how to use BCExplore, the software tool that she would use to trace crypto transactions. Apparently, Billy had thought Ange's idea of letting Bree range across the crypto landscape was brilliant. All too often, authorities were far too late to the table when crypto scams were being dished up. Also, authorities were already busy handling current crimes, leaving no time to watch out for new or potential scams. Increasingly regular data integrity breaches, where people's identities were being stolen and sold on the black market, combined with extreme volatility in the global financial markets, were creating fertile ground for scammers to farm.

'I'm going to start with initial coin offerings. You might have heard me refer to these as ICOs. To do it properly, minting an ICO is a lot of work. I'm planning to subscribe to a spread of these and see where that takes me. If they seem legitimate, then I'll exit the position and move on.'

'What about NFTs? Are you going to skip them?' asked Ange.

'No, not at all. I intend to keep a lookout for NFTs that are trending against the odds, plus keep my ears open on the Dark Web. The problem is that the NFT space has become so crowded. I would need an army of people to take positions in everything that looked suspicious. Most of them would be garden-variety suburban scammers or everyday fools, not organised crime like I presume we're on the lookout for. I've exited most of my NFT collection. It's looking like a massive bubble to me,' replied Bree.

'What, you've even sold your CoolCat tennis player?' asked Ange, referring to Bree's most valuable NFT.

'Yes, I figured now was the time while the Ash Barty effect still lingered. If my hunch is correct, many people are going to get badly hurt in the NFT space sometime soon. However, I'm all cashed up with nowhere to go!' Bree grinned, plainly enjoying her modest win in the NFT marketplace.

'Have you and the sarge sorted out the financial oversight arrangements with Sally Anders?'

'Yes, I need to supply a complete list of trades and open positions at the end of each month. All my trades will be audited at the end of the financial year. Apparently, Senior Detective Anders needed to "break a few eggs" to get this across the line,' replied Bree, making air quotes.

'The boss seems to enjoy breaking eggs in my experience. How are you juggling things at the station?'

'I can see how difficult it might be to have two bosses, so I plan to be careful not to abuse the privilege.'

'When do you plan to start trading?' asked Ange.

'I'm waiting to get access to an initial stake that was carved out of Ted Kramer's crypto portfolio. I've asked for a split of the majors, plus any dribs and drabs of minor currencies he had accumulated. I figure that I'll trade with the Bitcoin and Ethereum first up but also investigate the minor currencies. Perhaps I'll exit some of our positions if they check out, but those won't be worth much. The market still hasn't fully recovered from the last crypto crash.'

While Ange was no crypto trader, she knew full well about the last crypto crash, as this had precipitated the series of events that had led to her being shot. 'Sounds like a solid plan. We need to schedule some regular catch-ups once you start trading. Perhaps after Christmas?' Ange would not forget her last lapse of focus, one that had resulted in her being on a very different page to Billy, a slip-up that could have put Bree in danger. It prompted her to check on something. 'What name are you using to execute your trades? I presume you aren't using Lily White for that.'

'No way. I've set up a separate account under the persona of Matilda Mi, an all-too-cryptic homage to my hero Australian women's soccer team. It doesn't need to be a real name for the account holder. Billy helped set up the identity of the fake real person behind the scenes, someone called Matilda Smith—a very popular name, it seems.'

'OK. It sounds like you've given this plenty of thought. Let me know when your funding comes through and you're ready to trade,' said Ange before they turned to the sort of things that women catching up for a drink after work should talk about—as opposed to setting traps to ensnare organised criminals.

'Gus and I are heading back to my family's property for Christmas. We leave on Christmas Eve. Wish me luck with this meet-the-parents moment. The whole extended family will be there. I hope Gus can cope. What are your plans?'

'I'm staying around here. Given how soon the test series against India starts, I have a lot of training to do. It's my first Christmas in Byron and I understand it can get crazy here, so I guess work might keep me busy as well.'

Australia changed gears as the week progressed. The last few days leading up to Christmas were always a frenetic period of getting those last few jobs in, perhaps trying to make good a previous New Year's resolution to catch up for drinks with friends, other things having gotten in the way for the previous three hundred and fifty-odd days. Then there was the panic of buying last-minute gifts for people forgotten in the first tranche of shopping. Now that Ange was the plus-one to the ever-popular Gus Bell, the couple had a Christmas function every other night—sometimes two. Gus was exhausted and couldn't wait for Christmas Eve when the factory would shut down. Other than the major public holidays, the outlet shop would continue to trade, but the staff didn't need their CEO for that.

Kerrie invited Ange and Gus to her gala Christmas picnic, which was held the day before Christmas Eve. It proved an appropriate point to mark the start of Ange's own Christmas break, when she could put her new case aside and spend some time thinking about the nice things that people did for each other, a pleasant change of mood after her past two weeks.

The couple finally got away from Byron after an early lunch on Christmas Eve. Ange's new Prado was the perfect vehicle for the four-and-a-half-hour drive to the property in Tamworth. The route took them south to Grafton, where they then tracked along the wild and impressive Nymboida River before tackling the Great Dividing Range via the delightfully named Waterfall Way. Once on the central plains, they paused for a break in Armidale. Ange took Gus for a whistle-stop tour of her alma mater, a home-away-from-home for five years whilst she completed her schooling. Gus had also boarded during his senior school years, so he could relate to her experiences. They spent the last hour of their journey across to Tamworth trading stories about the many pranks and funny situations they had experienced during their respective boarding years. Before long, Ange was indicating to turn off the asphalt and wind down the long and dusty track that led to the family homestead. Her consciousness was suddenly brimming with memories of her life on the farm. She smiled to herself about the way her father still called the turn indicator a *flicker*, an Australian-only saying and a window into the simple way that bushies viewed life.

It was only then that Ange realised that she had forgotten to pack her trusty Akubra hat. Like the Stetson famous in the USA, one's choice of Akubra was part function and part fashion statement. Ange's father had two Akubras—one was beaten-up and weatherworn from years of hard work in the paddocks, and the other was his *town hat*, reserved for important occasions and a steadfast adornment at horse racing events. Hers had been a highschool graduation present from her father and would have come in handy as defence against the relentless summer sun. She hadn't thought about her Akubra for ages and it remained safely packed away in one of the cardboard packing boxes stacked in Gus's garage. As they approached the homestead, Ange wondered if this memory lapse had been a Freudian slip to signal that her transition from a country girl to a surfer girl was now irreversible. She noted that one of her brightly coloured surfing hats was stuffed in the pocket behind the driver's seat, and she hoped her father wouldn't notice such a telling lapse of judgment.

It was late afternoon and the light cast a magical quality over the landscape, softening the yellows and olive greens of a landscape parched by the early summer. In many parts of Australia, late summer was normally hot and dry, with storms and showers the only occasional relief. In late January, once the monsoon in the north was underway, tropical cyclones and low-pressure systems would travel south down the coast, fuelled by the warm water of the north Coral Sea. As these crossed the coastline, they would disgorge all their moisture and quench the thirsty land. Well, that was the theory; however, the weather patterns were changing right before Ange's eyes. The farmers planned their year and their finances around these rains, as well as the weather systems that moved across from Western Australia in autumn and early winter. A farmer's life was a constant lottery of weather and finances, one that all too often ended in tears after a depressing fight with their bank. It rarely matched the image of a gentle and time-rich life made popular in outback romance novels.

Ange and Gus stretched out tight muscles and took in their surroundings. The large and rambling homestead stood off to the left. Straight in front lay two large machinery sheds, overflowing with the tools of the trade. To the right of the machinery sheds was the obligatory junk heap, filled with the detritus of rural life. Ange recognised family cars that had literally been driven to the ground until they could go no farther than the junk heap. Naturally, nothing was ever thrown away in case it might come in handy someday. Ange knew few things made her father happier than finding the perfect widget lying in the junkyard, redeployed into active duty and rescuing him from a pinch. Even if the widget was available in town for purchase, the round trip would inevitably turn into a half-day affair. The rusty junk heap was more an asset than any liability.

To the right sat the ramshackle shearers' shed, an icon that had seen thousands upon thousands of sheep pass through; in one side all woolly and fluffy, and then out the other side, as bald as a badger, happy to be relieved of a heavy coat that was becoming totally inappropriate for the coming summer. Ange's parents came over to greet the couple. The raised eyebrows of her mother amused Ange when she introduced Gus. Ange could tell that Gus impressed her parents with his relaxed and direct manner, cemented with the obligatory bone-crushing handshake. A posse of kids came over to give Ange a hug. Being a detective carried a certain cache, and they all wanted to know if she had shot anyone lately. One could not imagine wider eyes, when she lifted her skirt to show them her gunshot wound, still purple and angry looking, adding to the legend of Aunty Ange. This newly earned reputation as a gunslinger was heavily overblown, but Ange saw no purpose in letting the facts get in the way of a good Christmas story.

Someone else moseyed up to Ange for a snuffle. She sensed by her father's expression that this could only be Buddy, the red cattle dog he had mentioned. Ange let Buddy have a decent sniff before she bent over to give him a solid tousle, taking the time to massage his neck and ears. Buddy lapped this up, relishing a level of attention rarely given to working dogs. He stayed and watched as Gus retrieved their luggage from the Prado and found some spare bunks in the shearer shed. Ange's older relatives enjoyed the air-conditioned comfort of the homestead, which was fair enough. The shearers' shed was stifling, so Ange took Gus for a walk around the homestead to ease stiff muscles before dinner.

The tradition in her family was for Christmas Eve to be a smallish meal ahead of the main feast the next day, when the family would crowd into the air-conditioning to partake in a hearty lamb roast, complete with all the trimmings that her mother and aunties had been creating for days. Once the evening meal was complete and everyone was departing to their bunks, Ange asked her father if she could feed Buddy and spent some time watching how he behaved around the other dogs. Buddy handled himself well, and Ange concluded that he would be the perfect companion.

She only needed to convince Gus about the idea. That could wait as a Christmas surprise.

Chapter 17

A New Buddy

Ange carefully extracted herself from the bunk bed and crept across the raw wooden floor of the shearers' shed. Mottled with stains, the floorboards were deeply scarred with the patina of a busy life, rich with lanolin and the smell of wool. The floor creaked under her weight, but it didn't seem to wake any of her fellow Christmas campers. Today was going to be a stinker, and she could already hear pings from the corrugated iron roof as it heated under the sun.

The morning displayed a brooding quality that signalled the start of a clear, hot day. The countryside shimmered in the distance as air molecules distanced themselves from each other, having already successfully squeezed away any moisture. Ange needed no weather forecaster to know that this shimmering was the best clue to the oppressive heat that would soon take all before it hostage, baking to a crisp the already parched land. Knowing that early morning would be her only opportunity, she had arranged her exercise gear the night before. She changed outside behind the tank stand and then sat on the rear stairs to put on her jogging shoes.

The land stretched out forever, a depth of field that only the ocean could offer fringe dwellers. The bulk of Australians lived pushed up against the sea edge and few experienced such a vista, lit with that piercing light reserved for dry places where the sun moved directly overhead. In this picture, using this extraordinary light as illumination, whether you looked left, right, forward, or backward, the landscape vista showed a sameness—yet somehow was not the same.

When learning that Ange had grown up on a property out west, most city dwellers commented, 'But there's nothing to see or do out there. It's boring.' To Ange, the bush was a place of work and industriousness, where business and lifestyle merged into one amorphous blob. Countryfolk often suffered from a case of confused identity because of this merger. The bush was also a place of great comfort, and she was ever grateful for the perspective on life that childhood had afforded her. Her father had often admonished that 'only boring people get bored', which was his way of saying that there was yet another job for her to do. Boredom had never been a problem, her imagination stepping in once chores were complete.

She looked over to see the dogs watching expectantly from the kennels, hoping to be let off so they could begin their working day. Kennel was a somewhat misleading choice of word, as they were, in fact, nothing more than a series of large hollowed-out logs, scattered around the centre of the large turning circle used by the long and ponderous B-double trucks that came either to pick up or drop off some animal or another, their smell unmistakable from considerable distance, an odour that applied equally to kennel and truck. Growing up, Ange used to refer to their collective pack of farm dogs as 'the logdogs'. That cute memory came and went as she walked across and unclipped Buddy from his tether. He didn't jump up or act crazy, just shook himself and looked at her with a tilted head, imploring her with his deep questioning eyes as if to say, 'OK. I'm ready. What are we going to do now?'

Ange started walking and Buddy fell in happily beside, seeming pleased that they weren't going to just stand around idle all day. Ange looked down at his steady loping walk, one of efficiency that could go forever, perfect for long days in the paddock and reminiscent of a rangy long-distance runner. The pair crossed the home paddock and Ange opened a wide metal gate. Buddy ducked through the opening and waited patiently on the other side as Ange used the dangling chain to secure the gate back against the large ironbark round-post. The track ahead dipped and wound its way to the furthermost extremities of the property. Ange stopped for a moment beside a large eucalypt tree to fashion herself a walking stick. Messy trees, there were plenty of branches to choose from. She looked up into the canopy, knowing that eucalypt trees were also dangerous, particularly after rain, when the tree would suck up as much water as it could. Large moisture-laden branches, perhaps weakened by drought, could suddenly snap off. Camping tragedies happened each year, often involving children and school camps.

Walking stick in hand, the pair fell into a peaceful rhythm, looking this way and that as the landscape unfolded. If one focussed on any point, a myriad of surprises would be revealed. Then, if one focussed again on a point within that point, another set of wonders awaited, and so on, ad infinitum. It was certainly not the boring view dismissed by city folk. To Ange, the bush evoked potent feelings: moody yet peaceful, frustrating yet seductive, beautiful at times, and ugly at others. It was addictive, and she felt herself falling back into its clutches as she wandered through the peace and quiet, an intense tranquillity reserved for the Australian bush, a quiet filled with noise and activity.

A crow looked down upon the pair of bushwalkers before barking its mournful cry to a colleague some distance away, ever watchful for an opportune moment to steal some food. A small flock of sulphur-crested cockatoos screeched their way overhead, causing Ange to look skyward. The bush was certainly not silent—unless it was sounds of the city that you were expecting to hear. Away off in the distance, she could see a flock of tiny finches or budgerigars weaving magically in tune with each other, morphing this way and that, dancing on the shimmering air. Across to the left, some fifty metres away, Ange could see a small mob of kangaroos silently grazing, eating grass that her father had carefully cultivated for other animals, a source of some conflict in times of drought. The bush was never boring, provided you took the time to look.

If someone had tasked a team of industrial designers with designing an animal that was perfectly suited to the Australian landscape, they surely would have developed a leopard or cheetah. Certainly, it was hard to imagine that they would have arrived at anything which remotely resembled a kangaroo. Yet there they were, the perennial survivor, standing over in the paddock, looking directly at Ange and Buddy, their oddly small yet pretty faces peering over the long grass, as cute as ever. There was no better survivor of all that this continent could throw at an animal, come hell or high water. The very colour of the landscape itself, the mob stood perfectly still, waiting to see if danger was headed their way.

A large male 'roo' reared up to his full height of some two metres before hopping away with his small harem. Ange marvelled at the ease and grace with which these large animals moved across the paddock. Their powerful legs could leap them over or across most things. Man-made fences or cattle grates posed no obstacle. This strength, combined with a super-low centre of gravity, made kangaroos fast and agile. Their long and muscular tails not only provided balance for darting this way and that, but also served as a third leg, one capable of supporting the animal's entire weight and useful for inching around when grazing peacefully.

The signature move of the boxing kangaroos famous on YouTube was to tilt back onto their tails and use those mighty rear legs to rip at the belly of any opponent. It was a deadly move, sharp claws making the male kangaroo something to fear. Ange was ever respectful of kangaroos. In fact, of all the dangerous animals who called Australia home, they were the animal responsible for the most fatalities—more from the carnage caused in car accidents than the occasional attack. Everyone who lived in the bush knew how unpredictable kangaroos could be around vehicles, especially at dawn and dusk, when they would come from afar to eat the green shoots along the tarmac verge, only to suddenly leap right in front of you for no apparent reason.

Yet, the true superpower of the species lay with the female kangaroo. Once conceived, she could hold her foetus in suspended animation for up to seven years, waiting for rain and a bountiful season in which to raise her joey. There was no cuter name for a juvenile animal than 'joey'. It was even cuter to see a joey bundle itself into its mother's pouch, low on her belly, diving in headfirst, usually leaving a jumble of legs sticking skyward before arranging itself to get a better look at the journey ahead. The brilliance of this pouch was undeniable. The mother, no longer hobbled and held back by minding her slower and weaker offspring, could whisk herself and her joey away in the blink of an eye.

Perhaps the team of industrial designers might have included more useful arms; or a set of opposable thumbs; or even a larger brain, fashioning them more in their own form. Despite these potential design flaws, kangaroos were flourishing. Anyway, why would they need these things? More brainpower and opposable thumbs would only conjure up lots of things they didn't really need. Eventually, they would design things to kill each other with, and then work hard to make these things ever better. Sure, the thumbs might have been useful, but the kangaroo remained a remarkable survivor and Ange had never seen a kangaroo die at the hands of another. She reasoned that there would be no need for a detective on a planet of the kangaroos.

Forever the daydreamer, Ange was meandering through these waves of thought and lost in a daze. Buddy suddenly started barking madly, urgent and insistent, causing her to stop and re-enter the moment. There, directly in front of where she was walking, slithered a large eastern brown snake that the vibrations of their footsteps had disturbed, rudely interrupted while warming its cold blood in the morning sunlight. This animal, unlike the kangaroos that she had been contemplating, could kill in minutes and was one of the deadliest and most feared snakes on the planet. Once bitten, Ange would probably be dead before anyone could come to help. This was breeding season, and 'browns' could also be highly aggressive, able to strike staccato style and deliver fresh venom with each bite. A fencer who was working on the property when Ange was growing up had suffered some seventy puncture wounds from a single snake. He was an absolute bear of a man, and his immensity and quick thinking by his co-worker were all that saved his life. He was never the same again, certainly no use as a fencer—at least according to her father.

The pair of walkers watched the snake slither away before cautiously making a generous detour. Over the years, besides losing a valuable fencer, the family had lost innumerable dogs to brown snakes. Ange was pleased to see that Buddy was smart enough to realise that this was a moment where discretion was the better part of valour.

Their walk took almost ninety minutes, a time that seemed to disappear in the blink of an eye. When the wanderers returned to the home paddock, Christmas revellers were spilling from the uninsulated tin shed, awoken by the rapidly rising temperature of the day ahead. It would get brutally hot inside the shed within a couple of hours. Her young nieces and nephews were poking around at this and that, and two boys kicked a rugby ball at each other. Gus was sitting on the steps watching this activity, and Buddy loped over for a pat.

Ange dropped her walking stick beside the gate, ready for tomorrow, and stepped across to the shearing shed. 'What do you think of Buddy?' asked Ange. This was a leading question, as she hadn't told Gus about her plan.

'Cool dog,' commented Gus as he gave Buddy's neck a roughhouse scratch.

'How do you think he would cope with the Byron Bay set?' asked Ange casually, as if this thought had just occurred to her.

'What do you mean? Isn't he a working dog?' asked Gus, stopping his patting to look Ange directly in the eye.

'Buddy got badly injured after being kicked by a bull. He's too smart, and he's now cattle shy, which isn't the perfect trait for a cattle dog. My dad can't bear to put him down, but he also can't afford to keep feeding a dog that can't work. The day will come eventually....,' said Ange, her trailing tone meant to pull on Gus's heartstrings.

'I feel like I've been set up,' said Gus, his big smile showing that he didn't mind being outmanoeuvred in this way. Buddy, for his part, almost seemed to know what was going on. He lifted his right paw and placed it on Gus's thigh. In truth, he probably just wanted Gus to resume his patting, but this timely and affectionate move settled the deal.

Chapter 18

Christmas and Beyond

C hristmas day settled into a familiar ritual. Breakfast was a time to revel in the excitement of young children opening Christmas presents, also for the grandparents to remember a time when they had enjoyed the thrill of their own children. More than once, Ange caught her mother glancing her way, reminiscing about Christmases past. Ange had packed her trusty Bialetti stovetop coffee maker, essential equipment for feeding her caffeine addiction. Her parents had never acquired the taste for decent coffee, preferring the efficiency of the instant variety. Ange would rather drink mud than stoop to that level.

Her father had gifted Ange a square dog mattress and hand-plaited a lead made from kangaroo hide, one of the strongest and finest-grained leathers one could find. She was initially surprised at her father's clairvoyance that she would hit it off with Buddy, although she really shouldn't have been. After all, her father had been around dogs all his life and probably knew more about dogs than people, such was the reliance on working dogs around the property.

After breakfast, Ange helped him with some chores, attending to animals that didn't realise that it was Christmas Day. He took in her colourful surfing hat without remark, but Ange read his thoughts and her face had flushed with guilt. She rationalised his lack of comment as a statement about his opinion of Gus. Had her father been displeased with her choice of partner, he would certainly have been vociferous about her completely inappropriate choice of hat.

Around 11 a.m., everyone reconvened in the homestead, pleased for the air-conditioning, and settled down to the long table for the Christmas feast, all noisy and frenetic as plates got passed up and down. Once bellies were full and the lunchtime conversation had stalled, everyone departed for their obligatory

Christmas Day nap to see through the brutal midday heat, finding whatever soft impromptu bed was available. By this stage, the shearer shed was an oven and a place to be avoided. The children waited patiently for the sting to leave the sun before dragging everyone outside for the mandatory game of backyard cricket, hoping that this might be the year when they could finally assert their dominance of the dusty and uneven makeshift pitch.

Showered and freshened up, everyone gathered once more on the lawn ahead of the evening BBQ. Sunset had always been, and always would be, Ange's favourite time of the day in the bush, where the baton passed from the creatures of the day to those of the night. Those final moments, when the sun cast its last long shadows, were magical, where a blanket of peace and solitude descended on the countryside. The dying breeze, having carried the cries of cockatoos, crows, and kookaburras, now became the domain of the insects. In the distance, Ange could hear the barking of an owl as it settled in to pick off any unwary rodents that wandered from cover, thinking that they were now safe from the hawks and eagles which patrolled the daytime skies. Ange reflected and marvelled at this cycle of life, humankind seemingly the giant disrupter of this perpetual motion.

After too many drinks and too many tall stories, another Christmas Day was over, an annual cycle of country life in itself. Ange and Gus collapsed onto their bunks, tossing and turning until the cooling air mercifully allowed them to drift off to sleep.

The next morning, Ange awoke at dawn again and tiptoed outside. This time, Gus joined her, looking far more relaxed than he had on the drive down on Christmas Eve. Ange suggested Gus go over and let Buddy off his lead, observing how the two interacted. After securing a quick pat from Gus, Buddy raced down to the gate and crab-walked back, dragging Ange's rudimentary walking stick from the previous day, ready for another mini-adventure. She probably would have forgotten that she had placed it there after their walk. Buddy was one smart dog.

Ange took Gus on a track that took in the stony creek and its magnificent ghost gums, one of Australia's most majestic trees. Now at the peak of dry season, the creek had stopped flowing weeks ago, reduced to a series of beaded waterholes, a string of life-giving pearls filled with precious water. The pair of walkers stopped to observe all the animal prints that had ventured for a drink under cover of darkness. She noted that there were some wild dog prints. She would need to tell her father. Packs of feral dogs regularly wreaked havoc on the property, killing indiscriminately and well past any need for sustenance. Often inbred with native dingoes, they were the scourge of farmers. Once the children had left the property, her father would probably start a baiting program aimed at keeping these killing machines under control. Baits were also tempting for working dogs, so this was a tricky and worrisome task for any farmer.

After coffee and a leftover breakfast, Gus and Ange packed up their things and said their goodbyes. Aunty Ange promised not to get shot again, and the kids thought she was being a massive killjoy. There was one last passenger to settle into the Prado and Ange opened the back door, where she had laid out Buddy's new dog mattress. The two looked each other in the eye before Ange summoned her best country accent, one that Buddy would recognise and respond to. 'In ya get.'

Buddy leapt into action and jumped up into the back of the car. After two quick laps to check out his new bedding, Buddy settled down and looked back out at Ange, giving his best 'OK, let's go' look. Ange's father looked at Buddy and muttered the word *turncoat*. Despite his downcast eyes, Buddy seemed to admit the truth in this accusation, accepting this promotion of sorts, choosing a new life as a companion and protector in preference to his old one as a servant. Ange and her father understood this look in Buddy's eye and father and daughter exchanged a knowing look of their own before Ange went up and gave her father a big hug, whispering 'Thanks, Dad' in his ear, bringing a subtle yet satisfied grin to his face. The knowing smile on Ange's mother's face made it obvious that she was more interested in Ange's relations with the other male in the Prado. Ange returned this smile, both knowing full well what the other was thinking. Scott Partridge, Ange's beau of three decades past, never even rated a mention.

As they drove back out along the dusty track toward the bitumen road, Ange figured it had been a successful trip, one where she had not thought about her work for a minute—until that moment. Ange suddenly conjured a vivid image of a barefooted Cua Kwm frantically running down a similar road in the middle of the night to elude her captors. Once they hit the paved surface, Ange noted how long it was before she could see another farmhouse, one that might provide refuge. She could only imagine the fear that the young woman must have experienced during her escape ordeal, causing Ange to shiver at the brutality that humans were prepared to inflict on others.

Gus pulled her from this dramatic, imagined, and cruel mind-movie. 'Can we swing by Angourie on our way home, Ange? There's something I'd like to show you.' Gus gave no further clues what that something might be. Ange wound the Prado back down the Waterfall Way and through to Grafton, where they picked up the M1, otherwise known as the Pacific Highway. They then took the turn towards Yamba and Angourie, a legendary surf spot that Ange had only visited once before. With Gus directing, they eventually pulled into the driveway of a low-set fibro beach shack, coloured a faded blue and white, seemingly unchanged from when it was first constructed, somewhat incongruous amongst the more substantial beachside mansions that had come since.

Gus finally explained what he had in mind with this detour. 'I thought we might stay here for a few days if you're able to. I'm not needed at the shop. What do you think?'

'Fantastic, but it would have been nice to be forewarned. We could have brought along some surfboards.' Gus ignored her admonishment, quietly pulling some keys from his pocket and walking over to the house. Ange let Buddy out of the back of the 4WD so that he could do his thing, wetting a few fenceposts and sniffing his way around the yard. Gus strained to open an old-fashioned sliding garage door, one that squeaked and groaned in protest. Once there was sufficient light to see inside, Ange spied racks of surfboards in all shapes and sizes.

Gus smiled her way. 'Oh, ye of little faith. I would hope that the CEO of a major surfboard company could find you something to borrow for a few days.'

While unpacking the Prado, Gus explained that this was his father's original beach shack, built when Angourie was first discovered by the burgeoning surfing set of the 1970s. As they opened the house to welcome in the fresh sea air, Ange could see that this was a simple dwelling meant for enjoying the outdoors and maximising precious surfing time. As far as beach shacks went, it seemed just perfect.

Over the next three days, Gus showed Ange his country, the Angourie where he had grown up during endless summer holidays. Almost all the locals knew Gus, and most showed him respect in the water. He explained how a new breed of aggressive surfers had taken over the iconic point break and how unpleasant it could become whenever the surf was pumping. Fortunately for them, light conditions meant that the back beach to the south of the point held all the action. Ange was certain that sharks did not discriminate, but beaches facing south somehow seemed more ominous than their north-facing counterparts. Pleasingly, the sun was out and the water crystal clear, easing away any pangs of discomfort over the prospect of any unwelcome visitors.

As they were walking back to the shack one day, Gus relived his connection to Jake Thomson. He'd been impressed with how Jake asserted himself in a testy Angourie line-up of surfers that was bordering on murderous. So exceptional was his natural ability that Gus had offered Jake a sponsorship on the spot. 'I sometimes feel that I'm responsible for what happened to Jake. If I hadn't offered him that sponsorship and mentored him while he matured as a surfer, Jake would never have become a pro and never would have been in Namba Heads. I still get upset at such a wasteful tragedy.'

'That's just ridiculous, Gus. What happened to Jake is not your responsibility,' Ange implored. She could see in his eyes that he did not fully agree on that point, which cast a sombre shadow over the pair as they drifted off on their own thought bubbles. Ange said a silent prayer for Jake and hoped that he had found some perfect waves in his afterlife, unfettered by earthy constraints and free from harm.

Having never seen the ocean before, Buddy took to it with gusto, running up and down the beach, chasing the breaking waves and making a nuisance of himself for twenty minutes each morning. Once that job was done, he would sit patiently beside his mistress's towel, peering out into the ocean as if imploring her to return. Now that Buddy was her surfing buddy, Ange figured she would no longer need to scratch around hiding car keys.

It was a magical few days and over far too soon. Once they had given the beach shack a cursory clean and cleared out the fridge, they packed up the car and headed for home. Ange settled into the drive back to Byron Bay with a deep sense of contentment. All it took was a single phone call to torpedo this sense of peace, blowing it all to smithereens.

Chapter 19

Disaster

Ange could see that the caller was Judy Ly. 'Hi, Ange, I have some terrible news,' she said, which turned out to be an understatement of some magnitude. 'I think you had better pull over.'

Ange felt an instant churning in the pit of her stomach and edged off the highway and into an emergency stopping zone. Once she had screeched to a stop, Ange took Judy Ly off speaker and put the phone to her ear. 'What's up?'

'Cua Kwm was found dead this morning at the Brisbane immigration detention centre.'

Emotions flooded through Ange as she took in this news. Within a split second, anger and indignation took control over her response. 'You can't be serious. How on earth could this have happened?'

'The person who I spoke to from the detention centre told me it's obviously a drug overdose. Those were his exact words, by the way. They found her during the morning roll call,' replied Ly.

Ange was furious. 'For goodness' sake, it's an immigration detention centre, not a Nazi concentration camp where people go missing in the night. Surely you don't believe this, do you, Judy? Even if it was plausible, how could she have gotten her hands on any drugs to overdose on? Bloody hell, aren't we supposed to be protecting these people?'

'I don't believe it either, but they're refusing to look any further. They plan to repatriate the body back to Vietnam in the next few days.'

'Over my dead body, they are. And not before we've completed a proper autopsy. Thanks for letting me know Judy. I need to make a few calls.'

She rang Sally Anders. 'Sorry to bother you, boss, but there's been a tragic development in our case. I need you to break a few eggs for me.' Ange then explained to her boss what she had just learned before getting to the point of her call. 'The mongrels are trying to ship her body out of the country without a proper autopsy. My guess is that they're trying to avoid copping any heat and pass this whole thing off as a terrible and sad tragedy of narcotics, probably even giving themselves solid pats on the back for keeping our borders safe. I'll bet that the same people who trafficked her into the country killed her. Do the feds have jurisdiction over this? Now might be the perfect time to cash another chip for me.'

'I agree that this all sounds sketchy. I'll see what I can do. At the rate you're going, you will have gambled away all my chips before I've gotten to use any myself,' rued Sally Anders before she hung up from the call.

Ange could not recall being angrier. Not trusting herself to drive, she asked Gus to take the wheel. The pair exited the Prado as traffic whizzed by and walked around the car to trade seats. Ange passed Gus in a daze, unspeaking. Buddy sat up and quizzically watched this procession. Once Gus was at the wheel and had re-joined the highway traffic, he looked across at Ange. 'I gather that was distressing news you just received.'

'I'm so angry and upset, I didn't feel that I was safe to drive any further.'

'Can you talk about it?' asked Gus.

Ange took a deep breath and held it for a few seconds before making a long sigh, trying to calm herself sufficiently to give Gus a decent explanation of what had happened. 'The case that I've just started working on involves a seventeen-year-old woman who was trafficked from Vietnam. Hers was a textbook case where a family member responded to an advertisement for well-paid overseas jobs that could help support her impoverished family. Sometimes victims are taken forcibly, often children as well. Once in their target country, they're sold as brides, or enslaved by domestic or menial work, even to assist with other criminal activities. Human trafficking is now the second most profitable form of organised crime and arguably one of the safest from detection and prosecution.'

'Why is that?'

'Not only is it hard to detect in the first place, but victims are fearful of retribution if they come forward and speak up—either to them or their families. Often, the families become hostage to the scheme and are paid a sign-on bonus, which is ostensibly a loan to be paid off by the victim's work. These supposed loans are inflated to cover costs of travel and accommodation, and high interest rates mean they can never repay them. The families are often hooked into becoming accomplices to help recruit other victims. Some brokers are operating under cover of legitimate migration or employment operations. The criminals handle all the paperwork and secure passports and visa documents, often forged or stolen, and then sell the victims for as little as ten to fifteen thousand US dollars. However, an Asian prostitute can earn as much as two hundred thousand dollars per year for the mongrels who ultimately buy them and put them to work. Victims are sometimes forced to perform other illegal activities such as transporting or growing narcotics,' explained Ange, giving Gus the basics of what she had learned during her research.

'What happened to the woman?' asked Gus.

'Soon after arriving in Australia, the young woman was essentially kidnapped and taken to an unknown destination, where she escaped in quite dramatic circumstances. I interviewed her just before Christmas in an immigration detention centre up in Brisbane. When I heard that the Border Force was planning to deport her, I intervened. She would have been in danger had she travelled back to Vietnam and I was trying to get her held in Australia under some legislation specifically designed to protect victims of trafficking. They found her dead this morning,' said Ange. She looked at Gus with teary eyes. 'I think I may have gotten her killed, Gus.'

'Ange, remember what you told me a few days ago? None of this was your fault,' counselled Gus, a wholly ineffective attempt at absolving Ange from feeling responsible.

'Gus, this poor woman has been comprehensively roached. First, by Covid and the collapse of her local economy; second, by her own brother, who essentially sold her off for a few dollars; third, by a series of heartless criminals who treating her like a pack animal to be traded; fourth, by an immigration system that turned a blind eye to this conduit into Australia; then finally by us, the authorities, who should have been keeping her safe in our so-called civilised country. It's a complete disgrace.'

'How did she die?'

'She didn't just die, they killed her. That's something I'm certain of. What's even worse is that the detention centre is trying to pass her death off as a self-inflicted drug overdose. There are so many inconsistencies in that presumption that

I don't know where to begin. Border Force is planning to cover up this mess by shipping her body back to Vietnam and washing their hands of the whole affair. The whole thing stinks to high heaven.' Ange's voice then took on a steely edge. 'There is no way that I'm letting these scumbags get away with it.'

Gus had no response to this intent, and the trio drove the rest of the way home in silence.

Ange's level of frustration and indignation about what had happened grew with each passing kilometre. Common sense, backed by her reading and research, told her that Cua Kwm would have met a similar fate once she had arrived back in her native country. However, what really riled Ange was the fact that the young woman should never have been held in immigration detention. A country that prides itself on giving people a fair go should have protected her. Life had not afforded Cua Kwm anything remotely resembling a fair go—the direct opposite, in fact.

Ange felt her focus shifting from outrage for the dead to concern for the living. There were five other women held alongside Cua Kwm, and who knew how many other similar cells were operating around the country? If this tragic death was to mean anything, Ange knew she must dig deep and strive to rescue the other women and succeed where she had failed Kwm.

As she drove into Gus's palatial estate, with its spectacular view over Byron Bay and the Coral Sea, she contemplated how fortunate was her life, one of privilege and excess by any standard—a stark contrast to the lives of Kwm and those other young women.

Ange's New Year's resolution was already a foregone conclusion.

Chapter 20

Bad Dreams

A nge let Buddy escape from the back of the Prado and gave him a big scratch around the head and neck, more for her comfort than his. Ange observed him as he ranged around his new home paddock. Her father was a superb trainer of dogs, and Buddy never strayed out of eyesight from his new mistress. The prospect that Buddy would be an inveterate wanderer had been concerning her, as Gus's fence line was more for delineation than incarceration. As soon as she picked up Buddy's dog mattress, Buddy loped back over beside her, sensing that whatever Ange was doing, it was related to him.

When Ange was a young girl back on the farm and mistress to Buddy #1, her life was split between boarding school and farm life. Buddy #1 lived a similar existence. When Ange was at school, he was a faithful working logdog. However, whenever she was home from school, he served as her companion, first and foremost. Buddy insisted on sleeping on the ground under the house directly outside Ange's bedroom. In the night, she would sometimes hear him trundle off to check on something not right or out of place, returning to settle back to sleep once he was happy with the state of things. She had loved Buddy #1 with a passion.

Gus's house enjoyed a wide covered veranda running the entire length of the house. The view over the ocean to the east was the principal attraction and the perfect place to sit and relax. The master bedroom sat in the south-eastern corner of the house and large doors opened directly onto the veranda and that view. Ange had fallen into the habit of opening those doors to make her first assessment of the day, the bird's-eye position ideal for considering what the weather might have in store. She decided that her new Buddy should sleep on the veranda directly outside the bedroom and plopped his new mattress on the floor in the corner. Buddy took a quick lap of his new quarters and lay down, thinking that this was expected, before jumping back up to supervise Ange with the unpacking.

She wandered around in a daze and Gus sensed she needed to be left alone to process what had happened. Ange rang Judy Ly mid-afternoon to tell her she was calling in some favours to ensure that Cua Kwm's body was properly autopsied. She asked Judy to organise an urgent Teams meeting for the next morning, where the task force could discuss the implications of this development.

That evening, in the middle of the night, Ange's Ndrangheta nightmares returned—the first time in ages. She woke up yelling out loud, waking Gus and eliciting a sharp yelp of alarm from Buddy. Thinking that she was over her problems, Ange had put aside her sleeping aids and was left floundering, tossing and turning, vainly trying to fall back asleep. After a good hour, knowing that she was also disturbing Gus, she arose from bed and went to sit on the veranda steps. Buddy lumbered over and put his head on Ange's lap and the pair took in the moonlit landscape. Putting aside her dreams of murderous assassins, it was a beautiful and balmy evening, with a cooling zephyr creating an almost perfect temperature. The moon was full and still rising to the east, reflecting on the ocean in the distance, creating a magical effect that helped calm Ange's racing mind and slow her heart rate. Every so often, when her terrifying thoughts returned, Buddy would look up and prompt her to restart her unconscious stroking of his head and ears, soothing them both. Eventually, Ange felt ready to catch that elusive sleep train and stood up to head back to her own bed. Buddy looked at her in disappointment before slowly wandering over to his own bed, appearing to fall asleep in an instant. She knew this feat would not be so easy an accomplishment for herself.

First thing the next morning, after apologising to Gus for inflicting on him such a restless night, Ange rang her psychiatrist. Luckily, Dr Hall was available to take the call and Ange gave her a summary of what had happened with Cua Kwm before getting to the crux of her call. 'I thought I was done with those nightmares. I'm really concerned that they returned so readily. Is this something that I must now deal with for the rest of my life?'

Kirby Hall's explanation of what was going on caused Ange to visualise her trauma as a discrete ball of pain. She imagined her mind working hard to build a protective cocoon around the pain and sequester it away, progressively deeper and deeper in the subconscious. As Kirby explained, significant shocks could puncture this cocoon and bring the memory flooding back. This could even happen with everyday events, sounds, or smells. As time went on, providing Ange didn't fall for the trap of internalising and dwelling unnecessarily on her pain, the protective cocoon should hopefully become tougher.

'Getting a solid night's sleep is essential, as is keeping up with exercise and surfing. Are you using the sleeping and meditation app that I signed you up for?' asked Dr Hall.

'No, I hadn't needed it lately and put it all away. One downside of that app is having my phone beside the bed overnight. I'll get myself sorted for tonight. I got a dog, though. Buddy, a red cattle dog from the farm. Buddy suffered his own trauma, courtesy of a bull's hoof. He was no use on the farm anymore, but I think he's going to be a big help to me. I sense a difficult period ahead dealing with the case that I'm working on. It's even more confronting than my last case.'

'OK, Ange. Treat this seriously and be diligent in the strategies we set in place. Remember to ring me if you ever need to talk things over,' concluded Dr Hall.

Ange hung up from her conversation with her psychiatrist, feeling much better. Unfortunately, her 11 a.m. Teams video call undid all of Hall's good work. Detective Wallace got under Ange's skin from the get-go. 'I don't know why you're being so insistent on this, Detective Watson. It's obvious to everyone that she was an addict who smuggled in whatever drug she craved. I'm now even doubting her story and if she ever presented a viable lead. We can't afford to be distracted from the main game and waste time and valuable resources exploring random dry gullies.'

Ange was not so easily dissuaded. 'That's absurd. There are way too many inconsistencies here for my liking. First, if we consider your assertion that she's a junkie, how did she smuggle in narcotics, and why would she overdose? Second, why didn't anyone see her overdose and call for help—I presume she was in a dorm room with others? Third, in response to your view that she may have concocted her story, the interview that Judy and I conducted with her just before Christmas was highly credible. She gave no inconsistencies or any sign that her story had been fabricated.'

'That is all quite subjective. What are you suggesting, Detective?' replied Wallace, his superior tone attempting to reassert his authority and realign the discussion back towards his original hypothesis.

'What I'm suggesting is that she was murdered. Making her death appear like an overdose was simply building on the narrative that Border Force had already started. If I didn't know better, I'd bet that whoever is behind this has a mole within the government—or the detention centre,' replied Ange, barely keeping her bubbling anger in check.

'That's fanciful, Detective. I realise that you may have conspiracy theories running around in your head after your last case, but there aren't commies under every bed,' replied Wallace dismissively.

At least Wallace had held himself back from the trap of alluding to her *pretty little head*, although Ange surmised that this diminutive may have been on the tip of his tongue. She was forming a distinct dislike for her supercilious colleague of sorts.

Ange needed to remind herself that the authorities were doing their darnedest to hide any failures. Unfortunately, and consistent with Wallace's viewpoint, their overarching strategy was for the public to remain within a delusional bubble where everything was just peachy.

'OK. I see how you might form that point of view. However, there's absolutely no harm in waiting for the results of the autopsy. If they come up clean and point to Cua Kwm as being a junkie, then I will agree with you and we can start looking elsewhere to tackle our broader objectives,' replied Ange, proposing a soft ultimatum of sorts.

'Fair enough. I'll do as you suggest and humour you in this case. Let's reconvene once the autopsy results come in, which I presume will be in the New Year. On that basis, let's adjourn today's meeting. Have a happy New Year, everyone,' concluded Wallace.

Ange noted that nobody else had spoken in the meeting and she made a mental note to find out who Wallace reported to, and why her Queensland colleagues were showing him such deference. Her own happy New Year was likely to be an elusive illusion.

The dreams that came to visit that night called for the help of her sleeping and meditation app on two separate occasions, along with one trip to the veranda to seek Buddy's counsel. Ange knew she couldn't go on this way forever.

Chapter 21

A New Year

A nge was in no mood to party in Byron Bay, so she prevailed upon Gus to host a small dinner party on the veranda of his house. Kerrie and Mike were keen to approach the New Year in this relaxed fashion, and Gus had an old school friend who was spending the holidays at Byron Bay with his wife. Ange rang Bree to see what she was doing; however, Bree was staying with Billy in Sydney and busy with her last-minute training. Ange asked that Bree put the call on speaker so that she could ask them both a question that had been running around in her mind.

'Hi, Billy,' said Ange once the call was on speakerphone. 'I had a question for you both about IP addresses.'

'Shoot,' said Billy. 'Sorry, I shouldn't use that word with you.'

Ange laughed at his Freudian slip, even though she had heard the joke before. 'You once told me you could easily determine the approximate physical location of an IP address but would need the service provider to help pinpoint a precise address. Is that correct?'

'Yes,' replied Billy. 'We usually need a court order to get the ISP on board. ISP stands for internet service provider, just in case you've forgotten.'

'OK. So, what happens if the user that we want to track is using data on their mobile phone? Does the same logic apply?'

'I think so. It should be easier. Each phone has a unique identifier and is logged onto a cell to receive service. Cells usually overlap, so as the phone moves around, it's progressively logged onto whichever cell has the strongest signal.'

'Good. Let's say that we're looking in rural areas. Do you think that the mobile service provider could pinpoint data usage that seems anomalous?' asked Ange.

'I see what you're getting at,' commented Bree. 'You want to know who might use lots of data in an area that seems out of place?'

'Exactly,' replied Ange. 'Going by what I've researched myself, the mobile service provider should be able to triangulate from the various towers and even approximate the actual address. Is that true?'

'Certainly, that would be true in the city where there are lots of mobile phone transponders,' replied Billy. 'But I'm not sure about rural areas where there might only be one tower in range at a time. You would need to ask one of the service providers about that.'

'OK. Thanks. What are you guys doing on New Year's Eve?'

'We plan to watch the fireworks over the Sydney Harbour. Tell you what, I wish we could get a key to Ethan Tedesco's old apartment on Point Piper. That would be something. As it is, we'll be mixing with the great unwashed trying to steal a view from the Botanic Garden,' Billy replied.

'That will still be spectacular. I suppose I have the pleasure of the Byron Bay equivalent of Tedesco's apartment with Gus's ponderosa on the hill. Bree knows what that view is like.'

'That will be awesome, Ange,' commented Bree. 'Have fun and see you on the other side of the year.'

'It's been an interesting one. Happy New Year,' said Ange as she hung up.

Ange could easily apply *horrific*, *painful*, *life-threatening*, *successful*, even *wonderful* as adjectives to describe her year. On balance, however, she would not be sorry to see the back of it.

New Year on the hill was a relaxing and peaceful affair. It was the first time that Kerrie and Mike had met Buddy, and Kerrie was smitten by Ange's red dog.

'He's so beautiful, Ange. Can I borrow him for a media shoot sometime?' asked Kerrie.

'Sure, he seems to like you. Can you use a media name when you refer to him in any posts? I wouldn't want him responding to your multitude of followers should they call out his name. Hopefully, he might ignore his media alias. Use Rusty, which is the name my dad will use for Buddy's replacement,' suggested

Ange.

Gus's friends Harry and Anna were lovely, and Ange learnt about the break-neck speed of merchant banking, not to mention the trouble Harry and Gus had gotten up to during their time at boarding school. A life as a merchant banker seemed far more ruthless and demanding than Ange's. Harry even had to break from dinner and take a call on some deal that was in the wind. It was New Year's Eve, for goodness' sake. Anna worked as a dermatologist on Sydney's North Shore—talk about a power couple. She was particularly interested once Kerrie blurted out that Ange had recently gotten herself shot. Anna was keen to see the effects, never having seen an actual gunshot wound before. Kerrie stuck her nose into the gunshot viewing, expressing her hope that it didn't happen again in the year about to start. Ange had formed a similar view.

Even when seen from afar, the fireworks over Byron Bay were a fitting end to the fireworks of Ange's year. Some of those fireworks had been terrible and literally involved people firing things; others had been terrific, notably the fireworks of her romance with Gus. Although their relationship had been a slow and steady burn, it had ultimately exploded, which was much to Kerrie's relief and a testament to her skills as a schemer. The Byron Bay fireworks display would be nowhere as spectacular as the waterfall of light that cascaded from the Sydney Harbour Bridge each year, reflected off the harbour and the Opera House. However, Ange figured she wouldn't change places for any money.

New Year's Day itself saw Ange and Gus find an almost deserted beach break for a surf. Now a veteran, Buddy seemed to understand what was going on. Ange had picked out an old towel that was now Buddy's beach towel, and he sat peacefully under a large pandanus palm and took a nap, keeping one eye half-open to guard their gear against opportunistic passers-by.

Even after her gentle and relaxing surf, enjoyed with her new partner, Ange was still seething with anger over what had happened to the young Vietnamese woman. Despite this simmering fury, she held herself in check for the last of the holidays, sensing that she was perhaps standing on the edge of a steep, slippery slide—destination unknown.

Chapter 22

Autopsy

T he autopsy report for Cua Kwm's body arrived in Ange's inbox early on Tuesday, the first actual workday of the New Year. It came attached to a Teams meeting invite for 11 a.m. that same day. Ange was furious to note that the report was dated December 28th, some six days earlier. She may have now entered the year of the rabbit, but as she read the report, Ange started feeling more like a tiger from the year gone past.

The toxicology report contained three crucial pieces of information. First, that Kwm had likely been rendered unconscious with a hefty dose of chloroform. Second, Kwm had died of a fentanyl overdose, something which the medical examiner found surprising. Of the commonly injectable drugs found on Vietnamese streets, heroin enjoyed a market share of almost one hundred percent, whereas fentanyl never rated a mention. However, the third and most telling finding stated that Kwm did not exhibit any other signs of habitual intravenous drug use. Putting aside any discussion on how Kwm may have obtained fentanyl while inside the detention centre, the examiner expressed serious doubt that Kwm's death was caused by any fentanyl addiction and self-inflicted overdose.

The question mark over the traces of opiates found in Kwm's hair follicles remained. Ange spent some hours hunched over her laptop, learning that passive inhalation of opium smoke could show in hair follicles for several months. This situation commonly provided false-positive drug tests, and Kwm's testimony about her opium addicted brothers offered a plausible explanation. There remained a remote possibility that Kwm could be a consummate liar and a habitual drug user, but that contradicted Ange's powerful impressions of the young woman. She was absolutely convinced that Cua Kwm was no junkie and had been murdered.

Ange walked outside and sat with Buddy on the veranda, giving him a pat as she mulled over this information. It bothered her that everyone had been so quick to dismiss Kwm as an illegally arrived junkie. She wondered if this was simply racial prejudice or whether someone was covering their tracks. More disturbing was the apparent rush to ship her back to Vietnam, be that either dead or alive. Perhaps this was just bureaucracy at its very worst, trying to pass the parcel and leave the problem on someone else's desk, maybe even to tick some box that might deliver a nice end-of-year bonus for keeping Aussie borders safe.

She had a dreadful feeling that something deeper and more sinister was at play, but was sufficiently self-aware to realise that she might very well have become the conspiracy theorist of Wallace's recent accusation. She was very much on edge when 11 a.m. came around—even Buddy had failed to work his magic.

Ange sat for some ten minutes in the Teams waiting room, impatiently waiting for the convener to let her into the video meeting. Wallace looked like he was still on holidays and Henry Chan was absent. Chris Lambert and Judy Ly looked sheepish, and it left Ange with the distinct impression that they had been talking about her while she was stuck in the virtual waiting room.

After the obligatory New Year's greetings, Wallace opened the conversation. 'So, Detective Watson, it seems as if you've gotten your New Year's wish and you may have a murder investigation on your hands.'

Ange seethed at Wallace's greeting. He made it sound as if the murder was her fault and the whole affair was a huge imposition. 'Well, it's not *my* murder investigation. I thought this was a task force. However, I am pleased that we've both reached the same conclusion. Anyway, the murder happened in Queensland, didn't it?' raged Ange, spitting out her frustration in rapid fire.

Wallace bristled noticeably. 'The immigration centre is not actually Queensland territory. It's on federal lands. Anyhow, I must go. I have a tee time to get to with Bernie Peters, so I'll leave this mess with you three to clean up while Henry is away on leave.'

With that, Wallace abruptly exited the call. Evidently, his tee time was far more important than a trifling murder investigation. Ange asked the obvious question of the others. 'Who the heck is Bernie Peters? Was I supposed to know who that guy is?'

'His name was dropped for our benefit,' said Chris Lambert in sombre tone.

'Peters is the integrity chief within the Queensland Police Service.'

'Interesting,' thought Ange to herself. At least she now understood the hold that Wallace seemed to exert over the others.

Judy Ly spoke for the first time. 'We need to interview the authorities at the immigration detention centre. I assume that someone over there already has a copy of the autopsy report. Do you want to be involved, Ange, or are you happy for Chris and me to handle it?'

'Why don't you guys deal with that, seeing as you're both based in Brisbane? I'm furious about this and I'm not sure I would be the best person to let loose on whoever was supposedly responsible for keeping Cua Kwm safe and sound. This all suggests a highly organised and sophisticated operation. We know from Kwm's testimony that there were multiple women involved. While they are now probably long gone, we need to assume that this was not an isolated case. More women will be at risk.'

'I agree,' said Lambert in quick response. 'Whoever they are, they were hell-bent on getting rid of Kwm. Sadly, I suspect that she would have suffered the same fate once she arrived back in Vietnam. Attempting to make this look like a self-inflicted suicide shows a certain level of planning and sophistication, as you say.'

'It seems to me they had someone inside the detention centre, perhaps another inmate, or a worker, perhaps even an official. We'll try to find out what we can,' added Judy Ly. 'What will you do, Ange?'

'I have some ideas about how we might locate the place where Kwm escaped from, but I need to see if my theories are plausible. Let me work with my team on that while you and Chris investigate Kwm's death,' replied Ange. She paused, assessing her two colleagues before she confided in them what was really concerning her. 'I feel Wallace would prefer I wasn't here. Even worse, I'm worried that we're just expected to pay lip service to any investigation into people trafficking. Am I on the right track here?'

Chris Lambert and Judy Ly sat in awkward silence for a few moments before a look of resolve swam into Judy Ly's eyes. 'He referred to you as a dodgy detective who has a habit of getting people killed.'

Ange wanted to scream out loud at this accusation and fought hard to bring her frustration under control. 'OK. If we're going to work together, it's best you know the facts.'

Over the next twenty-odd minutes, Ange gave her colleagues a full account of the Ndrangheta affair and how she had taken on the persona of a suspect cop, operating somewhat undercover on the Gold Coast. She also filled them in on how the Ndrangheta had infiltrated the department at the highest levels, and how this was being kept under wraps to protect the reputation of the New South Wales police service. 'So, you can see why I might be a touch sensitive to any obfuscation.'

Her colleagues sat in stunned silence until Judy Ly asked an interesting question, evidently something that had been bothering her, given the close relationship of Wallace to Bernie Peters. 'So, how did your own Internal Affairs react to all this?'

'Not well. They first tried to blame me for getting myself shot and then argued that my conspiracy theory was just a smokescreen for my benefit. The fact is that my boss and I knew we had a mole in our midst and we needed to keep everything as tight as possible.'

'So, why did Internal Affairs let you go?' asked Lambert.

'My boss, Sally Anders, is very smart and super cunning. When she sensed that something smelt, she started recording any key conversations, ultimately setting a trap for the chief superintendent. When push came to shove, those recordings worked a treat. I have a lot of time for Sally—she was the person who recruited me into Major Crimes.'

Lambert looked incredulous. 'Are you telling me that the Ndrangheta had infiltrated up to the position of chief superintendent?'

'You'll never hear that officially, but yes. I'm not even sure that's the end of it, either. We suspect they have a mole in the feds, perhaps even within the Ndrangheta task force itself. I'm certain that we only scratched the surface as far as the Ndrangheta is concerned. Can you now get a sense of why I might be prone to conspiracy theories? By the way, please keep all this to yourself. As you can gather, it's not a narrative that the service is keen to run with.'

Judy Ly concluded the meeting on a sombre note. 'OK. Thanks for confiding in us, Ange. It certainly puts a new light on our interview at the immigration detention centre. We'll report back to you as soon as we've run that to ground.'

Chapter 23

Plotting

A nge often thought of her investigations as a giant jigsaw puzzle. Usually, she could sit to one side and dispassionately assess each piece before slotting it into place. This one was different. She had become heavily invested once Cua Kwm was murdered, feeling in part responsible for this tragedy, even though she knew this was completely illogical. She surmised that the managers of the detention centre, or Border Force, would not greet Judy Ly and Chris Lambert with open arms. This was now a mess that both organisations would try to distance themselves from, and she knew that a professional finger-pointing tournament was about to begin.

Ange needed some help to get started on her jigsaw puzzle. While she had some strong clues, a second or even third pair of hands would be helpful, so she rang her boss in Sydney first thing on Wednesday morning.

'Hi, boss. I think we are about to stir up a hornet's nest in Brisbane, but I've left that to two of my local task force colleagues. Do you know if Billy will be around next week? I need his help with the technical aspects of some ideas I have. I also need to complete my firearms training as we, or should I say you, agreed with Internal Affairs.'

'Sure, Ange. I'm pretty sure he'll be in. When are you thinking of coming down?'

'Monday and Tuesday next week. I can stay on, but two days should about do it. How about I fly down Sunday evening and then spend the day with Billy to work through the practicalities of my theories? I could complete the firearms training on Tuesday morning and then have time to tidy up any loose ends before heading home.'

'Sounds like a plan. I'll block out the same apartment that you stayed in last time, the one just around the corner from the office. Unless something comes up in the meantime, I'll see you on Monday,' concluded Anders.

When Sally Anders was locking horns with Internal Affairs during the washup of the Namba Heads shooting, she had made a concession that Ange update her firearms training. Ange had been quite indignant. 'For goodness' sake, I never even placed a hand on my revolver, let alone pulled the trigger on the darn thing. What are they trying to say, that if I'd earned my Billy the Kid badge, I could have shot from the hip and taken them out?'

Sally Anders had simply laughed at Ange's analogy. 'I had to give them something, Ange. We all know how this works. IA has a massive ego and needs to have a win in there somewhere.' Regrettably, politics aside, Ange knew the memo on file at IA would be filled with terms like 'failure to respond and draw arms' and 'inexperienced marksman'.

Ange was about to book her tickets when she remembered she was now in a permanent relationship. She caught herself just in time and wondered if this sort of independent behaviour had been a factor in her long run of relationship train wrecks. She left her browser open and rang Gus at work.

'Hi, Gus. I need to go to Sydney for a few days. I'm planning to fly down Sunday evening and back Tuesday evening. Does that cause any hassles for you?'

'No, that's fine. You need to do what you need to do. What will we do about Buddy?'

Ange walked over and stuck her head out the door and called out Buddy's name. He had been at the bottom of the property, probably doing dog stuff, and he scooted back up to the house the moment he heard Ange's call. 'Yes, I'm not sure it's sensible to leave him roam around on his own and I wouldn't like to tie him up all day. What about taking him down to the shop? I hear a dog can be good for staff morale,' she said, a prospective inflection in her voice. 'Tell you what, why don't we give him a trial run tomorrow? If he causes any grief, I can swing by and bring him home.'

'Sounds good. I'll speak to the staff and we can chat about it this evening. I think I have a picture, or twenty, to show them,' laughed Gus. He was equally smitten by Buddy.

Ange completed her travel arrangements and then settled in to do some more research on the immigration detention centre and who was behind ImDm Corporation. The provision of government services like detention centres and jails flip-flopped between government and private management, subject to which side of politics ruled the roost. Some privatisation drives worked well and stood the test of time, while others failed miserably. From a politician's perspective, it would be convenient to have a third party to blame when things went off the rails.

Gus arrived home early for dinner, and the pair went for a stroll along the narrow road that led to Gus's estate. Buddy wandered alongside, sniffing this and that, cocking his leg to leave his mark where needed. 'Did you know that dogs have a sense of smell that's somewhere between ten thousand and one hundred thousand times more acute than ours? Can you imagine what the world of smells must be like for a dog? Think of all the secrets they can discern that we have absolutely no clue about. By the way, how did you go with the staff about having a mascot tomorrow?' asked Ange.

'I think they're quite excited. I'm sure Buddy doesn't think of himself as cute, but that seems to be the general opinion, at least of the female contingent. How about I take him down to work first thing, and then you can pick him up if it all goes pear-shaped?'

'Watch out for Kerrie. I think she has designs on our red dog,' replied Ange, some famous last words as things turned out.

Gus and Buddy headed off to work early on Thursday morning. Ange had to laugh seeing Buddy looking out of the back window of the Volvo, his first time in Gus's classic station wagon. She imagined all the unfamiliar smells that would assail him in the back of that old car. The Volvo had been one of Gus's first-ever vehicles, and Ange shuddered to think of what those residual aromas might mean to such a sensitive nose.

She rang Kerrie to ask about lunch and Kerrie suggested Ange join her for a Pilates class beforehand. She was just getting her gear assembled when Judy Ly rang. 'Hi, Ange. Just wanted to let you know that we've finally organised to interview the officials at the detention centre. Apparently, the minister has gotten wind of the matter and is sending a representative. We're scheduled for 11 a.m. on Monday. You're welcome to join us if you change your mind.'

'Thanks, Judy. I'm booked to travel down to Sydney for a couple of days. I plan to run a few ideas to the ground. Plus, I need to update my firearms certification—not that I'm planning anything after my last effort,' said Ange, her self-deprecating chuckle stimulating a similar response from her colleague.

'Me three. Being shot is one area where I definitely don't need any role models,' said Ly good-naturedly.

'Let me know how it goes,' replied Ange before hanging up, surprised by Ly's inference that she was any sort of role model.

Somewhat predictably given her recent past, Ange was becoming concerned that she was battling another leak in the system. There were far too many anomalies. First and foremost: why had Kwm been so rapidly earmarked for deportation? Second: how did anyone know that pressure was being exerted to have Kwm reclassified as a victim of trafficking and that she would likely stay in Australia? Third: how had they identified and located her? Ange had visited the facility and it must have housed hundreds of detainees. Finally, and most notably: how had the perpetrators gotten inside the facility? A break-in raid would raise one set of questions, and quite another would arise if a worker was responsible. Workers should be vetted and properly cleared before being allowed to enter such a sensitive facility. Conversely, someone breaking in to commit a murder was an oxymoron for a high-security facility like a detention centre. Perhaps a fellow inmate had been recruited to carry out Kwm's execution, which would mean a mountain of work sifting through all those people. Then there was the question mark over the lack of adequate surveillance. Surely there were security cameras placed all over the facility? Ange hoped that her two colleagues could discern solutions for some of those anomalies.

Ange found her Pilates class both demanding and fun. Midway through the class, she noticed that she no longer favoured her injured leg whatsoever, reaffirming how amazing the human mind was and a reminder of the healing process that her physiotherapist had so accurately described. She discussed her progress with Kerrie over lunch. 'My body seems to have healed just fine, but I still have terrible nightmares at least once a week. I sometimes worry that I'll wake up one morning to find that I strangled Gus in the night, you know, like in one of those horror movies. Come to think of it, I haven't heard from Gus. It must be going well.' She elaborated when met with Kerrie's curious look. 'I have to go to Sydney next week, and we're giving Buddy a trial run at the shop today.'

'Oh, that beautiful boy. Let's swing by and say hello. So, you're away Monday and Tuesday?'

'What are you planning, Kerrie?' asked Ange cautiously, suspicious of the intent behind her friend's seemingly innocuous question.

'Nothing you need to worry about. Keep focussed on catching those criminals, my dear detective,' replied Kerrie in her most breezy and flippant voice.

Ange was all too familiar with her friend's tone. Some scheme or another was being hatched.

Now that Ange had her arrangement for her trip to Sydney, she thought it wise to contact Bree and check in on how her crypto assignment was panning out.

'Sorry, Ange, but I've had no spare time. The station was super busy over the Christmas–New Year period. I totally underestimated the workload. On top of all that, I've been training like crazy for the test series against India. I don't want to disappoint you, but I think it will be February before I can make any genuine progress,' explained Bree.

'Don't panic, Bree. This is a long-range project. We've nothing specific to chase down, so just do what you can. That could change if we need to get deep into a specific case—like with Ethan Tedesco and the BuzzyBat NFTs. How is the market behaving?'

'The cryptocurrency market is going nowhere after the last correction, but I feel that the NFT marketplace is entering a dangerous place. One thing I have been observing with the help of my new software—which is amazing, by the way—is just how many trades are basically a person trading with themselves.'

'What do you mean, trading with themselves?' asked Ange.

'Well, imagine I have an NFT series that I want to pump up. An easy way to achieve this is to trade between two accounts that I own. To the normal person, this could look as if the NFT series was desirable and rising in price. It's normally quite difficult to tell a legitimate trade from a scam trade. However, the market is so soft right now that these sorts of pricing signals stand out like the proverbial. I'm monitoring some repeat offenders for future reference.'

'That would be very good for laundering money, wouldn't it?'

'Of course. It would be super easy. Let's say I have five thousand dollars in cash that I wanted laundered. I could convert it to Ether—that's the lingo for Ethereum, by the way—and then use the Ether to buy an NFT from myself. I can then either leave it in crypto or exchange it back to cash and, hey presto, clean cash.'

'How much would they lose in the process with all the transaction fees?' asked Ange.

Bree did some mental arithmetic. 'It depends on the exchange and the value of the NFT, but let's say five percent.'

'That is a very attractive rate to launder money going by what I've learned. Rates of ten or fifteen percent seem more usual with traditional methods, those involving banks and normal cash. I really think that we're on the right track with this project, Bree. Stick with it when you have the time. I'd love to see one of your hockey games. Are there any scheduled for closer to Byron?'

'Well, presuming that I keep getting selected, we have one in Warwick in Queensland on the fifteenth, which is four days after the Brisbane game. Being west of the Great Divide, the Warwick game will be a scorcher. I've heard stories of forty degrees, but at least that one is a night game. I looked on Google Maps and it's about a three-and-a-half-hour drive west-north-west from Byron.'

'That might work out rather well,' concluded Ange, thinking that Warwick might well be in the target zone for her case. Bree's hockey test match might be an opportunity to mix business and pleasure.

After dropping off Buddy at his new home away from home, Ange made a half-hearted attempt to have a surf early on Friday. Unable to find a parking space anywhere in Byron, she was forced to drive well south of town to find a mostly deserted beach break. The waves were mushy and poorly formed, courtesy of an aimless easterly wind, but at least she had the break to herself and one other surfer. Ange sometimes worried that surfing was being loved to death. In fact, the extreme holiday crowds had opened up a battleground on that front, one with tragic circumstances.

Back in the day, when surfing started, almost nobody wore leg ropes. This had been no major problem for anyone but the surfer, as hardly anyone surfed and the breaks were mostly deserted. Early leg ropes were nothing more than a piece of rope tied to the board's fin through a crudely drilled hole. The other end of the rope was secured to the surfer's leg via a standard dog collar. The idea caught on when other surfers saw how many extra waves their leg-roped cousins caught, no longer forced to make a long swim back to retrieve their board after wiping out.

Things progressed quickly until stretchy modern leg ropes became ubiquitous. Unfortunately, the rise of a hipster longboard movement had seen many surfers ditch their leg ropes, favouring a free-form approach to surfing, one not constrained by such unwieldy contraptions. Others simply considered themselves too skilled to require something as banal as a leg rope. Unfortunately, delusional surfers wiped out just as often as sane ones.

A tearaway longboard, rushing side on and hidden under white water, made for a terrifying weapon. Surfers were being maimed almost hourly, and the matter had reached a flashpoint when a young boy had suffered a serious head injury caused by a runaway longboard. Hipsters were clashing with other surfers every day, and the local council was considering bringing in a law that made it an offence to surf without a leg rope at crowded breaks. Somewhat predicably, the hipster longboarders were not taking kindly to this Big Brother approach.

As she stood on the beach towelling off after her solitary surf, Ange wondered whether this was simply another case where individual rights were more important than those of the community, or whether strict mandatory vaccination and lockdown laws had somehow played a part in fuelling such militancy. She guessed that there might be a strong correlation between the anti-establishment movement and a desire for a leg-rope-free world.

Whatever the cause, Ange figured that she would be the perfect undercover operative to police the council's proposed new laws. Perhaps if that job had been on offer, she might not have returned to Major Crimes. After all, she was unlikely to get shot while out surfing in the ocean.

Chapter 24

Influence

Ange arrived at her serviced apartment in Sydney just after 9 p.m. on Sunday evening. It was every bit as dull and impersonal as she remembered, and she could not shake the feeling that it resembled a bland waiting room of sorts, like that of a hospital, with its clinical design attempting to exude a sense of order and communicate that everything was under control. Yet, as Ange had recently experienced, drama and mayhem sat on the other side of those large swinging hospital doors.

As with her previous sleepover, barely six months ago, she sensed she was on the edge of something big. A shiver ran down her spine as she recalled the days leading up to her own moments of mayhem. At least she didn't need a new haircut and a fresh look this time around.

She was about to settle down in front of the TV to stream some Netflix, hoping to find something comforting to watch, when she realised that she had let her account lapse and was now using Gus's. It's sometimes the little things that highlight how profoundly one's life had changed. A fiercely independent person, Ange briefly wondered where this new era of co-dependence might lead. Would they stay as individuals whose lives overlapped for convenience, or would their lives merge into an amalgam where the identities of the parts were inseparable from the whole? She had seen both realities befall friends from university, and it was confronting to think how she might fare in either case. Then there was Buddy thrown into the mix. With him now spending time down at the shop, who would claim custody if her relationship with Gus failed?

Ange had no desire to be left alone pondering these unanswerable questions, so she wandered downstairs to walk around the city. The streets were buzzing with people trying to extract their last moments of weekend fun. It was a young crowd and there were loads of Asian students who lived in the city. They likely kept flexible diaries, where a late Sunday evening was of no concern. The juxtaposition of the carefree young women milling around and Cua Kwm's challenging life resonated with Ange. Whereas those happy-go-lucky Sydneysiders lived in a world of order, one filled with happiness and hope for the future, Cua Kwm's had been a world of peril, where daily life could see you captured and exploited—even killed. Ange knew full well that a flick of fate's wrist separated the two paradigms.

Ange arrived in the office early on Monday juggling takeaway coffee and a croissant. She hoped the caffeine might kick-start her brain after a wholly unsatisfying night's sleep. Billy, like most in the IT crowd, worked at the far end of the day and she knew he was unlikely to be seen before 9 a.m. She sat at Billy's desk and reviewed the notes that she had made following her interview with Cua Kwm. After a few minutes of contemplation, Ange walked around the office floor until she found a whiteboard that was not currently in use. She wheeled it over to Billy's work area and sketched out her plan.

1. *Target Area* – *Plot on map—Texas QLD as centre.*
   - *Assume Kwm travelled approximately 3 hours in vehicle following escape.*
2. *Geography* – *Manual review of search area.*
   - *Most likely held captive in cattle country accessed by gravel road.*
   - *Journey traversed a range or hilly zone after reaching a sealed road.*
   - *Highway or major road into Texas.*
3. *Site* – *Review satellite imagery.*
   - *House and donga positioned away from gravel road.*
   - *Separated from the road by a clump of trees.*
   - *Rectangular donga positioned parallel to road — window rattler a/c.*
   - *Neighbouring house estimated 2 km away, on right-hand side facing road, with silver 4WD ute.*
4. *Mobile Data* - *Contact phone companies who service target area. Cross reference phone towers.*

- *Captors using mobile data, perhaps for trafficking activities.*
5. <u>*Wheelie Bin*</u> *– Contact councils in target area.*
  - *Coloured wheelie bin suggests council refuse service.*
6. <u>*Food*</u> *- Manual review of target areas.*
  - *Captives fed chicken and frozen vegetables – suggests supermarket nearby.*

Once she was happy, Ange ducked downstairs to pick up some more coffee. On returning, she found Billy had arrived and was staring at the fresh addition to his workspace. 'I heard you were in town. I guess this is all for my benefit, then?' he said with a big smile. 'Run me through it.'

Ange briefed Billy on what she had learned before getting down to business. 'Billy, I'd like to start by mapping out the search area? Can you do that?'

Billy sat down at his computer screens and opened some software that Ange hadn't seen before. She watched as Billy pulled up a satellite image centred on Texas, not the one in the USA as was the first attempt, but the one on the Queensland/New South Wales border. Once they were happy that they were on the correct continent, he selected a tab called 'Drive Times' and entered three hours. He turned to Ange. 'What time of the day did she escape in the vehicle?'

'Let's assume 6 a.m.,' replied Ange.

Within seconds of Billy entering those parameters, the software shaded the map with an amorphous blob. Billy turned to Ange to explain what was showing on the screen. 'This map now shows us a three-hour drive-time radius that considers the route options, road conditions, speed limits, and likely traffic impacts. Pretty cool, huh?'

'That is cool, Billy. It sure saves a lot of work. The next thing we need is to look at the various councils that service the area. Can you do that?'

'Easy,' replied Billy as he clicked through some options and added an overlay of local government areas. 'Property developers use this software to look at catchments for shops, service stations, and other services. I see that you've targeted supermarkets. Let me add that.'

'You're kidding! I thought we would be here all day just getting this far. Remind me to schedule a regular update about your latest magic tricks, Billy,' commented Ange, eliciting a proud smile from Billy.

He went through another set of manoeuvres before a list of supermarket chains came up. He selected them all, and in a minute, every supermarket was identified on the map with an icon.

'Don't tell me you can also call up mobile phone tower data as well?' said Ange, not entirely sure of what Billy's answer might be.

'No. Sorry, boss. I'll need to put in the hard yards for that. This software was designed for property developers, but I find it useful for checking witness statements.' He sat and contemplated the screen for a few moments before drawing his conclusion. 'My guess is that we're only looking at the two major carriers for a regional area like this. My firm opinion is that Telstra will offer the best coverage out there.'

This made sense to Ange. Being from the country, she knew that the former national carrier enjoyed an extensive infrastructure network. Most bushies she knew relied on Telstra once they left the major towns. 'I agree, Billy. Given that we aren't asking for any personal information, hopefully they might help us out without requiring a search warrant. Can you see how you go with that? In the meantime, can you email me a copy of that map you just built?' asked Ange.

'Sure, boss. Getting the phone towers located might take a day or two. Let me see what I can do. I'll contact the service provider once we identify a specific phone tower that we're interested in, however we'll probably need a court order to access pings that identify individual clients.' Billy looked back at the screen before drawing his conclusions. 'This might look impressive, but it's going to take a hell of a lot of legwork to find what you're looking for.'

'You're right, Billy, but I'm still in awe that we've moved this far. Fingers crossed that the mobile phone tower data comes through, and we can find the proverbial needle in the haystack.'

Ange left Billy to his sorcery, figuring that this might be the right time to tackle updating her firearm certification, something that proved easier said than done.

Chapter 25

Firing Line

The last few months had rattled Ange's sense of self belief, challenging a steadfast belief in her ability to deal with whatever the world threw at her. The muted crack of a gunshot that came when the lift doors opened to the basement shooting range did nothing to help matters. Suddenly, the shock of being a gunshot victim punched her in the stomach with a debilitating thud.

As her subconscious sought to protect her from more pain, the room swooned and swirled. She became lost in a daze, suddenly vulnerable. Her heart raced and beads of sweat started forming on her forehead. The hand that gently touched her arm was like an electric shock, jump-starting her from that other state, a dangerous place where her very existence was at risk. 'Are you OK, ma'am?' said the female attendant.

'To be honest, I'm not sure,' replied Ange, wiping the beads of sweat from her brow, searching for somewhere to sit. She spied a hard beige plastic chair, the type ubiquitous in places where function had comprehensively won its battle over form. Ange sat down and folded her head into her hands, knees supporting elbows in an abject display of submission to her demons.

'Can you give me a minute to collect myself? First time back after being shot,' said Ange, sheepishly attempting to explain away her fragility.

'I presume you're Detective Watson. I was told you might pay us a visit. Don't worry, what you're experiencing is quite normal. Frankly, I would be more worried if you weren't stressing out. Take your time. Let me get you a glass of water,' said the woman kindly.

Ange was pleased to hear that her reaction was not unexpected. Hopefully, there might still be a chance that she hadn't devolved into a complete milksop, a loser who couldn't cope with her job—or worse, a broken veteran unable to enter the fray again. Ange took a series of deep breaths, slowly bringing her runaway heart rate under control, eventually able to watch her crisis disappear in the rear-view mirror. She stood and walked over to the attendant, unaware that her ashen face was a telltale sign of her shock. 'OK. Let's get this done.'

The attendant appraised Ange for a moment before turning and leading her to the armoury. Once Ange was appropriately attired in some safety glasses and earmuffs, the attendant handed her a standard-issue revolver, an identical weapon to Ange's own, the one that was yet to be fired in the heat of battle. Ange felt its weight in her hand and then immediately checked the safety catch, aware that the attendant was watching with the intensity of an examiner. Comfortable that it was safe—well, as safe as any firearm can be—she slid out the magazine and loaded it full of bullets. The attendant then led her to a bay on the shooting range.

Ange flipped off the safety catch and aimed the weapon at the target, a faceless avatar of a presumed criminal up to no good. She then fell for the cardinal sin, closing her eyes as she squeezed the trigger. The power and sound were unmistakable, and it instantly transported her back to Namba Heads and into that fateful moment, where her life had teetered on a knife edge. Her thigh twitched reflexively in a subliminal response to the trauma that had accompanied that sound. How could something so tiny as a bullet wreak so much carnage?

As a farm girl, she had grown up around firearms, taught to wield a rifle at the ripe old age of fourteen. Farms were dangerous places, yet a firearm was as much a merchant of peace as one of devastation, most often called upon to relieve a distressed animal of its misery. Ange had seen firearms in this light, a necessary tool that had allowed the farm to maintain its calm and equilibrium, not the harbinger of doom and destruction, as was commonly thought. Ange knew she would forever look at firearms with renewed respect.

She finally opened her eyes to see that her faceless opponent was completely unmarked. The attendant summed it up nicely. 'How about we try again with our eyes open?'

Ange made her best attempt but still blinked at the critical moment, sending the bullet high and to the right. Gritting her teeth, she dredged her soul, looking for the steely resolve that was part of her being. Her next shot at least caught an edge of the target, having missed any imagined body parts. Ange finally found some inspiration by imagining Lomax as the faceless target and she fired off a series of rapid shots, each scoring the outcome that had eluded her in the scrub that fateful day. The empty click of her revolver jolted her back to reality. She turned toward her examiner, clicked on the safety catch, and handed back the weapon.

'I think you'll be fine,' was all her examiner had to say, suggesting to Ange that she may have passed her test. Whether Ange would pass the same test in the heat of the battle remained unclear. This, it seemed, was not something to be tested on any firing range. Hopefully, she would never need to explore the answer to that challenge.

Sally Anders spied Ange coming out of the office elevator and came over to greet her. 'Hi, Ange. I hear you passed your weapons' certification.'

'It was touch and go for a moment, boss. I wasn't prepared for that mental torture. I know that what doesn't kill you is supposed to make you stronger, but I'm not planning to test that theory again.'

'Good work. It wouldn't do to have a lame duck as one of my lead investigators. How is your case going?'

'Better than I expected, thanks to Billy's magic tricks. The team from Brisbane is a mixed bag. I really like Judy Ly. She speaks Vietnamese, Chinese, and a smattering of Khmer. Chris Lambert seems very capable. Henry Chan is an unknown quantity, but that he's part of the team makes me think that there may be a Chinese angle that I'm not privy to. There is some testiness between Ly and Chan, but that might be just racial prejudice and a symptom of simmering Vietnamese–Chinese tensions. However, the chief of the task force gives me a bad feeling. He seems more of a scheming politician than any investigator. I wouldn't wish to get between him and his ambition.'

'How about I suss him out? You can imagine that I am equally gun-shy about scheming chiefs,' offered Anders with a pained smile. 'Let me know if you need any help.'

'I may need some court orders to access data traffic from mobile phone nodes. I'll let Billy handle that with you once we have a line of sight on anything interesting.'

Ange went downstairs to grab some lunch and browse through some of her favourite shops, picking up a few things unavailable in Byron. Billy's phone call caught her wallowing in indecision over whether to purchase some new shoes. 'Hey, boss, I got the usage data from the mobile phone towers in our search zone. I've plotted them on our map. Unfortunately, it's useless.'

'Wow, that was quick. I'm on my way,' commented Ange, instantly abandoning her aimless shopping excursion and racing back to the office and Billy's desk.

'They seemed keen to help. ISPs are required to keep data for two years and we don't need a warrant, which was handy. I had assumed we would need one. The woman I spoke to said that, despite what the public might think, they're not interested in spying on their customers, but they are required to keep the data and provide it to us when we ask. I sense they may lean on us to repay the favour at some point, but I don't see any harm in that. That is our job, after all.' Billy turned back to his computer and pulled up his working map of the target area. The map looked like it had suffered an attack of the chickenpox.

'There is absolutely nothing that I can glean from this,' commented Billy. 'Even when I reduce it to a per capita usage, it still doesn't help.' Billy clicked on a tab and the map changed marginally, erasing barely ten percent of the mobile phone towers in the target area. 'I think we need to take another approach.'

Ange asked the next obvious question. 'How good is the satellite imagery of those areas?'

'It's good enough for our purposes. I've been meaning to get a licence for a more up-to-date service, one which uses a combination of satellite and regular imagery taken from planes. Some of the free imagery can be many years out of date. With any luck, we should also be able to review a timeline, which can span up to six times per year.'

'This has been fantastic. I can't believe that we achieved all this in one day. Did I ever tell you what a genius you are?' said Ange with a big smile of appreciation.

'Nowhere near often enough, boss. Care to join me for a drink tonight? I'm catching up with Nelson. Six thirty p.m. at the Four in Hand if you're interested.'

Ange readily agreed to this. Another night in her sterile apartment was not overly enticing. The fact was that she was missing Gus, Buddy, and Byron Bay. Sydney was not her home, and she marvelled at how quickly things had changed. It made her realise that friends and family define home, not a city or town, not even a house or apartment. Needing to process her day, Ange glanced at her watch and realised that she still had time to catch some exercise. After a quick change, she was soon wandering around the Sydney Harbour foreshore and letting the kaleidoscope of light and colour seep into her subconscious. Once she was lost in contemplation, time slipped away and she arrived at her impromptu drinks catch-up almost thirty minutes late.

Billy and Nelson were already in full flight. Every so often, the conversation would stop and the pair would place a bet on some sporting event. There was something going on 24/7 in the world of sports betting. The deal, it seemed, was that the winner purchased the next round of drinks. Billy had just scored a modest win, so he quickly included Ange in his shout.

Once Billy was back with their drinks, Ange dived right into her ruminations of the past few hours. 'Tell me, guys, do any of you know much about the Dark Web?'

Nelson started Ange's crash-course education before Billy had time to take a sip of his beer. 'Well, it's certainly the go-to place for anything illegal, that's for sure. How much do you know already?'

'Assume nothing. However, I know it's a haven for anybody up to no good,' replied Ange.

Nelson continued his impromptu lesson. 'I like to think of it as a parallel online universe of sorts. To access the Dark Web, you need a special browser called TOR, which is an acronym for The Onion Router, a weird name for sure. Like the internet itself, the TOR Project was originally developed by the US military to communicate securely in the field. It's completely anonymous and users can't be traced. Allegedly, TOR and the Dark Web were opened up to the public so that the military could hide their stuff amongst everyday traffic.'

'Surely they knew that this would be a magnet for criminal activity?' observed Ange.

'That point has been made many times, and it's something that astonishes me,' replied Nelson, adding a resigned smile to his observation, showing that this was a conundrum that he might have grappled with in his own job from time to time. 'It's not the first time that military and government have stimulated illegal activity for their own means. However, not everything on the Dark Web is illegal, and there are legitimate reasons you might use the Dark Web. Things like political dissent or whistle-blowing. The tax office uses the Dark Web to receive anonymous tips about tax fraud and to out cheaters. It's been quite lucrative for us.'

Ange had noticed Billy looking sideways at her, and he entered the conversation. 'This wouldn't have anything to do with our conversation this afternoon, would it, boss?'

'You know me too well, Billy,' she replied before diving back into her lesson.

'So, tell me, Nelson, how does the Dark Web ecosystem function?'

'TOR isn't an indexed browser like, say, Google Chrome, or Bing, which allows you to find websites and information with simple search requests. You need to know where you're going on the Dark Web. Finding what you want can be painstakingly slow. Most of the interesting stuff gets exchanged through chat rooms, which are a weird world of their own. Given that everything is anonymous means the chat rooms contain some outrageous stuff.'

'Are you're telling me that there's no way to identify someone using TOR and the Dark Web?'

'No. That's not completely correct, but it is an incredibly complex and time-consuming task to peel back the layers. This makes the exercise expensive and something that only makes sense for high-value cases. A good example was the story of Bitcoin Bonnie and Clyde. Did you guys hear about that?' asked Nelson. The blank looks on the faces of his drinking companions provided the answer, so he continued. 'A couple in New York hacked a Bitcoin exchange and stole around one hundred thousand Bitcoins. Bitcoins were trading at around six hundred dollars each when the theft occurred, making the total of the theft worth some sixty million dollars, which was a huge deal. The couple simply sat on the coins for years and the trail went dead. By the time Bitcoin was trading at almost seventy thousand dollars apiece, the stolen coins were worth some seven billion US dollars, which made it a treasure worth chasing. The FBI ultimately tracked the pair down through a Dark Web online marketplace, one used primarily for the sale of illegal goods. The couple had set up a fake store to launder some of their stolen crypto. I guess sanitising that amount of Bitcoin would be quite an enterprise.'

Billy and Ange exchanged a glance, both recognising the similarities between Bonnie and Clyde and their recent case involving Eddie Falconi and his fake marketplace operation. Nelson saw the look pass between the two work colleagues. 'So why the interest in the Dark Web? Is this something you're working on?'

Nelson had already proven himself both discreet and trustworthy during their last case, so Ange felt comfortable bringing him into their confidence. 'We're trying to trace a people trafficking operation involving young women lured to Australia under false pretences. We suspect the criminals are going online to sell their products and it makes sense that they would use the Dark Web. It sounds like tracing them would be beyond the time and budget we have available. We have a broad idea of their last known location, but we were hoping to narrow down the search area somewhat. We know the perpetrators are big on using their mobile phones. Do you know if TOR is available as a phone app?'

'I understand that there is a TOR app available on Android, but I haven't used it myself,' replied Nelson.

Ange was on a roll and Billy was rolling with her. 'I wonder if the ISPs could tell us if the Dark Web was being used at any nodes on their mobile network,' he mused.

'I guess it might make things easier for you if they're using mobile data. If they have a fixed internet connection, then they would most likely go through a VPN,' commented Nelson. On seeing Ange's vacant stare, he elaborated. 'A VPN stands for a virtual private network. It's like a routing service. In the eyes of the ISP, the traffic will come from an entirely different location to where the user is physically located, having been routed around the world. It will be much harder to pin anyone down if they're accessing the Dark Web via a VPN.'

'I guess you'll find out the answers to these questions tomorrow, Billy,' observed Ange. She turned to Nelson. 'I can see why Billy enjoys your company so much, Nelson. I guess I need to buy the next round of drinks based on how valuable this conversation has been.'

Chapter 26

Progress

H aving checked out of her apartment, Ange wheeled her cabin bag into the office after 8:30 a.m. Her flight wasn't until late that afternoon, and she hoped to make some more progress before catching the train to the airport.

'You're up early, Billy. This is not like you,' observed Ange by way of a greeting, pulling Billy from his mental gyrations. Going by the empty coffee cup and pastry crumbs scattered across his desk, Billy had evidently been hard at it for some time.

'Turns out I already had all the information I needed. All I had to do was look more closely at the metadata file that Telstra provided.' He went to his keyboard and pulled up the target map the pair had been working on. The chickenpox infection was now reduced to six red dots. 'These are the six mobile towers where users had been using the TOR browser to access the Dark Web. Three of the dots cluster in the one general vicinity, so I think it might be safe to assume that these are a single user, or somehow related. My first impression is that this cluster represents a single user roaming around.'

He pointed to another of the red dots. 'I don't think that this one is relevant, as this sits in a more urban area. That location is too populated to line up with your description of the site.' He pointed to the last remaining two dots. 'I need to do some more work on these two towers. It looks like multiple users accessing TOR through the two towers. I'll need to drill down on the time of use data to work out what's what.' Billy looked at his boss in admiration. 'It makes perfect sense that the criminals would be using the Dark Web. When you think about it, the lack of searchability is essential for discreet criminal activity. You wouldn't want every Tom, Dick, and Harry stumbling across your Dark Website.'

Ange simply brushed aside Billy's admiring look, preferring to dish out some of her own. 'This is great work, Billy. Can you continue to work on the data? If you need any support to get your subscription to the mapping service, let me know and I'll give it a push along. Can you pull up the local government areas?'

Billy rumbled around on his keyboard and pulled up the map on another screen. 'I'll overlay this onto our working map when I get a chance, but it looks like the northern towers are within the Hillburn local council. The Green River Council covers those to the south.'

'I think some good-old-fashioned legwork might be required. If Cua Kim hadn't escaped, we would have absolutely no idea where to start and this activity would remain completely under the radar,' observed Ange. 'I need to leave for the airport by 3:30. How about we regroup around 2:30?'

'Sure thing. I'll keep plugging away until then,' replied Billy, appearing pleased with himself and the rapid progress he had made.

Ange went upstairs to search for a spare office so that she could join her weekly online meeting with the team in Brisbane. There weren't any free, so she found a desk in a discreet corner of the floor. Ironically, this was the very desk that Peter Fredericks had used to spy on his colleagues during their investigations into the Ndrangheta syndicate. Ange briefly wondered how Fredericks was faring over at Internal Affairs, reflecting for a moment on the carnage he had caused. It was cold comfort that his spying had been purely for his own career advancement. However, breaches in confidentiality and trust are rarely positive, no matter how innocuous they might seem. Perhaps his new position, where spying and probing others was part of the job description, might be a match made in heaven.

She saw Sally Anders walk out of the lift and had a thought. She raced over and intercepted her boss on the way to her office. 'Hi, boss, are you able to join my 11 a.m. meeting with the team in Brisbane? It would be an excellent opportunity to meet them. I'd appreciate your sense of the dynamics. We both have some big issues to discuss, and how everyone reacts to that might be enlightening.'

Sally Anders looked at her phone and reviewed her calendar. 'Sure. I only have thirty minutes to spare. Bring your laptop into my office and then you can move out at 11:30.'

When Ange and Sally joined the meeting online, her colleagues were all seated in their usual conference room. Once Ange had completed making introductions, Wallace got straight down to what was bugging him. 'I had a call from the immigration minister this morning.' He looked towards Judy Ly and Chris Lambert.

'Your interview yesterday seems to have stirred up a wasp's nest, and one of them came back to sting me. Bloody hell. What allegations did you make, for goodness' sake?'

The look on Chris Lambert's face turned to one of disgust. 'Talk about a bunch of arse-covering corporate spin doctors. They've absolutely no interest in finding out what happened to Cua Kwm, and we never got one straight answer. They hadn't bothered to bring a single person from operations into the meeting. Oh, but they had *two* lawyers to *help* us with our enquiries. In summary, the video surveillance blind spot was supposedly new information, although I seriously doubt this by the way they behaved. Honestly, these guys ducked and weaved like a Sydney taxi driver. I had to threaten them to get even the slightest concession.'

'And how did you threaten them, Detective?' asked Wallace pointedly.

'I suggested it wouldn't look good when I made an official report on them obstructing an investigation. I might have also suggested that I would front the Senate enquiry myself, if it came to that.'

'Hmm,' was Wallace's observation. 'Go on.'

'After a great deal of pushing on our part, they ultimately conceded it had been difficult to fill rosters over the Christmas holiday season. Staff shortages and Covid quarantine periods had placed them over the edge of being able to service the *inmates*—as they called them. Apparently, they needed to source service personnel from a labour hire company that they use from time to time.' Lambert looked down at his notes. 'Ample Personnel is the company that they referred to. I haven't had time to investigate them. When I asked for the staff logs, the lawyers told me that Ample did all the vetting and paperwork, and that we'll need to speak to them. The only concession I received was a comment that Ample use mostly Asian immigrant workers. Apparently, in their words, it's almost impossible to get *Australians* to do that sort of manual work since Covid. It was at that point that I lost my cool and suggested they weren't doing their job and making adequate provisions for the safety of the detainees.'

'That explains why the minister called me. So, what is your theory about what happened?'

'I think that someone slipped through the net via Ample Personnel and disposed of Cua Kwm. They must have had some insider knowledge of the workings of the facility and where to find the blind spot,' replied Lambert.

Wallace seemed dubious. 'Or, as the minister pointed out this morning—rather forcefully I might add—Cua Kwm was another drug-addicted illegal immigrant who killed herself in an overdose.'

Ange had been observing the body language of her boss during this exposé in political interference. It came as no surprise when Sally Anders entered the conversation. 'I'm new here, but there are way too many coincidences here. That this all took place in an isolated surveillance blind spot is the largest and most obvious. There is absolutely no incentive for the managers of the detention centre to look any deeper. Explaining this away as a suicide is the easiest route to washing their hands of the matter. I'll bet that they're secretly patting themselves on the back for getting Cua Kwm out of the country, even if it was in a box. That Detective Wallace got a call from the minister within twenty-four hours of the interview tells us they have strong connections. It's no surprise that the minister wishes to avoid harpooning his flagship immigration policy, spearheaded by a private sector partnership with ImDm Corporation. By the way, who was behind getting this task force assembled?'

Wallace screwed up his face in distaste before spitting out his answer. 'One of the newly elected independent senators, a Senator Deborah Vann. She's been raising hell over our country's immigration policy, and I gather the government commissioned the task force to shut her up. Apparently, people trafficking and child exploitation are pet projects of hers.'

By this stage, Ange had had enough. 'If you ask me, this sounds like a worthwhile *pet project* for Senator Vann to pursue. I agree with Sally and don't believe that this is just plain old bad luck. My vote is that we keep digging on the murder of Kwm. Perhaps look at Ample Personnel some more, but I reckon anyone this organised would have carefully brushed over any footsteps.'

Wallace seemed unwilling to concede anything. He turned his attention towards the video camera. 'Have you been able to make any progress, Detective Watson?'

Ange summarised where she and Billy were situated, explaining how they were piecing together the evidence provided by Cua Kwm during her interview. 'My theory is that the commercial underpinnings of this operation sit on the Dark Web, which has led us to two prospective locations, one to the northwest and one to the south of Texas, the town where Kwm had been found. I must admit that this is all quite circumstantial at this stage, but I should have a better sense once we can overlay some more current satellite imagery. I'm also planning to drive through both target areas and see if they line up with Kwm's recollection of her journey.'

'We have some cyber resources here, which we'll put into trawling the Dark Web for anything that lines up with Ange's theory,' offered Anders. 'So, are we agreed? We'll chase down Detective Watson's hypothesis and you guys will continue to investigate Cua Kwm's death.'

Ange could not help but notice that the thirty minutes that Sally Anders had available had slipped well past. Judy Ly and Chris Lambert nodded. Henry Chan continued to look as if he had someplace better to be, and David Wallace glared daggers at Sally Anders.

'Excellent,' said Anders. 'The ayes have it, then. If you don't mind, I'll sit in on these meetings from now on.'

With that, the meeting disbanded, and Ange left the video call. Sally Anders wasted no time in voicing her conclusions. 'What a supercilious tool that Wallace is. You were being way too kind when you described him to me. Why don't you get Constable White to do some lurking on the Dark Web? Tell her not to stick her head up this time. I don't need any more shootings to deal with.'

'Will do, boss. Thanks for joining in. I'll see you next week, then?'

'It'll be fun. I need some light relief and Wallace looks a worthwhile subject,' suggested Sally Anders with a broad smile.

Ange had barely walked from the office when her phone rang. It was Judy Ly. 'I want to come and work for Major Crimes. Your boss was amazing. You should have heard Wallace ranting and raving once you guys left the meeting. He doesn't respond well to women like your boss. I gather he now feels caught between a rock and a hard place.'

'I agree, Judy. Sally is amazing and I'm very lucky to have her as my boss. I hope she gave you some confidence to keep digging. I'll back my boss over yours, any day. Speak next week, if not before.'

Ange glanced back at Billy's desk but saw him intent on deciphering the metadata provided by the phone company. She rang Gus to tell him of her flight arrangements and that she should be home for dinner. 'By the way, how is Buddy coping without me?'

'I think he's doing nicely. He seems to enjoy the shop and greeting his many fans,' replied Gus.

'What do you mean, *many fans?*' she asked before reality checked in. 'Let me guess, Kerrie has been on the case?'

'Haven't you checked her blog yet? I suggest you do. We may have a celebrity in the house. I'll pick up some fish for dinner. Does that work for you?'

'Perfect, see you around 7 p.m.,' replied Ange. She glanced down at her phone, noticing that it was still on silent from the previous evening. Kerrie's blog had Buddy, aka Rusty Bell, in a whole series of shots, flitting between beautiful models and even more beautiful Bell Surfboards. 'Oh, Kerrie, you'll be the ruin of that dog,' Ange muttered out loud as she walked downstairs to find some lunch. She was pleased that Kerrie had resisted any temptation to dress Buddy up in anything ridiculous and his manhood remained intact, or maleness, or whatever term applied in the dog world. This seemed in stark contrast to Senior Detective Wallace, and Ange smiled at that comparison.

Before she left for the airport, Ange swung by Billy's desk again. 'Just about to leave, Billy. Any progress?'

'I built a macro to analyse the metadata, as I figured I might need to do this for future data sets. It's interesting. It looks as if we can discount the single user. That's spasmodic and always from the same cell tower. The cluster to the south lights up three cell towers and resembled a single user who moves around a bit. One of those towers is in the local town, so I guess all that makes sense. Those transmissions are always sequential, so I'm ninety percent certain of my conclusion. The cluster to the north was more difficult. I'm pretty sure that those hits represent two users and they come in waves. Whether they're connected is too hard to say.'

'Excellent, Billy. I'm planning a site visit, so I might be in and out of mobile phone reception. By the way, are you coming to Warwick to watch Bree's last test against India? I'm planning to swing by there on my way home from Hillburn.'

'Probably not. I've seen all her other games, and travelling to Warwick from Sydney isn't easy. Also, I just looked at the airfares and those things have quadrupled from a few months ago. Frankly, I doubt that you'll see me.'

'OK, Billy, I'll cheer on your behalf. Maybe I can teach Buddy to howl whenever Australia scores a goal. He could be like one of those football commentators who scream *goalgoalgoalgoal* without drawing breath.'

'Speak soon, boss,' concluded Billy with a smile as Ange started towards the lift.

Ange texted Gus from the Ballina airport that she was on her way. By the time she had walked into the house, dinner was in full swing. Buddy rushed over to greet her, evidently having moved into the house while she was away.

'I see Buddy is settling himself in,' observed Ange with a cynical smile.

Gus seemed to be buzzing with energy. 'I'm positive that we got a sales spike after Kerrie's posts of Buddy with a Bell Surfboard. I tell you, that dog is the best thing ever. The guys have pitched me an idea for a new range of boards that they've been sitting on. A cruisy single fin in the seven-to-eight-foot range. They want to call it the Rusty Cruiser. They've already started working on some prototypes. I've ordered a seven-footer, which should be perfect for you to try.' Gus went to his phone and pulled up an image to show her. 'Mal, the guy who does our artwork, did this sketch of Buddy when he came around yesterday. How cool is that? I'm going to introduce a new line of tee shirts with Buddy as the feature. *Rusty Bell* is the tag line I'm thinking of. Either in off-white with deep maroon writing, or rusty red colour with white writing. What do you think?'

'Sign me up for the first one. Although we might need dog therapy to keep Buddy from gaining a colossal ego. Now, Angus Bell, how do you feel about taking a few days off for a trip out west?'

'Where and when?' asked Gus, a halfway reply that hedged his bets between yes and no. He looked at her sideways. 'Are you deputising me for one of your crusades, Detective Watson?'

'I'm thinking that we could head west this Thursday and then cruise north before ending up in Warwick to watch Bree's hockey test against India on Sunday. Can the shop do without you for a few days? Or more to the point, can your team cope without Buddy?'

'I'll speak to the boss, but I'm pretty sure we can work something out,' replied Gus, full of irony, seeing as he was the boss. 'I'll need to break the news gently that Buddy will be on leave,' he added, smiling down at his new best mate. Buddy looked entirely ambivalent, although he was enjoying being tousled by his mistress. Ange had the distinct impression that Buddy had become a bit of a tart.

Chapter 27

Western Sun

The principal town which serviced the Green River Shire was the delightfully named Clearwater. Ange dearly hoped that the region lived up to its name and conjured up sparkling eucalypt-lined rivers and streams cascading gently between rolling hills. Her sat nav was showing a travel time of just over three and a half hours. To set the scene, she assailed her two travelling companions with a podcast about people trafficking. Gus was shocked by what he heard. Buddy, on the other hand, fell asleep in no time.

Clearwater looked like a thoroughly delightful town, nestled within a valley created by the Green River as it meandered between two large mountain ranges. Buddy appreciated the stop they made at a small park on the edge of the Green River and raced around smelling everything in sight, stopping here and there to mark his territory and signal that 'Buddy was here'. Ange made a mental note to check him for ticks each night, which was an interesting change of circumstances for a former logdog, where the concept of tough love had prevailed.

Clearwater and the Green River Shire seemed green and prosperous. The Green River itself was brimming with water and full of life. The region had enjoyed some solid late-summer rain, which was in stark contrast to her family property in Tamworth. In times of drought, the gently flowing river would wither into a series of precious waterholes. As a country girl, Ange fully appreciated the impact of drought on the psyche of rural folk. A drought was more pervasive than a flood, which was normally a disastrous but fleeting affair. Sometimes, one property might enjoy bountiful rain, and another just a few kilometres away would remain in drought. The weather was a mystery of some consequence.

The last major drought in Australia had run for almost a decade, destroying countless lives and livelihoods. As she was filling up the Prado at a service station, Ange commented to the attendant on the wonderful season that the region seemed to be experiencing. Barry, according to his name tag, was a glass-half-empty type of guy, something typical of countryfolk where seasons were concerned. 'We've just gotten through these floods, and now a strong El Niño weather pattern is developing in the Pacific Ocean. They reckon we'll be back in drought within twelve months.' Like most countryfolk, Barry also moonlighted as an amateur meteorologist and was fixated by the weather. Nourishing rains meant bountiful crops and healthy livestock, which brought prosperity to everyone in the region. Drought brought devastation and times of hardship. Ange said a secret prayer that the forecasters were mistaken and El Niño moved on quickly.

Ange had booked a cabin for the night, part of a caravan park on the outskirts of the town centre and one that allowed pets. Before Ange targeted the zones circled on the map that Billy had prepared for her, she dropped off Gus and Buddy at the cabin to get settled. While not quite up to the standard of her favourite riverside cabin in Namba Heads, it was very pleasant and certainly peaceful. Gus offered to take Buddy for a walk around the town and find somewhere suitable for dinner, leaving Ange free to survey the area.

There were three roads that resembled the description that Cua Kwm had made, each serviced by the cell towers which were located outside of the town. Ange knew she needed to be mindful that Kwm's recollections could easily have been distorted by the trauma she experienced during her midnight escape. The first road was a furphy. What had once been a dirt road was now paved with asphalt. There was a sign displaying the cost of this upgrade and proudly promoting the state's rural roads program. The cynic in Ange wondered when the next election was due and whether Green River sat within a marginal seat of Parliament.

The second road was more interesting and Ange drove its full extent twice before eventually discounting it because of housing density. Small hobby farms dominated the beautiful landscape, and Ange could easily see the attraction for anyone seeking a relaxed and peaceful slice of rural life.

Her last road was by far the most interesting. However, Ange couldn't fully join the dots of Kwm's testimony. There was a stretch of road, some ten kilometres long, that offered some possibilities. Ange rang Billy from her vehicle, noting the strong mobile phone reception, and asked him to send over some detailed imagery of the area. She then drove back into town and found the office of the local council. Ange saw no reason to be obtuse, so she showed her badge to the young man at the main counter and asked to see someone who could help her with the local refuse service. The guy gave her the strangest of looks, evidently wondering why council refuse services would be of any interest to a detective from Major Crimes, before leaving the counter and heading back into the bowels of the office.

Ange stood and waited patiently for some ten minutes. It was hardly bustling. Ange was the only person on her side of the counter. Evidently, Green River ran to a very different beat than Sydney, where everything needed to be done yesterday. Eventually an attractive forty-something woman came around to greet Ange, not at all the gruff middle-aged male rubbish collector that she had imagined. The woman did not look happy with this intrusion, so Ange turned on the charm to get her onside. 'Thanks for seeing me. I come from Tamworth, and I remember what my dad used to say around council elections. All that council needs to get right is the three Rs.'

'Yes, rates, rubbish, and roads,' said the woman with just the hint of a smile creeping into her expression. 'How can I help?'

'I'm just interested in council refuse collection routes. Can you show me the extent of your service area?' asked Ange.

The woman looked completely taken aback by this suggestion, so much so that the pair exchanged the oddest of stares for a moment. 'Oh. OK then,' the woman stuttered. 'I'll get some maps.'

The woman ducked back into the office and returned a couple of minutes later, holding a large poster-sized map. She unfurled the map onto the counter and pointed to the town. 'This is where we are. The areas shaded in pink are purely general waste and serviced weekly as part of normal council rates. The area beyond shaded in yellow represents areas which the council can service with special arrangements. Places like agricultural supply outlets, for example.'

Ange took some time to get her bearings. She pulled out her own map and then located her three target roads, ultimately focussing on the road of most interest. The refuse service to that area swelled out like a giant carbuncle. She pointed this out. 'Why does this area balloon out so markedly?'

The woman met this seemingly innocuous question with another even more curious stare. When she finally answered, her eyes were darting all over the place.

'Samsons Road. That was a special project of the CEO,' was all that she would offer, a rather bland explanation considering her fidgety body language.

Ange opted to leave that answer alone for the moment, sensing that something odd was underpinning this response. 'That's perfect. Thanks again for your help. Do you mind if I take a photo of this on my phone?'

'Be my guest,' said the woman offhandedly, standing back to allow Ange to take a series of photographs on her phone.

Once Ange was out of the council office, she emailed the photos to Billy, asking if he could overlay them on the high-resolution imagery that he was working on. Before she had gotten to her car, the woman with whom she had just been speaking rushed over.

'Hello, Detective. Sorry that I seemed weird just before. I thought you were here about Brendan. Brendan Tame. My name is Sandy Ellis, by the way.'

As the pair shook hands, Ange's instinct was to press the point. 'Why would you have thought that?'

'Well, refuse isn't really my job. That was Brendan's area before he got stood down. It was terrible what happened to him.'

'Tell me more,' probed Ange. While she needed no fresh crusades, she had learned never to prejudge which loose threads needed pulling in the early stages of any investigation.

'Well, the area that you pointed out was a bone of contention with Brendan. He argued until he was blue in the face that it was too sparsely populated and couldn't justify being serviced by weekly council refuse trucks. It was probably just politics, but our CEO was insistent. Brendan should have let it go, but he went on and on about it. Not long after that, Brendan was accused of sexual harassment, which came totally out of the blue.' The woman paused for effect, screwing up her face in apparent disgust before continuing. 'And guess who the alleged victim was?'

Ange didn't need Buddy's acute sense of smell to get the whiff of a rat. 'The CEO.'

'Exactly. There was no way Brendan would have done something inappropriate with the CEO. Apart from the fact that Brendan was in a long-term relationship, he didn't like our CEO much at all. Believe me, after I split with my husband, I gave Brendan every hint that I could muster. He never even made the slightest move. The whole thing was a set-up and Brendan paid a dear price, and all over the pathetic routing of a refuse truck.'

'How long ago was this?' asked Ange.

'I guess around six months ago,' answered Ellis.

'What happened to your colleague?'

'Nothing yet. They stood him down pending an investigation, but that's dragging on. I think we all know where it will end up. The word of a male subordinate versus his female boss?' she asked rhetorically. 'Whether Brendan has the wherewithal to take it further, I'm not sure. The trouble is that, once accused, everyone assumes he's guilty. I suspect he'll have trouble finding another job with that hanging over his head. At least his partner has stuck by him.'

'Thanks for coming forward. It's not really my area, but I'll keep my eye out in case anything lines up.'

'Can you tell me what you're in town about?' asked the woman, curiosity finally getting the better of her.

'I can't say. However, if you think of anything else out of sync, please contact me. If I can help with your colleague, and I'm not promising that I can, then I'll try. My visit here needs to remain low key. Given what you just told me, it probably should stay just between us. Are you OK with that?' asked Ange as she handed over her business card.

'Sure. That's fine by me. I'm afraid to say anything in case I end up like Brendan. I need this job to make ends meet and get my kids through school. Thanks for doing whatever you can, and I understand that might be nothing,' said a grim-faced Sandy Ellis before she took Ange's business card and walked away.

As she drove to the riverside cabin, Ange figured that the town warranted some further attention. Whilst none of what the woman had told her made sense, Ange knew that smoke normally signalled that a fire of some sort was burning.

Gus had decided that they should take dinner at a nearby historic pub. Apparently, when he had asked if they allowed dogs on the verandah, the publican had thought him deranged. 'If we didn't allow dogs, we wouldn't have any customers. Kitchen shuts at 8 p.m. sharp, so don't be late,' was the reply to Gus's enquiry. After a pleasant afternoon stroll in the cooling air, they ended up at the pub and found a suitable table. Buddy strategically plopped himself down beside them, making sure that he was well paced to observe the last of the day's comings and goings. The sign said to order at the bar, and rib fillet with salad and chips seemed an appropriate choice. When Ange asked if the beef was locally sourced, the publican assured her that this was unlikely given the influx of hobby farmers who had taken over the region. 'Most of the serious beef country is further west nowadays. There are a few local stud farms, but those don't supply much beef for the table. Certainly none of that comes our way.'

This confirmed Ange's sense of things as she had driven around. By the time their meals had arrived, the town was supremely tranquil, with just the odd vehicle running up the main street to disturb the serenity. Clearwater resembled any of hundreds of country towns on a weeknight after dark. 'Out for the count' was the term that Gus used to describe the deathly quiet that accompanied their walk back to the cabin. The meal had been simple but tasty, and Buddy had feasted on some juicy leftovers that the publican's wife had dished up. That dog carried some secret sauce around with him, that was for sure.

On the way home, Ange's sixth sense pinged loudly, the one honed by her years on the streets in Western Sydney. A drug drop was going down in a small riverside park, discreetly located off the main street. That was interesting. Ange refrained from busting the protagonists in the act, opting instead to text herself the registration number of the dark coloured 4WD twin-cab and a white midsize SUV.

Despite its current languid state, there seemed to be plenty going on beneath the surface of Clearwater, more than enough to suggest that they would not be breaking camp and moving on straight up the next morning. There was more work to be done.

Chapter 28

Digging

A nge was up early the next morning. While Gus dozed peacefully, Ange took Buddy for a walk to make a closer inspection of the town. A thick fog had descended on the valley, creating a muted and eerie scene. The odd barking dog echoed dimly in the distance and the usual morning avian cacophony was starkly absent. Streetlights had remained on, shining a weak haloed light over the scene, creating an impression that Ange was back in the Middle Ages, a scene from *The Hound of the Baskervilles*, perhaps. Muffled vehicles seemed to leap out of the gloom.

Luckily, she found a welcome cafe, the appropriately named Pam's Place, and ordered two large flat whites to go, both with extra shots. The friendly Pam evidently doubled as the town's watchdog and probed her alien customer for information. Ange was having none of that, opting instead for a vague excuse that she and her partner were looking at property in the area. Pam kindly recommended that Ange pay a visit to Glenda Webster. Just a few doors down the main street, apparently Glenda was 'the best real estate agent in town'. Ange embraced her persona of a homebuyer doing due diligence and explained that she and her partner were planning on having a family, asking what the schools were like and whether drugs were a problem in town.

'Schools are great and we're close to the boarding schools in Armidale once they get older, if that's your thing. All my lot went to school here, and they turned out OK. My daughter works as a teacher at the local Catholic school and my son is a dentist in Gunnedah, which is too far away for my liking.' A look of disgust came over Pam's face. 'As for drugs, we never used to have a problem, but the last couple of years have seen drugs appear in town—since Covid, actually. My daughter caught my grandson with some pot. Seriously, he's only in grade ten. Who sells drugs to a fifteen-year-old, I ask you?' she implored. 'I wish the authorities would do something about it. I suppose, in that respect, we're probably no different from most other country towns nowadays. Clearwater really is a wonderful place to live. I love your dog, by the way,' she added, as if remembering that her customer was a potential citizen, one with a well-trained dog who sat patiently at the door, intent on the pair's conversation.

Coffees in hand, Ange walked back to where she had spied the likely drug transaction. A small gravel carpark snaked down from the main street to nestle beside the river, placing it almost underneath the bridge that formed the northern crossing. The ramped approach to the bridge created a visual barrier, meaning that the site remained hidden from all but pedestrians. Weeknights after 8 p.m. would normally be a safe bet against nosy parkers. The location was perfect.

Gus was checking emails when she arrived back and was thankful for the coffee. Ange fired up her tablet and logged into the vehicle registration system. The white SUV was registered to a Mark Dole with a Clearwater address. The 4WD dual cab was registered at a post office box in Newcastle. She opened Google Maps and located Dole's house, which proved to be on the southern outskirts of town. Once her caffeine level was restored, she took a shower and changed into jeans and a light blue shirt. After rolling up her shirtsleeves and pulling on her R.M. Williams riding boots, Ange figured that she could easily pass the city slicker smell test.

Leaving Gus and Buddy at the cabin, Ange took a drive over to see where Mark Dole lived. By the look of the ramshackle home, his surname seemed appropriate. Tall scrappy weeds grew around a rusty old swing set, which sat abandoned in the corner of the unloved yard. A few rambling rose bushes tried their best to brighten things, but the overall effect was drab and depressing. The house didn't appear to profit from any woman's touch, and it was Ange's powerful impression that Mark Dole was the drug user of the pair she had spied on the previous evening.

She then headed to her target road some ten kilometres out of town, the one conspicuously delineated by a carbuncle of extended council refuse services. She drove slowly down the dusty road, overlaying the journey with the image that Cua Kwm had implanted. By the time she had driven a further ten kilometres, Ange concluded it was remotely plausible that this was the location. However, the farmhouses seemed closer together than she'd imagined. The night of Kwm's escape had been very dark, and it was plausible that she had missed one or more houses along the way.

Ange turned around and drove back towards town, taking the journey even slower this time. By the time she had reached the asphalt pavement, she concluded that this was not the site that Kwm had escaped from. Not a single property featured a cattle grid. Ange was certain that Kwm would not have been mistaken about this detail.

The time was approaching 9 a.m. by the time she had arrived back at the cabin, late enough that she didn't feel guilty for ringing Billy. She could hear bustling Sydney commuters in the background, suggesting that Billy was still on his way to the office. 'Hi, boss, how is the trip going?'

Ange explained her conclusions about the location, explaining that she was planning to drive north to the Hillburn shire. 'However, I saw something suspicious, Billy. Could you contact Telstra and get a feed from last night? I know it's a long shot, but see if there was any Dark Web activity in the township of Clearwater. I think we might have stumbled on a home-grown drug operation. When you get back to the office, can you pull up the latest image for Samsons Road near Clearwater and call me? I sent you a photo showing the extent of council refuse services. If you could overlay that and send me a copy of the combined image before you call, I can run you through my thoughts.'

Ange busied herself packing the car and checking out of the cabin. The manager seemed to have been hoping that they might stay longer. 'We're usually fully booked, but everybody is obsessed by the beach at this time of year,' he explained. Ange promised she would likely be back soon. She neglected to explain why she might be back.

Billy called when she was walking back to the cabin. She fired up her tablet and opened the image that Billy had just emailed her. 'Can you see how the council service area balloons out along Samsons Road? I thought it might be worth investigating who might benefit from this extended service. Let's start at the bitumen and work our way out along Samsons Road. See if we can spot anything out of the ordinary.' The pair went silent as they scanned the imagery. They simultaneously both spotted the incongruity—a very large shed covered in solar panels and with an equally large and newish-looking water tank alongside. Further away from the road sat a moderately sized dam and a small shed. Ange concluded that this was most likely a pump house that serviced the water tank.

Before they jumped to any conclusions, Ange insisted they continue the full stretch of road, well past the outer extent of the council service area. Neither of them could see anything else out of the ordinary.

'Thanks, Billy,' concluded Ange once they had completed their back-and-forth on Samsons Road. 'Let me know when you have yesterday's phone tower data. I'll take my suspicions up with Sally if they line up. There's no way a small hobby farm could need such a large shed with so many solar panels. Something way out of place is going on in that shed.'

Ange briefly considered paying the CEO a visit, but she suspected that something was amiss in council and didn't wish to blunder in and scatter the pigeons, so to speak. She could always swing back on her return journey if it came to that.

With some misgivings, she loaded Gus and Buddy into the Prado and headed north towards Hillburn.

Chapter 29

Texas—the Other One

The drive through to Texas was simply gorgeous. Even though the ocean, in all its many moods and guises, had forever stolen her heart, Ange would always remain hostage to her country roots, and her love of the outback ran deep. Both imbued in her a sense of calm and tranquillity, even though they could bare teeth in an instant. Ange well knew to stay alert when navigating country roads, where massive trucks, straying animals, and sleepy drivers claimed a disproportionately high number of lives. After a welcome stretch of fine weather, at least she didn't have to worry about flooded waterways on this trip, another hazard of outback travel that was often underestimated by the uneducated—or the plain old stupid.

The run from Clearwater to Texas took just over two hours, which was the lower limit of her expectations. Given what Cua Kwm had been through, her sense of time was likely to be scrambled. Notwithstanding being shorter than expected, the drive approximated her description in most other respects. Despite the many anomalies, Ange arrived at Texas feeling that Clearwater must remain on the watch list. She pulled over on the outskirts of the town and consulted the briefing papers that she had been provided.

Rather than use Google Maps, Ange crisscrossed slowly through the township, progressively taking in the small border town. She soon found the Anglican church where Kwm had hid. A service station sat approximately one hundred metres away, exactly as Kwm has described during her interview. Ange briefly contemplated speaking to the pastor at the church, but the officers who'd collected Kwm would have done that. She was more interested in the service station where the driver of Kwm's escape vehicle had stopped for fuel.

Ange pulled the Prado into the covered driveway and took in the facility, an older-style service station which fronted a key intersection connecting the highway and the town centre. By the look of it, the service station may very well have been serving customers since the very birth of the motor vehicle itself. While Gus watched Buddy have a wander, she walked around the side of the servo to find the toilets. Annexed off the main shop, and most likely a later addition, the amenities had been constructed from cinder blocks and covered with layers upon layers of white paint. Ange quickly concluded that it would have been relatively easy for Kwm to sneak out from the rear of her escape vehicle and slip unnoticed into the toilet block. She walked out to the street and looked back towards the church. Kwm's explanation of her movements that day and night was highly believable.

She went inside and made use of the women's amenities, choosing the right-hand cubicle, the one farthest from the door. As she sat there, she imagined herself as a petrified Cua Kwm, tired and hungry, wondering what fresh peril the next hour or day would bring. It must have been a thoroughly terrifying ordeal for the young woman. Ange observed that there was no graffiti on any wall or door, and everything was clean and tidy. On her way back around to the car, she stuck her head into the men's facilities, which were similarly respectable. While the service station was old and well worn, someone cared about how the business presented itself.

A Prado has long legs and a massive fuel tank. Although she still had ample fuel on board, Ange opted to fill up. She picked up a couple of drinks from the fridge and made her way over to the counter to pay. She could see several framed photos of winning racehorses on the wall behind the counter, the telltale signs of addiction to that species.

'Hi. Nice place you have. I was pleased to find such clean toilets. Do you know anything about the young Vietnamese woman that was found in the church around the corner? On December the sixth.' Ange paused and flashed her badge.

The man's eyes narrowed, easing back open once Ange flipped out her badge. 'Yes, as a matter of fact. That was quite a shock for little-old Texas. How did it go with her? Í understand that she was petrified of someone or something.'

'Not well. It's a tragic story that I can't really go into. Tell me, I guess most people are like me and regularly stop at the same fuel stop?'

'Been here for twenty-eight years,' said the man proudly. 'The big fuel companies keep pushing me to renovate and then lumber me with an enormous debt. I keep telling them I'm doing just fine. To answer your question, I get more than my share of the locals, along with regulars who travel the route. I guess your assumptions are correct. I know I always stop at my usual. We're all creatures of habit, after all.'

Ange waved her phone over the EFTPOS terminal to secure a reassuring beep. As the receipt was printing, Ange probed the proprietor some more. 'I suppose most people pay like this nowadays.'

'Sure do. Except for the local kids who come by on their push-bikes to buy drinks or ice creams, I hardly see any cash since Covid.'

'Would you be OK to hand over your EFTPOS transactions for the past six months? I could get a warrant if you would prefer,' Ange asked nicely, adding a subtle sting-in-the-tail to her request.

'No problem. I've got nothing to hide. It's a straightforward process now with online banking. Each quarter, I do the same thing for my accountant. I feel sorry for that young woman. I presume you're looking into how she got here. We use the same cleaner as the church. Apparently, the young woman couldn't speak a word of English, the poor soul.' He pointed to the split-screen monitor beside the counter. 'I see your dog found the water bowl that I keep out the back for thirsty travellers like him. He's a good-looking dog.'

She pulled out her business card and wrote Billy's email address on the back. 'I'd really appreciate you downloading all the transactions for the past six months and emailing them to the address on the back. Can you copy me in as well just in case you can't read my writing? Oh, and I don't suppose you remember any regulars who passed through around the day when the young woman was found.'

The man shook his head. 'No. Sorry. Texas may look like a sleepy hollow, but I have loads of customers that I service each day.'

'I guess it's also too much to expect that you still have some security video from back then?'

'Sorry again. I only keep the footage for a week before recording over it. It's an old system and more designed to deter fuel thieves than anything else. Texas is a nice little town, so I don't have many problems.'

As if on cue, a crusty man in his sixties walked in.

'Rob, I haven't seen you for a while,' said the proprietor easily, as if he had known the customer for ages.

'No. The missus talked me into taking a holiday. Two weeks driving around the South Island of New Zealand, stuck in a campervan with the wife nagging me what to do and where to go—and me with absolutely no escape.' The smile in Customer Rob's eyes suggested that this whinge was for effect rather than any actual hardship. 'If I'm being honest, the entire trip was excellent, even the missus. Beautiful country. Bloody expensive, but worth it. Anyhow, life is back to normal again. Any specials for the weekend, Vic?'

'She Can Fly in the fifth at Caulfield. Word is that she's being prepped for a run,' replied Vic in a conspiratorial tone.

'Brilliant. On the nose or each way?' asked Rob as he paid for his fuel.

'Definitely the win,' replied Vic emphatically. 'See you in a couple of weeks, then. Horrible accident on the Killarney road a few weeks back. Local family. Very sad. Anyhow, take care, Rob.'

Rob turned and made for the door. Ange knew to listen when the universe was speaking so overtly and quickly finished up her business with Vic. 'Thanks for your help. My colleague will be in touch. You have my card, so please ring me if you think of anything else.'

Ange scuttled out the door and caught up with Rob. 'I gather you stop here often, then?' she asked in a friendly tone.

'Wouldn't dare stop anywhere else. I usually come by this way every other week. Always call in on the way up or back. Vic is a bit of an institution on this stretch of the highway. Where else can I get a cracking tip with a tank of fuel? I've paid for my fuel tons of times courtesy of one of Vic's specials.'

Ange marvelled at the punter's predilection to exaggerate infrequent wins and forget habitual losses. 'Good to know. I'll start doing the same.'

'Places like this are a dying breed. We need to support people like Vic before the big guys steamroller him. I sure won't be getting racing tips from the massive roadhouses that those multinationals keep ramming down our throats.'

Ange knew this to be true, and the pair parted their ways on that sombre note. She would have confidently placed a bet that her own father would be one of Vic's many customers. As she watched Customer Rob drive away, she wondered how he might feel, knowing that his comings and goings were about to be analysed by Major Crimes.

Ange rounded up her travelling companions and settled back in the car. She had some calls to make, so inserted her wireless earbuds for the sake of probity.

As much as she trusted Gus, he didn't need to know all the intimate details of her dirty laundry. Gus took over the driving duties and Ange rang Billy as soon as they were back on the road. 'Hi, Billy. Any luck with the data from Telstra?'

'I should have it sorted by the end of today. I'll let you know as soon as I've had a look through.'

'No pressure. It's not on the critical path right now. However, I think that we might have caught a break. I identified the service station where Cua Kwm left her escape vehicle and hid in an amenities block. The owner is going to send you a dump of all his EFTPOS transactions for the past six months. It's a super long shot, but I'd like to see if any patterns emerge. Will that be difficult?'

'Very. There must be thousands of transactions from scores of banks. Is there any way we could narrow it down a little?'

'I've got a hunch that the owner of the pickup truck regularly passes this way, and it's not beyond the realm of possibility that he would stop there each time out of habit. December the sixth needs to be your reference point, as we now know the driver in question stopped for fuel that morning. I'd like you to look for any regulars. Maybe look for intervals longer than a week, which should weed out the locals,' explained Ange.

'OK, that should be easy. I can write a macro that shifts through the data looking for those sorts of patterns.'

'Perfect. Let's regroup after that. It could be a complete waste of time, but I'm hoping that we can identify a regular who comes from either Green River or Hillburn. It's not the best idea that I've ever had, but we might just catch a break that saves us a load of tedious cross-checking.'

'When you say us, I presume you mean the royal us—as in me!' correctly observed Billy.

'Billy, we all know that you love this sort of stuff. Speak soon,' concluded Ange, her smile reflected in the tone of her voice.

Ange called her boss the moment that she had hung up from Billy. 'Hi, boss. I think I'm making some slow progress on the people trafficking case. I may also have stumbled on a small-town drug operation. Billy is doing some more work on that, so I'll let you know if those ducks all line up.'

'Where are you exactly?' asked Sally Anders.

'We've just left Texas and on our way to Hillburn, the second prospective location based on our Dark Web theory. That's why I called. I get the distinct impression that nobody really wants to solve the Cua Kwm case.'

'Explain, Detective. And, by the way, who is *we*?'

'I'm with Gus and Buddy. We're making a weekend of the trip to watch Breanna White's final hockey match against India. It's being played in Warwick on Sunday. That isn't a problem, is it?' answered Ange, now wondering if bringing Gus and Buddy was in breach of some protocol, adding, 'I didn't feel comfortable making the trip on my own.'

'Normally it would be, but you can't help it when work interrupts your personal life, can you, Detective?' said Anders, graciously offering Ange a way out. 'Who is Buddy, by the way?'

'Didn't I tell you when I was in Sydney? Buddy is my new red cattle dog. Someone to keep me safe at night. He's proving quite a hit around town. If my friend Kerrie has her way, she'll be his agent for a movie deal or lead role in a miniseries.'

'So, you were saying about your case?' asked Anders, getting back down to business.

Ange took her boss through what had transpired after she had located the service station. 'The people who picked up Cua Kwm were either incompetent or disinterested. If Senator Vann hadn't started raising hell, I reckon that Kwm would have been whisked out of the country without another look. This task force has virtue signalling written all over it. Two token females, one recently winged in the line of duty, and a team leader more intent on his own reputation,' ranted Ange. 'Honestly, the investigation at Texas was pathetic.'

'Are you questioning the ability of your colleagues with that theory, Ange?'

'Not Judy Ly and Chris Lambert. They seem equally frustrated. I don't have any sense of Henry Chan. However, you witnessed David Wallace in full flight. That guy worries the socks off me. The trouble is, I'm not sure how far I should go it alone and when I should bring the team into my confidences. What do you suggest?' Ange asked her more experienced and politically savvier boss.

After a few seconds of silence, Sally Anders confirmed all of Ange's misgivings. 'I would suggest that you should bring your team into the fold only once you feel confident about your theories and conclusions. I agree with your sense of Wallace. He seems way too weasely and gives me the impression of someone chasing the fast lane to upstairs. Do you need any more resources? Two of our new recruits start next week.'

'Not yet. However, Billy might need a hand sifting through the EFTPOS transactions that I secured from a service station where Kwm hid. The owner was keen to help. Honestly, we could have gotten some CCTV footage from the service station if someone had simply done some legwork and asked up and down the street. It doesn't sound to me as if the officers who found Kwm were on the ball.'

After she had finished her calls, Gus looked at Ange, having heard her half of the conversation and voicing his conclusion. 'Careful that you aren't swimming with crocodiles, Ange. *Again.*'

Chapter 30

Hillburn

The drive from Texas to Hillburn took just over two hours and forty minutes, and Team Ange needed to stretch their legs. Ange hadn't bothered to book any accommodation, figuring that it shouldn't be a problem on a Friday night. How wrong she was. Hillburn was hosting a country cricket carnival that weekend, and players had come from far and wide to bake themselves under the summer sun and chase a red leather Kookaburra cricket ball around all day. Ange swung into a sports club that seemed to be the hub for sporting action. After availing themselves of the amenities, Ange searched on her phone for somewhere to stay. The options seemed limited, even more so when you clicked the 'Pet Friendly' tab. They settled on a detached cabin at a caravan park on the outskirts of town. By the look of the listing, the cabin was more a donga, a cast-off rescued from one of the many gas mining camps.

Ange left Gus and Buddy to find a shady tree and watch some cricket while she drove across town to check out their cabin. Hillburn was quite a large town—at least double, maybe even triple the size of Clearwater. All the major shops had a presence, and the place looked prosperous. The town benefited from being positioned on a strategic crossroads of highways running north–south and east–west. It was an excellent location for a cricket carnival, but also a major service centre for the many agricultural and mining businesses in the region. This was coal and gas country, sitting underneath some prime grazing land. As one could imagine, these two industries were not always compatible. Although these tensions were well publicised in the national press, Ange saw little evidence of this in Hillburn.

She noticed a large IGA which stood on the edge of town, the closest of the supermarkets to the highway crossroads. IGA represents the largest chain of independent grocery shops in the country, and the stores were family owned and run. Its strategic location and convenient car parking looked perfect for anyone looking to dash in and out and leave minimal footprints. Ange popped in to pick up some provisions for their stay in the so-called *holiday cabin*. As she walked around the well-stocked store, she noted the regularly placed security cameras scatted throughout. After filling her small shopping basket with some drinks, a litre of milk and some dog food for Buddy, she approached the checkout. She noted the manager was manning it.

'Hi. Nice shop you have here. Tell me—I'm planning a camping trip for a few family groups once the weather cools off. Do I need to reserve basic frozen stuff like chickens, meats, and mixed vegetables?' Ange asked with her friendliest smile. 'We're quite the battalion, so I wouldn't want to miss out and let the troops go hungry.'

'No, you should be OK. Our store services loads of properties in the region, so we're always well stocked up on the basics. However, once you know your dates, it would be worth letting us know what you need. We do occasionally run out of certain lines. Things are much better now that some of the Covid supply chain issues are being sorted out,' said the manager. He handed over a business card. 'Best to ring or email us a week before you arrive and we can make sure we have your provisions put aside. Take care with the frozen vegetables. They can't be allowed to thaw out. We had a bunch of people get sick last year on poorly refrigerated frozen veges. If you're camping, I'd suggest that you stick with fresh or canned. We always have plenty of both. Much safer if you're camping.'

Ange thanked the manager and walked back to her car. It was no smoking gun, or even a distant whiff of a smoking gun, but it supported Kwm's testimony of what they had fed her in captivity. One could imagine that her captors would limit their trips to the supermarket and make a single large purchase, perhaps even phone ahead, as the manager had suggested.

She then drove over to the caravan park on the edge of town, pushed up against the Emigrant Creek, more of a rocky gully holding a smattering of brackish waterholes than an actual creek with running water. There were many Emigrant Creeks scattered around the country, a constant reminder of early European settlement. Ange wished that more landmarks used indigenous names, even minor ones like Emigrant Creek. She found them more interesting and meaningful, usually connecting the role that the landscape played for the ancient peoples who had lived there long before European settlement. If one were lucky, there might even be a story from the Dreamtime that explained the landmark's very existence. Decreeing a new name for an ancient landmark, like Emigrant Creek, seemed like such a lazy copout by comparison.

After finding the manager's office, Ange entered through the fly screen door, setting off a chime meant to alert whoever was out the back. A middle-aged woman came out to greet Ange. 'How can I help you?' asked the woman pleasantly.

'I saw you had a cabin free for this evening. Would I be able to book it? I thought I should come and pay direct so you don't need to cough up the booking fees. We have a dog. Is that a problem?' asked Ange, making sure she was on the right side of the woman from the get-go.

'No problem. Dogs are fine provided you keep them under control—and they don't bark at night. You're lucky. We only have one cabin left on account of the cricket carnival, a last-minute cancellation. Do you want to have a look at it?'

'I'm sure it will be fine. It looks like you have a series of those cabins?' asked Ange.

'Yes, we snapped up as many as we could after the gas mining camps disbanded once their major construction works were complete. They were going for a song. I suppose the transport costs would have been significant, so it was better to sell them locally. Lots of locals picked one up. We would have purchased more had our development approval allowed it. With the current shortage of building materials, I reckon we could double our money if we sold them today. They work well for us during winter when the grey nomads and family holidaymakers swarm through.'

Ange paid in advance and picked up the key, then drove over to her cabin and unloaded the Prado. It was no suite at the Hilton but would do just fine. She snapped on the air-conditioning to start the long process of cooling down the stuffy cabin. Ange could see how six or even eight bunk beds could easily fit inside the rectangular metal-clad donga. The toilet amenities mirrored what Kwm had described. Once again, no smoking gun, but the case was slowly building for Hillburn to take the lead over Clearwater.

Ange drove back to collect her two travelling companions. She found Gus comfortably leaning up against a large tree. Much to everyone's delight, Buddy was holding court to some young boys and playing fetch with an old cricket ball.

He was most reluctant to leave his newfound cricket mates when Ange insisted they take a drive around the area.

The countryside around Hillburn was mostly flat or gently undulating, perfect for farming grains or cereals. Once they left the outskirts of the township, they crossed the expansive Condamine River, languidly snaking its way west. The Condamine is one of the main tributaries of the larger Darling River and part of the crucial Murray-Darling basin, the most extensive river system in the country. Ange headed towards the region supported by the cell tower that had registered the Dark Web activity. About ten minutes' drive west of town, she entered a heavily forested mountainous area and her heart started racing. This was looking more and more interesting.

After she crested the mountain range, the countryside changed markedly, with grazing land replacing the broad acre farms of the east. There were only a few roads to explore, but Ange noticed the properties were much larger than she had seen at Clearwater. Crucially, cattle grids adorned the entry to almost every property. She looked down at her phone and was pleased to see a powerful signal. Ange became convinced that this was the region she needed to focus on.

Rather than drag Gus and Buddy from pillar to post, Ange backtracked to town. It was now late afternoon, so she took her investigations online, courtesy of her aerial surveillance imagery. Gus sat on the porch making some calls while Buddy took a nap alongside. Ange set herself up on the small kitchen table and fired up her tablet and started running her eyes over the area she had just driven from. She identified three prospective sites that could plausibly match Kwm's testimony. Excitement coursed through her. She felt on the cusp of a breakthrough.

Ange sat back in her uncomfortable beige plastic kitchen chair and questioned herself. Was she at risk of confirmation bias, finding clues that were nothing more than random occurrences, convincing herself of a truth that was just a statistical anomaly? Ange was sufficiently aware of this flaw in her personality, an overactive imagination that was prone to creating patterns out of random background noise. Rather than race off half-cocked, she sat on her findings overnight. In the fresh light of day, hopefully, she could remain dispassionate and discern fact from fantasy.

As things transpired, she needn't have worried. Clarity came more quickly and easily than Ange had expected.

Chapter 31

Bingo

O nce dinner time had arrived, Ange and Gus drove back into town to look for somewhere suitable to eat. Like most rural towns, pubs were plentiful, scattered at various intervals around the township. Ange had often laughed to herself about this phenomenon, where a pub was never more than a short walk from all points. It was obvious to Ange that Hillburn was squarely a serious working town, as distinct from the more gentrified Clearwater and its many hobby farms. They found a pub which sported a large covered awning dotted with tables and chairs. Two other dogs lay tethered outside, so Ange figured Buddy wouldn't cause any grief for the other diners.

Gus ordered dinner and secured some drinks at the bar while Ange looked after Buddy at their chosen table. Evidently, the games were over and white-clad cricketers were streaming into the pub, looking to slake their thirst with a cold beer after a long hot day in the field. It was lucky that Ange had ventured out to dinner early. By the time their meals had arrived, all the tables were full, and the bar was a cacophony of noisy banter as happy cricketers exchanged stories of runs scored, catches taken, and opportunities missed perhaps. It was nice to be a bystander to such camaraderie. Country sport was a glue of some strength for rural communities.

The couple awoke the next morning just before 6 a.m. feeling refreshed, having slept well despite their unfamiliar surroundings. Taking advantage of the cooler morning air, they went for an early morning walk around town and picked up some breakfast at a coffee shop. It was doing a roaring trade and several customers came over to give Buddy the attention he was getting used to. He had well and truly shaken off his former life as a neglected working farm dog. Ange chatted

to a few of the more obvious cricketers, asking where they came from and how
the games were progressing. Some cloud cover had developed overnight, much
to the delight of those scheduled to take the field that morning. The prospect
of rain clouds was bittersweet for the players, potentially upsetting the games
but perhaps providing some respite from the heat. Ange expressed her hope that
they could make it through the three-day carnival before the heavens opened and
drowned the carnival.

They were just walking back to their cabin when Ange's phone buzzed with an
incoming call. It was Billy.

'Hi, Billy. What are you doing working on a Saturday morning?'

'With Bree being away playing hockey, I'm banking up some leave. I didn't
want to ring you late last night, but I think I may have found something interesting.'

Ange's heart rate quickened as she waited patiently for Billy to elaborate. 'I
spent yesterday writing a macro to analyse those EFTPOS transactions. It's always
a temptation to dive right in, but I'm pleased that I took the time. I included a
variable whereby I could play with the interval between visits. Your hunch was
spot on. I found three travellers who used the service station regularly. One of
them is very interesting. His visits are like clockwork and he purchased fuel on
December the sixth.'

'Let me guess. That traveller comes from Pineridge?' guessed Ange—the location that she had scoped out the previous evening.

'How did you know that?' asked Billy, amazement showing in his voice.

'I'm in the area now, and it lines up perfectly with the description Kwm gave
of her journey. There are also lots of smaller clues. I was about to head back out
there and take a detailed look over a few prospective properties. Do you have an
address for me?'

'I searched vehicle registrations for the person's name. A certain Joel Francis
seems to be the owner of a property called Four Gums. Drives a Nissan Navara
twin-cab. He also moonlights as an academic at my old university in Armidale. I
looked up the property, and it's on Reedy Creek Road,' explained Billy, a flat tone
having crept into his voice.

Ange sensed Billy's disappointment at having his thunder stolen so easily. 'This
is fantastic, Billy. You have just saved me a day's work and prevented me from
blundering in and alerting someone I shouldn't. I know that you've heard it

before, but you are an undoubted genius.'

'Oh, and by the way, there was someone using TOR in the town of Clearwater
the night before last. My contact at Telstra was tiring of my requests, so she's
given me a link to a portal where I can download the data myself in real time.
She asked for some paperwork, which I'll get sorted with the boss on Monday. It
might come in handy,' explained an upbeat Billy, as prone to flattery as the next
person.

'Thanks, Billy. I hope you have a fun weekend. I'll send you a picture of the
hockey game tomorrow,' offered Ange as she hung up from the call.

Packing up the car, Ange and her two companions drove back out towards
Pineridge. She easily found Reedy Creek Road, which wound west along a
wide-open valley. She spied the incongruously named Four Gums. The property
featured a large grove of eucalypt trees, far more than the requisite four suggested
by its name. Ange drove slowly past Four Gums and continued for another few
minutes before coming to a property that perfectly matched Kwm's description.
A large grove of trees obscured any decent view, and she drove well past the
property before pulling over to the side of the road and checking the map on her
tablet. It was one that she had earmarked, and the imagery showed a farmhouse
and two sheds nestled behind the grove of trees. The larger shed seemed the type
used to house farm machinery, and the smaller shed approximated the dimensions
of their holiday donga of the previous evening. Ange was certain that this was the
spot.

She weighed up the options. Should she leave it alone and wait for backup? Or
should she make some cautious investigations herself and possibly save a lot of
fuss and bother if her hunch was incorrect? After a moment's deliberation, she
chose the middle ground, deputising her travelling companions as cover to pay
Joel Francis and Four Gums a visit.

'Gus, I need to speak to one of the property owners. I don't wish to risk alerting
anyone or getting in too deep. How about we masquerade as a couple looking to
purchase a property? I'll take the lead, but it would be helpful if you could play
out the ruse,' Ange asked of her partner.

'Sure. However, I hope it is a ruse. I really don't think that I'm cut out for rural
life. It's way too solitary for my liking.'

'Don't worry. My days as a country girl are well past, Gus,' laughed Ange.

She drove slowly back along the dusty road towards Four Gums. As she passed the target property, she peered down the entry road as best she could. The front gate was closed and there didn't appear to be any activity on the property. She noted the cattle grid and could see some cattle grazing in the distance, suggesting that the property was still in active use.

She came to Four Gums and turned through the open gateway, driving slowly down the gravel road that led to the farmhouse. A silver Nissan Navara twin-cab 4WD was parked near the house. She noticed some wheelie bins pushed beside a tank stand, their different-coloured lids hallmarks of refuse collection services. As they pulled up, a thin and bespectacled fifty-something man came out to greet them, his longish grey hair combining to create a distinguished impression. 'Can I help you?'

'Hi,' said Ange as she hopped out of the Prado and walked across to greet the man, meeting his eyes with a good-old-fashioned country handshake. 'Gloria White,' she said, bringing her alter ego back into action. 'My husband and I are looking to buy a property and we really like this valley. I saw the gate was open and thought we should call in on the off chance you might know of someone looking to sell. Perhaps even yourself?'

'Joel Francis. It is a lovely valley. I'm probably not quite ready to sell yet, but stranger things have happened. I've applied for a permanent teaching position at the university in Armidale. If that comes off, then we'll probably put the place on the market.'

'I went to boarding school at NEGS in Armidale. Nice town. There are certainly worse places to live. What are your chances of securing the posting?'

'Better than even money. I've been teaching some courses there for a while now. I enjoy the teaching part, but the travelling is killing me. Every fortnight, I head to Armidale for a couple of days. I know that road like the back of my hand. Just over five hours on a good day. Six with the ever-present roadworks,' Francis replied with a resigned smile.

Gus took on his new role with gusto. 'How big is your property and how many head do you carry?' he asked, gesturing toward the smattering of cattle grazing in the distance.

'Almost a thousand acres,' answered Francis. He looked toward the hills further to the north. 'Some of the property becomes a touch hilly on the ridge, but it's mostly useful land. The creek is spring-fed from the mountain range. It was the permanent water that originally attracted me to the place. Maximum holding capacity for me is three hundred head. I try not to overstock the place, but it's always a balancing act depending on the season. We're enjoying an excellent season right now.'

'Wow, that's larger than I thought. It might be too big for us. What about the property next door? I like the sound of permanent water,' asked Ange.

'That property is unusual. The owners are mostly absentee. They must use it as a retreat of some sort, as they suddenly show up for a week or ten days and then leave overnight. I've never met them, but they've not caused me any trouble. The grazing land is probably on an agistment to someone from out of town. Cattle get dropped off or picked up from time-to time, but I haven't seen anyone living there for weeks now.'

Francis peered into the rear of the Prado. 'I see you have a cattle dog. Recently lost mine to a snake bite. I'm waiting for a new one, but cattle dog pups are almost impossible to find since Covid—not to mention expensive. Everybody seems to want a dog nowadays. Where did you get yours?'

'From my dad. Buddy got himself kicked by a bull and wasn't much use on the farm anymore. He seems to enjoy his new life as a pet,' said Ange as she looked affectionately over at Buddy, now sitting up and looking their way, somehow sensing that people were talking about him.

Ange fumbled around in her wallet and found one of Gloria White's business cards, being careful to ensure that she didn't flash her badge around. 'Thanks for your time. Let us know if you secure the posting in Armidale and decide to sell. I think that a thousand acres may be too much for us to handle, but we'll certainly give it some consideration—should things come to that. Good luck with the job.'

'Thanks. Will do. You should look at some of the country further north, perhaps take a drive along Wilders Road. It runs down a much tighter valley and most of the properties are smaller. It might give you some other options.'

Having said her goodbyes, Ange drove back down Reedy Creek Road convinced that she had found the location where Cua Kwm had been held captive. That Francis had lost his dog was yet another fact that lined up perfectly with Kwm's testimony.

What to do next would need some thought. Whatever that was, Ange knew it needed to include her team.

Next stop was Warwick, and Gus took over the driving while Ange thought things through. An interesting idea was forming in her head.

Chapter 32

Game On

Given that Bree's hockey game wasn't until Sunday evening, the three travellers enjoyed a delightful night and day, staying in a winery in Stanthorpe en route to Warwick. After a leisurely start, they arrived in Warwick mid-afternoon. Given that it was a night game, Ange had already booked a pet-friendly motel, and they arrived at the game with plenty of time to spare.

The Hockeyroos won the test match over India, securing the series two games to one. Ange felt that Bree had played well, but it was always difficult to shine brightly amongst the very best in the world. Ange kept Buddy on a tight lead lest he dash across the field and spark an international incident by stealing the hockey ball. He still got into the swing of things, barking loudly in tune with Ange and Gus's cheering.

Ange caught up with Bree not long after the game. 'We're going to head back to Byron first thing in the morning. When do you start back at work?'

'I've got tomorrow off, but I'll be back at work on Tuesday,' Bree replied.

Ange gave her a brief history of her case and the events of the past few days, before explaining the idea that she had been hatching on her drive up to Warwick. 'Can you spend some time lurking in the shady chat rooms of the Dark Web? I figure that the people responsible need to move their product—if you could call real people a product. The Dark Web would seem to be an obvious platform. I'm not sure whether the women are being trafficked to serve as brides, sex workers, or perhaps to work in sweatshops.'

'The Dark Web is a big place, Ange. Let me think about it. Perhaps I could pose as a buyer looking to secure an Asian bride. I can tell you that the stuff that swirls around the Dark Web would make your skin crawl.'

'That sounds like a decent plan, Bree. Keep me posted. Now, celebrate with your teammates. Well done, by the way.'

Bree squatted down to give Buddy a rough-and-tumble pat, much to his delight. 'Thanks. I might have a headache tomorrow morning, at least going by the plan I heard being hatched in the dressing room.'

Seeing as Ange saw no immediate need to retrace her steps, the trio of travellers left at daybreak on Monday and chose the fastest route home, passing through Killarney and Kyogle, skirting just south of the Border Ranges, through to Lismore and then home. They stopped once for a comfort break at a beautiful roadside park and listened to a flock of bellbirds chime while Buddy did his business. Bellbirds are curious and innocuous little birds, their chime one of the most piercing of Australia's native birds. As beautiful as their call sign is, they are also completely intolerant of all other birds in their territory. As Ange sat there admiring the beautiful chiming bells, impressive camouflage for a nasty side, Ange thought back to the CEO of the Green River Council and wondered if she was also of that ilk.

The troupe arrived back at Gus's house mid-morning. Buddy looked happy to be back at his new home and set about scouting the perimeter for any fresh smells. The moment Gus made a move toward his Volvo station wagon to head straight down to the shop in Byron, Buddy raced over and insisted on jumping on board. 'Social butterfly,' called out Ange as her dog abandoned her and jumped up into the back of Gus's ride. As they drove away, Buddy sat up happily and looked at Ange through the back window, seemingly not in the least bit concerned about this slight on his character.

Before Ange got down to unpacking and doing some chores, she sent a Teams meeting invitation to both Billy and Sally Anders for 1:30 p.m. She was pleased to see that both had accepted her invitation by the time she had her washing pegged onto the clothesline. Once her colleagues had joined her online, she briefed them on her findings over the past four days.

'So, Ange. Where do you want to go from here?' asked Sally Anders.

'I see the two sites as separate matters. Regarding my suspicions at Clearwater,

I don't see that this is relevant for the task force, even if I stumbled across it while investigating the people trafficking operation. I'm reasonably convinced that they're unrelated. Also, seeing as Clearwater is in New South Wales, I think we should take the running on that. What are your thoughts?' asked Ange.

'I agree, at least based on what you've told me. If they turn out to be connected, then we can cross that bridge when we come to it. What I propose is that we send Jim Grady across from Byron and get some help from the drug unit based in Tweed Heads. Ange, if you could send me your report by the close of business today, then I'll get the ball rolling. Seeing as you have a handle on the area, I suggest that you accompany Jim. What about Hillburn and the task force?' asked Anders.

'I have my weekly meeting at 11 a.m. tomorrow. That's Queensland time, so midday at our end on account of daylight saving. It would be helpful if you could join again, boss.'

'Sure. How do you plan to handle it?' asked Anders.

'Now that Billy has secured a real-time link to the cell tower traffic, I think he should monitor that for Dark Web activity. My theory is that they come and go from the Pineridge property, using it as a waypoint for the women. It makes sense, being pretty much directly west from Brisbane, out of the way, yet close to shops and services. Hillburn also enjoys excellent road access in all directions. If my hunch is correct, the women are being used to service the mining towns. Once Billy raises the alert, we can mount an operation and swoop in. Also, Bree will be lurking in various Dark Web chat rooms looking for something useful.'

Ange took a breath and checked that her colleagues were keeping up with her. Seeing no questioning expressions, she pushed on. 'I want to get the Queensland team to secure video footage from the three major supermarkets, starting with the IGA.'

'Why the IGA?' asked Billy.

'It's the one that I would choose if I was trying to duck in and out for provisions. It's on the edge of town, close to the major roads, and has convenient car parking. Except for a small bottle shop, it's stand-alone and not complicated with a raft of speciality shops,' replied Ange. Seeing the nods of agreement with her logic, she continued. 'We might get lucky and spot a person of interest in the video feeds. I think we can be confident of the dates when Kwm was held in the facility. Billy, how many patterns can your amazing video analysis software look for at one time?'

'I'm not sure, but I can't imagine that there's any limit. I expect that adding more patterns to the search function may slow the software down. But how would you decide who to look for? I don't think it's workable to run every criminal in our database through the algorithm. That would yield too many false positives and just confuse things.'

'That makes sense, Billy. I might hand that question over to the Queenslanders. Who knows, they might have a shortlist of potential suspects that they could focus on. Is that software hard to use?'

'Not really. Once it's properly configured, an hour's training should do the trick.'

'It would also be useful to get a live video feed of the compound. There's a high ridgeline about a kilometre from the property. It wouldn't need to be picture-perfect, just enough to pick up any activity.'

Sally Anders had heard all that she needed to. Evidently, any more conversation was just chatter, for chatter's sake. 'Take up your ideas up with the team tomorrow, Ange. I'll get cracking with the preparations and paperwork for the drug bust in Clearwater. Remember to send me an invitation to your meeting tomorrow? I presume it will be online?'

'Absolutely. I don't have time to drive up to Brisbane and back again. I'll forward you the meeting invite as soon as we finish this call. Oh, one last thing. Billy, when you process the cell tower feeds looking for Dark Web activity, do you think you could configure an alert system and tag me in?' asked Ange.

'Sure. It might not be the most elegant solution, but I'm sure I can cobble something together that will do the trick,' replied Billy confidently.

As Ange concluded the video call, she caught Billy looking up to the right, the telltale sign of someone deep in thought. Ange felt very confident that her colleague would bring home the bacon. Maintaining a live feed of the comings and goings of the protagonists was going to be critical.

That evening, once they were in bed, Gus tackled an elephant that had been creeping progressively into the room over the past few days. 'Ange, I hope you aren't getting in too deep and putting yourself back in the line of fire. I can't imagine that any group who are happy to abduct young women and sell them into prostitution would have many boundaries.'

'Don't worry. I think I've learnt my lesson. I promise to be careful and stay safe,' said Ange tenderly. Her track record suggested otherwise.

Chapter 33

A Somewhat United Front

A nge awoke just on 6 a.m. on Tuesday morning, summer sunlight imploring her to get out of bed. The day was well underway, and she walked out onto the veranda to greet an absolute cracker of a morning. The ocean glittered in the distance and a light offshore wind wafted, beckoning her. She felt the excitement and anticipation stir in the pit of her belly, the DTs of a surfer who was neglecting her addiction. In any event, her brain somehow worked better while she was surfing.

She woke up Gus and suggested that they take their morning exercise beachside. Gus was keen, as he wanted to try the first of the new Rusty midsize surfboards that his shapers had created. With the state of Queensland having spurned the concept of daylight saving, Ange had until midday local time before the start of her meeting. She would never understand Queensland's resistance to something that the rest of the world enjoyed. Sunrise at 4 a.m. seemed a crazy waste of the best part of a hot summer's day—but each to their own.

Gus assembled his work gear, and the pair drove separately down the hill towards the ocean, agreeing to meet at the southern end of Tallow Beach to check out the less crowded beach breaks. That Buddy had once again chosen to ride with Gus in the back of the Volvo had secretly annoyed Ange at first. However, as she followed them down the drive, she could see the attraction. Buddy had expansive views from the old station wagon, especially when he sat atop Gus's new Rusty. Even though this seemed entirely sensible, appropriate even, Ange still felt spurned and gave Buddy a mocking glare to drive the point home. He didn't seem to care.

Buddy was now a seasoned towel and car key watcher and seemed to enjoy the action. When she was waiting for a wave, bobbing out the back on her longboard, Ange often looked back to the beach and observed Buddy wandering around, checking out his immediate surrounds. Occasionally, he would seek some company from another surfer as they readied themselves, as if giving them a surf report and asking them to say hello to his master and mistress. If anyone walked towards their gear, Buddy would scamper back and sit down on his own special surfing towel.

The surf was small, and the session was more about enjoying the morning and being out in the water amongst such splendour. Gus caught the two best waves of the morning and was enthusiastic about how his new Rusty Cruiser performed. While they were sitting in the line-up after each wave, Gus would explain some of the small design tweaks that he would instruct his shapers to make to the next prototype. At one point, they swapped boards and Ange agreed with Gus that the Rusty seemed a winner, although she was a vastly less experienced surfer than Gus and no expert judge. As Ange called the session and made her way to the beach, Buddy came rushing down to the water's edge to greet her, barking at the waves and running up and down the wet sand excitedly. He added a delightful touch to the end of a surf session.

While she was standing on the beach, towelling off and waiting for Gus to catch his last wave, a guy came over and asked if her dog was called Rusty. 'Only in the movies' was Ange's obscure reply. Buddy was intent on Gus's whereabouts and appeared disinterested in his fame, taking the persona of a seasoned celebrity in his stride.

After partaking of brunch in town, the pair parted ways. Ange took Buddy home in the Prado and then readied herself for the weekly video call. Billy called just after 11 a.m. 'Hi, boss, I've built some software that sends you a text whenever we detect TOR is being used through those cell towers. We're only looking at three in Clearwater and two in Hillburn. The third tower in Clearwater hardly ever shows up. I had a look at the imagery of the area supported by that tower, and it makes no sense. There's a large agricultural supplies company, which is the only thing that I can think of. Here, let me insert a dummy event and you can see how it works.'

'Wow. That was quick, Billy,' observed Ange. She could hear his keyboard clicking madly away in the background as he set up the trial run.

'I was up all night working on it. Once I had the problem running around in my head, I just couldn't let it go.' Billy paused for a moment before Ange heard the responding thump of Billy hitting the Enter button. 'There you go. You should receive a text in a few seconds. I'll currently set the algorithm to run through each fresh data set at thirty-minute intervals, but we can change that anytime. I set up a variable for the interval, as I figured we might need a finer grain once we get into the thick of things.'

Ange's phone buzzed. She put the call on speaker and opened the incoming text message. It came from Billy's phone.

> *11.47: Clearwater 1: Start*

'I routed the texts through my mobile number. That way, I receive a copy as well. Anyhow, when the Dark Web session has been dormant for over five minutes, you'll get another similar text to tell you that transmission has ended. I've numbered both town-based cell towers as Clearwater 1 and Hillburn 1, and then 2 and then 3 as they radiate outwards from the town,' explained Billy. 'By the way, there has been regular activity in the Clearwater area, but absolutely nothing around Hillburn.'

'That's brilliant, Billy. I'm impressed. When will you start the software running?'

'I could activate it now, but it might get annoying until you need it. How about I send you a daily summary of movements? When you head into the field, I can then fire up the algorithm and you'll start receiving the text alerts. I wouldn't want to interrupt your beauty sleep, boss.'

'That ship had already sailed, Billy,' joked Ange before getting back to business. 'I like your idea of the daily summary. I can also forward your summary to my colleagues and keep them up to date. Anyhow, I need to jump on this video call. Thanks again. I'll let you know if anything comes from the meeting.'

After having some trouble with her microphone, she joined the meeting just as Sally Anders was explaining her attendance to Wallace. 'This investigation is tying up quite a few resources, Detective Wallace, so I need to stay on top of this. I presume you realise that we have one or two other investigations going on in New South Wales.' Anders saw Ange was online and passed the baton before affording Wallace any right of reply. 'Detective Watson has been busy. Why don't you fill in your colleagues, Ange?'

Ange spent the next fifteen minutes updating her Queensland colleagues on her findings in Hillburn, answering questions from both Judy Ly and Chris Lambert along the way. Chan had evidently returned from leave, but sat there impassively. Wallace looked as if the discussion was above his station in life. Once Ange's backgrounding exercise was complete, Sally Anders interjected. 'Detective Watson also may have stumbled over something else during her investigations. It seems to be an entirely separate matter, and being in New South Wales, our team will investigate that. Obviously, we will update you if any connections emerge.'

'What sort of matter?' asked Wallace, his first utterance since Sally Anders had dismissed him earlier.

'It looks like a localised drug operation. I came across it during my surveillance of the Dark Web, quite by accident. It was a plausible location for where Kwm might have escaped from, so it will be a lucky side benefit—if it pans out,' said Ange. 'Which reminds me. Why didn't anyone properly investigate the area around where Cua Kwm was found? I realise that there was likely a language barrier, and Kwm didn't fully explain how she got from the back of the utility vehicle to the church where she was found, but somebody should have canvassed the immediate area at the very least. It didn't take me long to find the service station where she first escaped to and hid. The proprietor was happy to assist and we may have been able to secure valuable CCTV footage. That would have saved us loads of time and we might even have been able to save the other women who were being held captive alongside Kwm.'

A look of indignation came over Wallace's face at this thinly veiled accusation; evidently he preferred to make the pointed accusations and not the other way around. 'It was a jurisdictional matter. Once Kwm was identified as an illegal immigrant, Border Force insisted on taking over. I suppose this detail fell between the cracks.'

'More like lost interest in a supposed illegal immigrant,' replied Ange, her face darkening in disgust at such shallowness, before turning the meeting's focus toward the future. 'It is what it is, I suppose. Moving on—my colleague has set up a feed from the cell towers in Hillburn. I'll be sent a daily report on any activity, which I'll distribute each morning. Hillburn has been quiet.' She then explained her theory about the supermarkets. 'Can you guys organise an order to source the video footage from the three major supermarkets? My strong hunch suggests the IGA. If you guys could sift through for the ten days before and after Kwm's escape, then we might spot someone or something out of the ordinary.'

'That could be thousands of people, Detective. We have better things to do than monitor shopping carts,' said Wallace, not giving up on his role as a stick-in-the-mud.

'I've been thinking about that,' commented Ange, doing her best to stay on an even keel amidst Wallace's petulance. 'I reckon these guys would use cash and avoid any EFTPOS transactions. Perhaps you could do a first cut and look for cash transactions. My colleague has some software that's brilliant for picking up stuff like that in video feeds. It might save you a lot of time and energy.'

Henry Chan then spoke. It was the very first utterance that Ange could recall since their initial introduction some weeks back. 'Can you get your colleague to send me the details on the software and we'll purchase a licence? Do you know if it's hard to use?'

'Apparently not. Billy, Constable Basset, has already offered to give you a training session online. He suggested an hour should be plenty of time to learn the basics. I'll get him to contact you.'

'Is there anything else?' asked Wallace impatiently. Ange ungraciously wondered if their meeting was keeping him from another tee time.

'We need some video surveillance of the property,' said Ange quickly, before explaining her ideas about that. 'Can you guys sort something out? I think we should do it straight away while the property seems to be unoccupied.'

'We don't have the resources for that sort of stuff,' replied Wallace, equally quickly.

Sally Anders was having none of this. 'That's OK. We have some friends in the federal police in Brisbane. They're very skilled in this stuff and I'm sure that they would love to assist.'

'We don't want anyone else involved in this case. It's already too crowded as it is,' spat out a gruff Wallace. Evidently, this discussion was not going how he had planned.

The *crowd* he was referring to was quick to rebut. 'This is probably as much a federal matter as a state matter,' said Sally Anders sharply. She moved on before Wallace could protest further. 'Now, there's still the detention centre to deal with. I suggest that you and I approach the immigration minister, Detective Wallace. If you could let me know your availability over the next few days, I'll set something up. Ange will send you my email address.'

Before Wallace had any time to react, Anders cut him off at the pass. 'Detective Watson and I have another meeting to attend. If there is nothing else critical, I'll look forward to getting that email, Detective Wallace.' Without waiting for any reply, Sally Anders hung up, leaving Ange in the spotlight. Her phone started ringing, so she promptly thanked the others and exited the meeting. It was Sally Anders calling.

'What a tool. I had to leave. I couldn't bear it any longer and I probably would have said something totally inappropriate. Now, down to business. Operation Clearwater is on for Friday. I've already secured a search warrant and sent it to Jim Grady, so I suggest you pop by and see your old boss this afternoon if you can.'

Somehow, the universe seemed to speed up whenever Sally Anders was in range.

Chapter 34

Operation Clearwater

After checking that Jim Grady was at the station, Ange dressed in something appropriate and readied herself to head back down to Byron Bay. Before she left, she fired off an email to Billy containing the contact details for Henry Chan, asking him to include details of his video analysis software and how Chan should go about getting a licence. She suggested Chan would appreciate some guidance on how to navigate the system and get the best out of it.

Within thirty minutes, Ange was on the road back to Byron. She dropped off Buddy for a royal visit at the shop. Ange was like a wallflower compared to the reception that Buddy received from the staff and any customers in sight. Ange just shook her head and drove over to the station. As she walked through the office, she brushed off the pathetic greetings of Walton and Lynch as she passed by their desks, driving home the message that they had crossed the line with their puerile gossip-mongering. She popped her head into Bree's little office to say hello. She looked tired and Ange said as much.

'I didn't realise how much the test series would take it out of me. Once the adrenaline of competition was behind me, I sort of collapsed physically. Anyway, I've started my skulking around the Dark Web. It's a tough place to navigate if you don't know specifically where to go. Do you have any clues that might help me narrow my search window?'

'No, sorry. Don't worry too much about it. It was just a thought. I figured that stalking the Dark Web was unlikely to be a waste of time for us in the longer term anyway,' answered Ange.

'I'll keep looking. My current alter ego is a guy called Merv the Miner from Moranbah. I'd like to say that he's a rough diamond, but he's actually a bit of a pig. Merv is lonely and wants an Asian bride. Apparently, he's suffering from the delusion that an Asian bride is like a slave with benefits,' replied Bree with a wicked smile. Ange grimaced at the vision of Merv from Moranbah, skulking on the Dark Web to buy an Asian slave for a wife—had he been a real person, that is.

Jim Grady was ready for her, having already spoken to Sally Anders. They agreed to set off Thursday after lunch and get settled for the following day. Ange suggested they pose as father and daughter, with Jim Grady taking on the role of helping Ange look for real estate. Ange planned to bring Buddy, as he was probably already recognisable by a few of the local townspeople. The plan was for the drug enforcement guys from Tweed Heads to deal with the property that Ange had identified. She was at pains to reiterate that she couldn't be one hundred percent sure of her theory. Ange and Grady would tackle the council CEO once the drug farm was under control.

Ange busied herself over the next few days. Now that they had set a date for the operation, Billy had activated his text alert system for Dark Web activity and she was receiving regular text alerts from Clearwater, sometimes three or four alerts in a day. There was nothing happening in Hillburn and she was happy with this, as they weren't ready to pounce on another shipment of trafficked immigrants.

She reasoned it would be wise to get a better sense of whatever was going on at the Green River Council. Ange contacted Sandy Ellis to get the phone number for Brendan Tame and she rang him straight away. Tame answered with a tentative 'Hello', the modern-day gold standard for how to greet an unknown caller.

'Mr Tame?'

'Yes, who's asking?'

'My name is Detective Ange Watson. I wanted to ask you a few questions about your time at Green River Council.'

'Don't tell me she's pressed charges. What a crock. Talk about kicking a man when he's already down.'

'No, not at all, certainly not that I'm aware of. I'm investigating a separate matter. Your colleague, Sandy Ellis, suggested that I contact you. Can you tell me what happened that led to your leaving the Council?'

'Let me state at the outset that I never touched the woman or acted inappropriately towards her. She disgusts me if I'm honest, breezing into town with her grand plans and an even bigger ambition. I felt she was acting above her level of authority and should have been involving the Council in her ideas. Bennet didn't see it that way, intimating that the Council was overly conservative and holding back progress.'

'Can you tell me about Samsons Road and the problems that you had?' asked Ange as gently as possible.

'Well, she wanted to extend council services further down the road. I pushed back, feeling that it wasn't fair for other ratepayers to be subsidising a scant few properties. She had this idea that we should attract more intensive industry to the region and had targeted Samsons Road. I don't have a problem with that idea, but that was a decision for the Council, not Julia Bennet. I threatened to take my concerns up with the mayor, but I shouldn't have been so transparent. She immediately accused me of sexual harassment. With all these high-profile cases swirling around in the media, I understand that my guilt will be assumed.'

Tame paused for a moment to catch his breath, such was the rising intensity in his voice. 'The crazy thing is that I probably gave her the idea when I pushed for the council to adopt a workplace harassment policy. My sister had been a victim two years ago, and her employer had offered no support. Other than going through the wringer of a police investigation, she had no mechanism to pursue her concerns and was left feeling helpless and vulnerable. Knowing that the offender remained untouched and free to do it again has turned my sister into a bitter woman.'

As Ange listened to Tame, she concluded his story had the ring of truth about it. Unproven, for sure, but credible enough for her to doubt the validity of Bennet's claim. Even after the *#MeToo* movement, Ange knew from the data that men still perpetrated most sexual misconduct crimes. However, Ange didn't like the way society instantly assumed the worst. Despite her age, she was old-school about the notion of a person's presumption of innocence. Even though she was guilty of jumping to assumptions from time to time, this was a bias towards her own theories, not shallow stereotypical assumptions.

'Did you ever speak to the mayor about your concerns?'

'No, I never got around to it. I was stood down from work almost immediately. At least she paid me a decent termination payment. She told me that the council didn't need the scandal and it would be better for everyone if I just slipped away into the sunset. The trouble is that I'm having trouble getting a new job without a reference from my previous employer. My pride won't let me grovel up to that woman,' said Tame bitterly.

'Did you have any other issues or concerns?' asked Ange.

'Not really. I figured that Julia Bennet would soon lever herself into a more prestigious job in the city. My original plan had been to see her out, but when I saw what she was doing, I felt I had to speak up. We would have needed to clean up her mess once she was off grazing in greener pastures. Confronting her and being upfront was certainly a big mistake on my part—one that I won't make again.'

'Thank you, Mr Tame. You've been most helpful. I'll contact you should I find anything that might help your situation,' promised Ange as she hung up the call. Brendan Tame was one bitter man—that was for sure. Ange wondered what part of Tame's explanation was fact and what was self-justification. She held herself back from making any snap judgements until she had fronted Julia Bennet herself.

Ange and Grady had taken turns at driving the Prado to ease the burden of the longish drive to Clearwater. At each change of driver, they let Buddy out to relieve himself. The drive took them in and out of mobile reception and Ange's phone beeped with three messages at one point, which was unusual for her new work arrangements. She waited until Grady was driving again before attending to them.

The first message was from the Tweed Heads team, who were expecting to arrive in Clearwater at around the same time as Ange and Grady. They would be staying in a unit behind one of the three pubs in town. Ange had booked a larger family cabin at the caravan park, one with two bedrooms and a separate kitchen. She texted back a message suggesting that the team meet up at her cabin for some takeaway Chinese. Even though Ange hadn't specifically scoped out any such establishments, every country town in Australia enjoyed at least one Chinese restaurant.

The second message was from a number which she didn't recognise. Expecting that this had been a scam caller, she was surprised to hear the voice of Henry Chan asking that Ange call him back urgently. The third message was also from Chan, reiterating his earlier request.

Ange asked Grady to pull over lest they fall out of mobile reception again. Henry Chan got straight down to it. 'I'm pleased you got my message, Detective. Something has come up that I thought you needed to know about.'

'Please call me Ange. What's up, Detective?'

'Your hunches have been spot on. I didn't need to go any further than the IGA, and it didn't take long to identify what I was looking for. That software that your colleague helped me install is impressive.'

'That was quick. I wasn't certain that focussing on cash transaction would work. There must still be scads of cash sales in a place like Hillburn,' commented Ange.

'Maybe, but I added a further twist and searched for anyone with a tattoo as well. You can imagine that this might narrow things down somewhat. Even though tattoos are common amongst younger generations, few of them pay with cash, mostly doing everything via their mobile phone.'

'Why the tattoo?' asked Ange.

Chan avoided any specific answers to Ange's question. 'I found something disturbing. The guy who paid for the food had some very enlightening tattoos on his hand. These are very serious guys, Detective—I mean Ange. We need to be careful. Are you certain that Clearwater and Hillburn aren't connected?'

'I guess I can't be certain. Why do you ask?'

'The business of trafficking women for prostitution is a bit of a loss-leader for the Chinese Triads. Once they get their hooks into someone, their arrangement will often extend to include drugs, protection, and even gambling. The Hillburn operation will be one of many cells operating around the country. This is not a one-hit wonder that we have here, I'm sure of that. It isn't beyond the realm that the drug operation in Clearwater could be another line of business for them.'

Ange needed a moment to process this new information, as well as come to grips with Chan's fresh attitude. 'Chinese Triads. Out here? Surely you can't be serious. Anyway, I thought you weren't particularly engaged in this investigation. Why the sudden change of heart?'

'Oh, you are completely mistaken. I was always engaged. I just didn't see that we were ever going to get anywhere. Wallace is nothing more than a social climber and Judy Ly is still green. Chris Lambert has some solid experience, but this would be his first time on a case like his. Frankly, if you hadn't come along and tipped over the apple cart, I would have kept working this case on my own. And, yes, I am deadly serious about the Chinese Triads.'

'That explains a lot, frankly. I have time for Judy and Chris, but I share your thoughts about Wallace. I think my boss has his measure for the moment. So, are you suggesting that we take a deep breath until we totally rule out any connection between Clearwater and Hillburn?'

'Yes, that's my advice. If they turn out to be separate operations, then no harm is done. However, if there is a link and you move on Clearwater, they will quickly pivot and we will lose the trail. Remember, we're only here because of Cua Kwm's bravery. I, for one, don't want her sacrifice to go to waste.'

Ange felt as if the universe had shifted slightly, giving her a view of another world, one where Henry Chan was a chameleon who had been hiding in plain sight. 'OK. I hear you. We'll look to scale back the operation to purely surveillance and report back. I'll need to clear this change of approach with my boss, but I'm sure that she'll back my judgement. Thanks for the heads-up, Henry. I appreciate it,' concluded Ange, before she had another thought. 'By the way, I have someone trawling the Dark Web looking for anything that might connect with the people trafficking operation. Once the victims are in Australia, they surely need to be placed into the field and start earning money at some point. The trouble is that she has absolutely nothing to guide her and filter out all the noise. I'm no expert, but I'm told that the Dark Web is very hard to search and look around unless you know specifically where you're going. Do you have any ideas that might help?'

There was silence at the end of the line while Chan thought this through. 'I really can't point to anything, but I have had the word *shama* mentioned by one of my informants.'

'What, as in the mystical medical man?' asked Ange.

'No, that is a shaman. Shama, spelt S-H-A-M-A. The word has two potential meanings, either as a woman's name or an Asian songbird. I think the latter is more likely, as the woman's name is more of Middle Eastern origin. There's a massive illegal trade in Asian songbirds, and various shamas are highly prized. Maybe the name points to illegal songbird trafficking rather than people trafficking. I can't be sure. Sorry, but that's the best idea I have.'

'OK. Thanks for the heads-up, Henry.'

She ended the call and sat back in the passenger seat. 'Huh. That sure caught me by surprise.' Using the car speakerphone, she dialed Sally Anders so that Grady could also listen to the update.

'You make the call, Ange,' replied Anders once Ange had completed her briefing. 'You and Jim are in the field and in the box seat. By the way, did you ever do
any background work on Henry Chan, Ange?'

'No, I didn't. I don't have that sort of clearance to look into Queensland police
officers,' pleaded Ange, realising this failure to understand her team. Relying on
her own shallow assessments was a grave error on her part. So much for avoiding
stereotypical assumptions.

'Ex-Cabramatta vice before moving to Queensland two years ago. It seems a
big step backwards to end up working under the moronic David Wallace. Maybe
I should try to lure him back to New South Wales and into the fold. Anyhow, I'll
leave this to you guys.'

Like all good bosses, Sally Anders knew when to trust the judgement of her
team and not helicopter every situation. Once settled into their cabin, Ange took
Buddy for a walk, planning to pick up their Chinese takeaway meal on the way
back. She was approaching the restaurant when her phone pinged with a text.

18.04: Clearwater 1: Start

It tempted her to race off back to the cabin, but she resisted this urge. The
text alert didn't really change anything. They still had a lot of work to do, even
considering the scaled-back operation. She put the phone back in her pocket and
walked in through the front door to pick up her takeaway meal. Luckily, as things
transpired, the force of habit had made her assume the identity of the useful
Gloria White.

She threw her residual misgivings about any link between Clearwater and
Hillburn out the door when she noticed the guy sitting down to a meal in the
restaurant. Well built, mixed race, Eurasian, an appearance that leaned neither
one way nor the other. The guy remained fixated on fiddling with his mobile
phone and never looked up at Ange. She surveyed him from the corner of her eye
and there was an iciness that sat within his eyes that made her skin crawl. Ange
instinctively looked back to check that Buddy was safely outside. She felt sure he
would have growled deeply and attracted attention.

She couldn't help but notice that his right arm was heavily tattooed.

Chapter 35

A Lucky Catch

It took all her will to walk slowly and calmly back to the cabin, acting out the part of a plain old tourist, walking her dog on the way to pick up some takeaway dinner. When she arrived at the cabin, she could hear the debate raging inside as the two guys from Tweed Heads pushed Jim Grady to agree that the operation should continue as planned. She caught a thick South American accent in the mix, adding some distinct colour to their discussion. Before she had even introduced herself, Ange pulled them up quick smart. She told them of the coincidental happening of a few minutes before and the corresponding Dark Web text alert. 'Guys. Pulling down a local drug operation is one thing, but we cannot afford even the slightest possibility that we might mess up our investigation into the people trafficking case.'

'What do you mean, people trafficking? We were told that this was a home-grown drug deal.'

'Sorry, Ange,' said Jim Grady. 'I didn't think it was my place to brief them on your other operation. I don't know all that much about it myself.'

It was the first time that Jim Grady had deferred to Ange like that, and she took a moment to acknowledge this. 'That's OK, boss. It's my fault. Until just now, I was convinced that the two sites weren't linked. How about we start from scratch?'

Ange took a moment to introduce herself and get to know her temporary workmates. She soon learned that Andre Martinez was ex–Brazilian military, the narcotics unit. Apparently, Martinez had rattled the wrong cage and had to leave the country several years back. Gary Franks had come up through the ranks like Ange and had over ten years' experience under his belt. Ange took in both men as they narrated the abridged versions of their careers. She figured Martinez was the muscle and Franks the tactician.

Once the makeshift team had a sense of each other, Ange explained how she had first seen the likely drug exchange under the bridge one evening. Buddy slunk his way inside the cabin, obviously feeling left out of the party. After he had received pats from everyone, he lay down comfortably beside the door, evidently now satisfied with the state of things.

Ange pulled out her tablet and went through the logic of how she had identified the subject property and why she suspected it to be a drug factory. She realised how many times she had used the words *likely* and *possible* during her briefing, bringing forth a rush of self-doubt to rattle her confidence. She shoved those doubting thoughts from her mind and pressed on. 'I'm making the call that we use this trip to set up some surveillance. Did you guys bring any useful kit with you?'

'Yep, our usual stuff should be in the vehicle. What are you thinking?' offered Franks.

'Can you guys install some cameras under the bridge, focussed on this small car park?' said Ange, pointing to her tablet to identify the precise location where she had seen the likely drug trade.

'Easy. Do you know how busy the car park is? It would be easier during daylight, but we could do it after dark. Nothing good happens after 2 a.m., we all know that,' said Martinez in his thick Brazilian accent, bringing some levity back to the situation.

'How about you scope it out early tomorrow morning? It's going to be a stinker, so we might find a window late morning. How long would you need?' asked Ange.

'Just a couple of minutes once we have the installation planned out. Five tops,' replied Franks.

Ange's phone buzzed with another text.

> *19.06: Clearwater: End*

'Great. I need to speak with my colleague about what I just saw. You guys should tuck into the food. It smells pretty good.'

It was tempting to rush over to the bridge to see if she could identify someone or something concrete. Ange suppressed those precipitous thoughts and rang

Henry Chan's number. Chan must have been at home, as she heard the lively chatter of a young child in the background. After apologising for ringing him at home after hours, she summarised what had just happened. She then tackled something which had been bothering her all afternoon. 'What I don't understand is, if Chinese Triads are behind the drug farm, why would they risk selling product locally? This would seem a tiny marketplace and not worth the risk in their grand scheme of things.'

'I agree. Maybe he's earning a bit of cash on the side and skimming some cream from his bosses. That would be dangerous and could offer us some leverage if we can bring him in. Did you get a look at his tattoos?'

'No. I was trying to stay inconspicuous. I'm pretty sure he never saw me. Except for one council worker, who has agreed to remain discreet, nobody in town knows I'm a police officer. I'm ostensibly looking at real estate. We're putting together a plan to install some video surveillance gear where the drug handoffs take place.'

'Great. If I could get a decent look at him, I might identify which Triad he works for. The video imagery of the IGA was quite low resolution. What about surveillance of the drug farm you identified?' asked Chan.

'That's going to be trickier. I might waste the time of a local real estate agent and get them to take a run past the property to scope out that possibility. I don't want my car to be seen too often. They probably have their own surveillance cameras guarding the place.'

'OK. Let me know how it goes. By the way, your boss is all action. She has a federal police officer heading out to Hillburn to install some surveillance on the ridge you identified. She mentioned you know him from a previous operation. A guy called Andy?'

'Top-shelf,' was all that Ange was prepared to admit about her relationship with the feds.

'Let's stay in touch. Good luck,' said Chan as he hung up from the call.

Ange rejoined her colleagues to map out their plan for the next day. She explained a desire to get some surveillance on the drug farm. She had a sudden brainwave and pulled up the map that Billy had provided, the one that showed the cell tower that had alerted them to the location. It was constructed on a ridge, perhaps two kilometres away from the property as the crow flies. She turned to her new colleagues. 'Tell me, what sort of resolution could you get at, say, two kilometres?'

Martinez looked at Franks, who took a moment to finish a mouthful of Mongolian lamb before answering. 'It's a chicken and an egg thing. The higher the resolution, the higher the power drain. Also, I can't really set a motion activation at that distance. It would pick up everything. The battery would die in no time.'

'What if you had a power source?' asked Ange.

'I could read your business card,' said Franks confidently. 'What do you have in mind?'

She pointed to the cell tower and explained her brainwave. Franks brought a reality check to the party. 'I'd need to know my way around the installation. I don't expect it would be in our interests to take the tower offline. Also, I could only make that sort of installation during the day, and someone scaling a cell tower would be obvious.'

'Point taken. Leave that with me,' said Ange, shovelling a few mouthfuls of fried rice down her throat before ringing Billy. As he answered, she could hear the unmistakable sound of a pub in the background. 'Yes, boss? What is it now? Can't you do anything without me?' he jested.

'Sorry to interrupt your online gambling, Billy. Can you get hold of your contact in Telstra and tell them we need the services of their local technician? They'll need to drop everything. It must be tomorrow. Give them my number to ring with an ETA. And, Billy, don't take no for an answer. Get the boss onto it if necessary.'

'Are you going to tap into the comms? That's technical stuff, boss.'

'Nothing so fancy. We just want to install a surveillance camera. Not only will the technician provide cover, but they will also give us the technical advice that we need to tap into a power source without blowing up the tower.'

'I'll get onto to it first thing. Tomorrow, you say?'

'Yes, Billy, it must be tomorrow. Use all your boyish charms on your Telstra contact. Oh, and say hello to Nelson for me.'

There was little more that the team could do that evening, and they departed to their respective digs. The next day was shaping up as a busy one.

Chapter 36

Good Service

A nge woke early and let Buddy off his leash to do his business, following along obediently with a plastic bag to collect his inevitable ablutions. She wandered down towards town and was pleased to find Pam's cafe getting ready to open. Pam remembered Ange immediately. 'The coffee machine will take a few minutes to heat. Flat white with an extra shot—isn't it?' Ange nodded at this accuracy. 'I knew that you'd come back to Clearwater after your look around the other towns. Everyone does. Tell you what, why don't you walk down and have a look in Glenda's window and see if she has any properties listed that you might like? I never got your name?'

'Gloria White. Pleased to meet you. I presume your name is Pam?'

'It would be a silly name for a cafe if it wasn't,' laughed Ange's friendly barista. 'Come back in ten minutes. I assume you want two coffees?'

Ange rammed home her cover. 'Yes, but I'm here with my dad this time. He's a bit more experienced in real estate than I am.'

Pam's eyes lit up, as if sensing that she had a live one on the line. Perhaps she might be due for a spotter's fee from her friend Glenda. 'Webster's First National. It's just around the corner on the main street. See you in ten.'

Ange made a show of wandering Glenda's way before collecting her coffees and heading back to the cabin. Jim Grady was grateful for the caffeine hit. 'The guys were busy last night. Gary came by while you were out. They scoped out the bridge in the early hours of the morning and already installed the camera. He's just bringing it online now. You should go for a walk and check it out. It's impressive. I couldn't see it.'

Ange wandered along the riverfront to the bridge, finishing her coffee on the way. She also could not spot the camera at a casual glance. Her phone buzzed with a text.

I gather you couldn't spot it either. Excellent. Gary

Evidently, the camera was now online. Ange texted back a smiling emoji and a thumbs up, an accurate description of her thoughts. This was terrific progress. Now they could spend the day focussed on securing video from the cell tower.

As soon as 9 a.m. came around, Ange took Grady up to visit Glenda Webster. It came as no surprise that Glenda was expecting a Ms Gloria White to swing by. She probed Ange for information on what type of property she was looking for. Ange explained she had been driving around and liked the valley serviced by Samsons Road. Either that valley or the next one further to the north. Glenda offered to give them a tour. Ange had thought this scenario through and suggested that her father needed the car to visit an old friend. 'Perhaps we could go in your car, Glenda?' suggested Ange, not wanting her white Prado seen too often driving along Samsons Road.

Glenda did what real estate agents do and made a detour to several alternative places along the way. Ange expressed disinterest in all of them. 'So, tell me. What are the key attributes that you are looking for?'

Ange had also concocted a story during the night that would almost certainly lead them down Samsons Road. 'Well, my husband runs an online marketplace and I dabble in cryptocurrency and the like. We need strong and reliable internet service. Also, strong mobile phone reception is critical. My husband is always on the phone trading something or other. And when he's not doing that, he likes to play the drums. It would be best that we have some distance from any neighbours. It's one reason we plan to move to the country. We can manage all our business remotely, but my husband fancies himself as a rock star in the making. Believe me, I've tried to dampen his enthusiasm. Luckily for me, those new noise-cancelling headsets that I recently purchased work a treat.'

'Oh well, you were on the money, then. Samsons Road has some of the best mobile phone reception in the area—well, out of town at least. I have nothing for sale in that area just now, but let's take a drive that way. I can approach the owners of any properties that you like.'

They chatted aimlessly on the drive over. Glenda worked hard to extract as much information as possible and Ange was enjoying expanding on the fantasy world of Gloria White. She made another mention of having children and wondered where this proposition had sprung from.

Once they reached the dirt section of Samsons Road, Ange pointed out what she liked and didn't like about each property that they slowly passed by. As they passed the suspect drug farm/lab, Ange commented that the property seemed overdeveloped. Apparently, Glenda felt the same way. 'Yes, it's a bit out of character, that one. I don't really know the owners.' She pointed to a cell tower on the ridge. 'There's your cell tower. I think this valley is better than the next. It opens out, so we have more options with strong reception. The next valley closes in on itself and reception isn't as good.'

After completing a slow and steady drive up and down Samsons Road, Glenda chattering real estate stuff the whole time, Ange insisted on taking a drive through the next valley—just in case. Once there, she could see what Glenda had meant by the valley closing in, and there were only a couple of properties that would suit the highly specific needs of Gloria White. She took special note of the dirt road that snaked up towards the cell tower. Her phone buzzed with a message from Billy with a business card attached.

> *Hi, boss. Doug from Telstra is coming across from Gunnedah. He should be there by 11am. Give him a call.*

Ange had seen and heard enough, so suggested that she needed to head back to town. 'Dad is having lunch with his mate and I need to check up on my dog. I think you have a good sense of what I'm looking for. If you give me a card, I'll text you my contact details and we can stay in touch.' Glenda Webster felt that her sale might slip away and suggested some other locations in the area.

'We're in no desperate hurry, Glenda. Something will come up, I'm sure. I love Clearwater and I think we would enjoy living here. You've been a terrific help,' said Ange, ending the debate but giving Glenda a glimmer of hope that a future commission might be coming her way.

As soon as Ange was back at the cabin, she forwarded the contact details to Gary before ringing him. 'Can you contact Doug, the Telstra technician? I just texted you his contact details, so how about you guys sort out the details? I just took a drive out that way and you should have a clear line of sight from the cell tower. Frankly, I doubt that you'll need to climb to the top, but I'll leave that to you and Doug from Telstra.'

After she had hung up from the call, she turned to Grady. 'Boss, you need to go for a drive. I told the real estate agent that I needed to be back to mind Buddy while you had lunch with a mate. This town has big ears and eyes. There's nothing we can do now anyway, so find somewhere nice to have lunch. I read a story about a gastropub that's only ten minutes' drive south of here. Apparently, some high-end chef left Sydney for the good-life in the country. I had it scoped out when Gus and I came by, but our timing didn't work out. It gets terrific reviews. Enjoy yourself.'

Ange did some admin, preferring the air-conditioned comfort of her cabin to the oppressive heat outside. She imagined how hot it would be for the guys scaling the Telstra cell tower. By 4 p.m., Grady was back from his 'exceptional' lunch and the video camera was in place on the cell tower. Ange suggested the guys pick up some food and pop over again to show Ange the fruits of their labour.

When they arrived with the food, Gary installed some software on Ange's tablet and logged her in to both camera feeds. 'The one on the tower is permanently online, but the camera under the bridge is motion-activated and only works after sunset. It's infrared and I've set it up that way to preserve the battery, but we can change the settings from here.' He pressed a tab and toggled the camera on and off, the video feed distinctive with its grainy green hue. He then pressed on the tab for the other camera. It was dark, and the vision was poor. Gary tapped on a slider and pulled up some earlier recorded imagery and zoomed in on the property. 'That's incredible.' Ange could read the number plate on the car parked beside the house. She jotted it down and sent a text to Billy, asking him to check if it was the same vehicle she had seen during her last trip to Clearwater.

'What's even better is that I can train the system to alert us to specific movement. For instance, if I select that dual-cab, we can set up an alert whenever it moves. I've still got some more configuring to do, but I'll let you know when I'm done. Are there any specific things you want to look out for?' asked Gary.

'No, I think the vehicle would make sense for the moment. Once we get closer to raiding the place, we should also focus on any human movements, but I guess that might drive us crazy in the meantime.'

Even though their operation hadn't followed their original plan, it had been a successful trip. After dinner, they agreed to go their separate ways until next time. Ange hoped that the Hillburn installation was going equally well.

After breakfast at Pam's, sticking with their father-and-daughter charade, the pair left Clearwater just on 9 a.m. and were back in Byron by lunchtime After seeing her old boss off and grabbing some lunch, Ange drove home to change clothes, pick up her longboard and head back down to the beach for a late-afternoon surf. The breeze was out of the south-east and she figured The Pass would provide the best chance for a surfable wave.

With rangy dogs unwelcome at The Pass, Ange called by the shop to drop off Buddy and say hello to her other favourite male, who promptly handed her a new retro-orange surfboard. 'Here. Give this new Rusty Cruiser prototype a try. It's a shorter version of the board I was riding last weekend.' He pointed to the square tail. 'I moved the fin further up the board, and the new square tail should give some more volume for smaller conditions. Let me know. I presume you're headed to The Pass. I plan to knock off work in about an hour, so how about Buddy and I swing by and see how you went? Perhaps we can catch an early dinner in town. We're down a staff member and were so busy today that I missed lunch.'

The surf was crowded despite the small conditions. Ange found her new Rusty Cruiser an interesting change from her other boards and soon started forcing long carving turns off the bottom. She loved how she could maintain her momentum and re-join the wave with speed. She had only enjoyed eight or nine rides before she noticed Gus and Buddy standing on the foreshore, so caught a last wave in and joined them. The pair discussed Ange's opinion of the board as she towelled off. Seeing as it was too early for dinner, she suggested that they take a walk up to the lighthouse. As Ange returned her gear to the Prado, she noticed that a WhatsApp message concerning Hillburn had arrived while she was in the water.

> *All done. I'll call you on Monday and tell you how to log in. Wife and kids with me. Stargazing tonight at Hillburn. Should be fun. Andy*

Everything was now in place. All they had to do was wait patiently.

Once the trio stood atop the headland beside the Byron Bay lighthouse, Ange gazed out over the expansive ocean from on high. She felt good about where things were and her role in getting there. Cell towers were sitting close to the surface of her subconscious and she mused that the lighthouse was an ancient form of cell tower, standing tall for generations and communicating across the ocean in constant vigilance.

The calming ocean scene below, accompanied by her two lovable friends, blended into a notion of confidence. She would not realise her lapse in judgement for days.

Chapter 37

A Waiting Game

'Billy,' said Ange when she called her colleague first thing on Monday morning. 'I can't believe that we never checked this before now, but would it be possible for you to check the cell tower feeds to see if there's been any two-way conversation between both sites? I guess that could be by text or phone, but I reckon they'd use one of the end-to-end encrypted messaging services like WhatsApp.'

'That should be pretty easy to do, boss. But they might have a fixed internet connection as well,' he replied.

'I thought about that. These guys are all mobile and transient. I can't see that they would risk the intrusion of installing and maintaining a fixed-line connection when both locations have excellent mobile phone reception. How long would it take to check it out? Focus on the period where we know Cua Kwm was being held captive. It was sloppy of us not to check this earlier. I was so convinced that these locations weren't connected. We could have blundered into Clearwater and blown the people trafficking operation to pieces.'

'I'll get back to you in a couple of hours. It's not a hard algorithm to write. Speak later, boss.'

Ange then rang Sally Anders and gave her an update on the situation. Once she had briefed her boss on the significant progress of the past few days, Ange confessed her error of judgement. 'I'm worried that I've lost my touch, boss. That was a rookie error I almost made. I should never have so blindly assumed that the two sites weren't connected. Even the most inexperienced investigator should have realised that activities like people trafficking, prostitution, and narcotics go hand in hand,' admitted Ange in a bout of self-flagellation.

'We all made that same error, Detective. You should add *trust nobody and assume nothing* to your list of favourite sayings. *Follow the money* hasn't exactly brought home the bacon. I assume that we're still on for tomorrow's meeting?'

Ange took in that thought and wondered if the job doomed her to become that person who trusted no one, or whether she could compartmentalise such a cynical view to her cases. 'Thanks, boss, I'm still not happy with myself. Yes. The meeting is still on at midday our time, at least as far as I know.'

'Good. Detective Wallace and I haven't been as productive as you have, although I am expecting a call from the minister's chief of staff this afternoon. If anything comes from that, we can cover it off tomorrow,' surmised Anders.

After Ange had hung up, she checked her messages. The phone had been buzzing with texts far too often and she had put her phone on silent. She saw that Clearwater 2, the tower near the drug farm/lab, had been active at various times, but there were no alerts showing for the other towers. She pulled up her tablet and checked the video feed, scrolling through the video on fast forward and observing two men, one familiar and one not, moving around the property at various times. The car hadn't moved.

The drug farm seemed to offer a lonely existence and Ange reflected on Gus's resistance to join the hobby farming set. Even though she had grown up on a rural property, she could not imagine returning to that former life, removed and isolated from the hustle and bustle of her new one. Who knew—maybe she would change her opinion as she aged? As things stood, the chances of Glenda Webster ever earning any commission from Ange/Gloria seemed remote at best.

Hopefully, Billy could resolve her concerns and either prove or disprove any connection between Clearwater and Hillburn. While she was waiting, she rang Bree to pass on the weak lead to the Dark Web that Henry Chan had offered. Bree had the same first medicine-man thought, so Ange spelt out the word for her, explaining the parallel crisis in Asia regarding the trafficking of songbirds. 'Who knows, it could be a clue for either songbird smuggling or a people trafficking operation. Shama is also a woman's name, so this could also be a complete dead end and just the stage name used by some Ethiopian online porn star. Sorry, but it's the best I can do.'

'Thanks, Ange. It's better than nothing and certainly better than floundering around as I currently am. How is the investigation going?'

Ange kept Bree somewhat in the dark and more focussed on prowling in the

Dark Web. 'We're making progress, but the general view is that we've only just scratched the surface and are most likely facing multiple cells. Keep going with your work where you can, please, Bree.'

Billy rang just after 10 a.m. 'Boss, your hunch was spot on. They were using WhatsApp to communicate. Not all that often, mind you, but I'm certain of my conclusions. There's been no synchronous communications for over a month.'

'Excellent, Billy, would you mind adding in another alert to tell us when you detect a connection? What's the word you used—synchronous? That's a good way to describe it. I'll use that myself. I might sound intelligent for once,' Ange smirked, pleased to have confirmed a connection between the Clearwater and Hillburn sites before any harm had been done.

Andy called soon after and told her how to access the video feed from the mountain ridge outside Hillburn. 'There's been zero action on the property, so I didn't see the need to bother you on the weekend.'

Ange followed his instructions and soon had a superb bird's-eye view of the Hillburn property on her screen. 'Wow, that's great. How long will the battery last?'

'Seeing as I didn't need to worry about size, I carted up the biggest battery I could get my hands on. It should last for over a month. Hauling all that gear up the ridge was hard work. I hid the installation amongst some rocks. Someone would need to step on it to find it. Mobile phone reception was excellent, so I don't see any problems with data transmission. Anyhow, we'll monitor this site and let you know when we see any action. Your boss said that she hoped to use us to take down the facility. Will you be joining us?'

'Not this time, Andy. Our last adventure was way too much fun. You guys were too slow off the mark for my liking,' she joked before getting back on track. 'We've stumbled across an associated location further south. My guess is that we will want to coordinate our moves and take them down simultaneously to limit any communications. We've installed surveillance there also, and we'll monitor that site. Thanks for your help. By the way, how was the stargazing?'

'It was incredible. I never knew about the dark emu. I've always just looked at the Milky Way as a big smear of stars. When I look at that galaxy now, all I can see is the emu that lurks in the darkness between the light. We had an Aboriginal man explain his traditional stories about the stars and the constellations. The kids were agog and they haven't stopped talking about it. Anyhow, got to go. No doubt we'll be speaking again soon,' said Andy.

Ange twiddled her thumbs for the next twenty-four hours, the regular text messages interrupting her attempts at assembling any worthwhile chain of thought. She was pleased when the time came around for the weekly meeting with her Queensland colleagues.

Henry Chan was an entirely different person from the one who had attended previous sessions. He briefed the team that they were almost certainly dealing with Chinese Triads, reiterating how serious they were. Ange piped up and told them how her team had now confirmed the two sites had been communicating during the period that they held Cua Kwm captive. She also explained that multiple video surveillance installations were active in both locations.

'If the guy in Clearwater is dealing on the side, we might use that as leverage to get him to talk. He won't want it known that he was skimming from his bosses,' added Henry Chan.

'We need both operations to happen simultaneously, as we don't need to risk one group alerting the other. My view is that, should something go pear-shaped, we must prioritise the Hillburn incursion. Protecting anyone being held captive must remain a priority,' said Ange.

'I agree with Detective Watson. Why don't we set up a WhatsApp group so that we don't need to wait for any meetings to be convened? Also, we need a mobilisation plan. How about we work on that and shoot something around by close of business today?' offered Sally Anders.

The look on Wallace's face showed he felt control slipping through his fingers. Whereas before he had looked disinterested and convinced that the task force wasn't worthy of his full attention, he now seemed eager to get involved. 'Why don't we work out the mobilisation plan?'

Chris Lambert crossed the floor, much to the obvious contempt of Wallace. 'I agree with Detective Anders. You guys at Major Crimes seem to have the relationships with the SWAT teams and understand their capabilities.'

'Our two field teams need to be top-shelf. These are scary guys that we're dealing with here,' added Henry Chan.

'I can assure you of that, particularly the guys from the federal police. I wouldn't be here if they weren't,' confirmed Ange.

'OK, that's settled, then,' said Sally Anders firmly, killing any further discussion on that topic. She then threw Wallace a bone, knowing that having a recalcitrant on the team would help nobody. 'David, can you fill the group in on the progress we've made with the minister?'

The mention of Wallace in the same sentence as the immigration minister seemed to perk him up to no end. 'The minister had agreed to open a more fulsome investigation into Cua Kwm's death in the detention centre. I'm still not convinced that they will find anything, but it might bring some improvement actions to the table. The minister has also agreed that his department will process any victims under the Support for Trafficked People Program and ensure that they are treated more appropriately. Detective Anders here kindly brought the matter to the attention of the human rights commissioner.'

'Yes. I'm not sure what she said, but Commissioner Low seemed to put a giant rocket under their bonnets,' said Sally Anders with a sideways smile. 'OK. We've got work to do. Once we have the draft mobilisation plan, we'll share it around for comment. I suggest you guys lead the Hillburn operation, and we'll look after Clearwater.'

Once the meeting had concluded, Ange spoke to Sally Anders on the phone. 'I'm thinking it might be best to convene a meeting with both ground teams. Is that what you're thinking, boss?'

'Yes, bring me in on the planning this time, Detective. Since we can't be certain how many bad guys we might encounter, I think we need to be overcautious. By the way, how did you find the guys from Tweed Heads?'

'Very good. They both seem to know their stuff. However, I agree we should add another member to each team for safety's sake. After all, not counting Billings and me, we had a team of five supporting us on the ground in Namba Heads—and that almost wasn't enough. I'll set up a meet-and-greet between the two teams and send you a meeting invitation.'

Ange convened the meeting with the field teams post haste and was back online inside two hours. Sally Anders set the scene. 'We need to settle on a mobilisation plan. It's our view that we should take down both sites synchronously.'

Ange smiled when her boss stole her word, having stolen it herself from Billy. 'The trouble is that we don't know when the next shipment of victims will pass through the Hillburn facility. Once it gets recommissioned, we'll need to act quickly to limit any stress on the victims. They need to take priority over everything else,' Ange said, restating the obvious. 'My view, for what that's worth, is that we keep both teams on alert and ready to mobilise the minute we detect action at Hillburn. When we're in position, we can watch and wait to ensure the Clearwater site is occupied and then move in simultaneously.'

Matt, the chief technician from the federal police SWAT team, took over. 'Thanks for the background, Ange. That all makes sense. How about we map out an ops plan and send it to you guys to review? I think we have all the information we need,' he said, soundly dismissing the two detectives and leaving the formulation of an ops plan to the experts.

Ange was OK with this, but the look on the face of Sally Anders suggested she wasn't used to being dismissed like that. 'Sounds good to me, Matt,' replied Ange quickly. 'You guys are the experts. When will you have something for us?'

'Tomorrow morning at the latest,' replied Matt.

Sally Anders admired efficiency more than anyone and seemed mollified by Matt's air of quiet competence. Ange, for her side of the argument, had one more thing that she wanted to wrap into the operation. She needed to work that over in her mind and would confront her boss at an appropriate time.

Chapter 38

Action Stations

Ange had learned not to become upset with the everyday criminals who she locked horns with, and she sometimes found their antics downright amusing. It was those types who behaved as if the law didn't apply to them that riled her intently; those hiding behind their money, fame, or station in life, acting as if they were smarter and better than everybody else. Worse still, was that such arrogance came at the expense of others, those often less fortunate because of circumstance.

Ange had a bone to pick with the CEO of the Green River Council. Focussing her animosity, Ange imagined the CEO sitting in her expansive air-conditioned office in Clearwater, directing her staff to rush off and do this and that, perhaps using their endeavours to feather her own nest. These types rarely believed what they were doing was illegal, considering instead that they were simply playing the system, exploring loopholes that shouldn't have been there if the authorities weren't so stupid.

Playing the waiting game was never one of Ange's strong suits, and the next days, weeks, or even months suggested an excruciating time ahead, where her imagination would run rampant. The CEO was the perfect foil for such boredom.

She rang Billy to explain her latest idea. 'Billy, do you think you could set up another alert for synchronous communications between Clearwater 1 and 2 cell towers, and would it tell us anything?'

'Yes, we could do that, boss, but I doubt it would tell us anything. Residents would contact each other all the time through these towers.'

'How about WhatsApp? Is this used much in the area?' asked Ange.

'That would narrow it down, at least based on what I saw. It's possible, I suppose,' said Billy, sounding as if this was more a thought bubble than any statement of fact. 'I'll set it up now for WhatsApp comms. The alert will say Clearwater, colon, one, colon, two. Let's see what happens.'

Ange didn't elaborate any further and immediately ran her idea past Sally Anders. 'Boss, I want to bring down the CEO of the Green River Council as part of this. Not only do I suspect she's complicit in the Clearwater drug farm, but she also ruined the life of one of her employees, just to protect her own position.'

Ange explained what she had in mind and was pleased to secure her boss's blessing to put the plan into motion. She then rang the Green River Council offices, posing as Gloria White and asking to speak with Sandy Ellis, the officer responsible for refuse collection.

'Hello. Have we met, Ms White?' asked Sandy Ellis as she came onto the call.

'Not as Gloria White. I use that name occasionally when needed. It's Detective Ange Watson on the line. We met the other week when you told me about your colleague, Brendan Tame, and your suspicions about the CEO. Have you kept my presence in town confidential?' asked Ange.

'Absolutely. I don't even want my involvement known. I think I told you how much I need this job. What's up?'

'Would it be possible to stop refuse collection for a certain property for a couple of weeks? Perhaps for someone who hasn't paid their rates bill?'

'Well, I've never heard of such a thing happening here. I suppose it could. It wouldn't be hard to get the driver to skip a property or two. Why do you ask?'

Ange's plan relied on several properties being missed. Those that were innocent would undoubtedly ring Sandy Ellis to complain, and she could immediately put things right. If her suspicions were correct, the drug farmers would make their complaint directly with the CEO. They would want to keep their heads down with the council staff as much as possible. 'Sandy, I'd like you to direct the driver to skip three properties on Samsons Road, the area which has the incongruous refuse route. You could tell the driver that there are some biosecurity issues that you're working through and that the council doesn't yet have the authority to take anything off the properties. If any of the residents ring and speak with you, perhaps you could ask them some questions about whether they feel well and ask about any mystery rashes? You could then send a vehicle around to drop off a new bin and pick up the old one.'

Sandy Ellis went silent as she thought about Ange's proposal. Ange felt her support slipping away and went in for the killer blow. 'There's something odd going on out there, Sandy. It's potentially the reason your CEO got rid of Brendan with her harassment claim. We're only going to get one shot at exposing the truth, and this is the best idea I can come up with. There's more to it, of course, but you don't need to know the full extent of what we have planned. You can blame me if anything ever blows back on you. Major Crimes trumps local council—any day of the week.'

Sandy Ellis stayed silent for a moment longer. 'OK. I think I can pull off the plan you have in mind. With foot and mouth disease, monkeypox, and Covid, that story should hold up. I can tell the driver to keep it confidential. We wouldn't want any more pandemic hysteria sweeping through the town. Terry is a terrific guy. He'll be good,' said Sandy Ellis, getting comfortable with her role as a deputy in Ange's sting operation.

'Great, Sandy. Now, if you get any sort of sense that this might not stay confidential between you and the driver, or you aren't confident fibbing to any resident who calls you, we need to abandon this plan immediately.'

'I get it. Which properties are you looking at?'

'It's 242, 250, and 264 Samsons Road. Even though the numbers don't run sequentially, they're three properties in a row. When do rubbish collections normally take place?'

Sandy Ellis took a moment to answer as she checked her route map. 'We service Samsons Road on Mondays. What do I do if the CEO finds out?'

'Excellent point. If my theory is correct, the CEO will find out for sure. Perhaps you could say that the driver had some mechanical issues? You could explain that a few people had the same problem and that you're onto it.'

'That would work. It happens from time to time that a property or two gets missed. Rather than go through the whole mess of picking up their rubbish, I'll just offer for a spare bin to be dropped off and then picked up the following week. Will we need to go through this charade again?'

'No,' replied Ange definitively. 'Once will be enough. You can tell the driver that it was all a false alarm and to keep the matter strictly confidential. I like your idea of just dropping off a fresh bin and minimising any contact. Can you let me know which of the three residents contacts you directly?'

'Sure. I expect we'll know that by Monday evening. People don't mess around with a failure of the council to deliver a service—particularly when it relates to rubbish collection.'

'Perfect. You have my card. If anything comes up, or you have any second thoughts, please ring me straight away. We can always abandon ship and take our chances that the CEO slips up somewhere else.'

'No, it's all good,' replied Sandy Ellis. 'I trust that you'll have my back if necessary? I don't know what I would do without this job.'

'You can count on me, but I doubt it will come to that,' said Ange with conviction.

Ange reflected on how difficult it would be for a single mother to raise a family. Sandy Ellis's job was an essential component in keeping her life and her family together. Perhaps the same applied to Brendan Tame. It was always good to find something to keep the fire of rage burning brightly, and the image of Brendan homeless on the street worked wonders. The CEO was a marked woman.

Chapter 39

Preparations

The days stretched on interminably, save for the regular discrete text alerts from Clearwater 1 and Clearwater 2. At least they had secured video footage of two drug handovers going off under the bridge in Clearwater. Ange distracted herself with some surfing and doing her exercise each day. Surfing was less relaxing than usual, as her phone didn't like water and she was forever worried that the fateful call would come through while she was out at sea sitting on her board. She tried to limit her surfing time to before 8 a.m., something easily managed in the midsummer heat. She almost wished she had spent more money on a high-end smartwatch so she could answer calls while surfing. Well, almost...

The Australia Day holiday had come and gone, a day that had become a battleground of sorts. What used to be a day for all Australians to celebrate was now called Invasion Day by many, a day to feel guilty and ashamed. Aggrieved protestors had marched in cities and towns all over the country, something that had taken the shine out of the holiday. Some wanted the day moved, others insisted that the date stay put, and still others wanted it cancelled altogether. Ange had formed the view that a day for all Australians to celebrate what's great about their country seemed a wonderful idea and a true luxury, but the actual date appeared less important. It sounded easy, but finding a new date on the calendar that everyone supported would be difficult. After all, every date in history was significant, and it seemed easy to offend someone these days. Unfortunately, some of these protests had turned violent. She spared a thought for the perilous way that some of her uniformed colleagues had spent their holiday.

Bree checked in on Friday to tell Ange that she had a weak lead on the clue that Henry Chan had provided. 'I have to tell you, Ange, there are some sick puppies out there,' admitted Bree. 'I normally do my Dark Web skulking in chat rooms that are focussed on crypto and NFTs, but I started following every obscure lead I could find. It wasn't until I threw the word shama into the mix that I got anywhere. Merv-the-Miner took me to some dark places—excuse the pun. However, I have a feeling that I might be onto something, but I can't break through the front door.'

'What do you mean?' asked Ange.

'It's a niche Dark Web marketplace that appears to be offering a set of NFTs called The Songbird Collection. The only trouble is that the collection is password-protected and I have no way in. Nobody in the chat rooms knows anything—well, nothing they're prepared to disclose. It could be nothing, but why would anyone lock up an NFT collection like that if it was legit? Merv will keep digging. Once again, excuse the pun.'

'I agree. That makes no sense, Bree. Keep me posted. I look forward to hearing about your Dark Web journeys over a drink sometime,' said Ange.

After an aimless weekend and a slow Monday morning, Ange's phone pinged mid-afternoon with the alert that she had been hoping for.

Clearwater: 1: 2

Sandy Ellis phoned last thing that same day. She had received two calls from the unhappy residents of 242 and 264 Samsons Road, along with a generic complaint from the CEO about rubbish collection in the area. This not only confirmed Ange's misgivings about the CEO but it also added further weight to her suspicions about the middle property at 250 Samsons Road. Ange probed Sandy Ellis on confidentiality, and Sandy has assured her that everything was as tight as a drum.

It wasn't until Wednesday afternoon that the action started. The surveillance of the Hillburn property picked up some movement when two men arrived in a nondescript SUV. Henry Chan rang Ange to give her the news, adding that he had also checked CCTV footage from the local IGA and found that someone suspicious had made a substantial purchase of frozen goods and paid in cash. All of this pointed to the prospect that a fresh shipment of people might shortly arrive at the Hillburn property.

Ange and Henry convened an urgent online meeting of the task force, where they reviewed the status of the two operations and sense-checked their assumptions and conclusions. Sally Anders, now a self-invited fully-fledged member of the task force, got straight to the point. 'We need to mobilise the teams immediately. Assuming all our theories are correct, then once the trafficked victims arrive, we will want to extract them as quickly as possible. The longer we wait, the higher the risks. Neither location seems aware of our surveillance. However, and I know I don't need to say this again, we must always keep the safety of the victims paramount. Ensuring that the two incursions happen simultaneously should limit any communication between the two sites that might compromise our actions. Ange, you've been to both locations. What are your thoughts on how we might do this?'

Ange patiently explained her thinking to her task force colleagues. 'I've given this some thought. For efficiency's sake, it would seem logical to expect approximately six women, at least going by the testimony of Cua Kwm. Once we're confident that all the victims have arrived in Hillburn, I think it's safe to assume that they won't be moved again on the first night, but each passing day will add to the risk that one or more of the victims will be moved. Therefore, the timing rests with the Clearwater site. Based on our monitoring of both the Dark Web activity and our surveillance cameras, we should be able to predict when the perpetrators are present at the drug farm. My vote is that we get both SWAT teams to move into place on night one, and then we make the call from Clearwater once we're sure the drug farmers are on site. Of course, it's possible that all our theories are just that and nothing untoward is going on whatsoever.'

'I agree with all of that logic, but I seriously doubt this will turn into nothing,' said Henry Chan, proving to be much more of a leader than Ange had thought when they'd first met. 'Detective Watson should be the one to make the call. She'll be on the ground in Clearwater but also has the best feel for both sites.' The team nodded their assent to this proposal.

'Which brings me to a crucial element of this operation,' said Ange. 'We suspect that the group uses WhatsApp to communicate. We need to secure their mobile phones as a priority, preferably unlocked. If the perps are given any chance to shoot off an alert, my fear is that the wider operation will scatter and disappear into the background.'

'That makes sense. We should bring the field guys into the meeting and run through the arrangements. I'll invite the Clearwater team if you guys can get the Hillburn team into the meeting,' said Sally Anders.

There was a period of awkwardness, the type common in online meetings, waiting for everyone to arrive, where idle chatter seems inappropriate. Eventually, the meeting of six became fourteen. Everyone briefly introduced themselves. Joining the task force were Jim Grady, Andre Martinez, Gary Franks, and a new member of the Clearwater team, Nick Eastwood. The Hillburn team comprised Ange's old sparring partners from the Namba Heads shooting, Matt Wilks, Andy Barnett, and Will Fox, joined by a fresh-faced Sam Jessop. Ange noted an air of confidence in their respective introductions. She gave a full briefing of what they were involved in, going right back to the start.

David Wallace interrupted at one point and suggested that there was no need to go over every element. Sally Anders pulled him up, insisting that the team needed to get a full sense of this investigation. Henry Chan gave the group an understanding of who he felt was behind the people trafficking. Ange watched the body language of the team as he exposed the prospect of dealing with Chinese Triads. That is one problem with video calls comprising large numbers of attendees; body language is reduced to mere facial expressions, a poor subset of the full gamut of unspoken human interactions. Nobody flinched, except perhaps Jim Grady, whose seat seemed suddenly uncomfortable.

The meeting eventually stalled, as it hit the point in the briefing where everything that needed to be said had been said. Ange moved the proceedings on. 'Can you guys decide which of you should lead team Hillburn and team Clearwater? Henry and I will join the two team leaders in a WhatsApp group.' This proposal did not go down well with David Wallace. He made an issue about being included, seeing as he was *head of the task force*. Wallace graciously conceded that Sally Anders should also make the team.

Anders quickly shot him down. 'We need to keep the ops team as tight as possible and minimise any debate or discussion. If anyone has any misgivings about the plan or the people charged with executing the plan, you need to speak now. Otherwise, we should let them execute. We don't need to be second-guessing their every move and adding to the possibility of hesitation and the consequences of that. Anyway, David, you need to get a search warrant for Hillburn organised as soon as possible. We already have our warrant for Clearwater and you should get onto securing yours. Having someone of your standing take the lead on that should ensure the magistrate doesn't mess around.'

Wallace had been positively fuming at being cut off like that, but Ange was grateful that her boss had stepped in. The prospect of running around securing a search warrant was plainly not the role David Wallace expected to play, although Anders had buttered him up nicely. Nobody said a word, and Sally Anders pushed the meeting along. 'So, let's get the leadership group sorted now. Who's it going to be, guys?' There was no hesitation from either SWAT team, appointing Andy Barnett for team Hillburn and Gary Franks for team Clearwater.

'Guys, there remains a possibility that we've gotten it all wrong, and one or both sites are innocuous. Let's not be too heavy-handed until the situation demands it,' added Ange, misgivings over her recent experience with Internal Affairs coming to the surface.

Andy Barnett balanced those concerns with a voice of experience. 'Ange, I know what you're saying, but we can't come in all nice-and-friendly-like. We need to plan for the worst but hope for the best. We can apologise later if we need to. Now, if both teams are going to move in at the same time, we need to decide what time we're using, daylight saving time or eastern standard time. My vote is that we use daylight saving time.'

Wallace couldn't help himself. 'Why can't we use Queensland time? I'm sick of always kowtowing to southerners.'

'Queensland's out of step with the eastern seaboard over its refusal to adopt daylight saving. We're used to making the correction up here, so I figure we'll be less likely to make a mistake,' shot back Barnett.

Sally Anders then finished the meeting in fine style. 'I agree with that logic. Daylight savings time it is. I also agree with your tactics, Andy. We can't afford to be half-baked in our approach. OK. We all know what we need to do, so let's get on with it. Good luck, everyone.'

As soon as the video call was complete, Ange contacted Jim Grady and agreed to their travel arrangements. She decided it was best to leave Buddy with Gus. Ange was certain this would be no problem for anyone and braced herself for Rusty to make a much-awaited return to Kerrie's lifestyle blog.

After creating the leadership WhatsApp group, she sent her first message to tell everyone that she and Jim Grady should be in Clearwater by noon the next day, and each group should make their own accommodation arrangements.

Once her gear was packed, she set about preparing dinner. Seeing as she was heading back into the field, she went the extra mile to add some romantic flair, hoping that candlelight and flowers would set the scene for the after-dinner moves she had planned. As she stood at the kitchen bench, cutting and dicing her way to a chicken stir-fry, she struggled to push thoughts of a 'last supper' from her overactive and overstimulated mind. Sex would be the perfect segue to sleep, and she hoped her efforts would help put Gus in the mood. Not wanting to leave anything to chance, she chose a nice bottle of wine from Gus's wine fridge to help smooth the way towards this diversion.

The dinner and the sex were both superb, but neither proved effective in delivering a restful night's sleep.

Chapter 40

Clearwater Revival

During the drive over to Clearwater, Jim Grady broached a sensitive subject. 'Ange, you've only just recovered and you don't need to put yourself in line of fire again. Leave it to the SWAT team this time.'

'Don't worry, boss, I'm not planning any heroics. Hopefully, the only action either of us will see will be bringing down the CEO of Green River Council. After all, I'm too delicate and you're too old for that stuff anymore.' Grady railed strongly against the latter charge.

The pair rang Billy on the drive. 'Hi, Billy. I'm in the car with our old boss on our way to Clearwater. Just confirming that the alert system for Dark Web activity on the cell towers is still active. That's going to be critical. Can you also monitor for any synchronous communication between Clearwater and Hillburn?' asked Ange, using her new favourite word.

'Gee, boss. You've really made that word your own, haven't you? Yes, I will keep my multichannel comms surveillance system on high alert. You're free to appropriate that saying as well. I've just sent a dummy alert to your phone. It should say Clearwater, colon, Hillburn, colon, Active. That will alert you whenever the two locations are communicating. Did you receive it?'

Ange's phone buzzed mid-call. 'I'm driving, but something just came in. I guess that was you, but I'll let you know if we have a problem. Don't assume I'm monitoring everything. If you see something suspicious, call me or send me a separate message. How about I include you in the WhatsApp group for our ops team? I'll attend to that when we've arrived in Clearwater. Speak then, Billy.'

Once she and Grady were back in the familiar surroundings of their cabin, Ange sent a message to the ops team explaining the role Billy would play in monitoring Dark Web and communications activity, also checking that everyone was happy for her to add Billy to their WhatsApp group. After an especially uneventful few hours, she received an interesting call from Gary Franks.

'That makes sense about adding in your colleague to our WhatsApp group. We're fully setup on site in Clearwater. We've tucked our van down by the creek off Tolley's Road. That's in the next valley over from Samsons Road and the drug farm. It's a pleasant spot.'

'What? You guys are living in a van?'

'Yeh, sure. It's not the first time. This way we can each take turns to grab some sleep while another monitors the video feeds,' added Gary. 'It's OK for a day or so, but it gets smelly after that.' Ange wrinkled her nose at that thought.

There was no respite from this anxious waiting game, holed up in her cabin watching the paint dry, so to speak. Grady was no better, cleaning his weapon and mumbling about the work that would pile up on his desk back in Byron Bay. In desperation, Ange checked her social media feeds. She saw a post from Kerrie was getting a lot of attention and clicked on the link, only to find the face of her dog staring adorably back at her. He was promoting pet insurance. Ange rang her. 'Kerrie, you'll be the ruin of that dog.'

'You'll thank me when you hear the fee that I negotiated. Free pet insurance for five years!' said Kerrie, trumpeting her ta-da moment. 'I couldn't bear to think of anything bad happening to that beautiful boy.'

Ange couldn't help but laugh as she hung up from the call. How could one get upset with a friend like Kerrie on your team? A WhatsApp message from Andy Barnett pulled Ange out of the doldrums.

> *Ange, a large white Mercedes van just pulled into subject property. Six women on board. We're prepped to go whenever you make the call.*

Ange sprang into action and joined each of the team leaders in a conference call. After weighing up the options, they settled on a go-time of 12:15 a.m., around five hours from now. The two SWAT teams were keen to be in place well before their planned incursion, and they agreed to move into place at 9 p.m. Realising that it would likely be a long night, Ange ordered some more Chinese takeaway for collection at 8 p.m. and Jim Grady did the honours to retrieve their food.

They were just finishing dinner when Ange's phone started pinging with multiple Dark Web alerts for both locations. She rang Billy straight away. 'Billy, are you seeing this? Are they communicating? I hope our cover's not blown.'

'Yes, boss, I've been watching it as well. It's too early to tell what's going on. Give me thirty minutes and I'll come back to you.'

Ange immediately sent a message to the operations team.

> *Comms are underway at both locations. Suggest we temporarily suspend operations until we have reviewed at our end.*

Ange received a series of replies comprising a mixture of OKs and thumbs-up emojis. She paced around the tiny kitchenette, still reeking with the pungent smell of stale Chinese food. Other than her pensive footsteps, only the air conditioner droned on, straining against the omnipresent heat and pervasive silence outside. Billy took a full fifty minutes to reply, longer than she would have liked, and testing her patience.

The clanging phone startled the pair, and Ange swooped before it had time for a second ring. 'Hi, Billy. What do you think?'

'I'm pretty sure that these are separate communications. Sometimes they're both communicating at roughly the same time, but I'm confident that this is coincidental. There are two separate individuals at Hillburn and only one at Clearwater. I'm sure that your cover is intact.'

Ange breathed a heavy sigh of relief. 'Thanks, Billy. Can you keep on top of this and let me know if anything unusual pops up?'

No sooner had she hung up from the call than she received a call from Gary Franks. Ange imagined Franks sitting in his van, a discordant object set amongst the serenity of their hidden creek-side location. 'Hi, Ange, our drug farmer has just driven out the gate. It might be another delivery in town. We're monitoring this, but you should pull up the video feed as well.'

After letting Henry Chan and Andy Barnett know of this late development, she sat glued to her laptop screen. Twenty minutes later, the camera surveying the bridge blinked into action and Ange watched two cars drive slowly into the small car park under the bridge. Once their headlights were dimmed, Ange could see the grainy imagery of the drug handover. Within thirty seconds, the two protagonists had hopped back into their cars and driven off. Twenty more minutes elapsed before Ange saw the taillights of a car driving down Samsons Road and turning back into the drug farm.

She breathed a sigh of relief and rang Billy. 'Billy, can you keep monitoring Hillburn? Those guys are still busy on the Dark Web. I'm thinking we need an hour or two of silence before we move in. I'd prefer that most of the perps were asleep when the SWAT teams roll in. What are your thoughts?'

'Yep. I agree, boss. Going by the regularity of their recent comms, I reckon an hour's silence should be enough. I'll let you know when things have been quiet for an hour and then you can make the call.'

'Got it. Stay alert, Billy,' cautioned Ange before she hung up the call.

Ange then sent a text message on WhatsApp.

> *Drug farmer back from visit to town. Queensland mob is still active online. Suggest you guys move to position and we either wait one hour after online activity ceases or until 2am before we move in—whichever is earlier. Any thoughts?*

Andy Barnett messaged straight back.

> *Good news. Rather than risk confusion, why don't we just make it 2am? If you're still seeing activity at 1am, we can review the plan.*

Gary Franks added his opinion.

> *Agree. Will check messages at 1am Failing further instructions, will move in at 2am.*

Henry Chan was the last of the field teams to reply.

> *Good luck, everyone.*

Ange was anxious and jumpy. It promised to be an all-nighter, and she remonstrated herself for not catching some sleep mid-afternoon. She rang Henry Chan, and they had a long conversation, ultimately agreeing that once Hillburn was secure, he and the Queensland team would process the site and deal with the formalities. Ange and her team from Tweed Heads would do the same at Clearwater. Although they would still keep in touch, they agreed that there was no reason to wait before calling in any extra resources deemed necessary.

Just on 1 a.m., both SWAT teams had confirmed that they were in position.

Since Billy was also in the WhatsApp group, he messaged the group soon after, to say that there hadn't been any further online activity since 11:47 p.m. Ange resisted the temptation to send another message, but this would have been just unnecessary noise. Everyone knew exactly what they needed to do.

By 1:30 a.m., Ange was crawling up the walls. Annoyingly, Jim Grady had fallen asleep on the couch, evidently a much more experienced hand at dealing with this sort of pressure. She shook him awake. 'Boss, I think we should start heading out there. The property is a twenty-minute drive away, and I'd like to be close by in case they need help.'

Grady rubbed his eyes and checked his watch before sprinkling a dose of reality on the situation. 'Ange, I seriously doubt that we would be any help to those guys. But, yes, let's get kitted up and we can move out.'

'What do you mean, kitted up?' asked Ange.

'Put your vest on and check our weapons. Surely you weren't intending to roll in there armed only with your notebook and pencil?'

'Of course not,' lied Ange. She had been so amped up over her job as the team leader that she very well could have leaped into the car and driven off unprotected. They went to the back of the Prado and rummaged around in a large duffle bag that Grady had brought along, pulling out two navy-blue bulletproof vests emblazoned with the words POLICE in large white block text. These bulky adornments were not the high-tech nanotube vestments of her last fateful operation, capable of being concealed under one's clothing. These screamed a warning that guns were involved and danger lay just around the corner.

Ange checked her weapon before navigating the Prado slowly toward the entrance to the caravan park. She then made her way north along the main street and across the bridge. The pair drove in silence until Ange pulled off the road and stopped the Prado at the point that the asphalt ended and the gravel started. She looked across to check that her old boss hadn't fallen asleep and was pleased to find that he was still with her. The deathly quiet that replaced the clattering diesel engine did nothing to calm Ange's nerves. The pair waited impatiently.

The soft ping of Ange's phone came like a klaxon blaring, such was the silence cloaking their roadside vigil. It was Gary Franks, brief and to the point.

Clearwater secure.

Chapter 41

Secure

Ange started up the Prado and drove further along Samsons Road, turning left into the subject property and then shuddering across the cattle grid. She could see that the lights were on in the house. As she pulled up, Gary Franks came over to the car, kitted out in SWAT paraphernalia and fully armed, an ominous sight appearing out of the gloom. He stated the obvious. 'This was a piece of cake. Only two people in the house.' He handed over an Apple iPhone. 'One guy went straight for his phone, but we didn't give him a chance to use it.' He then pointed to the large shed. 'It looks like a substantial hydroponics cannabis farm with some sort of drug lab tucked in the front corner. It appears to be a highly professional operation. Any word from the other guys?'

Ange looked down at her phone. There was no text from the Hillburn team. 'Thanks, Gary. No, nothing yet. Where are you holding the perps?'

While Jim Grady walked over to the shed, Franks led her inside the farmhouse to the kitchen. Two thirty-something men were trussed up on kitchen chairs. Ange recognised one of them as the same man she had spied in the Chinese takeaway restaurant. Franks gestured his way. 'The phone belongs to this one.'

Ange walked over and stood directly in front of owner of the phone, his enmity towards her obvious. She pressed his phone to life and held it up in front of the man's face until the facial recognition software did its magic and unlocked the device. She fiddled with the phone's settings and permanently turned off the screen lock. Scrolling through the WhatsApp messages, she found a message sent from the phone on Monday afternoon. It simply referred to the recipient as 'B'.

No rubbish collection today. Need you to fix asap.

Ange suspected who 'B' was, and planned to test that theory later that day. Her own phone pinged, and she placed the iPhone on the kitchen table while she read her incoming message.

Hillburn secure. 3 perps in custody. 6 women rescued.

Ange didn't even have time to rejoice before the captured iPhone buzzed loudly on the kitchen table. She already had WhatsApp active on the screen and she skimmed the message, more out of interest than thinking it might be important. It was a message from someone called Wally to an unnamed group.

We've just been raided.

Ange took a moment to process the meaning of this. Her heart jumped when she realised what was going on and she rang Andy, worried about any potential delay. Anyway, there was no further need for radio silence.

'Hi, Ange. It all went well. They didn't know what hit them.'

'You've missed someone. One of the men we're holding here in Clearwater just received a warning message.'

'Stand by,' was Andy's sharp response before he abruptly hung up. Ange imagined him forcing the team to undertake a thorough sweep of the property.

Ange spent a pensive fifteen minutes waiting for Andy's call. 'We got him. He'd been asleep in the van that they used to transport the women. Sorry, Ange. Once we had the house secure, we moved straight to releasing the women. It never occurred to us that anyone would sleep in a vehicle with this heat.'

Any element of surprise had been comprehensively flushed down the toilet. Ange knew that they probably only had twenty-four hours at most to extend their dragnet to include other trafficking cells. As things stood, they had no active leads, so she was doubtful that they had lost any ground and cut her colleague a break. 'No worries, Andy. We probably gained more from the messages than we lost. They not only prove that the two sites are linked, but they also suggest that this is just part of a bigger operation. Nobody had any idea that we were coming, so that's a positive. You might imagine how touchy I am about leaky boats. Well done on getting this done with no shots fired.'

'Thanks, Ange. I know we slipped up, even if you won't say it. We were just lucky he wasn't the type to come out of hiding with all guns blazing.'

'I'd love to say that you owe me one, but I already owed you one. Let's call it even, then.' Ange laughed, breaking the extreme tension that had been circling for the past twenty-four hours. Her tone then took on a serious edge. 'I'll leave the details of processing the site to you and Henry, but I would appreciate you monitoring what happens to the women for me. They must be processed under the Victims of People Trafficking Legislation and not made out as criminals themselves—like happened previously.'

'Will do. Well done on cracking this cell apart, Ange. It looks like the facility has been operational for some time. Who knows how many women have passed through here?' observed Barnett. 'Now, I'd best get back to the team.'

This sombre thought brought Ange back to earth. She turned to Gary Franks. 'Gary, I presume that you have people from your team coming down from Tweed Heads to start the job of processing these guys. I'm not sure whether upstairs will want to deal with the Clearwater and Hillburn perps separately or lump them together. That decision is above both our pay grades. Anyhow, I'll take Jim back to Clearwater and catch a couple of hours' sleep. We have something to clean up in town as soon as the council offices open.'

'Will you need any support?'

'No, this is more white-collar. We can handle it ourselves. Well done and thanks for all your help. That was a very slick takedown.'

'Thanks. This is a significant operation here. I think my bosses will be very pleased with this seizure.'

By that, Ange assumed that a press release would be forthcoming. She was fast becoming an old hand at the politics of crime enforcement. With that, she walked over to the shed to find Grady. Once she opened the door, she could see the purple glow of UV lights spilling under some large plastic drapes. She pushed the heavy drapes aside and gasped at the multilayer growing facility that stood before her. It resembled something from a space colonisation movie. She couldn't see anyone and called out. 'Boss. Where are you?' at the top of her voice.

'Over here. In the lab in the front corner of the shed,' came Grady's yelled reply.

Ange walked back through the drapes and found Grady standing in the lab. It looked more like a pathology lab than the grimy meth labs from the television shows. He stated the obvious. 'This is certainly no novice set-up. Whoever is behind this knows what they're doing.'

'I agree. The hydroponics set-up is no less impressive. Boss, we should catch a few hours' sleep. I need to be on my game when we front the CEO.'

With that, the pair got back in the Prado and drove back into town. Despite one minor glitch, it had been a supremely successful day. Even the glitch might benefit them. Satisfied with her lot, Ange set her alarm for 8 a.m. and dropped instantly into a deep sleep.

She might not have slept so soundly had she known what the day would reveal.

Chapter 42

It's Complicated

As things transpired, Ange slept soundly through her alarm. The soothing tune that she used for her alarm became the background music of the train she was travelling on, finally roused by a conductor knocking loudly on the door and calling her name. She reluctantly and painfully clawed her way back to reality, disorientated and unable to work out where she was. Completely lost, she took a moment to retrace her steps of the past twenty-four hours. Suddenly, like an out-of-focus camera finding its target, her imagined sleeper cabin transformed itself into the bedroom of her little Clearwater abode. The conductor calling out her name was, of course, Jim Grady, telling her she had slept through her alarm. It was still happily playing its soothing tune in the background, so Ange leaned awkwardly across the bed and tapped her phone to silence.

'Got it, boss,' she called out in a croaky voice, just one of many body parts that refused to accept their new reality. She collapsed back on the bed feeling physically ill, such was the trauma her body was fighting with this rude interruption. It took a full five minutes before she felt well enough to escape from her lovely bed, the same bed that she had previously complained of being lumpy and hard. She stumbled out into the kitchen, still dressed in her clothes from the night before, and mumbled her thanks to Grady for rousing her, adding the word coffee into this incoherence. She pulled on her shoes in silence and stumbled towards Pam and salvation.

Pam's homely little coffee shop had already been open for hours. Ange must have looked a sight, as Pam greeted her with a concerned look. 'Goodness me, you look terrible. Did you have trouble sleeping, dear? Let me get you some coffee. Flat white with an extra shot, isn't it?'

Normally, Ange would rail against being called *dear*. Along with *love* and *darling*, *dear* sat atop her list of banned diminutives. However, it somehow seemed entirely appropriate for the kindly Pam. 'Two, please. I had a couple of disturbances last night. I'll be OK after your coffee. Can you add in two bacon-and-egg wraps to go with the coffees?'

Ange was not the first sleep-deprived customer Pam must serve each day, and she was grateful for the silence. Making use of the small rickety table and chairs outside, she sat down and planned her day. The prospect of confronting the CEO proved to be the tonic she needed, combined, of course, with a sip or two from her coffee. 'You have a pleasant day, dear,' was Pam's parting comment as Ange paid for breakfast. Ange promised to follow her kindly advice.

She was walking back to the cabin, juggling the coffee and breakfast, when Gary Franks called from the drug farm. 'Hi, Ange. Something's not quite right with this lab. It didn't look like any meth lab that I've ever seen, so I went and picked up the van and ran over the building with a drug-testing kit that I'd brought along. There wasn't a trace of anything other than cannabis. The lab is very high-tech and makes little sense to me. I thought you should know. Oh, by the way. Our prisoners seem smug and not at all concerned by their situation. It feels like they're waiting for something or someone to spring them. We found some dried blood in the small building closer to the dam. I'll get that tested, but the rest of the operation is far too clinical for this to be something as sloppy as human blood. It looks like someone uses the shed as a home abattoir. Either that or the place is a torture chamber of some horror. Given the small gantry and meat hooks, my guess would be blood from cattle being butchered, but let's run the tests before we jump to any conclusions.'

'Thanks, Gary. That wasn't the news that I expected. Great work running some tests before I made a fool of myself. Keep me posted if anything else drops from the sky.'

She discussed this development with Jim Grady over breakfast, also outlining her plan for the morning ahead. At 9 a.m. on the dot, she rang the Green River Council offices and asked to speak with Sandy Ellis. 'Hi, Sandy. I'd like to pay your CEO a visit today if possible. Can you let me know when she arrives at the office?'

'That's easy. She has her weekly meeting with the mayor at 10 a.m. today. He lives on a cattle property north of town and isn't here every day. Alan Cameron.

He's a really nice man. Please don't dob me in, Detective.'

'Don't worry, Sandy, I will do my very best to stop that from happening.' Ange hoped that this would be true. More than once, she had needed to backtrack on similar commitments when the tide of an investigation turned against her.

Ange and Grady got dressed in their most official clothing and took the short walk across town to the council offices, arriving at 10:10 a.m. The captured iPhone, Ange's smoking gun, was fully charged and safely tucked in the pocket of her jeans. No longer needing to stay under the radar, she showed her Major Crimes badge at the front counter and asked to speak with the CEO. The person manning the front desk did the right thing and suggested that the CEO was busy with the mayor. He asked if the pair could come back later.

'No. Now will be fine, thanks. The mayor might want to stay as well,' stated Ange in her most authoritative voice. 'Tell her that Detective Angela Watson and Sergeant Jim Grady are here to see them.'

After a full five minutes of toe-tapping frustration, the pair were led into the wood panelled office of the CEO. A large gold embossed nameplate announced they were in the presence of *Julia Bennet—Chief Executive Officer*.

Whereas CEO Bennet stayed seated behind her nameplate, Mayor Alan Cameron came over to introduce himself, offering the two police officers a firm country-style handshake. Ange took in his weather-beaten features and noted the well-worn Akubra hat on the sideboard. Cameron had the familiar bearing of a bushie, the word *cattleman* branded on his forehead.

'I presume you're here about the cattle rustling I reported a few months ago. I expected something before now, but better late than never. With the beef prices so high, I expect rustling is rife everywhere,' said Cameron.

Ange had endured the endless tirades of her father when she lived at home over stock that had mysteriously gone missing. Rather than burst his bubble immediately, Ange eased into the conversation, friendly and country-like. 'Nice town you have here. I grew up on a property just out of Tamworth. I probably came through Clearwater as a kid.'

'What's your name again?' said Cameron.

'Watson. My parents are still on the property. I'm the black sheep who left for the coast. Sergeant Grady and I are both stationed in Byron Bay.'

'I know your father. He's had some nice racehorses in his day. I dabble in the dark art myself. We all have our weaknesses,' said Cameron conspiratorially.

'Byron Bay, huh? I don't suppose you've ever run across an old friend of mine who moved over your way. Fellow by the name of Terry Scott. I believe he's also a local councillor.'

'Small world. Terry and Jenny are close friends of mine. I met them during a terrible case I worked on in the town where they now live. I presume you purchased some farm machinery from him—just like my dad.' Ange silently thanked her bushie connections yet again, where long familial lines meant that two or three degrees of separation were closer to the truth than the fabled six.

'Yep. Sure did. Give him my regards when you next see them. So, any news on my cattle rustling problem?' In bushie terms, cattle rustling was the original major crime, so Cameron's assumption didn't surprise Ange.

If looks could kill, Julia Bennet would have razed Ange to the ground by now. She hadn't taken kindly to the way Ange had quickly won over the mayor. Ange took a moment to appraise her. Well groomed and with the carefully curated air of a CEO. Perfectly matched to an air of superiority, Bennet's high-end designer clothes seemed unlikely to be found in any local boutiques. The Green River Council was a mere stepping stone in the burgeoning career path that Julia Bennet had laid out for herself. Ange had locked horns with plenty of highly ambitious women and knew that she presented as an instant adversary to Bennet's ambition. The glare in Bennet's eyes told her that no man or woman was going to get in her way, certainly not another woman posing as an accomplished professional. Ange realised in an instant that Brendan Tame hadn't stood a chance.

'Actually, Mayor Cameron, I'm here for another matter. While investigating a very disturbing case, we stumbled on a cannabis operation in Green River.'

'Please call me Alan. In our shire? Really? Where exactly?' Cameron promptly responded, his cattle rustling problems forgotten in an instant.

'Along Samsons Road, about two kilometres from where the bitumen ends,' replied Ange. 'We raided it in the early hours of this morning.'

'I hope you had a search warrant, Detective,' stated a haughty Bennet, seeking to stamp some of her own authority on the situation.

'We did, actually—although we didn't need one. We had reasons to suspect highly illegal activity,' added Jim Grady in a show of solidarity with his colleague.

'Well, Detective, those assumptions were incorrect. The property that I presume you're referring to is a properly licenced medicinal cannabis facility.' Julia Bennet smiled, brandishing a smoking gun. Ange's heart sank a notch as she realised her own smoking gun had just turned to dust in her pocket. She had been looking forward to the theatre of ringing Bennet from the seized iPhone.

Luckily for Ange, she had some other irons in the fire. 'I doubt the licence extends to selling cannabis under the counter to townsfolk. We have video evidence of this in case you were worried.'

Alan Cameron's face had gone so red that he looked in danger of exploding. 'What do you mean, Julia? Are you telling me that there's a cannabis farm in Green River and the council knows nothing about it? I doubt the ratepayers will be happy. How did this happen?'

'I saw it as an executive matter, Mayor. The Minister for Regional Development called me directly and asked for our help. Council has been wanting to encourage investment into more intensive agriculture in the area, and the company has big plans to expand the facility once they prove up the location,' replied Bennet, confirming Ange's suspicions about her ambition.

'When we said intensive agriculture, we had in mind poultry or horticulture, perhaps a native tree farm. A narcotics facility is squarely something that the council should have been across. We're a deeply conservative region here in Green River, Julia. I'm surprised you didn't consider that before you allowed a drug farm into the shire,' glared Cameron.

Ange upped the ante. 'The disturbing thing is that we believe this cannabis farm has links with organised crime. In fact, we simultaneously raided another property last night after we learned of the link. I can assure you, the second raid yielded something far more insidious than medicinal cannabis.' Cameron stood still, glaring daggers at Bennet. Ange could not have been enjoying herself more and went in for the kill. 'And then there's the unfair dismissal claim coming council's way.'

'What unfair dismissal claim?' exclaimed Bennet and Cameron, almost in unison.

'Your former employee, a certain Brendan Tame. I understand he started questioning the extended council refuse services along Samsons Road.'

'I remember Brendan,' stated Cameron. 'He left a message that he needed to speak to me a while back, but I never heard from him again. What happened to him?'

'I understand that Samsons Road was more a symptom than the cause of his concerns. Ms Bennet accused him of sexual harassment and then dismissed him.

He knew the reality of defending himself and left with his tail between his legs. However, I understand that he's about to reconsider his position,' said Ange knowingly, not bothering to disclose that this change of heart would be of her making. Ange's radar remained on high alert over how Julia Bennet had disposed of the inquisitive Brendan Tame. Sexual harassment was an insidious problem in the workplace and people like Julia Bennet, who used the shifting sands of public opinion to their own advantage, did nothing to assist women who had experienced genuine harassment.

'Julia. Council should also have known about any claim of sexual harassment. You know how these things can easily spiral out of control. We take such accusations seriously.' Cameron paused for a moment, thinking through the implications of the past twenty minutes. 'Can you please call an urgent meeting of councillors at 8 a.m. tomorrow morning?'

'But tomorrow is Saturday, Mayor. Anyway, I'm heading to Sydney this evening,' protested Bennet.

'Suit yourself, Julia. I still want to meet tomorrow at 8 a.m. You and the town clerk won't be required until 9 a.m. at the earliest. You can join online from Sydney. The first part of the meeting will be a non-executive session.'

Bennet's face turned ashen as the mayor uttered the words 'non-executive session', meaning that she was not invited, a prospect that struck fear into the heart of any CEO, even more so when they were feeling on shaky ground.

Bennet set about retrieving her reputation from the coals and turned on Ange. 'I'm sure that the minister will have a word or two to say about your illegal raid on a properly licensed facility.'

'And I'm sure that it will thrill the minister to learn that said facility has links with organised crime. It also won't help that the staff were selling drugs directly to residents. I doubt that the legislation allows for that side gig. Someone should have done some due diligence on the operator of the cannabis farm.' Despite her bravado, Ange had a sinking feeling that the minister could very well be aware of who was sitting behind the Clearwater operation and had played Bennet's ambition to his own advantage.

'Anyhow, we just wanted to bring this to your attention. We'll be in touch,' concluded Ange. She looked Bennet squarely in the eye. 'I expect we will need to question you more formally at some stage, Ms Bennet.'

On the assumption that Julia Bennet would white-ant Ange the moment they walked out of the room, Ange fired one last shot across the bow of the CEO. She opened her wallet and retrieved a business card, which she handed to Alan Cameron. 'Alan, can you send me any correspondence on your cattle rustling issue and I'll try to have a look into it when I get a chance?' She cast a conspiratorial look at Cameron. 'People jump to attention when Major Crimes comes knocking at the door. No promises, but I'll do what I can.'

'Thank you, Detective. And thanks for your efforts in dealing with this issue in town. Drugs are a modern scourge and have no place in Green River,' said Cameron. He looked at Bennet before completing his sentence. 'Even with the approval of some faraway minister. I'll bet he chose Green River because he knew what would happen if he approved any such facility in his own electorate.'

As the two officers left the building, Grady stated the obvious, his ever-present dry humour coming to the fore. 'I get the impression that Julia Bennet just crossed you off her Christmas card list, Ange.'

'That didn't go as I had thought it might, but I think we got there in the end. What's the bet that Ms Bennet is a *very* close friend of the minister? Anyhow, now that the drug farm makes more sense, we'd better have a quick meeting before we all head back to base.'

As soon as she was back at the cabin, she rang her SWAT team colleagues and filled them in on the latest shifting sands. That there was no longer any drug seizure to report upstairs shattered the mood of the team from Tweed Heads. Some local dealing in cannabis amid a potential and unproven link to organised crime was a mere trifle in comparison. The Hillburn raid was an entirely other story and a significant development. Ange made Andy Barnett feel better about his slip-up when she commented that the message between Hillburn and Clearwater had been a lucky break. Presumably, they would find other communications once they started digging. Before the meeting wrapped up, Ange asked Henry Chan to stand by while she convened an urgent meeting with the task force.

Everyone was keen to learn how the two operations had gone down. Chan first briefed the others on the success of the Hillburn raid, receiving resounding congratulations from the team. Ange's news was more subtle and not the result that everyone had assumed.

Sally Anders was right on it. 'I guess I can expect a call from the Minister for Regional Development sometime today or tomorrow. I've handled worse. It will be interesting to see how he plays it. I'm sure he won't be happy to learn that his big idea is already a haven for serious organised crime. Investing in a business like that would be an excellent way to launder some ill-gotten gains. Then again, someone might have him in their pocket. Depending on how close they are, he might try to lay this all on the CEO. I'll look forward to his call—it should be interesting.'

Ange once again marvelled at how savvy her boss was and how quickly she had assessed the situation. Ange concluded she had struck the tip of a very large iceberg.

Chapter 43

Vogon Logic

As soon as Ange had arrived back in Byron, she had become embroiled in the doldrums of administration, dealing with the detritus of the Hillburn and Clearwater operations. That there would be ramifications for herself and Major Crimes seemed predictable. After all, arse-covering was a sport much favoured by administrators and officials everywhere.

Taking the time to document a case forced a justification of conclusions made and actions taken. This was always more difficult and complicated than expected. Ange understood why many of her less diligent colleagues would cut corners with this process, often with disastrous consequences when a case was exposed under the glaring light of a courtroom.

There were two things that grated on any sense of achievement or closure. Missing the fact that the drug farm was actually a licenced medicinal cannabis operation perplexed her. Why didn't council officers like Sandy Ellis know about this? Even the mayor seemed in the dark, for goodness' sake. Apart from any planning or development approval within the jurisdiction of the Green River Council and any alleged delegated authority of Julia Bennet, surely something as sensitive as a cannabis production facility must have needed an intense and comprehensive state approval process.

Ultimately, after many hours of searching, Ange found an obscure register where the Minister for Regional Development had signed off on the facility. This seemed an opaque approach for a government that extolled the virtues of transparency and its record in that regard, especially for such a contentious matter. However, the government was not entirely without form. When she was a constable in Western Sydney, she had been called to placate some angry business owners who found that a methadone clinic had opened right beside them, without warning or consultation. The justification that these arrangements were for the public good seemed a shallow excuse for expedience.

Ange was reminded of a favourite chapter in *The Hitchhiker's Guide to the Galaxy*, when Ford Prefect learns that Earth is to be destroyed to make way for a new intergalactic superhighway. Any protestations fall on deaf ears when the contractors for the new superhighway, the delightfully named Vogons, confirm that nothing more could be done. After all, the plans for the project had been on public display in the basement of an administrative building in another galaxy. Earthlings only had themselves to blame.

The proprietor of the cannabis farm in Clearwater was a company named C2Z Pharma. Their slick website explained that C2Z was at the forefront of the medicinal cannabis revolution. Some more digging around showed that C2Z also boasted a 'potent' nasal spray for men to assist with their sexual prowess, some secret concoction of ancient Chinese herbs and spices. C2Z was a clever name, also an acronym for close-to-zero, which hinted at some sort of environmental stewardship. Ange made a mental note to check in on Billy and his friend Nelson from the tax office. Hopefully, they could shed some light on the business affairs of C2Z Pharma and who sat behind the corporate veil.

However, her more galling concern was how the people trafficking operation and the Hilburn facility even existed. With all the noise about strong borders, the benefits of Australia's distant island location, and a society with a testy relationship to immigration, how could such a sophisticated operation elude the authorities? She suspected multiple agencies of having been compromised. Border Force and the Immigration Department remained top of mind. The performance of the corporation who ran the Brisbane detention centre was questionable. Then there were the Vietnamese authorities, who must surely know people were being taken from their country and trafficked to another in servitude. It was all one epic clusterfuck.

If Henry Chan was correct and the Chinese Triads were involved, the perpetrators of this operation would have significant resources with which to bribe officials and grease palms. These same Triads had a terrible reputation for ruthlessness and brutality. This menacing thought forced her final and confronting revelation. Henry Chan had provided her ample warning that the Triads might be involved, yet Ange had been quite prepared to race off and put herself at peril, apparently with little thought for who she might have left behind.

The realisation that she was no longer carefree and single, able to do whatever she wanted and take any risk necessary, came as a rude shock. Ange now had a loving partner and an equally loving dog to consider. It could scar their lives forever, should anything happen to her.

A trip to the beach for a surf with her two favourite boys suddenly seemed far more important and consequential than any report that needed to be written. She closed her laptop and called out to them. Nothing else really mattered—until tomorrow, at least.

Epilogue

When Ange opened her inbox early Monday morning, she saw an email from a Detective Trevor Clarke, suggesting that she should call him. The signature block at the bottom of the email showed that Clarke worked in drug enforcement and was based out of Tweed Heads. Seeing as the email had been sent that same morning, Ange figured that her colleague was already hard at work. Curious, she dialled his number and Clarke answered immediately.

'Hello, Detective Clarke. My name is Ange Watson. You sent me an email early this morning asking me to call you.'

'Thanks for ringing me so promptly, Detective. I got something big going down today and will have my hands full,' replied Clarke. He paused briefly, as if taking a sip of coffee or tea. 'The guys that helped you with the Clearwater raid told me you were convinced that Chinese Triads were involved. What made you think that?'

'One of my task force colleagues tweaked me to that. A Detective Henry Chan. I understand he's ex-Cabramatta vice, now based in Brisbane. He said that he recognised some tattoos. Well, not the ones on the guys you processed, but some of his associates who were running a waypoint for trafficked women further north in Hillburn.'

'And Detective Chan is of Chinese background?'

'Yes. I gather that's why he was added to the task force. I came late to the party, but I assume there was already some intel on Chinese Triad involvement,' replied Ange, a kernel of concern growing in the pit of her stomach with the direction that the conversation was taking.

'What exactly is this task force about, Detective?' asked Clarke, a sharper edge creeping into his tone of voice.

'It's looking into people trafficking. Behind your area of narcotics, people trafficking is the second most lucrative form of organised crime—mostly women who are sold as slaves, brides, or prostitutes. We recovered six such female victims in Hillburn. Why do you ask?'

'Well, either Detective Chan is blind, or he doesn't read Chinese. Those tattoos on the guy we collected from Clearwater had nothing to do with Chinese Triads. I ran them by one of my colleagues—someone who actually does read Chinese. She said that the three tattoos on the guy's arm were symbols for courage, strength, and glory. They are some of the most popular Chinese symbols used for tattoos. Did Detective Chan actually see these tattoos?'

The kernel of concern in Ange's stomach swelled. 'No, not in the flesh. He saw the tattoos on the Hillburn suspects via CCTV and alerted me to the potential involvement of Chinese Triads, something which upped the stakes considerably.' She paused for a moment to collect her thoughts. 'Why do you ask?'

"When we accused your guy of being involved with the Triads, he burst out laughing. I understand that he has a degree in biochemistry from the Queensland University of Technology and works for the company behind the cannabis facility, an outfit called C2Z Pharma. He was being well paid for his services and is quite aggrieved about the possibility of losing his job. His student work visa relies on him remaining in gainful employment,' replied Clarke.

'I understand,' lied Ange, not yet understating much at all. 'What about the localised dealing charge? That was where this all started. When we realised that the traffickers in Hillburn were communicating with the guy from Clearwater, we took a cautious approach and assumed the worst.'

'I ran the dealing matter past our prosecutor. She told me not to waste everyone's time. Let's face it—the guy supplied minor amounts of medicinal cannabis to someone with a valid prescription. At the very worst, he might receive a warning,' answered Clarke.

'That doesn't explain why he was in touch with the trafficking cell in Hillburn,' remonstrated Ange, now scrambling to validate the logic that had led to the Clearwater raid.

'The guys who helped you seize the farm filled me in on that connection and I quizzed him about that. He assures me they all met at a mixed martial arts gym in South Brisbane. Apparently, they became mates and use WhatsApp to egg each other on and help keep up with their training.'

'That's a convenient story,' replied Ange in a mocking tone of voice.

'He showed me a series of messages that convinced me of that story. I'm firmly of the view that he didn't know what was going on in Hillburn. If you ask me, I think it's best for everyone that we just drop this whole mess and hope it doesn't come back to bite us. I'll send you a link to the video recording of our interview with the guy and his lawyer. I think you'll agree with our conclusion.'

'OK. Thanks for the update. If I'm honest, that isn't what I wanted to hear.'

'By the way, when Chinese Triads were mentioned, the guy's lawyer suggested that he'd never seen such a stark example of inappropriate racial profiling. I really couldn't argue with that. Let's hope the gang responsible for trafficking has actual links with the Triads. That might give you some defence.'

'Great,' muttered Ange sarcastically, the only reply she could muster.

After she'd hung up from the call, Ange sat back in her chair and pondered this development. She craved some caffeine, but her stomach was going crazy, and coffee would only make that worse. 'What the hell is going on?' she said out loud to herself.

The assumption that Triads were implicated had made perfect sense—symmetrical, even. Judy Ly was of Vietnamese descent, Henry Chan Chinese. Cua Kwm had been lured from her home on the Vietnam-China border, where stories of young women being captured in lighting raids by Chinese gangs were well known. Once Chan had seeded the idea of Triad involvement, had she been blinded by this proposition, failing to probe and prod all other potential explanations—like any worthwhile investigator should have done?

On top of looking into C2Z Pharma, she needed to get Billy to review the video retrieved from the IGA supermarket, the footage which had alerted Chan to the possibility that Chinese Triads were involved. Hopefully, there was some logical explanation for Chan's conclusion, and more to the WhatsApp connection between Clearwater and Hillburn than Detective Clarke seemed prepared to believe.

However, even in her most optimistic appraisal of the situation, in her heart of hearts, Ange knew that things were about to get messy.

Coming Soon.
Green River
Part Two of The Songbird Tragedies

Now read the beginning of Green River...

The man glanced furtively over his shoulder as he walked towards a car parked on the street. He had faced up to his obsession some time ago. Like any addict, he had little or no control of the urgings that came to steal his soul away, arriving unbidden and out of nowhere in particular, starting as the tiniest of tiny itches, deep within his core. He would love to say that there was a specific part of his body that was the problem, the source of his itch, but his weakness was a complete surrender of body and mind. Once started, the itch would spread like wildfire, like an insidious infection. However, this disease was different. His illness, far from making him weak and incapacitated, thrilled and energised him like nothing else had, or ever could.

By the time he had slipped behind the wheel of his car and started the engine, he was shaking with excitement and anticipation. He glanced back towards the house he had just let. He still loved his wife and children, having convinced himself long ago that this addiction had no effect on that part of his life, such was his sickness. His wife and family were his rock, the secret to his success; somehow separate, sacrosanct, enduring; the face of who he really was, the very image of himself, the guy in the mirror who looked back when he shaved, mister dependable, the nice guy who everybody warmed to.

Had his fever been less intense, he may have noticed the nondescript silver Toyota Camry parked further back up the street. His leg was shaking as he drove away. It was all he could do to concentrate on his driving, let alone see who might be watching.

He had always loved women. His wife knew that—surely she did. The many secret affairs had kept that part of him alive, the part that she loved as well: his confidence and assuredness, the charm, his sex appeal, the ability to make women love him back. It was all part of the package that he had so carefully curated over time. This skill, to project one image that hid another, had been well harnessed in his career.

His excursion today was borne of something entirely different to his rank-and-file affairs. He had never experienced such lust. To have a woman so completely under his control was intoxicating. Of course, her youthful, almost ethereal beauty was part of the attraction, but it was her complete submissiveness that really turned him on. It didn't matter that the face of this intoxication changed. It was the whole experience that thrilled. His other conquests, even his wife for that matter, didn't treat him this way. Their nagging demands never ended. For the next hour or two, he would get to escape and play king, one with irresistible powers, perhaps a sultan with his own personal harem.

The man on the door let him in without a word. No identification was needed. He was well known. That was lucky, as any words or explanation would have been incoherent, such was the excruciating level of his excitement.

Afterwards, when his itch had been thoroughly scratched, he would inevitably experience a brief spasm of guilt. However, soon enough, thoughts of what had happened would dispel these fleeting misgivings. Within days, he would feel the first tingle again, something he would suppress as long as he could. That was part of the thrill, keeping his desire bottled up, perhaps distracted by the other women in his life for a while. Letting the itch grow and build pressure made the release even more spectacular—more addictive.

It was the perfect situation, being able to have his cake and eat it too—so to speak. He planned to keep this arrangement going forever.

Read The Saltwater Crimes Trilogy

Join Ange as she hunts a sophisticated criminal syndicate operating along Australia's rugged coastline.

 Scan or click here to buy The Saltwater Crimes boxset on Amazon:
https://www.pg-robertson.com/the-saltwater-crimes-boxset

 Scan or click here to see the individual books in The Saltwater Crimes:
www.pg-robertson.com/books

 facebook.com/profile.php?id=100090607141784

 instagram.com/petergrobertson/

 amazon.com/stores/P-G-Robertson/author/B0BY4B55VP?ref=ap_rdr&store_re f=ap_rdr&isDramIntegrated=true&shoppingPortalEnabled=true

Author's Note

The characters in this book are entirely fictional. I have created them from good friends, work colleagues, acquaintances, strangers I've encountered, some people that I've met in the surf, and others that are purely imaginary. Likewise, except for any household names, the companies, and enterprises that underpin the plot are figments of my imagination and similarly fictional. My heroine, Detective Ange Watson, is a mixture of close friends—some who surf and some who do not. I trust you have grown to like Ange as much as I like my friends.

Places like Byron Bay, Texas QLD, Warwick, Tamworth, Sydney, and Brisbane are real. Namba Heads is a purely fictional town but is based on the iconic coastal villages in the Northern Rivers region of New South Wales, Australia. Clearwater and Hillburn are similarly fictional, but have their roots in the many small country towns found just west of The Great Dividing Range. I hope my writing has done justice to these spectacular places.

Even though the storyline is purely fictional, the idea behind the plot theme came from a trip to Vietnam with my family. We were trekking in the hills near the China-Vietnam border. Our guide was a delightful and enterprising young Hmong woman who told us about the perils faced by young woman growing up in that remote rural region. The impact of her astonishing stories stayed with me, making them a compelling subject to write about and the perfect crusade for Ange.

So Many to Thank

T hank you for reading Trashed. I hope you enjoyed the journey and the slight change of scenery. Spending your precious time reading my books is incredibly gratifying for me. I hope you are looking forward to reading Green River, part two in The Songbird Tragedies.

Of utmost important, is the need to thank all those who gave me the encouragement to push on and write a second series. I probably should list you all individually, but the list is long and I risk missing someone important! Hopefully, I have already told you in person how much your input has meant to me. I cannot thank you all enough.

The Island Book Club always deserves a special mention. I will forever remember the scene of our inaugural book club meeting, sitting on the beach in our camp chairs one glorious afternoon, champagne in hand and laughter in our hearts. This year, I was pleased to proffer an actual paperback in the form of an author's proof copy. The crew had loads of fun deciphering who and what may have provided inspiration for my characters and their story.

I am also grateful for my 'media team', Sophie Robertson, and Ben Hall, whose skills and comfort with new media amaze me. I must also thank my editor, Eliza Dee, and my cover designer, Karri Klawiter, for their dedication and forbearance in enduring my many and continued rookie errors.

Finally, if you have a spare minute, I would appreciate you posting a review of Trashed on Amazon via your purchase history.

Surfing Terminology

A brief description of some of the surfing terminology follows:

'**Tombstoning**' occurs when a surfer is held under the water by a wave following a heavy wipeout. Whilst the surfer is being dragged deep beneath the water, their surfboard is straining on the surface, connected as they are by a fully stretched leg rope. An obvious metaphor for a perilous situation, tombstoning is never a good sign and rarely fun for the surfer, although bystanders or fellow surfers will invariably find it all most amusing after the fact.

A '**left-hander**' is a wave that breaks to the surfer's left. That is, as the surfer catches the wave, he or she will turn to the left. Obviously, a '**right-hander**' breaks to the surfer's right.

A '**goofy-footer**' is someone who surfs with the right foot forward, and a '**natural**' is someone who leads with their left foot. The decision to choose one side or another is instinctual and set for life.

Surfing '**forehand**' indicates that a surfer is facing the wave face, '**backhand**' is the reverse. Most surfers find surfing forehand easier, particularly in steep demanding waves. Hence, a 'right-hander' favours a 'natural', and a 'left-hander' best suits their 'goofy-footed' cousins.

The '**line-up**' is the term used for the queuing area where the waves start breaking.

'**Out the back**' means the smooth clear water beyond any breaking waves. It offers a zone of calm where a surfer can sit up on their board to take a breather and enjoy their surroundings—well, until the next ride rolls in.

The '**peak**' of a wave is a term commonly used for beach breaks. It defines the apex of the wave face. Once perfectly positioned at the 'peak' of a wave, a surfer can choose to go left or right. The other descriptor for perfect beach breaks is 'A-frames', but these dreamy situations are disappointingly rare.

A '**rip**' is where seawater, carried in by the crashing waves, combines into a channel and rushes back out to sea. Dangerous for swimmers, they can be a godsend for surfers to help ease a long and tiring paddle.

Being '**inside**' means the surfer is the one closest to the breaking point of the wave, which is the surfer who is farthest inside on the line-up. On a headland or reef break, this would be closest to the rocks or reef, and inevitably the most ambitious take-off point. The surfer sitting farthest 'inside' technically has a right of way, a case of fortune favouring the brave. It does not always work that way, wi th **'drop-ins'** being the scourge of surfers around the world, usually spoiling the wave and often dangerous to all concerned.

Jostling for the premier position at the take-off zone is part strategy, part bravado, and part aggression. Called **'hassling'**, this can easily spiral out of control, and fights in and out of the surf are not uncommon in crowded surf breaks, and where localism is rife. **'Dropping in'** on an aggressive local will usually end badly. The old way to surf was to take turns. As the 'inside' surfer departed on their wave, the next would slide across and assume the vacated spot in the line-up, gaining rights to the next wave, and so on. This type of surf etiquette is now relegated to isolated or sparsely populated breaks.

A **'grommet'** is surfer slang for a young school-aged surfer, a term usually reserved for those with talent, their lightness, speed, and flexibility sometimes grating on the older surfers around them.

The **'rail'** on a surfboard is the outside edge, the shape and taper of which are critical in how a board performs.

The 'rocker' of a surfboard describes how the nose turns up. Boards made with a pronounced rocker are more forgiving when tackling powerful, steep waves. Boards fashioned with minimal rocker make catching smaller and fuller waves easier, but are prone to nosedives during steep or late take-offs—but this might be my age talking.

'Longboards' and 'shortboards' create quite different surfing styles and favour different wave formations. Longboards typically range from eight to eleven feet, or 2.5 to 3.3 metres. Shortboards are under seven feet, or 2.1 metres. The weight of a surfer will often dictate the type of board they choose, and the division between a longboard and a shortboard has blurred over time.

The number of fins on a board varies depending on the style of board. **'Single fins'** are mostly reserved for longboards or surfers wanting a traditional style. The original surfboards were all single fins. **'Twin fins'** are highly manoeuvrable, usually earmarked for small wave boards. A **'thruster'** sports three fins and is the most popular and versatile configuration for shortboards. **'Quads'** have four fins and sit somewhere between a twin fin and a thruster in terms of functionality.

A **'quiver'** is simply a collection of surfboards used by a surfer, as in a 'quiver of arrows' used by an archer.

Finally, a **'tube ride'** is when the surfer positions themselves within the curl of the wave, precariously covered over by the breaking lip, but remaining relatively untouched within the eye of the storm—so to speak. It's the most exhilarating of all surf manoeuvres, and waves that are 'tubing' are highly prized, yet relatively rare. Surf spots that regularly produce tube rides are usually very popular, difficult to travel to, or jealously guarded secrets.

Australian-isms

For the benefit of non-Australian readers, some idioms that I have used occasionally are explained below:

'Back of whoop whoop'. Far away from everywhere and anywhere. Beyond the black stump is another synonym.

'Bad egg'. Someone who is rotten to the core.

'Berko'. Going crazy mad, angry and out of control. The Tasmanian devil goes berko if cornered while eating their dinner.

'Buggered, stuffed, screwed, rooted'—you get the drift.

'Bushie'. Someone who lives in the country, most commonly on a rural farm/property/station, and well away from any major towns or cities. One's degree of 'bushie-ness' is usually proportional to the distance one lives from the coast.

'Curly request or question'. Refers to a difficult request or loaded question.

'Deckie'. A shortened name given to the deckhand working on a fishing trawler.

'Feeling crook'. Feeling sick or unwell.

'Firey'. Slang for firefighter.

'Jackeroo'. Is the term used for a young man who is working on a sheep or cattle station as an apprentice of sorts. A jackaroo can also describe a spit-roasted kangaroo used for food, which I guess explains the day-to-day life of a Jackaroo, the person.

'Jillaroo'. The female equivalent of a Jackaroo.

'Kargaroo Court'. An impromptu or unofficial court used to try someone without due process or evidence, a stitch-up in other words.

'**Larrikin**'. Part rogue, part joker. The sort of person to enjoy a beer at the pub with, but not someone to risk with the family jewels. Larrikin is often used to describe the affable kookaburra, one of the coolest and most personable birds in Australia, also a ruthless killer of small birds and animals.

'**Nong**'. An idiot or fool, a term used endearingly and in jest toward a friend or loved one.

'**A park**'. A park can refer to either a park with grass and trees, or a single parking place for a car. Go figure!

'**Roached**'. Has its roots in the word cockroach. Being roached normally refers to the situation where someone has scuttled behind your back to do no good.

'**Roo**'. Shortened nickname for a kangaroo.

'**Rort**'. Another word for scam or con.

'**Seachange & Greenchange**'. Seachangers leave their lives in the city and move to the coast. Greenchangers move to the country.

'**Smoko**'. A remnant from the time when most everyone in the country smoked. It now refers to morning or afternoon tea.

'**Spit the dummy**'. A dummy, in Australian vernacular, is also known as a pacifier. When a baby is about to throw a tantrum, their face with turn sour, before they spit out their dummy and go berko. It's a wonderfully descriptive phrase—part facial expression, part change of mood, part warning for the carnage about to be unleashed.

'**Stunned mullet**'. Refers to someone who is in a form of temporary shock. An actual stunned mullet will be floating helplessly on the surface and unable to swim away.

'**Whinger.**' Someone who complains a lot, an approach to life that Australians have little time for. Sadly, whingers, in all their forms, seem to be on the ascendency.

Made in United States
Orlando, FL
13 December 2024

55580727R00147